In memory of
Harold Faulkner, 1890-1980
My father, Allan, 1906-1982
Gordon White, 1915-1983
Ted Hoskinson, 1912-1987

And for Jim Scott and all those who serve

They're heading back into trenches
At platoon-strength almost daily now,
So it looks as if we're soon going to
Have to either forget it or
Think about it for them.

—Don Coles

I have watched my body carry my head around
like a lamp, looking for light among the broken stones.

—Robert Bringhurst

UNKNOWN SOLDIER

BY

GEORGE PAYERLE

BOOKS

Cover artwork and book design by Włodzimierz Milewski

Note for libraries: A catalogue record for this book is available from Library and Archives Canada
at
www.collectionscanada.gc.ca

Revised edition
ISBN: 978-0-9812476-8-7

MW Books
Garden Bay, BC
Canada
www.mwbookpublishing.com
info@mwbookpublishing.com

10 9 8 7 6 5 4 3 2 1

ACKNOWLEDGEMENTS

I wish to thank the Canada Council, the Ontario Arts Council, and several private supporters for financial assistance during the writing of *Unknown Soldier*.

Special thanks to Dennis Lee, Robert Bringhurst, Anne Holloway, Fran Diamond, the late Ted Hoskinson, and the late Gordon White. More recently, Hoskie's grandson Liam Maloney rekindled my faith that the young do remember.

Parts of this book have appeared in *Grain*, the *Malahat Review*, *Negative Capability*, *Prism International*, and the *Vancouver Literary News*.

Other than individuals in the public eye who are identified by their actual names, all the characters in this book are creations of the author's imagination. Similarly, the battlefield scenes, while attempting to achieve verisimilitude, are imaginary and not intended to represent actual events.

This second edition would not have appeared without the perceptive kindness of my friend Zeev, another unknown soldier.

TABLE OF CONTENTS

BELGIUM,
1944

IN THE SILENCE, he imagines he can hear the mist fall.

He looks out past the barrel of the German machine gun. The rain has stopped. The storm of exploding steel and men's flesh has stopped. The madness has drained from him.

Precious little remains. Exhausted men sprawled in the straw, the lees of two rifle companies consumed between tea-time one day and lunch the next. His men, the smell of wool battle dress damp with sweat and blood and the weather, safe for now in this barn in Belgium still stinking of cordite. His men, and not one officer left to get them killed.

So I guess it's up to me, he thinks.

His eyes meet those of the young German propped in the corner like a slender sheaf of wheat. The German's eyes stare straight through him, pale blue as a winter sky with the clarity of final things. Precious little for him, too. A cigarette hangs from his lip and smoke curls out his nostrils. At least it's no longer coming out of the hole in his chest, now stuffed full of sulpha and bandages. The light in those eyes won't last until morning.

Through the opening the Germans had used for their gun and the farmer had used for manure, he can see the field of fire down the slope dotted with bushes and bunches of grass and punctured bundles of field-grey and khaki that had been men. More of the same invisible in the murk of the bottom. Among them the remains of Hugh Young, eyes that were bluer than this German's gone dark, a gutted corpse stiff under a groundsheet, and what the Belgian girl had buried. He can only guess at the shapes of the shellholes through the thick grey air. If they'd been able to see us any better, we'd all be dead.

For six months I've been trying to keep people alive. These precious few have made it through the breach, safe for now. Except the German, they should all see tomorrow.

His foot aches in its bloody cotton binding and he feels too tired for tomorrow. There's an outpost in the farmhouse to warn of ominous movement up the road. Trenches are dug and a position chosen for the Bren. He looks at Phillips the Brengunner asleep with his weapon, uniform dark from the blood of the last officer, the criminally stupid Halldorsen, Peter, Lieutenant. The captured German gun covers the valley. The panzer-grenadiers went that way and he doubts they'll be back. They'll bump into First Army and try to break through the same way they overran elements of the Vancouver Light Infantry. Us. God, he thinks, we were supposed to mop up pockets of resistance and secure the area. A soft touch after France. He closes his eyes. They feel hot under their lids.

Tonight he's not going to ask anyone to sleep outside if they don't have to. Braithwaite is stewing the sack of onions from the farmhouse with Bovril and tinned meat over a sterno fire, clucking at it like a mother hen. Good old addled Al Braithwaite, always a little crazy and blown up twice since Normandy to boot. Here we are, a fine pair of sergeants, you with shell shock, me the senior NCO with a hole in my foot, eighteen half-dead guys and one dying German. Thank God those SOBs didn't have any armour. Great steel beasts with 88mm snouts and roaring engines. His chin drops to his chest and he opens his eyes. The air smells delicious.

"Here we are, Sam," says Braithwaite, holding a mess tin under his nose. "Get this down you and sleep a while. I'll be around."

"Yes, Mother."

"Mother you, Collister." Braithwaite grins. "Tomorrow we'll go fishing." The Second-in-Command hums like a spinning reel and jerks his arms to set the hook. He pauses, looks blank, then shouts, "Right!" as he snaps to attention and turns on his heel more or less like you're supposed to. Get that man to a hospital. Or a nice quiet lake with trout in it. The 2-IC shuffles back to his stewpot calling, "Mess parade! Don't fall over yourselves." Turning war into a tour of KP. Not a bad idea.

"Sergeant," says a faint voice from one of the figures shaking themselves out of the straw, "what happens tomorrow?"

"Sims, if I knew what was going to happen tomorrow, I'd be God and I wouldn't have to sleep in a barn with you bastards. Tomorrow we're going to proceed in good order toward some R and R."

Sims covered in Halldorsen's brains, screaming. How many hours ago, in another life, had he kicked this kid to snap him out of the panic?

He eats the stew, which tastes almost as good as it smells. Tomorrow he'll have to get this bunch to a nice rear echelon. Too many damaged bodies to go far without transport. Get Al to a hospital, and himself, and even the German if he lasts, and the other crocks. If they all stay alive that long. Maybe he can wangle leave to London and find Dot and take her to Devon, and maybe the war will be over.

Then they could all go home to Vancouver and Victoria and little places like Duncan and Cowichan. Him too, with his English girl walking down peacetime streets, summer snow on the green mountains. But not Hugh. No – I'll never forget, my friend. Hugh's blood hot and thick on his hands. His skin tingles where it carries that memory.

He yearns for large warm presences, cows and draught horses to share the barn, munching their fodder, pricking their ears as the farmer stumbles out before dawn like Mother Braithwaite and the world starts moving again in time to their slow bells and swaying great sides. The smell of hay and forests and the western sea.

▷·◆·○·◁·◁

A voice calls him out of the night. Sam, it says. Sam! Collister! And the hand shaking him belongs to the voice. A prickle of fear tightens his muscles. It's tomorrow.

"Armour in the valley, Sam," says Braithwaite.

He can hear it clatter and squeak, leaps up, and falls cursing as the foot shoots agony through his leg.

"Fuck off, Braithwaite," he says to the fumbling hands and crawls to look out.

The squat dark shapes in the dawn are tanks that could belong to anyone. The wraithlike infantry deployed among them make the whole scene look unreal. But the noise is real enough.

"Where's that flare pistol? They must be ours, but if they're not we're leaving pretty damn quick."

The green-and-white globules arc over the hillside like incandescent spit. After the horrible moment in which nothing changes, two green dots brighten out of the mist. Cheers ring around him. He clambers onto his good foot and Braithwaite grabs him.

"Collister, you're crazy and you're too big to carry. Sims! Help me with this lug. What'd you have to leave your foot out to get shot for?"

The German lies pale and still. With Al wiry under one shoulder and Sims tall and skinny under the other, Sam says, "You rest easy, Fritz. This war's over."

They gimp him out to the brow of the hill.

The monsters in the mist take on the angular shape of Cromwells. The infantry are the right colour, their tin hats shallow and wide.

"Form up!" Sam shouts, but knows he's grinning. "Try and look like soldiers or they'll think you're Belgian farmboys. Braithwaite, go act like a sergeant. I'll keep Sims for a crutch. Call in the outpost."

He looks at Phillips standing easy with the Bren, his face clear in blood-stained repose. Hurtful warmth seizes the region of Sam's heart. That's what a good soldier looks like, he thinks.

I hope you never have to use that thing again.

"Sam," says Braithwaite quietly in his ear, "you brought us through. You ought to get a fucking V.C.," and has the sense to leave before Sam needs to answer.

11

As the lead Cromwell lumbers up the slope, he wonders that anything so ugly and awful can look so welcome. The tank commander peers down from his turret and calls in a Limey voice, "You gents need a lift?"

"Yeah," shouts Sam, "we won the war. Where's the dancing girls?"

THE CANADIAN

STUBBS'

"WHAT DAY is it, Sam?" asks Fred.

Collister looks at the pewter-blue water and the glare on it, gulls' wings. Someone's crab salad arrives. "Tuesday," he says. The summer evening of the Inner Harbour in Victoria. Across the table, Fred looks military and trim in his pale blue shirt, the Loomis insignia rising and falling on his chest like a big bright bug.

"Thought it was Wednesday," says Fred. "Week's not even half over."

First Armoured Couriers, thinks Sam. Rattle of light-arms fire on the vehicle's hard skin. Mud roads. Crack and clatter of airbursts. The driver's eyes squinted against the metal trying to stab through with the light. Here in the filtered sunshine of Stubbs' Restaurant and Lounge more than three decades later, Fred bitchy after a day piloting his yellow van through this colonial town that wants to be England. Fred who drove for the Service Corps back then and didn't see any front lines or shelling.

"At least you're workin'," says Sam.

"Why aren't you?"

"Whaddya mean?"

"Playing handyman and living in a dump and grousing all the time like a fucking zombie."

Sam straightens, startled. Fred ploughs on. "I've known you what, eight, ten years, and it's getting worse. You can scare hell out of people, Sam. God knows you scare it outta me often enough, when you decide to ramrod some guy. And the damnedest women don't mind you. But will you get your ass in gear? No. Use your brains for something, instead of brooding over what's gone."

"Fucking Jesus," says Sam.

"Well, it's called dignity, if you had any sense. Hell, get some decent clothes on and somebody might even hire you."

"To do what? Run a rifle platoon?"

"For chrissake, you can cook. You can carpenter. If I'm good enough to drive courier, you oughta be good enough to run a construction crew or some damn thing. How come you never bucked for a commission, anyhow? Easier to fuck the dog and mouth off about the brass?"

"Shut your face, you stupid bastard." Sam's fists knot and muscles bunch between his shoulder blades.

The long silence, in which reflected light flutters inside Sam's head as he concentrates on breathing rather than thinking. Waiting for the beer to cool them both off. Knowing Fred's right.

"Anyway," Fred says at last, "come Friday, I'm going to leave Mum with my sister and go kill some fish."

"Yeah." Sam leans forward. "Look, Fred, you really oughta put her in a home."

Fred's smooth, sad face looks at him with the mournful look dogs get. "Now you're sticking your oar in. She'd die, Sam. It's her house. Her things."

She'll do that anyway, he thinks. Eventually. And grunts. "We're not getting any younger, Fred. Everybody's dying off." Fred's eyebrows go up. His face looks a yard long.

"I got word Al Braithwaite's been bunged up in a car crash."

"Don't think I ever met him."

"He lives in Vancouver. Came out of the war a little funny in the head. Never got past pushing a broom for the Post Office. We were sergeants together all through France and Belgium. A good man, Braithwaite." Sam twists his beer glass on its coaster. A float plane hangs in the sky over Esquimalt, dropping down to land under their window. Harbour to harbour, Vancouver–Victoria.

"You going to go see him?"

"Yeah. Take a boat to Tsawwassen tomorrow." He lets a lungful of air out his nose and rolls the beer glass between his palms. "Next year I'll be sixty, Fred."

Fred laughs, a child of fifty-five. "You sound like you think that's the end of the line."

Sam stares out the window as the heels of the plane's floats feather the rumpled water of the harbour mouth. His insides twist like cardboard in the warm spill of light. "Yeah," he says, "maybe I do."

He doesn't look at Fred, but feels the weight of his eyes. Reproachful. Waiting to hear more. Clink of glasses in the table-talk as the Twin Otter settles onto its waterbug feet and unfurls a rainbowed roostertail of spray. You fucking beauty.

"Here comes Air Death," says a cheerful male voice from the next table.

He snaps his head around to look. There's their waitress bent over the two young guys in suits, slit up the back of her dress to show she's naked under the black crêpe.

"Such talk," she says. "That's the last plane. You better get out of here if you're going to catch it."

"Right on, dearheart. Gotta be brave to do business. Now stop waving your sweet flesh at me and gimme the bill."

Kids. "How do we get to be the way we are?" he says to Fred. "Lookit that broad. When she stands in the light it's like she's got no clothes on."

"Makes you feel young and foolish."

"Makes me feel old. My kid's probably older'n her. Hell, Dot's your age by now. Old Jameson in Devon's pushing seventy." How can I make enough dough to get back to Devon? "It's just no one tells your dick to curl up and die and you end up useless as tits on a boar."

"Any more here?" the girl's voice says. He hadn't seen her coming. Mascaraed hydrangea eyes that don't give a damn, in a pale triangular face. Blood tingles up into the roots of his hair.

"Two Export," he says, and digs a homemade cigarette out of the plastic case in his pocket. "Why don't you get some Whitbread in here?"

"There's just no call for it, sir. Sorry." She flounces a hip around the back of a chair and goes to order.

"Fucking hypocrites," he says. "They like to pretend they're in England so they stick out double-decker buses for the tourists, but you think they could bring in some decent beer?"

He imagines a fat pint of Bass, just cool in the July heat, a mirage in the dim interior of Stubbs'.

"I better go see to Mum after this. How about dinner later down in the Vic Inn? I never did try your young friend's rack of lamb."

"I dunno," Sam says. "Not tonight."

"You short of cash for Vancouver? I could spare a few bucks."

"Naw. Thanks. I'm okay this month – did the widow Simpson's garden and a few other bits. I can always wash dishes in the V.I." And shudders. His young friend the cook. Any time you're short, Sam. And he'd done it, the steaming machine, sweat rolling off him like a warm sea, scraping the leftovers of expense accounts into waste bins. The beer arrives. A slim arm plunks the bottles down and flips the tab between the salt cellar and the cardholder that lists Stubbs' Specials. A Silver Sled – soda, Cointreau and cream. The Love Boat – a margarita for two. Hmpf.

"Sam!" Fred says.

"What?"

Fred chortles. "Sam, you are becoming morose. Let's drink this up and I'll give you a lift home. We can meet at the VI. about eight."

"Go to hell, Whiteacre! Anyhow, Frenette's not cooking tonight. I'm gonna head over to the Beaver."

"I thought we stopped going to the Beaver because we never got out till closing time."

Kind Fred. *I* never got out till closing time. He sees himself in Fred's eyes, the night of the brawl he couldn't resist. Sam! Sam, get your ass back here! But he'd sailed on like a freight car gone off its rails, drunkenly into that swamp of punks.

And oh, its axles broken, Fred, its axles broken. The anger of the old soldier gone to war had slammed like a big fist in his chest, and he'd come to with a nurse looking at him as though he were an unexploded bomb.

"I promise I won't have another heart attack," he says.

"Your funeral," says Fred, hoisting his Export.

"Yeah. At least it got me over to England. Or Charlotte did, bless her. Don't know why I ever came back."

"Because you couldn't afford to live there. What would you do? Sponge off your sister and her buddy Jameson?"

"I dunno if I can afford to live anywhere." He stares off across the barroom, dreaming of good bitter beer in a place like the Earl of St. Vincent, which had changed just enough with the centuries to put light bulbs everywhere except the outdoor loo. Good old Jameson among the sheep farmers, when they'd gone down to stay with that young fellow in Cornwall. Jameson's kid wife Elizabeth. Her impish smile and Pre-Raphaelite curls. He sees the palisade of logs separating Stubbs' from the fluorescent boutiques of the shopping mall. No sheep farmers or slate cutters sitting over there – only a flock of after-office public employees. Other ranks of the grey army fighting paper wars for the provincial government. A lean-faced woman looks back at him and he realizes he has been seen.

Fred downs his beer, stands, and says, "Well, sometimes you scare me. You're old enough to know better or maybe too old to learn. Phone if you change your mind."

Sam grunts.

Fred puts a ten on the table. "Here's for the beer."

"You only owe about half that."

"Collister, don't argue with me."

They look at each other. Fred's uniform sags at the waist now that he's up. So you only got as far as rear echelon, Sam thinks. RCASC. So what? We're both old soldiers. The Home Guard. We won a war for this. The generals bungle the killing and the pinstripes bungle the peace. Now we wash their dishes and carry their mail.

"You want to come fishing when you're back from Vancouver?"

Fish, he thinks. A dead string of them trailing their colour away in clear water. "No," he says. "Where you going?"

"Up to Lasqueti."

"Well, that's another story. When?"

"Saturday. Soon as I get Mum over to Katie's."

"Maybe I'll go. Haven't been out in the bush for a while."

"Okay. Gimme a call when you're back."

That would be all right. He watches Fred manoeuvre his loose, broad-beamed shape out through the tables to the portal in the palisade. Two codgers in a car to French Creek and across the ferry to Lasqueti Island, laden with whisky and grub among the fugitive hippies. Catch the mail truck down-island and tromp through the bush, to the splayed old cabin someone dropped a tree on once. Its mullioned windows gaze out over the rock cove, bottle-green water deepening to black under the bluffs of the island beyond, where a man of vision and little sense had tried to raise fighting bulls, like so many bygone loonies on this coast. The steep slopes of Bull Island that look like Spain to anyone who knows the tale. Trolling from a water-logged boat, gazing back at the cabin's glass eyes in the viscid forest green. Oysters and thick-armed purple starfish among the barnacles at low tide, and red snapper to grill over open coals. That would be all right. Nights in the cabin smelling of aging men, decaying wood, coal oil and time washed by the tang of cedars and the sea.

He looks out those remembered windows and sees a lamp on the far shore. Someone lives there. The woman by the palisade in Stubbs' looks back at him – her lean, slavic face, dark hair blurred into the dimness of the bar. A loosening runs up from his toes through his innards to the roof of his head. That's how you know you're going to be afraid, he thinks. He looks at her and thinks, There's a woman over there – something he hasn't thought for a long time. He feels the blood in his muscles and breathes down to the bottom of his lungs. The waitress bends over the table in the window light. That made me blush, he thinks. This makes me breathe.

The last plane for Vancouver claws its way out of a cloud of bright spray into the air, sound of an earful of hornets. The waitress says, "Want another one?" He looks through her dress at the tops of her legs and the black triangle of pants and slowly up her gauzy torso tinged charcoal by the cloth to the luminous curve of dark-tipped breasts and the pale, sharp face. You wouldn't blush if I grabbed you by the crotch and squeezed juice, he thinks.

"Something else," he says. "Take that lady over there one of your all-day margaritas. And bring me another Ex." One eye-brow curls. "Which lady?" she asks, looking over her thin shoulder.

"The one twice your age over there with the office kids by the logs." The one with a face like a lamp, you peepshow.

He drains off the warm beer in his glass. How am I gonna deal with this? He looks at her talking to the kids, lively lines flickering around her eyes and mouth, one long arm bent upward like a heron cocked for fish. Where are your chevrons, lady? An NCO for drinks with the enlisteds. The dusky-green summer blouse open halfway down her soft chest. What a way to make a fool of yourself, Collister, he thinks as the black-crêpe waitress slides the big bowl of lime-cream margarita through the air onto the table. She startles like a bird, tilts her face to the waitress, then looks across at him, expressionless.

I *am* blushing, he thinks, and clenches his fist on the tabletop but doesn't dare look away. He feels like a lobster uncovered on a platter, but the room notices nothing. And then she laughs, her head thrown back like someone who's heard the right answer, and his blood goes back where it belongs as he grins across at the bright wreath of her face.

The peepshow brings his beer and says, "She says thank you."

"She would," he says.

The waitress's face gets disorganized around the edges but she says nothing.

"It takes all kinds," he says.

"For sure."

He looks out over the harbour's silver skin, his arms snugged down on the arms of his chair, thinking, Tomorrow is for tomorrow, and watches a big white sloop motor in. The easy slouch of the bare-chested sailor in the well of the scrubbed teak deck. The pinafored boys on the Round Pond, their boats standing in on the evening breeze while old men remember Empire in their bath chairs and watch the nannies bend over to marshal the sailorboys for home.

Beyond Laurel Point he sees the masthead of something big about to arrive. Ship coming to harbour. Forest suburbs of Metchosin beyond that and off into the blue history-book distance of Sooke and Point No Point and George Vancouver, Mad Dog Meares, Bodega y Quadra and the Nootka. The open sea.

"Gone sailing?" she says.

He looks up, startled. "Yeah," he says. Trim white trousers and the green blouse. The face shining down at him, long lines in it, and the eyes. You might not be pretty, he thinks, but you're sure as hell there. Here. Say something, Collister.

"I guess you've seen some weather," he says.

She nods. "It's unpredictable."

What do I say next? Here she is, for real. He looks past her to the vacant litter of bottles and glasses where she had been sitting with her troops.

"They went home," she says. "It's only Tuesday. But you left me with this." She waves the huge bowl of margarita, its foam subsided.

"Humungous," he says. "Have a chair."

"Thank you," she says, laughing. "That's the silliest thing anyone's done for me in years. Do you want to help me drink it?"

"No."

"I didn't think so. Cheers." She pours into the cocktail glass in her other hand. "One silliness deserves another."

She's as nervous as I am, he thinks. Then she says, "Do you always send drinks to women that look at you?"

"Hell no." And he feels the blush again. "Those your paper soldiers?"

She grimaces. "Yes."

"What outfit?"

She laughs. A sinewy, timbred sound. "Ministry of Education, Information Branch. And you?"

"Old Soldiers," he says. They both laugh. "Rifle company sergeant about the time you were born."

"That might be stretching it. I've got two boys as old as you were when you joined up."

They look at each other, and out the window at time gathering itself off for business in the Sandwich Islands.

"Sometimes I wish I was in England," he says, "but this is one of the great windows anyplace."

"It feels like a holiday," she says. "Your margarita got me thinking of Mexico. Why England?"

"I dunno." His face wrinkles to catch at an answer. "I was there a long time in the war. Brought an English girl back and married her. That didn't work out. Went over again a long time later and it was like going home. This place mostly feels like it's the wrong size. And the wrong age. Christ, I'm half as old as the fuckin' country."

He glances at her, thinking to say, Sorry for the language, but her profile tells him that would be dumb.

"Funny," she says, "about place."

They sit looking out their window as the fat bulk of the *Coho* slides around the point like an overgrown bathtub toy. Something big in plain view. The ferry from the U.S.A. Sam's mind wanders among the possibilities of Japanese submarines beneath the waves half a life ago. Another life ago. Musty posters and ration books. Hirohito's Bathtub on the other edge of this ocean, where the Yanks *had* blasted shipping out of tranquil domestic water. Cargoes of human flesh spilled into the sea. Sadly he remembers the crowds on Regent Street coming down to Piccadilly, the warm sea of humanity.

"My people were Russian," she says. "A long time ago. I still dream of churches shaped like onions and villages I've never seen."

She's just like me, Sam thinks. She's from someplace else in her head. He sees German armour snaking through burned-out villages. And himself standing there in khaki without a rifle, beside him this girl in a dark skirt and white blouse, her hair wrapped in a kerchief iconic gold and red. Like the cover of an Edna Ferber novel painted over Esquimalt's dour industrial shore.

The margarita is almost gone. She raises the glass to her mouth and he thinks, This has all been going on for a long time, as he watches her throat take a swallow down under the tanned, fine-wrinkled skin. That brown skin pulses in the hollow between her collarbones and opens out over the gentle contours of her chest to the moss-green edge of cloth. Green hills, the forest and the sea.

When he looks up, her eyes are on his. He feels guilty, like a voyeur. "I'm tired of Mexico," she says. "I'm tired of going places with people who talk all the time and don't say anything. I have to do that for a living, where most of them think the language was meant to cover their asses." She pauses. Sam feels dizzy, a big space inside that he might fall into. "So here I am making a speech," she says, and pauses again. Her eyes search his, as though she were afraid of what she wants to say next. "But it's nice to be able to tell the truth for once. Were you thinking about breasts just then?"

He startles and says, "Uh –"

"A woman gets used to being looked at, but she can get pretty cynical about why."

"I was thinking about breasts," he says. Her eyes are grey with green shadows in them and splashes of gold. "I was thinking you were the daughter of Mother Russia," and as he says it he hears the silence they're sitting in, and has a fleeting notion of why people might want to build churches.

Her mouth curves out and her shoulders shake in a laugh he feels more than hears. "I'm not sure what I'm the daughter of anymore," she says, and smooths one hand over her breast and down in a sweep the length of her thigh, gazing at herself. She joins her hands behind her head and stretches back, chin tucked in, looking away as far as one can look. She looks happy, he thinks, surprising himself. Or pleased. Or like herself.

"My gran grew up in Wisconsin and went to Ontario with six kids and no husband. I was born near Barrie and came out here with two kids and no husband. It seems to run in the family." He can see the muscles around her eyes take hold of something and say, What's that? "Run," she says. "I wonder." Save that and come back to it, he thinks. "I don't know why she chose Ontario, but I didn't want to go east and this was as far west as I could get."

"Where'd the husbands get to?"

"Hers just disappeared. Mine –" She smiles. "Some ladies don't bother with them anymore, but I kind of predate that. I did have one. He was building nuclear power plants and I was researching public affairs. We saw different things when we looked out the window. So he's living in Rosedale with a woman who likes to serve aspic salads and I'm living down there in James Bay with two sons who won't need a mother much longer," she waves her arm, "and my paper soldiers, who always will. What happened to you?"

"I disappeared into a bottle … Hadn't seen my son in twenty years till he came to find me last month."

"What was that like?"

Sam grunts. What was it like? Drunk and crazy.

"I think I scared him off."

He feels like she's looking at him from far away. Hugh's letter. *Can I come and see you?*

"You probably scared the hell out of each other."

"Yeah," he says and pulls out a cigarette. A drink of tepid beer.

"This doesn't seem like the kind of place for a man who disappeared into a bottle."

"No," he says. He swallows. Do sheep feel sheepish? "Fred brings me here, mostly." He nods toward the door. "The guy who was sitting here. I was just gonna finish this beer and go. Wanna come down to the Beaver?" He shifts in his chair. "It's more my style."

Her eyes sparkle. Quietly mocking, like the light on the water. "I don't know if that's the sort of invitation a lady should accept."

"The chili's cheap," he says, "but it tastes like chili."

"I better phone the boys," she says, "and tell them I missed dinner."

⊳┄⊷┄○┄⊶┄⊲

He holds the door for her as they go down the steps to the pavement. He feels like he's marching, next to her easy, long-boned gait. Halfway down to Humboldt, in the shadowed air, she takes his arm and says, "How do you live?" He stops and looks at her face there by his shoulder. The two of them standing in front of the blank façade of the Customs Building. A place that sells furs across the road. Her arm in his, her light body six inches away, easy in the air as a flag unfurling. He notices she smells good, among the floral scents of July Victoria. Good the way a woman does who's a little warm in her clothes and not worried about anything.

Her face looks at him and says, "Was that the wrong question?"

"No," he says. "I was just wondering how come you haven't been making me horny."

She laughs, and stops laughing. "Because it wasn't the wrong question," she says.

He starts walking again because he thinks otherwise he might seize up. "I got a bit of pension and a cheap place on Battery Street. Down where the old folks live." He laughs. "Next year I get the Mincome. And I do odd jobs. Used to be a bush cook till my ticker blew a fuse one night. Construction before that." He shrugs. "You get older."

They stop for the complicated junction of Humboldt, Government and Wharf. "I used to figure if I couldn't talk to it, I could out-fight it or out-drink it. Or both.

23

Now I dunno." He looks straight up, where there is nothing but blue air.

"I don't either," she says as they start across. "You could start living."

He grunts. "A fine time. More like getting ready to die."

Her hand clutches at his bicep, once, a spasm. I shouldn'ta said that, he thinks.

"What did you do about women?" she asks.

You bitch! he thinks. The loosening runs up his spine like a wind gone through him. You bitch? No. You scared me.

"After I left Dot I was a hosebag. But you get older."

"And now?"

He hesitates, but she's taking it all in stride. "Now I pull my wire a lot." He shudders. "And get mixed up with young stuff once in a while."

"And what did Dot do, besides bring up your son?"

They reach the little flying bridge out to the door of the Beaver. How much talk can you have, he wonders, getting from one bar to another? He opens the door for her.

The Beaver is winding into a hot summer night. Heads float in the uneven light and a hundred voices speak against the jukebox and the working noise of glass, cash register and washing machine. Home again, he thinks. A kid in a T-shirt, hollering over his shoulder, comes bustling for the door. The girl skips aside and the kid bounces off Sam like a ball off a bumper in a pinball machine and out into daylight.

As they pass the bar Sam shouts, "Hey Ralph! Frenette been in tonight?" The tapman shakes his head and keeps drawing beer.

"My word!" she says in his ear. "This place is like they say it is."

A motley crew in house-painter clothes sprawl around a table near the open window in the corner. "Can you guys make some room back there?" he bellows.

"Grab a chair, Sam."

Sam hoists a chair over his head and shoves it in next to the window sill, which will serve them as a table. "Sit," he says, and squeezes past her to the empty seat in the corner. He shifts the chair around and plants himself. There she is, white-trousered knees tilted out, one hand in her lap, shoulder bag slid down over the arm of the chair, elbow propped on the broad window sill, gazing out into the breeze and the marigold light filtering through the trees. He shakes his head. What are you doing here, woman?

"Dot," he says, leaning forward to cut through the racket, "married a guy who owns buildings."

She turns her face to him. "Oh," she says. This is what it's like to be looked at, he thinks. Himself in a chair just like her, a casual pile of human parts. Amazing.

"Does she serve aspic salads?"

"I don't know," he says. "She used to fry bread, but that was way back. I haven't seen her in twenty years either."

A tidy looking young guy picks up glasses from the house painters. "Paul!" Sam shouts. "Four beer and some chili," pointing his finger back and forth between her and himself. Paul nods. "Bring lotsa bread!"

The look on her face has nothing to do with food. It makes him want to do something, so he reaches out and squeezes her arm and she touches his shoulder. Her eyes seem to be seeing something remembered from another life.

"A woman in my position – or Dot's – has two choices. Either she learns how to be someone's wife, or she meets men who are just on the make."

The beer and chili arrive all at once. She opens her purse and says, "My turn." Paul slips an ashtray onto the window sill among the glasses and bowls and the plate heaped with bread and more butter than a sensible man should eat. He takes her money and Sam says, "Thanks," and Paul grins, and she says, "Have one yourself," and Paul says, "Thank you, ma'am."

"They seem to have a better class of waiter than you'd expect."

"Empress staff, that one was. Some adjust better than others."

They drink beer and eat chili with white bread baked in the French style. "You're right," she says, "it tastes like chili," wiping a rusty smear from her chin. She burps and grins. "I'm beginning to understand the merit of having a beer parlour in the Empress Hotel."

Then a round face leans over her shoulder, wide smile, round gold-rimmed glasses, round torso behind her.

"Frenette!" says Sam.

Frenette turns to the woman whose shoulder his hand is on and bobs his head. "Hello," he says to them both. "Don't introduce me. I'm just looking for Woody."

"Haven't seen him. We were in Stubbs'. Squat down and have a beer. Or swipe a chair off those painters."

Frenette looks at the woman who hasn't been introduced. "Next time," he says.

"Come on, what kinda soldier are you?"

"I'm not, remember?"

Sam grins. "Later," Frenette says. He pats the woman's shoulder and bounces away through the crowd.

Sam looks at her.

"Lily," she says. "Bristol. Formerly Baranova."

"Sam Collister," he says. She shakes his hand.

"Who was that – Frenette?" she asks.

"Jack Frenette. Friend of mine," he says. "Cooks in the Victoria Inn. He came up from L.A. Used to be a speed freak, but the cooking plumped him up." He pauses. "Dodged the draft."

"How do you feel about that," she says, "Sergeant?"

Again he feels like he's sitting in a church and the church looking at him.

He barks a laugh and bangs his glass on the window ledge. "Well," he says, "I learned a few things." He stirs the condensation around on the thick, chipped paint. "We had two wars to end all wars. Now we have 'police actions'. Dirty," he says. "And the next big one's gonna end everything." He looks out the window where the day is lowering its last and reddest flag. "That kid could soldier with anybody." The winds of time and Douglas MacArthur, bugles. He looks at her.

"There's sergeants in funny places," he says.

"He's good at leaning on people," she says. "He pays attention." She looks at the same flag, the ruddy glow on her slavic face, and turns to him. "Is that what sergeants do?"

"You should know. You're the sergeant with those office kids of yours. And *they* know it." He pauses, awkwardly. "Whenever you look at me I feel like I've been seen." He gestures at her face. "You carry that around like a lamp and shine it on things."

She smiles. "That's nice," she says. "Pretty as a flashlight. Lovely as a lanthorn." And laughs. Stops laughing. Looks at him, as he orders more beer and wonders if he said the wrong thing. Is this "gently mocking"?

His blush returns, sudden and scared. "I didn't mean to say anything wrong," he says.

"It's not you," she says impatiently. "Most men my age are too scared to do anything except get laid." Her anger jolts him. "Not that I object to sex. But I can't stand affairs anymore. You get some tarnished Adonis who plays tennis and takes you sailing and says you're beautiful. Then he lets you about as far into his life as he gets into yours." The corner of her mouth twists and she flops an imagined penis out of her fly into her hand. "About six inches."

Sam glances around nervously to see if anyone saw, and thinks, If she ain't worried, why should I be?

"You sound damn pissed off," he says.

"It's the truth," she says, her hands turned up in a shrug, "when I stop to notice." Her elbows come in to her ribs and he can see her closing up like a darkened flower. It chills him. The beer arrives and is paid for.

In her silence the chill seeps through him. It was too good to be true, whatever it was they'd been doing these few hours. He notices the house painters, notices they are loudly allowing him to be with her as though they weren't just two feet away. As though something were happening. The chill hardens to decision. Nothing's happening. She doesn't need an old fart like me.

He starts to stand up. "Let me get you out of here," he says.

She turns her face on him again, an accusation. "You said this place was more your style," she snaps. "Don't start acting like a polite asshole."

"So whaddya want me to do, you stupid bitch?" he flares, ready to kick back the chair and leave her there, another mistake in his trail.

Her face flattens as though he'd punched her, but she sits still, tight, fighting something.

At last she says, "I'm sorry. I get bitter sometimes."

"So do I," he says.

They sit like a knotted island between the noise behind them and the afterglow of the gone day.

He hauls in air and lets it out. "This might not sound like an apology exactly, but it feels like one. I am an asshole. Last month my son Hugh came in here to meet me. This same kid was slinging beer. I recognized my boy because he was wearing his hockey jacket like he said he would. But mostly I recognized him because he's got Dot's face."

"What happened?" she asks.

He stares off into the smoke and noise and cluttered drinkers of the room, brighter now than what's outside. "We got drunk," he says. "Wound up on the Ogden Point breakwater. And he went back to his hotel instead of coming to my place. That was that. I felt like the end of the world."

He looks at her. "I know I'm an asshole. You are not a stupid bitch."

"I haven't met a man for a long time," she says, stretching out her hand. "It's scary, but it feels good."

He takes the hand, remembering, oddly, the story of the airgunner stopped by an MP for wearing the ribbon of the Victoria Cross. *Who told you you could wear that?* said the one. *King said I could,* replied the other.

"And now I'm going to pee before I burst," she says. "It's behind the bar," he says.

He watches her weave through the crowd. Sees Hugh coming toward him that night. Sam, half-pissed already, saying, "My boy!" shaking his hand, the two of them awkward as virgins.

><>○<><

"You are the fruit of my loins!" he says.

The boy grins and blushes and his eyes look fixed and loose at once.

"Paul!" Collister hollers. "Bring us whisky, dammit!" and slams his hand on the table.

"You do drink whisky," Collister says.

The whisky comes neat in heavy glass. Collister feels the heat in him and his eyes belong to someone else as they watch the boy lift his glass and swallow everything. Tears in his eyes. "Yes," he says. "I don't usually take it straight."

Collister drinks and rises and says, "Let's go."

He goes, the lights and shadows, tables and drinkers of the Beaver bouncing off him. He can feel the boy trailing along, into the Nootka Court mall and up the stairs into the courtyard where it always rains and up the stairs to the LCB, through the glass door he always thinks he'll break and for the whisky shelves. Two bottles, in two bags because that's how they do it, and money, which is always difficult at a time like this, with change and the rightness in all that. *What* time like this? The fruit of my loins! And knows, all the times like this, drunk and full of it all, and out the other glass door – God knows how he knows which is which, too far gone to read IN and OUT

"Where are we going?" the boy asks.

Collister stops and hands him a bottle and says, "I don't know. But we're going to get drunk."

Along the esplanade of the Inner Harbour, he says, "This isn't England. But it's not bad." By the time they pass the wax museum he's braying about manliness and his band of brothers in battle dress.

A long march later, through the battles of Normandy, around the shores of James Bay and out the sweep of the Ogden Point breakwater with his bottle half gone and no railing between him and the night sea twenty feet below, careening through the history of Caen and Falaise, he says to Hugh, "If only I'd had more like you, we could've licked anybody." Then he stops and thinks what he's saying. The boy's face looking like what the hell is this, the way they all did. Children old enough to die but not to drink or vote, and their sergeant the shepherd with the authority of death.

He feels very warm. The rain like blood. The landing-boats in the Channel. The lights; there were no lights in the day-holiday ports. The sea rising and falling with the lights on it like a great ship passing into the dark. The smell of rain and wool and oil and warmth among crowded men, the smell of fear. The barrage went off like a blow in the spine.

"Dad," says Hugh, "Dad!" shaking his arm. Out under the red and white light-tower among night boats passing.

Cold. The heat drained off him. Shivering. Clenched teeth aching. He opens his mouth and coughs.

"Are you all right?"

A glass of wine in Calais. "Yeah," he says. "Let's go home." And levers himself up, swaying a bit on the wet concrete, the granite blocks down there breaking the swell, twenty feet below. Collister sloshes the bottle in his hand. A bitterness in him wants to give it to the granite and the sea. Sharp glass and the reek of Scotch belching up out of him. He stuffs it in his pocket.

"Home," he says.

"My bags are at the hotel."

⊶⊷⊶○⊷⊶

"Sorry I took so long," she says. "Lineup in the powder room." He looks up, feeling his face droop like a basset hound's. She frowns. "Where have you been?" she asks.

"Back on the breakwater."

"I did take too long."

"It's not your goddam fault I made an ass of myself with the kid. I used to be good at looking after people, when there was a war on. What the hell happened?" God knows it'd been hard enough to learn.

He looks around at what's left of the house painters. They have acquired women. One of these, a consumptive-looking child with huge breasts in a loose polyester blouse, smirks at him.

"Speaking of which," he says to Lily.

"Some of the young stuff?"

"Yeah. She was in here one night, blasted out of her head – seemed more like smack than booze. I got her down to my place and she took all her clothes off and said, 'Fifty bucks, dirty old man', and passed out."

"Sam," she says, "I want to tell you something."

"Okay," he says.

"Since you live on Battery and I live on Menzies, why don't you walk me home?"

29

DEADLY NIGHTSHADE

"IT'S WET," he says.

"Yes," she replies.

"Like frogs," he says. "After the rain the frogs sing." The exultation of frogs that they are no longer dry.

He licks her delicately between the legs, her little erection a nib of intensest light in the wet dark of his mouth.

"Wet," he says, "like the fish," moving up to her mouth with his.

"Yes," she says. The silver trout slippery in her hands. Their loins joining then, in a cascade of fish in which they thrash like a single drowning land-thing.

"It's all true," she says. "I've always thought it was all true, what they say about fish and fucking."

Were there fish the first time? he wonders, easing himself through her and through her, as she eases him in herself. What was it like, the first time? Of course he remembers some things. The colour of her labia, livid even by lamplight. Cunt-bright. Of course that wasn't the first time either. But the first with her, the marriage, that chunk of his life. Dorothy. Dot. Dotty. Who had fried bread for his breakfast. And he'd eaten the thick stench of grease, thinking kind thoughts. A brave people, the English. Hardship. Wondering if a bite of the griddle itself could taste worse. Fried bread like lead in his stomach. No, the lead was in that boy's belly in the Belgian mud. Frozen. Now in his own gut as he lies with Lily in the musty rooms of the King Edward Apartments. No, not the lead. Dotty saying, "What a lovely morning!" as he realized that only the English could find a way to eat the stove itself. "How can you eat the stove?" he said, watching the pigeons of Ladbroke Grove shit on the bricks beyond Dot's window. "What's that, luv?" "The stove," he said. "Oh, you mean the cooker." Yes.

He caresses Lily's hair and cradles her skull, thinking, I shouldn't be thinking all this, while he watches what he feels in his loins spread over her face like a sweaty vision of paradise. It's been going on so long and I'm a sixty-year-old trout heading up this stream one more time. And he grunts in a rush of the waters which aren't cold. Wet. Her flesh all around him, all around her.

"What are you thinking?" she says.

Thinking? Her fingers curl in his hair.

"How old are you?" he asks.

"Forty-four," she says. He hears a smile and lifts his head to look.

"You're beautiful," he says.

She laughs. He feels her breasts under him and himself slipping out of her. A feeling like nothing else on earth. Except the blood and the heart and the liver in your hands when someone's been gutshot and no one can do a thing. He grunts again, differently.

"That's funny," he says.

And furrows around her eyes as she says, "You don't look like it's funny."

"No." His eyes and her eyes begin doing that thing he knows about, in which two people fall into each other and come up wondering which way, or what day, at all, is it since they've been down there in that big, ancient, quiet place. Tears slide down from the corners of his eyes to the bridge of his nose, and roll uncertainly toward the tip.

"I love you," he says, gripping her skull as though it needed holding together. "Not too much, you understand. But enough." He swallows something. "Lord," he says. "Enough."

She looks at him. Quizzically, he thinks. Strange old familiar in my bed.

"I pray sometimes," he says.

"I know," she says. "You were praying all along, weren't you? While we were making love."

He smiles, and the warmth in his loins moves up through him like they said benediction was supposed to.

"I wish I had been," he says. "Thank you. But I was thinking too much."

She smiles. "You didn't feel like you were thinking."

"I keep thinking you're a girl," he says. Her sons almost men. Forty-four. Slim. Sapling birch. Some guy bending that birch tree to the ground. A poignant, queasy feeling.

She grins. "Thank you. I'm hungry," and slips down to nibble his ear and his neck and kiss his chest, like a girl.

"Nothing," she says, grinning up at him, "tastes like sweat." Blood, he thinks, and knows he shouldn't think it.

She licks the sweat from his navel and pecks, birdlike, soft-mouthed, along his abdomen and the angle of his hip. His surprise becomes anticipation. She giggles, wickedly, "Dessert," and slips his dozey cock into her mouth.

He looks at her, curled up like a girl at his hip, and can just reach her ribs with his fingertips.

She mouths his balls, one at a time, sucking them up over her tongue, and he wonders if this is how it feels to be a plum in a virgin's mouth.

⊷⊶○⊷⊶

Why does it have to be a virgin? he thinks. A blonde girl in a lane in Devon, blue-and-white print wrapped tight around her hips, hollows in her buttocks as she bends into the tangled foot of the hedgerow. New breasts languidly pointing around in her white blouse. Fourteen? He goes to look at what she's looking at, prickly in the August heat.

Bright hair swinging and blue eyes looking up, strange in the wild matted green of the hedge. Near her parting hand, a spikey, livid thing tipped with reddest orange among the cowslips and what he thinks are kinds of worts.

"Deadly nightshade," she says, sounding embarrassed.

"Yes," he says, wanting to touch her buttock with his fingers' ends, to feel if she vibrates as she seems to. He can smell her light, evaporating sweat and feels his pores gushing. I must look like a bloody aging consumptive, he thinks. His hands blunder into each other. He sees himself tearing her soft skirt away and reaching under her taut bottom to the sweet, sweaty young flesh there between her legs and his vision blurs. Cunt, he says, cunt, how can it be so lovely? And hopes he hasn't said it aloud.

She removes her hand from the hedge and says, "Well, I must be off now," and swings away. He watches her, unhurriedly quick and swaying, out of sight between the twisting hedge-rows, tasting bitterness and wrong. There are red hills and green, dotted with sheep and cows in the humid, dungy, febrile smell of England the good. He hates the flies with a brief concentration of hatred. Bends down and parts the good English weeds of centuries. Deadly nightshade.

Awesome, malicious, necromantic fruit. Delicious and dangerous to the eye as pointy red peppers. Deadly. He takes it in his fingers and crushes the stem, pulls it into his hands, mashes the berries in his fingers and palms, just barely avoids cramming the whole mess into his mouth.

He picks another, carefully, and takes it back with him to his hosts, who look at him in horror as he enters their kitchen. "That's deadly nightshade!" Jameson and Elizabeth cry. "Yes," he says. "Odd how pretty it is."

"Throw it out! In the dustbins, man. Don't you know it can kill you? And wash! Scrub! Immediately."

He stands looking at them like a ten-year-old, and feels for a moment that he is not in England, or anywhere, and the pit in him draws hoarse sucking noises back through his throat.

On the terrace of The Seven Stars he sucks at a pint of murky Bass and longs for company. It's closing time, the bizarre English hiatus in public hours to allow drunkards' wives the feeding of their men. A few tag-ends of tourists sit at the white enamel tables under gaudy canvas tilted all wrong for the sun. They stare over the beer-sticky tables as though there were no flies. A half-hearted bustle along Fore Street before the greengrocers close. A beery old Canadian, he thinks, and pretends he's sober enough to cross the street, pint in hand. On Vire Island he stares at the beer-coloured river. Tour boats blue and white float like the beer tables, stinking of diesel. The river sucks at the silt along its edges and laps over pavement that is gradually sliding in, its iron rails tilting rusted and bent out of the water. The underside of the road-bridge dully reflects its river on mud-skimmed concrete. He badly wants a place to piss, and that looks inviting. In Flanders' fields there is room to piss. He pours the dregs of his Bass onto his bootcaps and looks down. He isn't wearing boots. Civvy shoes. Soft leather. Comfortable for walking. Splattered with beer. He sways out over the river and hauls himself back. No place to piss. No place to sit. The benches either broken or occupied by young handholders.

The bushes rustle behind him and a girl's voice says, loud enough to be mean, "Strange 'un, is'n 'e?"

▷─▸─◦─◂─◁

"Breakfast," she says, peaceably sliding herself to and fro astride him. "Let's get up."

He looks at her out of what feel like haggard eyes. "Lily," he says, "I want to tell you something."

"Yes?" she says. She's not too hungry to say yes, he thinks.

"But I can't. There was a girl in Belgium." The waters well again behind his eyes. "She wasn't my girl. And things happened there. A lad in my platoon. One of my lads. It keeps coming back on me …"

"How old were you?" she asks.

"Twenty-five."

"An old man." She smiles, someone who has a son twenty and has lived long enough.

"He got his guts blown out in a field of parsnips in the mud." She had come to the shell hole at twilight and no one had stopped her. The Germans had been kind.

"Should you think about those things?" Lily asks, having been ten at the time, in Ontario.

"No," he says.

The girl had wanted to bury him, him lying on the slope of the hole like the filthiest bundle of rags and meat. Lise. She had said, "Before you came, I was raped once." Her hair brown, and her eyes brown enough to be black, fine bones under her brown, hollow-cheeked skin. "Five Germans who took turns holding each arm and leg. One for each, and one for me, turn by turn." Her French was schooled. Her Walloon he wouldn't have known. There is a fountain in the garden.

"Then you should tell me," Lily says.

"No," he says. He feels that all of him is up in his chest and face and eyes, spilling out even his ears. "There is a fountain in the garden," he blubbers. "It's a Belgian love song."

She had asked to bury him, but there was no way. She couldn't have moved him alone, much less dug him under. Hugh. Filthiest bundle of rags. And no one could help her. He could send no living man up there to dig a hole for the dead. Not even himself. Lord, if only he could have sent himself. He looked at the two boys in the hole with him. Not Hugh. They were looking at the coming night and the Germans they couldn't see, and at the freezing ground. In his head he saw the other boys in the other holes, the dozen or so left to him. He could send himself least of all.

She had laid her hand on a long, evil shard of shrapnel in the mud, fingering its broken-razor edge. "Give me your knife," she had said. And he had pulled out the dagger from his boot. It hadn't much edge, meant for plunging amongst ribs, mostly point. But it was long. The knife in her hands and no one could bury Hugh. Lord. Himself least of all, who had tried already to make whole flesh of the bloody wreckage in the mud. That dark slender girl intense as the blade in her hand. Love and death nameless in her eyes. The thing she was about to do inevitable as a bad dream.

"Give me your hands," Lily says, and tries to lift him up. "Breakfast," she says.

He makes a noise and twists away beneath her, hands clutched to his chest, eyes clenched tight on the darkness and palpable horror of Belgium. "No!" he says, guttural in the bedclothes. The darkness wants to burst out of him and throw her warm body away.

Her hand touches his hair. "It's okay," she says.

Christ, don't blow it. He drags his eyes open to see her there, dark-haired and real in early light, her eyes frightened, stubborn, willing him to be whole again. He feels her tense muscles begin to ease against him.

Her hand touches him again. "It's okay." He remembers how one speaks to frightened animals.

"Thank you," he says.

She looks at him like that again, sitting on his thighs with her legs wrapped around him. The big, ancient, quiet place. The Walloon Lise. All the women and men. "You're a good man, Sergeant Collister." And he's not sure which way or day at all. "Funny," he says, "she said the same thing."

"Being remembered by someone like you," Lily says, "is living in a holy place."

"I'm not so sure," he says, "about going down to breakfast with your sons old enough –"

"Shush," she says, rising. "They're old enough to know their father when they see one. Give me your hands."

And he sits there looking at eye-level at her cunt, thinking, yes, that's what cunt means. A wedge. A woman. And he puts his hand there, saying thank you to a woman. Yes.

And he gets ready to go downstairs, scared.

BATTERY STREET

HE SITS IN his room and waits until it's time to go. His eyes wander over the photographs on the dresser. Instead of those yellowed grey faces he sees Lily's eyes looking back at him, their green and gold shadows warm with delight, and wonders how that was possible. He shakes his head. It wasn't possible. He'd gone downstairs and seen two young guys, one just the man-side of boy, the other just the boy-side of man. And her place in which she lived with them, the old oak table stripped and refinished and stained with eating and drinking and life. The china the same. The macramé flowerpot holders. The elegant vases of dried pampas grass and eucalyptus, the gentle, worn couch and the oriental rug you could roll up and live in. He'd taken a trembling cup of coffee from the older polite boy and mumbled and fled before breakfast, her eyes startled. Down Menzies to the old place by the sea where Stone Age Indians had fortified their camp between the forest and the cliffs.

There are buses every hour to catch the ferry, but he's not ready yet. Not ready to see Braithwaite smashed up and dying, by the sound of it – after all these years and the times the Germans couldn't kill him. Four hours' travel with the tourists to see that. And he can still almost see Lily, as though she had really been there, her smell in his nostrils every time he breathes. His eyes caress her dim length and hit the coffee table, the mottled-green ashtray lying on it like a dead starfish. The knife in Lise's hands, the blood on his.

He grunts and reaches to roll a smoke from the pouch on the table. Gotta get some tailor-mades for the trip. Other than that, he's packed – toothbrush in his pocket and a handkerchief and a hundred bucks folded neat: his bank balance for the month. Better take a razor. He nips off the ends of tobacco, drops them back in the worn Export pouch, and sniffs his fingers, wondering. Nothing but nicotine. She's gone from there.

His eyes wander again, sweet smoke curling before them. The bed. The couch. The chair he's sitting in. Newspapers and books. The spines of books tell him things like *Basic Carpentry* and Steinbeck and *Better Gardens*. Liddell Hart's histories and Guderian's *Panzer Leader*. William Manchester and *The Diviners* and Hammond Innes and Haig-Brown. But they look like any books spilling out of shelves anyplace with dirty yellow walls and lumpy furniture. The blank eye of the

TV tells him nothing except the dust's getting thick enough to cut.

He stands up and the movement reminds his body of Lily's and he feels fleetingly twenty years younger. He sucks in his gut and fills his chest. His shoulders feel big and solid. He bellows TEN HUT! and goes to the kitchen to see if there's any beer left. Anyhow, the ferry serves better food once the afternoon buffet's open.

The remains of chicken in a pan in the sink tell him he better take out the garbage if he figures on coming back here. There are empty bottles on the table and the counter and a stack of old cases by the fridge. The fridge is near empty and there isn't any beer. He rummages through the case on the floor by the table, knowing he'll find nothing but dead soldiers. Dumped an ashtray in there, which was an asshole thing to do. Bit of a party around that chicken. Surprised I ain't dead yet.

Lily's hand on his arm. Don't think dead, Collister. Will she be here when I get back? Two sons, with macramé and eucalyptus. He puts down the beer case and goes to look for the phone book. There she is, on Menzies. And she'll be in an office somewhere in the Douglas Building – while he's futzing around here not leaving for Vancouver – doing whatever she does. He sees typewriters and telephones and hears her voice giving orders for the deployment of information. Doing something useful.

His hand reaches around chicken bones in greasy water to drain the sink and there's a knock at his door. Damn. The towel he wipes his hand on says things about the laundry he doesn't want to hear.

Outside the door, the round face of his deaf-mute neighbour smiles up at him. She's short and plump and reminds him too often that people can be brave. The paper she holds out for him to read says, "Can you come and fix my hot plate, please?" in careful pencil.

"Sorry, Jean," he says, then curses himself as she keeps smiling and shakes her head and taps her ear. He takes the pencil and writes, "I'm catching a ferry to Vancouver."

She smiles and nods and he closes the door. You prick, he says to himself. But he can't face fiddling with burnt wires and more grease. And she always tries to pay him. He'd better get out of here. Not that she'd hear him leave.

He rolls another smoke. You just don't want to go, do you? To see Al in a hospital bed, run over by some jackass civilian because he's a little funny between the ears and slow on his feet. And Dot lives three blocks from there with her small-time real estate baron. Too close for comfort. Al nearly dead. Ain't we all.

He finishes packing the garbage and takes it with him out the door he's gone in and out of so often.

iv

AN OLDTIME MOVIE

ON AN ORDINARY afternoon in the Buffet Lounge of the ferry from Swartz Bay to Tsawwassen, the chesty dude in Levis ahead of him in line says, "How about a furburger and a side of thighs?" The serving girl just pretty enough to ask. She flushes.

"Don't serve him," Sam says.

Her glance is cynical. "You I don't need," it says.

She says to the Levis, "I'm sorry, sir, full meals only. You'll have to try the cafeteria."

The Levis turn a pale, expressionless face on Sam. "Butt out, Pops." Iron Cross around the Levis' neck.

Sam takes the cross in his hand, its points digging into his flesh, and rips it away.

The pale eyes in that pale mask flicker as the right fist leaps at him. He catches it in his left hand and shoves the right with the cross in it against the thin lips below the eyes, which start looking empty. Lips are soft, he thinks. I'd love to break your teeth, punk, he thinks.

"This thing," he says, feeling the words in his chest, "used to be worn by guys who went out to get shot at by guys like me." The young German in the mud with a hole in him the size of a big fist. The eyes looking straight through him.

"Eat it," he says.

He can feel the lips wanting to say something, but nothing happens.

"Eat it, you young fucker, or I'll shove it down your throat, teeth and all!"

He cocks his fist and someone behind grabs the arm, so he delivers an elbow in the ear and turns around to find a steward sitting on the floor holding his head.

Oh shit, he thinks.

He looks at the punk and holds out the cross. "Here," he says, "something to remember me by."

Amongst the commotion and a lot of people saying No, he hears the punk say, "Crazy old bastard" and the Tannoy sound of the PA calling, "Chief Steward to the Buffet Lounge." Sam shrugs his way through cluttered arms and bodies to the companion way, where he meets the chief steward coming up.

"Do you have a brig in this thing?" Sam asks.

38

The chief steward is a small, doughty-looking character who would have belonged in corvettes. "No," he says. "Are you the nut?"

"I guess so. I'm the one that smacked your boy. The other one's back there. Motorbike punk that's tired of living."

The steward pulls a face. "Go wait in my cabin outside the cafeteria. The police will have a car at Tsawwassen."

"Marvellous."

Curious faces as he finds a door marked "Chief Steward's Office." Inside, an oak desk and padded chrome chairs. A lot of paper. What are you doing, Sam? he thinks. Christ, waiting for the RSM to come boot your ass around a parade ground. A fine way to go see a friend in hospital – Al over there smashed up in Vancouver. That asshole kid upstairs. Why doesn't this scow have a bar?

After a while the chief steward comes in and looks around as though he needs a safety valve and can't find one. His uniform looks like he's carrying spare parts. He glares at Sam. "You're too old for this bullshit. What d'you think you are, John Wayne?"

Sam looks out the porthole. The passenger lounges have windows. This porthole is a talisman. He sees the bottom of a lifeboat that looks like it needs to be chipped and painted, and a seagull holding formation on the ferry.

"Do you know what the punk said to that poor little bitch? He asked her for a furburger and a side of thighs! Then he turned on me like something out of a motorcycle movie. I wanted to kill him."

The steward rolls his eyes. "Thank God you didn't."

"Him and his Iron Cross … Were you in corvettes?"

The steward cocks an eyebrow. Sam looks up at the seagull, which cocks its head and looks back.

"No," the steward says, "Merchant Service."

They look at each other for a while. Cream-coloured steel walls, stuff that looks like old porridge on the ceiling. Bulkheads, deckhead, dead head. The cluttered desk. Green plastic upholstery. Sam shifts his bottom.

"I know," he sighs, "I know. I'm fifty-nine years old, I've had a heart attack, I shouldn't drink, I shouldn't smoke, I shouldn't get in fights with kids, and one does not bash stewards."

The steward sighs. He opens a bottom drawer of the desk and hauls out a bottle of Queen Anne. He rubs the green glass shoulder of the bottle with his thumb. He has thick nails trimmed short and hands that look as if they've earned their keep.

"Moral terpsichore and drinking on the job are about the only ways you can get fired anymore."

Sam laughs. "Moral terpsichore?"

"Dancing with depravity." The steward fixes him with a slightly bloodshot eye. "The only way you and I are going to get a furburger any more is to pay for it." Sam grins, feeling a bit sickly. The steward pulls out two glasses and pours.

"You in the army?" he asks. "Last guy I asked that, turned out he flew B-25s. Smart old farts, aren't we."

Sam grins. "Vancouver Light Infantry."

"Christ. No wonder you're an asshole."

Sam swallows the Scotch whole. It ignites a long laugh in him. He flaps his arms at the seagull, which skids and looks embarrassed. Settling into his chair, he smiles beatifically at the chief steward.

The chief steward shakes his head. "I should write books. This job. My kids keep telling me I should write books."

"You get that too, do you?" The steward looks at Sam as though he'd seen something that shouldn't be there. "When you get old," he says, "you gotta do something or you're dead."

The PA says, "Chief Steward to the cafeteria, please. Chief Steward to the cafeteria."

"Now it's the Lone Ranger with bits of copper wire in his gravy." And he goes.

The seagull banks suddenly and is gone. Sam sits in space, helping himself to the steward's Scotch, his mind as empty as the sky out there beyond the grablines hanging arced under the lifeboat's bottom. A nagging voice tolls, "Or you're dead," as the davits sway against the upper blue. Or you're dead.

At Tsawwassen two Mounties put him and the Levis in the back seat of a purple and white cruiser. The kid says, "What about my bike?"

"Never mind your bike, fella, it's not going anywhere." One Mountie sits between them.

"Can't you put him in the trunk?" says Sam to the horseman in the middle.

"You been drinking, sir?" inquires the Mountie.

"Hell no. It's this car. Smells like a whorehouse."

"He's crazy," says the punk. "Put him in Riverview."

Sam looks at the Mountie. "You poor fucker," he says, and sits back and falls asleep.

⊱──◈──⊰

The next morning a sceptical magistrate fines them both $50 for assault. Complicated. The kid poked Sam. Sam poked a steward. They both broke the peace. Cheap at fifty bucks. The punk is not wearing his cross.

"Where's your medal, kid? You get KP for not wearing your medal on parade."

"Why aren't you dead?" says the punk.

Sam grins. "Call me Sergeant, kid. Now go along and fetch your kit and get back here on the double. We're going to have a little square-bashing for a while."

"You two get the hell out of here!" says the magistrate. The court reporter looks up at the magistrate. The magistrate looks down at his docket of cases.

Sam heads for the door, wondering how he's going to get through the month fifty bucks short. You gotta do something or you're dead.

BEING STABLE

THERE'S TUBES sticking out of Al's nose and arms and a piece of plastic flex in the hole they cut in his throat so he could breathe. A bag of bloody urine hangs from under the bedclothes. Al's feet are in traction and his hands are in casts. His nearly naked body sprawls like a sack of meat on the dump.

Christ, thinks Collister.

"He's not responding well," says the nurse. "Don't stay long." A fat pale cloud, expressionless and watery.

Not responding well. No wonder you're not responding well.

Al's foggy breath comes snorting out of the flex as though his lungs were half full of water. Skin like parchment. Dry, translucent. Lizard skin, with bones poking out.

I've seen dead people look better than you, Al, he thinks. He feels cold, watching the fog come out of Al.

Further down the ward an old guy is saying over and over, "Something's wrong. Something is definitely wrong."

They blew you up twice in France, Al. A Tiger tank and a land mine. Jesus.

He goes up to Al's shoulder and says, "Al! How ya doin'? It's Sam."

Al's right eye flickers toward him. Sam puts a hand on the shoulder. It's hot and rough. Desert places. Corpses in the sand. The blood of the panzers. Freezing by night and frying by day. The sun comes up in the time it takes to piss.

"Hello, Al. Glad to see ya lookin' okay." The hands don't move, the eyes don't move. Al is looking out past the fog, but it doesn't look like he's seeing anything.

The old guy has called Security to correct what's wrong. Improbably, Security appears. The hospital rent-a-cop looks like you could break him in half like a breadstick. He looks like he believes old guys should be dead.

The Tiger had blown Al out of a hedgerow. The land mine had lifted him off a road near the Belgian border. But he'd been a little crazy before that, from the beginning. Sergeant three times, busted to private twice. "That's what noncoms are for, Sam. We're not officers and we're not men. We're sergeants. It's up to us to keep these poor fuckers alive so some asshole with trinkets on his collar can send 'em out to get killed."

Al led by example. The Wehrmacht had been able to do no more than leave him with a more peculiar mind than he'd had before.

"Al," he says, "don't just die."

How long is not long? What do you keep saying to a guy that might not be there?

He goes to find the fat cloud nurse. To think that she might be someone's mother …

"Is he going up or down – or do we know?"

"They say he's stable," she says.

"That means he's not in danger."

"No." She looks at him appraisingly. "It means that he's stable."

"We were in the war," he says. "I've known him thirty-nine years." He pauses. "I feel like family." It still doesn't sound convincing. "I live in Victoria." I forgot the fucking razor and I look like I spent the night in jail.

She says, "The stimulus is good for him. Even if it seems like he doesn't know you're there."

Oh. He feels like a great saggy "O" standing there.

"We don't know how much he's aware of," she explains.

Oh, he thinks. Do we know how much anyone is aware of?

How much are you aware of, you fogbank, you bag of shit.

"Oh," he says, "I see. Should I come back?"

"Yes. It does him good. You should come in as often as you can, just don't stay too long."

He regards her pale, puffy flesh and insipid eyes. Why, he wants to say, Why? And can't.

"I'll go now," he says. Am I supposed to shake your hand?

He goes back to look at Al. Iron hair and woodrasp cheeks. A man's face on something that looks like broken broomsticks in a bag.

Sam reaches to spread the thin sheet bunched at Al's middle. Al shivers quietly and steadily as an ill-tuned engine. The threadbare cotton stretched over his limbs is flecked with old blood.

You're bleeding everywhere, pal, he thinks. Except your face, your Goya, skinny, fucking face. Oh Jesus.

He reaches under the translucent sheet and tenderly shifts Al's tubed penis more nearly in line with the bloody urine bag. Touch him, you mothers! Every day. Every time. A man.

><+<>+0+<>+><

"He's cold!" he says as he passes the nursing station. "Warm him up." He hears something about blankets muttered in his wake and thinks, I should have done that, Al. Jesus.

Outside, in the air, he crosses the street before he starts to think. Back in the building full of broken men and bits of tube there is the end of everything. Sunlight here.

He turns around and looks at it. Ugly pile. Concrete and stone towers left from some fantasy of Edinburgh fifty years dead. A shadow against the July sun.

On this bright side of the street there are people. Strangeness fills him. A portly pair strolling by the Cancer Clinic as though it were a local attraction. He far more ugly than she in three-piece polyester airforce blue, all expensive-looking jowls and horn-rimmed glass. A kind of Florida florid oldness here on Heather Street. Ugliness. The postcards home. Sunsets the colour of flamingos. Sad flamingos the colour of crêpe paper in the gutters after a rainy wedding. Popcorn sellers in the zoo. Popcorn sellers along the esplanade at English Bay, twilit, their lamps burning in glass wagons. The smell of hot butter in glossy colour to send to Flo in Florida. Like coals to Newcastle. Ugliness. Off-register photographs of people on beaches, a pink rim slipping out of their skins while the sand beige seeps in on the other side and the sea looks like someone had poured it out of a soft-drink can.

What the fuck do you know about flying? he thinks, wildly, as the short blue airforce back strolls away from him with its fat wife waddling along beside. What the fuck do you know?

The Cancer Clinic and the Heather Pavilion and this narrow canyon full of cars dropping off and picking up the acolytes of death.

That man's as old as I am, he thinks. From the same time. How do I know he never flew an airplane called Halifax or Stirling? P for Popsie, M for Mother?

Jesus. I need to get drunk.

THE WAY DOWN

ON BROADWAY, barely a hundred yards from the hospital, he remembers that Dot lives only a few blocks over. He shudders and turns the other way, tempted.

He wants someone to talk to. But he never could talk to that woman. His mind doesn't want Al, doesn't want to see himself lying there ready for the morgue. He wants a beer and sees himself in some bar with some kid saying, So you were in the war. Did you kill anybody? What was it like? Why don't you write it down? And smashing a chair over the fucker's skull. But he doesn't see anywhere else to go. What's in his head feels like broken glass. Broadway looks like a shattered mosaic of human bodies among storefronts and cars and signs. A boutique called Neue in Fad, staffed by orientals. He walks away from where he was with Al's bones inside him like news of the end of the world. Shrapnel in the guts. What Hugh's innards had told him thirty-four years before.

The jagged light from chrome and polish hits him in the eyes as he pushes through the intersection traffic, north toward down-town. Punk music pounds from open windows and summer bodies glisten in bright machines, gunning their engines.

They gotcha, Al, the bastards. The stench of exhaust, hot dizzy air. Faceless condensation-trails arc across the central blue to mark death in 1940 over Britain. The sweet Merlins sing piercingly through the leaden throb of Germany. He looks up to see them there. So long ago.

A horn honks in his ear and he throws himself into the hedge of the traffic island at 2nd and Cambie. Chevy three-quarter-ton pickup, candy red, shouting mouth soundless and full of teeth. *Watch it! you old fart* – This nearer death.

Where are you going, old fool?

Looking for a beer, forgetting where to find it except that a memory of the Sylvia Hotel floats out somewhere by English Bay in seedy grace. Far the other side of downtown. Across the Connaught Bridge, past Catholic Charities that used to be Northern Electric with a blue neon lightning bolt, where a priest had tried to forgive him when he stumbled in looking for a bed.

"Are you married, son?" the priest had asked.

"I don't think so, Father. I was married to an Anglican. She's married to someone else now."

"Do you practise your faith?"

He had laughed. "I never was any good at it, so I quit."

The priest had not been pleased. A furrowed brow. One more leak in the hull. Iceberg warnings. The priests had never been pleased.

Creosote stench from the new planks underfoot. The bridge goes on and on. I could jump off that. Frail, pitted iron rail. Or go back. He looks back. Broadway seems too far away. His legs have begun to ache. A breeze no stronger than breath cools the sweat on his neck and cheek. The traffic vibrates along beside him at a broken crawl. Stench. Brown haze everywhere over the gentle curves of Vancouver – a woman's back, the limbs of lovers under the clear brassy blue. There is a condensation trail arrowing west, silver-tipped. He pictures a Wardair booze-up around 40,000 feet. He puts a hand on the railing and marches on northward, gimping a bit, the bridge shaking gently. I'm near as old as you, you pile of iron, but the day you walk away for a beer you're dead.

By the time he gets to Davie Street he knows he doesn't know where he's going. The bar of the Sylvia looms like a dismal beacon in his imagination. His feet hurt. His pants feel like sweaty newsprint wrapped around his thighs. No headlines. Things shake inside him. He sits on a bus bench on the north side of the street. A man in summer polyester that looks like mactac reads the news beside him.

News breaks, Sam thinks. This is not news. This is ordinary. Not even Al is news. Just an obituary. This is not ordinary. Keep this up and you're as much a goner as Al. He pushes himself up from the bench, feeling large and old and obvious.

Further down Davie he sees newspapers stacked outside the greengrocers', and girls in tight pants patrolling for the Thursday evening trade. Pigeon hawks in the golden light, red talons and far-seeing eyes. He longs to touch someone. Touch a whore. How many bucks for a quick throw? He feels no excitement, only glumness, his whole body longing for a place to sit down. Booze, food, a room. Lady, I can't afford the time of day.

He eyes them furtively as he passes. They look past him, above him, through him. I need a beer, he thinks. The Hotel Vancouver all brass and glass and stone hadn't wanted any sweaty old folks there. The girlie clubs with Mafia doors and cover charges. The Rembrandt full of punks and near-new threadbare carpet.

I'm a stranger in this town, he thinks. Blown out of himself by Al's bones. Al crawling out of the dust and cordite stink like a hallucination, mumbling, "Let's go fishing." Let's go fishing, lady. He imagines the cold amber taste of hops in his mouth. At least in the Sylvia a man can sit down and think.

In front of a restaurant he sees a slim girl in tight jeans and high-heel shoes. Tweed jacket over a white blouse. Fine features with dark hair and dark eyes, a purse clutched to her ribs, staring up the street, looking cold. Looking like someone's daughter.

Maybe, thinks Sam. Her lips the colour of Queen Anne cherries before they fall. The robins at the cherries. The fissures split open by rain.

Beyond her he can see down the long swooping hill to the foot of Davie Street, the trees in front of the Sylvia Hotel, the band of water between the buildings off into the tawny haze of distance and the blue mountains of Vancouver Island. The lightness of Maybe rises up in Sam and begins to clear his confusion for speech.

He veers toward the girl, eyes on the grotty pavement, candy wrappers, her toenails the colour of her lips, plaited leather pressed against delicate tanned feet, the surprise of ankles and the sudden blue legs tapering up to the plumb-bob of air beneath her groin's soft folds clamped in thick denim stitchery. And the broad flare of her hips under the jacket's edge.

Her eyes are almost black. "Hi," he says, "got a little time?"

She looks at him from the other side of her eyes. "You got any money?" she says.

The breast of her jacket swells outward, but there isn't much inside – cinched up, discreet. Good business, he thinks. Show 'em your crotch but not your tits.

"I don't want to fuck, I just want to talk," he says. Her expression goes from neutral to no. "I'll buy you a drink in the Sylvia." He laughs. "Hell, I'll buy you all the drinks you want. I came to town to see a pal in hospital. He's a mess. I need some company."

She looks away, up the street. "Talk don't pay the rent," she says.

"Aw, come on, honey, how many times you been propositioned for a conversation? There's nothing happening here anyway. Too early. We could have something to eat and a few drinks –"

"There's a place down the street where they get paid to talk to bums. Move on, Daddy. You're bad for business." She takes a few steps. Two sleek young guys come by, tanned and smooth. A fitted leather jacket and transparent cotton shirt. Nice asses in white pants. Ignoring the girl. Ignoring Sam.

"Talk about bad for business," he says. "They oughta be holding hands."

The girl moves away toward the corner of Jervis Street. He watches her, dark head floating above the sway of her bottom, abstracted and unreal as a pony in the paddock before a race. You bitch, he thinks. The dirty restaurant window says Schnitzel and Goulash. A dim interior beyond his bulky shadow on the glass. He imagines flies circling the gummy flans on a shelf by the coffee urns.

No, he thinks, eyeing the girl's easy motion again, you carry it around in that bone cradle as though it was the answer. Not your fault the answer might be wrong. All the hip bones yellow and stinking in all the charnel houses of the world.

He goes on, past the Rogers mansion huddled like a blind ghost behind stone walls, past the Sands, past the last tower on Davie Street. There English Bay suddenly opens like a huge silence before him and he catches his breath as though a wind had sucked it away. "I forgot," he whispers. The empty ships riding high to anchor on the liquid gold sea. The sun grown large and quiet between the broad arms of Point Atkinson and Point Grey. Blue tinges beyond the suntrack taking the first ships into the cool edge of night. Tears on his cheeks as he follows pedestrians across the traffic of Beach Avenue and blunders down through dusty sand to the water's edge. The last of the swimmers glisten, faint laughter in so much space. The last sunbathers, the fading babble of day, debris on the beach. Water laps at his feet. He turns to his left, where Kitsilano glimmers like a watercolour in the filtered light as the blues deepen from the east. Over there, beyond the bright pinpricks of the Molson clock and the crenellated toadstool Planetarium, under the indigo sky, somewhere over there among the mercury vapour lamps lives Dot.

"Dot," he says, crying now, "why couldn't I ever talk to you?" What's improbable about a shapeless old man standing in the tide at English Bay crying? "Dot," he says. Jesus. Little Dot clearing up Sid's dinner. Poor Dot. Poor Sam. Where are we now? Al's trussed up in a basket waiting to get his name spelled wrong in the Last Post, I'm on the beach with nowhere to go, and you're getting organized for – for what? Do you still sleep with that slum landlord? What can you be like now? What am I like now? Yeah, I wanna see you again, you little minx. If only because you're the only act in town.

The quiet in Lily's eyes touches him suddenly from the great distance of two days ago. No! That can't be real. Women with love in their eyes and knives in their hands. He looks around. Don't get too close, he thinks, as the first of the evening lovers and nightstalkers make random movement about him. I look haggard, he thinks. I am haggard. In the air he sees the face that looks at him from mirrors. Enough to frighten children. The figures on the beach. What happens after the crowd goes. What happens after the battle. Random figures. To name the dead. To loot. To bury. To be forlorn. To be frightened by the face in the mirror, red eyes in raw eyelids in a face like a leached-out wheatfield under stubble. An old man standing to his ankles in sea water. In here it's the other way around. I'm scared.

He looks back toward Dot under the darkening crest of Shaughnessy. "If only to remind me why I left," he says. There's no going back. He sees himself trudging further and further out until the water closes cold over his face. The end of the line. He sees corpses spread-eagled on the sea. Hugh and the German boy and all the rest gone under. Now Al. Me too, boy. They shoulda got us all then. So much garbage to toss in the drink.

He sees nowhere to go but the hotel perched like a faded dowager above the beach. He goes to the Sylvia with wet feet and an inkling of what will happen if he gets drunk. Sleeping in the park. Puking in the drunk-tank. He goes to the Sylvia to get drunk enough to stop thinking and figure out where to go. He opens one of the doors that look like they can't go anywhere but the foundation and climbs the stairs. In the upper Sylvia lounge bottles glitter behind the bar and women who look like they want to be Dietrich sit with men who probably wish they were. Red leather. He goes to the lower lounge, which looks more like home in two shades of dingy lit by candy-coloured lamps.

vii

SYLVIA

THERE IS NEVER an empty table by the windows of the Sylvia lounge. Instead, there are two punks at one end eyeing a table of working girls no one in his right mind would mess with. At the other, a bored couple fighting middle age. In between, a lone woman of forty going on sixty with bottle-black hair and a mean eye behind glasses, wearing a winter coat navy blue.

Sam sits at the table in the middle of the floor, hating it. At least by the window he could put his elbow up and stare through his reflection at the popcorn sellers across the road. He waits the usual long time for an old guy in a red jacket who looks like Frank Clair the football coach to come along and take an order. The black-haired old bird keeps eyeing him out of the corner of her glasses while he sits growling to himself. The noise in the Sylvia bar is like dust blown off the titles in Fraser's Book Bin.

"Black Label," he says to the old guy. Did you used to coach the Ottawa Rough Riders? No. Frank's a general manager now. This guy looks like he should be a general manager. Or a Professor of Accounting. Whatever. Always drink Black Label in the Sylvia Hotel. It matches the decor. And the staff. And the clientele. Me. Ha! He slams the beer into the glass and drinks it down in one squaf. Bang! on the table with the empty glass. If you think I'm a slob who drinks outta the bottle – This is the Sylvia Hotel, man.

Frank Clair appears at his shoulder, having been cleaning ashtrays, looking offended.

"Sorry," Collister says. "I was dry."

"Well, I didn't think you were Khruschev," he says.

Sam brightens. "I want some smokes," he says.

The waiter looks at him. "The machine," he says, "is over there. Do you need change?"

"You bring 'em. And another beer. Make it a pair."

"Yes, sir," the waiter says. "What brand?" Sam says, "Export Plain," and hears a football field and the coach shouting, *Get out there and do ten laps, you lardass!* The sound of happiness. The woman by the window looks at him as though he were a mistake.

When Frank Clair returns, he delivers drinks like a tired vending machine to the punks and the girls and the woman and comes to Sam as though it were a considered afterthought. "What's your name?" Sam asks.

"Nick," the waiter says.

"Oh. Not Frank."

The waiter raises his eyebrows. "A few years since I've seen you. I didn't think you'd be back."

"Yeah. I seem to remember some jackass called the cops."

Nick's eyebrows go up again. "Yes sir. I'm surprised you remember that." He delivers an unzipped pack of Exports and the beer and starts poking through the change from a five still on the table. Sam tosses out a deuce.

The woman by the window cackles. "A man with a past," she says.

You got a past, it must of been an accident, Sam thinks. Her face like dried-up meringue with rouge on it. "Take half a buck," he says to Nick.

"Thanks. I don't remember names."

"Sam."

Nick nods. "Be good, Sam."

Sam chews a mouthful of bland Black Label and stares out through the window and the trees at the spectacular turquoise sky beginning to darken over Kitsilano. Maybe Dot's beginning to look like her, he thinks, and shivers, staring out over the empty chair across from the woman by the window, out over the heads of anyone on Beach Avenue. The trees make it impossible to see much of anything. A canopy for the glow of the popcorn sellers below his sight.

"Not likely," she says.

He looks at her, refocussing in the inside light that is beginning to make reflections on the glass. She looks terrible. "Not likely what?" he says.

"That Sam will be good. Why don't you come over here for a better view?"

Yeah, he thinks, but gets himself up, stiff, his sweaty clothes cooling on him. Wet feet.

He settles heavily into the chair, which faces east. The wrong direction. And twists around to see the last of the day going out in bright yellow behind the Englesea Lodge.

"Those stupid Frenchmen," she says.

"What stupid Frenchmen?"

She looks at him. The eyes behind the reflection of the light from behind the Englesea Lodge are black. Bright. Nasty. "You're not French," she says.

"No. I'm not French. I'm from," he waves his right hand around, "out here."

"Well, that's where we belong. And those darn Frenchmen can just separate all the way back to France. Serve them right."

Outside, a pair of youths on ten-speeds teeter up to the nearest popcorn seller like giant wheeled insects.

"If Rennie Lévesque don't go up in smoke first, he'll probably take 'em there." He regards the rubbery face with paint-pot cheeks and two black holes in it. Snake eyes, he thinks. "I'm in town to see a friend in hospital," he says. The two cyclists ride slowly across Beach Avenue, drinking popcorn from their bags. He cranes around to watch them sweep by the corner of the Sylvia, bright faces in the streetlight, gone up Gilford.

"What's wrong with him?" she asks.

"Who?"

"Your friend in the hospital – what's the matter, you drunk?"

"No," he says, and swallows his beer. "He got run over. All smashed up."

He eyes the level in her glass. Almost gone. She's drinking Blue and the bottle's empty. Maybe she'll go home.

"Tell him to be more careful."

"Lady," he says, "he's next to dead. Tubes sticking out all over him and oxygen pumping into a hole in his throat. We got shot at by the same Germans in the war and he got through that and all the bullshit since and now he's busted up like a squashed chicken coop. I don't feel too good and I don't need you to tell him to be careful."

"I know what it's like," she comes back, sharp. "I had a husband just like you. Got himself killed crossing that street right there, drunk as a judge."

Acid in his stomach climbs up under his ribs. Outside, the night begins to look like an Italian movie in the greenish light of the popcorn wagons.

I need to eat, he thinks. This old bitch. If only that girl had been different. Like a ghost in the acid-green foliage of the trees, his dim reflection looks ready to cry, and saddens him. I can't be drunk yet, he thinks, and swallows the lump in his throat.

Behind him the bored woman asks Nick about Stanley Park. She has a voice to go with the good face she doesn't believe in any more and the strands of grey shot through her wiry black hair. He pictures her softly moulded face and discreet double chin instead of the woman in front of him. Her pointy maroon sweater.

"How big is it?" she asks.

"Pretty big," says Nick, "a thousand acres."

"How big's an acre?" He imagines the wrinkles gather mildly, like ripples across her brow. He smiles.

"What are you gaping at?" snaps the one in front.

"One hundred and sixty square rods, ma'am," says Nick to the one behind. "Would you care for another drink?"

She laughs. "After that, I think I'll have a Manhattan. Dry."

Sam twists around to make sure he collars Nick. The woman back there looks like boredom came up three plums and she might consider taking her husband upstairs before he gets too pissed. He imagines a bed bouncing somewhere over his head in the Sylvia Hotel. Acres of plump tanned flesh.

"Bring me another beer," says Sam.

"Make that two," says meringue-face. Fuck. His old table long since taken by a tired young guy in a tan suit behind a newspaper.

The waiter picks up empties.

"Nick," says Sam, "would you mind if I called you Frank?" Nick looks down his nose. You have eyes a fish could use, Sam thinks.

"Call me anything you like," Nick says, "most people do. You'll know if I mind when you don't get served."

Sam laughs at Frank's retreating back.

"I know your name," says his table mate. "I bet you don't know mine." Jesus. I shouldn't have ignored her. It's gonna get worse.

"No," he says. "I don't bet long shots, but what the hell. Winona."

Damned if she doesn't giggle. "You'd never guess," she says. "Sylvia. Just like the hotel. And I live right across the street in the Gilford. That's where Bert was going when he got killed by that hopped-up kid in his flashy car. Just across the street home."

Oh oh. And I'll bet she's got Bert's best pants for any old soldier that splits his arse getting up there.

"What do I win?" she asks.

"The beer," he says. "I was married too. My wife lives over there on 10th with a guy that owns buildings."

"Shame!" she says.

"They're married," he says, and picks up the food menu. The clubhouse sandwich is the only thing that looks reasonable. "Don't get the clubhouse," she says, "it's terrible."

"Yeah. I shoulda guessed." Probably delicious. His stomach feels like someone dropped a manhole cover on it. He pays for the beer that Frank brings. Outside, a phalanx of young toughs marches along Beach Avenue in the Fellini light. As they do along the front at Penzance. Tight pants and biceps showing. The seaside night for the salt of the earth too poor to go to St. Tropez or Waikiki. Greasy pasties and morning sausage like tallow-soaked sawdust stuffed in a condom. No wonder they're assholes.

Cold fuzz of beer going down his gullet. Outside, a shapeless sack of a man lumbers up the slope from the beach and carefully props himself against a tree. The leaves begin to shimmer under glass – the seabreeze freshening. The man turns up his collar. Another old guy comes along in a hound's tooth jacket and orange shirt, mincing, a bagged bottle under one arm. Off to party with some Doris in a flat near the bandstand. The man by the tree stares away over the sea. Arc lamps of the ships. Maybe it's not the end of the line.

He remembers this window on a squally afternoon, mist closing in to take the ships one by one, releasing them again, over and over like the wet breath of being here while the glassy sea went rough as a rasp under the flails of rain. This water touches everything. Why don't we think of air that way? The idiot charm of rain wet faces. A kid with binoculars who stopped and looked at things. Another armed for tennis, striding through puddles in white shoes and short pants, grim. It's hard to stop and look. People wonder.

"You are a talker, aren't you?" says Sylvia.

More beer. He flags Frank. The place is full. The newspaper has been replaced by four jock types in team jackets, two each, men and women, guzzling suds. Damn. If I paid attention –

"That's probably why she left."

Sylvia sounds gauzy and his face feels warm. I'm drunk, he thinks, and realizes he has to piss like a fireplug.

"Your wife. You sit there drinking and mooning like a cow. Now Bert would talk my ear off. Never stopped about Tobruk and tanks. You'd think for a mechanic he'd done something. All he could talk about was tanks."

Al comes back at him, the broken glass in his guts.

"Sylvia, I told you –"

"I know you," she says. "You're all the same. Doornails waiting to drop dead. Drunk. I know. I work in the laundromat and all I see is weirdos."

He pulls himself to his feet. "If I wanted to go to the bloody Legion and listen to you I would!" he says.

"The West End is full of them. Nuts and drunks and addicts."

"I'm from Victoria," he says. He puts a twenty on the table. "Pay Frank." And he turns for the pisser, talking to his legs because they feel like they belong to someone else.

He pisses with vengeance, realizes he's spraying his pants, and backs off, propping one fist against the tiles for comfort. What am I gonna do? There's another twenty after that one and then it's the beach. His balls feel like they'd hang to his knees if they could. Christ, if she wasn't so ugly I'd fuck her. At least she's got a bed.

Who do I know in this town? Dot. Hugh. A bunch of buzzards in bars. Guys who might as well be dead. Hugh. He shakes his dick as though he could blame it for something. "I better phone Hugh." The rasp of his voice hangs tangible in the tile-bright air. The urinals flush.

54

In the phone book he finds two Collisters, but he doesn't know either one. He stares at the grey page, listening to his own breathing in the telephone alcove. The sound of his tubes rusting out. Al's clotted breath. The last sound in a dark room … Collis. Collishaw. Collision. Collison. Collister N. Collister R D … Collister N. Collister R D. The blunt end of his finger smudging ink.

A grey light dawns in him. Wilson. My son Hugh Wilson. Flipping pages. A sea of Wilsons. Wilson H J on Haro Street. The number. I could dial that. His breath feels dense around him, like aspic about to set. He closes the book.

A beer awaits him on the table, beads of condensation running down its sides. The window hangs the clear night before him. Bright points of light in the trees. Dead still. Something in him tries to step through the window and disappear.

Sylvia greets him with her chin stuck out like an aggressive knob of piecrust. "Don't put on airs about your Victoria," she says. "I know about those widows over there. It said right in the newspaper that there's more women in Victoria than anywhere else in Canada."

He pours cold beer. Slowly the striated glass mists over, long-bodied and narrow-waisted, an almost female shape with blotches where his fingers have grasped.

"I thought that was horses," he says. He could call Hugh. Hi. It's your Dad. The one from Victoria. I'm broke. Got a spare bed?

Sure. If Hugh's even home. What would a young guy be doing home? Later, maybe, with a girl.

"Don't you even count your change?" she says. Sylvia. He tries to focus on her, out of the shadows of Hugh's apartment. Hugh had gone back to the Dominion Hotel on Yates Street that night, and that had been that. His eyes don't want Sylvia's face. They go queasy in their sockets and jump over her to the two punks quiet as dogs staring at the working girls. None of 'em more'n twenty. The girls arguing over shift rotation. Flushed cheeks. The solid, buxom one with honey-blonde hair, shining eyes and rabbit teeth.

He looks down and picks up a ten, a five and a two. "Not with an honest woman like you, Sylvia."

"I think you're trying to hustle me," she declares. "Well, I can tell you it won't do you any good, Sam Whateveryournameis. I know you."

Right as rain, he thinks. The blonde says, "Watson's an old prune. That's how you get to be Matron. Your insides dry up. She thinks social life means the girls on Davie Street."

He gulps down three mouthfuls of beer. One of the punks stands up with a rod in his jeans you could see across the room.

Sylvia says, "I'm talking to you and you better listen!"

Sam waves a finger for more beer.

A tall kid with clear blue eyes and a lucid face. He leans over the dark-haired girl nearest him and says something in her ear. Sitting across from him, the blonde stares at his pants, glows from the neck up, and says, lifting her eyes to his face, "We wondered why it took you so long." They all laugh.

Sylvia's mouth is working like a dry pump. She bends herself around to see what he's looking at and snaps back with blood in her eye.

"There, you see! You're just a dirty old man drooling after those nurses. I know them. They're nice girls. Not for the likes of you –"

"Sylvia, shut up."

The meringue sags. "Well! I never –"

The beer arrives, with a dour look from Frank. "No," Sam says. "You never. Never had any sense and never will. Now go take a piss before you blow your plumbing, and go home."

"It's my table. You came over here and –"

"I've been buying you beer the last hour and letting you run off at the mouth. Your table, my ass."

She fumbles with her hands in her lap and looks like she's trying to cry. Your effects are slow, lady, he thinks. The other tables, the kids and the jocks, turn curious faces.

"Men like you think they can do anything they want," she says, finding her handkerchief and talking through it.

"Sylvia, just because you're sitting in here looking for something to stuff up your cunt doesn't give you the right to mooch beer and drive a man crazy."

She pushes her chair back and stands, not much higher than she was sitting, purse clutched to her stomach. "I've got money!" she hisses, and starts for the door, saying to the air, "They're all alike. They're all animals."

The darkness boils up in him. "You ugly old bitch!" he yells. It stops her. The Germans dancing death on the Bren gun's fire. "We won a war for this shit? For the likes of you? It wasn't some drunk killed Bert, it was you. You pissy-prissy women that got no use for a man except his pay cheque and getting laid when you get the itch and remember how. No wonder all he talked was tanks. They meant something to him, the poor sod."

Her effects aren't slow. She crumples into the handkerchief and shakes as though she had been hit. In the immediate silence around his table, Sam watches her spindly legs stilt up the steps and scissor stiffly to the Women's. He blows air through his teeth. Shoulda got rid of her before it went bad. But she earned it, the bitch. His arms tremble. He pours more beer and swallows it, bitter hops amongst the astringent bubbles of tinny Canadian domestic.

The amalgamated nurses and punks look at him like the young ones in battle dress who have seen their first death. About time.

"Hey!" says the tall kid with the beautiful face. "Enjoy yourself?"

"Whadda you know? You never had a war. Get your ass in a uniform and see how you like watching your best friend's guts blown out!"

He looks out the window, ignoring what sounds like *Get fucked.* The beer's almost gone. He takes what Sylvia left and waves for more. Outside, the nearest popcorn seller walks over to the next one down the line. It's near the end of popcorn time. The man by the tree moves like a great burl detaching itself from the trunk and materializes into the lamplight of the abandoned wagon. An old brown coat that could be leather. Shabby pants.

If things get old enough, thinks Sam, they all look the same.

Without seeming to mean it, the man drifts over to the wagon and scoops a big handful of popped corn out of the glass box. He shuffles up towards Denman, leaving a trail of tiny white puffs behind as he crams the handful into his mouth.

The popcorn seller comes running and stops a few steps past his wagon, hands on hips, apron fluttering. A man who missed the kill after a day's boredom. The lamps begin to go out. Good on you, Sam thinks, you got away with it one more time. Sadness in him dark and without names, into which he collapses like a burned-out building. All the soldiers are old ones. He drains the glass. That dry old bastard does take his time. He waves again. Nick that he wanted to call Frank so it would hurt less. Where do we go from here?

In a desert place a dusty, grease-stained man holds a spanner in his hand. He curses the flies that buzz his torn knuckles, the shattered tread wedged in the bogie wheels. Guns over the dun hills. His mates sit in the shade of the lorry drinking tea. "Knock off, Bert. Flamin' Jerry won't miss that'un."

"Bloody hell," he says.

Sam waits for beer and dreams of Bass. A sunny day and crowds at Marble Arch. Poor bastards drink their tea in Africa and a troop of Jerry armour crests the hill. "This is supposed to be a fuckin' rear area!" Mad scramble as the lorry roars away in clouds of gritty dust and AP pitches into the sand about it like skipping stones. To die of booze and traffic and a screwy broad like Sylvia in Vancouver. Among the colonials. Like Braithwaite.

A police cruiser outside, slow along the esplanade. Keep us safe from ourselves.

Sam grunts. He looks at his watch and stares outside. A couple hours to closing. He hears the sea in his ears. I should get outta here, he thinks. Outside looks empty. A night for people to pass through between one place and another. The last postcard from Vancouver, riddled with bright teredos where cars moved through the long exposure. He imagines waking from hard sleep under a dew-dripping rhododendron. Will some lawncutter see my feet and call the cops? Or booking himself in: puke-slimey tiles of the drunk-tank. He sucks the thin, metallic dregs out of his glass. The streaks of foam on its sides look like dried spit. Maybe the one more …

After a while he becomes aware that he hasn't been thinking. A knot in the middle of his forehead tells him, Zero. Null time. At the corner of Denman and Davie where the lines of his sight meet like crossed fire, there is a hole in reality. A lot of air comes out of him, as though he had been holding his breath. High up the tower at the corner a figure stands silhouetted in a window. A man or a woman. The eye in the last postcard from Vancouver, looking out unblinking to the place where the sun was.

I'm going somewhere, he thinks. He can feel himself going somewhere, passing through his flesh as though it were an eddy of wind

>-+>-0-<+-<

He comes to. Nick is serving drinks to the young ones. "Nick!" he shouts. The fish-eyes flatten on him and approach with measured, butler tread. Fish-eyed owl. Bald-faced owl. Fine wrinkles of his skin at the fingertips of Sam's sight. Like putting your hand on a leached-out stone. Arizona might look like that from high enough.

"That's my name."

"Where's the beer? I musta ordered yesterday."

"Still the same day. In case you haven't noticed, you're not being served, no matter what you call me. Cut off."

"You heard."

"The whole bar heard. Just like they did last time. I thought you'd changed."

"Aw, she had it coming. I've had it up to here with her kind of bullshit. Be a pal and bring me a beer."

Arizona shakes its head. "Effie was in here since lunch. If she had any place else to go, we'd bar her out of here. You should of known better."

"I thought her name was Sylvia."

"She thinks she's a hotel. And you're a royal asshole."

Sam lunges to his feet, chair flying one way, table the other.

An empty smashes. "You dried up old relic," he snarls, hauling back a fist.

Nick looks up at him, wrinkles square at the corners, eyes hard. "You got problems, Sammy boy. We all got problems. Take 'em outta here."

The young ones are looking at them. What have I done? Their eyes like bullets plucking at him as he begins to move, hooks tearing out of his flesh. He catches a foot on the fallen table and near-misses the table of jocks. Everyone is looking at him. He blunders up the stairs. The late show. The shambles he's left behind him.

At Falaise the stench of burned and ripening flesh. Carnage of men and horses and machines in windrows along the roads. A lone shell that crashed into a hedge and the infantry captain screaming at an antitank battery commander, *Was that one of ours? Was that one of ours?*

A GRAVEYARD

GOD. WHAT HAVE I done? He blunders on through the lobby, looking for a back door that doesn't lead to Gilford but does lead toward Haro Street where Hugh lives. I can't go to Hugh's. He wants to run but can't, legs strange and heavy as though the air were gumbo. To get away from Effie and the stinging eyes. The mud full of deadmen and exploding steel. Blood flowers. To run anywhere that's away. Labyrinthine passages where every way seems wrong, a place that wasn't meant to be gotten in and out of. Heavy glass doors.

And then he's on a dinky street that might be in St. John's Wood except for the patio-brick fences. Haro's over that way, where Lord's would be if he'd walked out of Charlotte's flat on Abbey Road. But Abbey Road was the main drag there and Denman is the main drag here. What country am I in? He heads for Denman that isn't Abbey Road. Sister Charlotte in St. John's Wood who isn't here. You never came back.

A blue metal wind rushes past him, white ring around its nose and staccato thunder of the overrun as the driver gears down for the corner of Gilford. Its tail says Trans-Am in the red flash of brakes. *Tremendum dei.* Frantic heart. Lord.

The wet shoes feel square on his feet, heavy as combat boots. Walking feels like he's leaning forward to follow his belly and sticking his legs out to keep from falling. A sack of dark guts pulling him down. Blood would be black in this light.

At the corner Denman Street blares at him. Harsh glare, noise like a dozen jukebox cafés. He leans both hands against the lamp post and sidles around it, craning his neck to see what street he was on. Where do we go from here? The beach. The bushes in the park. The lockup. The dark. Denman Street pummels him. A large old guy in a seedy jacket praying to a streetlamp. Waiting to puke. Flashes of light. Blue-white airbursts of Belgium.

He swings around the lamp standard as though it were a maypole and wraps his arms around his head to make darkness. Damn them! Plunging back down Pendrell toward the thousand acres of darkness there. Damn the gunners who strew the fields with his boys' flesh, and the pale civilians who think they're not responsible. Damn them all to the pit where their bones stink. Something that isn't him pours out of the ground beneath his feet, the madness of all the ancient warriors gone down to death, his own ghost in the Belgian mist splatched with everyone's blood. It fills him with shattered bodies and staring eyes, Hugh's freshly dead heart among the parsnips, the knife in her hands and eyes, the clear faces of his boys gone grey and hollow staring into the ground. It pumps through his legs and fills his chest with a sound that raised them out of their holes to follow him into the mist full of shadows raining fire upon them. To meet death with death. To drive for the high ground and peace. Cessation. He goes for it. The enemy visible. Death in the shape of solid men broken by the fury in his hands. Life stopped in their faces. Effie crumpled into her handkerchief.

He groans. I'm death, he thinks. Bert was death. I showed her death. Bert showed her death. A man with a spanner in his hand, drunk with an apocalypse from which no one was raised.

At the corner of Gilford an apartment block old as himself says Effie lives here. Bert's mausoleum. Quaint fussy arches and bow windows. Many entrances and dowdy orange eyes peering glaucously into the night.

I should go in there and find her, he thinks. Awkward feet and hands. What do you want! I came – the slamming of the door – to dry your eyes and say it's okay, we'll all be gone soon. You stupid bitch.

He looks at the stairs and tiny nameplates sequestered in shadows of the weird blue light. His body sags. No forgiveness from Effie. No absolution there any more than from the priests who called God the Supreme Commander. As if God chose sides. An Eisenhower above Eisenhower. A bigger toothpaste grin. As if supreme commanders were entitled to forgive anybody. Can we forgive them? More churches in beer parlours than were ever filled on a Sunday. The eyes chasing him out of that good grotty Eden, a death's head amongst the generous and kind and lonely-hearted.

I'm dead, he thinks. The only thing alive in me is death. Hugh's heart. Lily looks at him out of the dark. The knife between his ribs. He had recoiled from her because he felt the knife in her hands. Lise in Belgium. The angel of love. I showed her death too. Lily full of grace. Bury me. What right have I got to be buried? Waiting to die, like a civilian. You gotta do something or you're dead. You gotta do something to be dead or you're an abomination in the sight of them all, the dead soldiers and the living men and women with light in their faces.

He trudges down the hill into the high looming blackness of the park. A few yellow lights in the Englesea. Traffic crawling in and out of the dark mass of trees. How many lovers have got knocked up out there? Pecker tracks on the upholstery, plastic Jesus on the dash. How many kids have pressed noses against car windows, watching the lit ships flicker through the trees? Skulls found now and then in the mulchy soil. Vancouver Common. Big as a town. I'm going down there. Tombstones and monuments among the fir and cedar that blot out the stars. Mark me. Acres of white crosses in the fields of honour. Mark me one of the fallen, some shade of honour who should have fallen long ago.

He feels eerie in his limping march out the fringes of the West End. He can smell the forest, fetid and musty beyond the Park Board building's floodlit, antiseptic angularity. He crosses the perimeter into the edge of preserved coastal jungle. A queer place, the common covered with trees, just a hundred years old. Tombstones in Cornwall of men twenty generations dead. In St. Mabyn he'd left the Jamesons with their friends and followed the centuries through long grass and weeds along the footpath to the pub. The publican had told him to go home before he'd finished his final argument with a pint of disagreeable bitter. Going back, that common seemed eerie as a graveyard, the stone houses backing onto it fallen dark as ruins under a moon. He felt himself go ghostly, insubstantial as moonsheen on the green-black grass. It scared him then that he'd be a deadman before he got across, a strange Canadian ghost among the ancient Cornish dead. The wild did that to you, the roar of meltwater and whisper of wind above the tree line got after your soul. Not this place men had made. He stumbled on uneven ground and bruised his knees against the road's macadam edge. Jameson drinking tea before bed by the fire. "Ruddy publicans treated you unkindly, Sam," he said, before Sam had said anything. "I hear they're new. A close pair, trying to please the tourists and the locals both." Jameson's eyes twinkled. "A problem of philosophy, don't you see. And you're a great shaggy question they haven't heard before."

A long silence later, bruised Sam finishing off the dinner wine, Jameson had said, "Fires burn, they do." Sam had gone for a piss in the moonlight.

No moonlight here. A prickle of tears tricks his eyes. He trips on a curb lying below the spill of distant streetlamps. Steady on. Bone weary but afloat in the air. Good Jameson, this is the answer. I won't go into history. This place hasn't any. Not ours. With luck I'll go to fertilizer under some enormous fir. But they'll likely burn what they find and throw it away.

In a clearing among the spaced boles of birches and fragrant tents of cedar the rhododendrons hulk like camouflaged armour. You're not getting me. The cage of a tennis court vague to his right. The lagoon stretches black ahead of him under willow fronds and his feet start slipping on the slope greasy with mud and bird droppings. Twin lamps of cars glint on the water like ghost-eyes reflected from a Stygian shore. He teeters at the edge, swaying.

Out there, chimerical swans slide away from his arrival and he sees the dead men float, large and lumpy offal amongst the pale eyes that blink and vanish and blink. The fountain shoots a blossoming column into the air. He hears it fall. The fountain in the garden. A Belgian love song. Then the thing's lights come on, garish red and green. The stench of the edge beneath his feet rises into his nostrils.

Slime of the drunk-tank. Cops and provosts and red-tabs and cages. His gorge rises and spews into the black water. He falls to his knees without falling in and heaves until his innards want to tear loose with the bile and the tears in his eyes make glittering spectres of everything.

God. He breathes. God. And wipes his mouth with one hand, his eyes with the other.

A lagoon and a fountain and swans. He pushes himself to his feet. There was a fountain you could drink out of somewhere. He follows the crunching gravel path. Everything seems too far to get to. He drifts off through the trees beyond the tennis court, closes his eyes and twists his head around as he forces air to the bottom of his lungs to try to get things right and thumps his shoulder into a gnarly trunk.

The water rinses his mouth and floods his stomach and washes his hands. He leans on the concrete pedestal and looks around. A phone booth glimmers blue and pale through the foliage.

I gotta phone Hugh.

THE LATE SHOW

HE LISTENS TO the phone digest his dime. He dials. The burr of Hugh's phone. He's out with a girl. Worse, he's in with a girl. In bed. In her.

"Hello?"

"Hugh. It's Sam."

He hears Hugh breathe and stares at the instructions for making phone calls. "I'm here."

"What are you doing in Vancouver?"

"Al Braithwaite. You know about him? Anyhow, he was a guy in my outfit and he's in the General so I came over to see him. Anyhow, look, I need a place to crash."

"Oh. You want to stay here?"

"Yeah. Jeez, look, I know it's late and you've prob'ly got a girl there, but –"

"No, no. Hate to disappoint you. I was just surprised."

"I'm feeling kinda drunk and peculiar." His stomach belches acid into his gullet.

"I can tell. Sure. The place is nothing to write home about, but sure. Where are you?"

"In the park."

"What are you doing in the park?"

"I got lost."

"Tell me where you are and I can come and get you."

"Hell, I can still walk. You got a buzzer?"

"Yeah. Name's on it. 1807."

"Pour me a drink, boy. I'm going to need it."

Going back up Pendrell it seems solid and ordinary, and vaguely objectionable. The road to hell should have shell holes in it.

When he passes the building he's sure houses Bert's memory, he pauses and says, "Good night, Effie. Don't lose sleep over assholes." Some hope. Most of the building's eyes are dark, but he wonders what she'll be doing to fend the demons. Late-night horror movies. His hand rises to ring a doorbell or touch a cheek. Some fucking hope.

By the time he reaches the tawdry din of Denman he feels like he's staggering. The lamp post a monument. A fiftyish bonzo in a dressing gown walks by, pizza in a box balanced on one hand, nose up. The aroma of pepperoni follows him.

Jeez, I should worry. Fucking West End is full of nuts, like she said. Blood rushes around in his head.

His stomach hears the pepperoni call and makes wet noises that slosh drunkenly in him, like sea movies. *The Wreck of the Mary Deare.* He turns north.

Denman Street begins to smell good. A big red and green dagger painted on a sandwich board in front of him. Topkapi Restaurant. He stands outside the open door. Belly-dance music twangs and shimmers at him in the spicy lamb scent of donner kebab. I'm starving, he thinks, staring down the candle-flickering length of the narrow, storefront place to the bright kitchen. Some meat still hangs on the vertical spit a woman is starting to clean for the night. I'm starving. Taste of puke still in his mouth.

A short Turk fellow in a white shirt and big grin bobs out the door at him.

"Come in, come in," he says. "We are still open. Good food. Good coffee." And you don't mind a guy who looks like me. Shadowy people at tables. Snatches of conversation. Are there cards on the tables and bottles under them? I'm in Soho, he thinks. Bayswater. This doesn't happen here.

The Turk waits. His eyes smile. "I wish you no offence," he says, "but if you are thinking we cost too much money," he shrugs, "it is the end of today and the meat is no good tomorrow ..."

He's inviting me to heaven, thinks Sam. It hurts. The generous and kind. Hooks tearing out of his flesh. "Thanks," he says, "but I gotta go or I won't get there." Who would think St. Peter was a Turk.

Another flash of white teeth. Another shrug. "Come back," he says. "We are here. I have the best."

"My nose told me that," says Sam, and turns north.

The Turk laughs behind him and calls, "Ask your nose to tell his friends. Say Yusuf at Topkapi."

I hope that young bastard has something in his fridge when I get there. Up in the air. The eighteenth floor. Hugh nearer to God. Hugh went to meet his maker.

He shakes off Hugh's blood in the shell hole. Other Hugh. Dead Hugh. Father of his son's name. And looks up. High. His son Hugh smoking dope on the eighteenth floor. How can I go there? But he said Sure. Up there, a funny blue-green curl at the top of Denman Place, near the sky, a lit-up sign, a plastic yin-yang among the stars. Oops, that was a curb, Sam. And where else is there to go?

The Dover Arms stands open to send out people who don't want to go home. "Don't give me your lip. Take it up with 'Arry." Someone's going to catch it in a minute.

He bumps into a large ugly guy who looks at him like something someone should get rid of. "'Scuse me," says Sam, and thinks, Naw, your shit don't stink either, mister.

This is the right way. He remembers that Haro comes before Robson and keeps falling off curbs until he finds it. The left foot aches. Haven't heard from you in a while, he thinks. Keepsake from the Germans. A busted foot, lest you forget when you get old. He's walking bent, right shoulder hunched to shift the weight onto the foot that wasn't busted. You sorry-ass sonofabitch, Collister. You could just keep on walking and hit the harbour and sleep on a boat. Rocking under the starshot sky. Quiet night water lapping hulls in the sleeping city hum. Bullshit.

He's shivering and cramps knot his stomach. Even in July he'd spend the night chattering in an aching ball on the deck, and probably get nabbed for trespass. Or fall in the drink and drown. He shudders. The Lagoon an evil-smelling dream.

Blessed Haro Street. He squints at the number on the sign. Three blocks up the hill to Hugh's. Three long blocks, past several acres of concrete bunkers that must be a school.

Which one of these singles tenements has Hugh in it? In the southwest tower of the complex at Haro and Nicola he finds 1807 H. Wilson. Press the button. Up there in the air, twenty-five years of a life he hardly knows.

"Come on up," says the louvred aluminum plate in the wall.

The door buzzes. "It's me!" he shouts. Dumb kid. Grab the door before it locks again. How does he know it's not some other drunk wanting to sleep in a bucket room?

He steps in. A visceral red foyer, plastic runner leading off to the elevator. He steers off the plastic to feel the carpet and sinks into plush pile. Touch the wall. Velvety. Come into my womb, he thinks. But stay off the rug.

A door says Exit. Inside it, concrete stairs go down into what smells like a parking lot. Another door has concrete stairs going up. Not eighteen floors, pal. Two more doors past the elevator won't open. Any drunk with sense would stay outside.

The elevator, Sam. He presses the button and stares at the ceiling. Puce. That's what this is. Puce. Puke. He laughs. Puke this colour and you're dead. The doors roll open sounding heavy and oiled. No one inside. Brushed steel and woodgrain. No one to wonder who let that in. Push 18.

The door stays open when he's inside. He looks out through the puce womb and the glass wall and the space odyssey courtyard to a clapboard house on Haro Street. All its windows are dark save one on the second floor where a woman in a dress puts her hand to the sash as the doors roll closed and he is whisked to the top of an eighteen-storey hole.

>──◆──◇──◆──◁

66

Hugh stands in a doorway down the hall that works like a wrong way telescope. Not tall. Solid. In cutoffs and a white singlet.

"Hi," he says, "I thought you got lost again."

"Hugh," says Sam. He feels his hand being shaken in a firm grip. "Gimme a drink."

"Sure. Come on in." He looks awful serious. What in hell must I look like?

Sam marches into a brown-carpeted entry hall with pumice walls. His ears buzz and his eyes feel like they want to cross instead of looking at the posh, soft-lit room opening ahead of him. He glimpses the glint of a toilet bowl in the shadows through a door on his left and wheels for it, colliding with Hugh.

"Sorry," he grunts. "Gotta piss." Like running into a wall. "Light's on the right," says Hugh.

Sam fumbles at switches. A whirring sound comes out of the ceiling, and hot red light. He growls. Need a fuckin' manual to use the can. Kill those two and try the third. Five bulbs come on over the mirror. I'm in the movies, he thinks.

With careful aim at the water's edge in the brown bowl, he lets fly. Keep an ear on the slosh and burble to make sure you don't piss on the rug. Look around. Cream tile. Yellow walls. A poster of Guy Lafleur and one of Cheryl Tiegs, who seem alike somehow, except she's wearing more clothes. On the toilet tank a flowered box. Among the flowers a man and woman make the beast with two backs. ConCept Foam, it says. A plastic plunger thing beside it, like a syringe without a needle. His curiosity goes edgy. On the smooth yellow countertop he sees a basket of hair curlers. Nail polish. He hears himself moaning and quits. Out, he thinks. Little bastard lied to me. Can't stay here if he's got a broad. This is my Dad the derelict.

Shake and tuck. Not a drop on the shag. Good thing I closed the door. Flush the john.

He makes for the entrance, thinks better and cautiously sticks his head into the kitchen.

"Hugh," he says, stage whisper. Hugh looks up from bottles and glasses. "You got a woman here. I'll go find a hotel."

"What?"

"All that stuff in the can. You got a woman here."

Hugh's gathered-up face spreads into a smile. "Oh that. Nancy forgets things so she keeps a spare drugstore in there. She's got her own place. But even if she was here, what the hell?"

Sam stands between two impulses. I just been told something, he thinks. But what do I do next?

"I hope you drink rye," says Hugh. "It's all the whisky I've got."

"I drink anything."

Hugh laughs. It doesn't sound pleasant. "Ginger ale? Seven-Up?"

Sam's tongue clacks dry in his mouth. "Just gimme a shot."

"You look like you need one. Go sit down in the living room and I'll bring it."

The room has a white woolly rug laid over the brown wall-to-wall; glass-topped chrome coffee table; low, rounded brown couch and chairs. A colour TV shows a chesty blonde at a garden party. Sleeping bag on the couch. He sits in a chair that gathers him in like a big catcher's mitt. The whole end of the room is glass. The Point Atkinson light winks at him.

Hugh hands him a short thick tumbler and goes over to flick off the TV. "Cheers," he says, sipping his rye and ginger.

Sam throws down the warm spirit and closes his eyes as its sweet raw fire stuns his gut and burns through him. Inside his eyelids a blue-white aurora dances and ripples. Muscles jump in his arms and legs.

When he opens his eyes, Hugh is standing where he was by the darkened television, looking at him from a face with Dot's bones. In the soft fall of light from one hooded lamp, Hugh's eyes are shadows. Sam looks into time. His eyes are grey like mine, he thinks. His father's eyes. His father's father's eyes, in the shadows under Hugh's brow, all the fathers and sons and time. His eyes in Dot's face. Hugh's thick shoulders and trim hips, legs like tree trunks. Bare feet sunk in the brown pile. Sam shakes his head. The images tumble queasily inside him.

"Nice pad you got here," he says. "Sid got a piece of this place?"

Hugh eyes him. "No, this is a bit out of Sid's league."

"Sorry. I just figured – I dunno what I figured. Sid owns buildings."

"That's okay –" Hugh stops. He doesn't know what to call me, Sam thinks. "You just thought Sid's my – dad, and –"

"Look, Hugh, we gotta get this straight. Thought we did in Victoria. You call me Sam, or Collister, or the old drunk, or whatever you like. Your mother married Sid, and he's been your dad for a long time. I just – was, I guess."

Hugh smiles. A grimace. "I think," he says, "there's more to it."

"I think I better get another drink."

Hugh eyes him some more. "Why don't you lay off it a bit?"

The shivering runs through him again. "Can't. I'm cold and sick and it'll settle me." He struggles to climb onto his aching pins.

"One way or the other. Here, I'll get you one."

Sam holds out the empty. "Put some water in it this time, and a little ice, or I'll pass out on the next one."

As Hugh makes clinks and clunks in the kitchen, the fear creeps again into Sam's muscles like the touch of cold damp air. I shouldn't be here, he thinks. What right have I got? In this kid's posh, squeaky-clean life. Smoking dope, hell. Hardly even drinks. Girl probably a fitness nut. No deadmen here. Leave him alone. Shoulda left Effie alone. Christ, Al, where have we got to?

He levers himself out of the chair's grasp, needing to move. It's not a great success. He heads for the couch as an excuse and sits, shoving the down bag over, working his hands together between his knees.

Hugh comes back, eyebrows up, a tall, pale-amber glass held out.

"I think I oughta have this and shove off," Sam says.

"Oh? What's wrong?"

Sam shivers. The battered booziness won't handle doubletalk. "I don't belong here."

"Bull. Where else would you go?"

"I can get a hotel. Still got a few bucks."

"You didn't call me because you can afford a hotel. What the hell happened to you anyway?"

The barrage at dawn. "The war," he says.

Hugh makes a face. "I know about the war. I mean tonight. You're a wreck."

"The guy I came to see was a buddy of mine in the infantry, another three-striper. And we both shoulda been dead over there. One time he decoyed a Tiger tank so we could get close enough to hit it with a PIAT. Damn thing blew him out of the hedgerow but he walked away and now he's meat for the wagon up in VGH because some goddam civilian ran over him with a car. It got to me." A bag of broken bones. "We're all dead, Hugh. Waiting to be buried. I got no right to bring that here."

His insides feel like they're breaking up and the pain shakes him. The kid says nothing. How can he? Not again, Sam, not again.

"I went down to the Sylvia to get drunk and dumped all over some poor broad named Effie when all she was was lonely and hopeless. I walked out on you and your mum twenty years ago, and when you come to find me I act like an asshole. I'm just no good, boy. Fucked. When I was your age I learned how to look after people and I was damn good at it, as long as there was a war on. What happened?"

"At least you had the sense to call," Hugh says. He gets out of his chair and walks over to the window. The ships float far below like jewelled black ducks on a pond. Unreal. A glow way off in the sky.

"You can see Victoria over there," the boy says, "that light in the sky."

Cities burning. The flickering barrage.

"Since I went to see you I sit here some nights and wonder what you're up to. You were awesome. Like you owned the whole world and I was one of the boys in your private army. I couldn't handle it. Now you're a wreck. What did you do to that woman in the bar?"

"I told her she killed her husband."

"What's that supposed to mean?"

He can feel his voice dying away in his chest. "He was an old soldier. Like me and Braithwaite. Got hit by a car crossing the street drunk. I said it was her fault for being an old bitch."

"Oh yeah. Not too heroic. She must've done something to tee you off."

"Said I was too much like him. I guess it's the truth."

Hugh shrugs, like a man assessing his own pain. "I don't know," he says. "I don't have to carry that kind of stuff around." He laces his fingers together and unlaces them. "Has it been like this since you left me and Mom?"

Sam looks at years, a deck of cards tumbling out through the night window. "When I was younger," he says, "I didn't notice so much. But it's been like this a long time. Too long."

Hugh sits at last, leaned forward like a hockey player between shifts when the score's wrong and time running out. "What are you going to do?" he asks.

"I'm not gonna live much longer, and it's not good enough. You can only go from day to day so long. But damned if I know what I'm gonna do." *You could start living,* Lily says. "God, I'm tired."

"You've got a bed here, Sam. You can clean up in the morning and do a laundry if you want. I'm glad you felt you could call. I know what it's like to need a friend. Never occurred to me I could do that for you."

I'm welcome here, Sam thinks. As Fred would be to his couch on Battery Street. As he'd wanted Hugh to feel welcome that stupid night on the breakwater. As anyone should be, old soldiers or young soldiers or the girl who took her clothes off and passed out. It's easier with men, he thinks. The couch feels snug and his stomach growls.

"Maybe we could get to know each other better," Hugh says.

"You got any food?"

Hugh laughs from the chair across the glass table. "You never say what I think you're going to say. Yeah, there's stuff in the fridge. You should've told me when you called. I could have phoned in a pizza."

"Here," says Sam, "lemme go looksee." He starts dragging himself up.

The kid bounces like a lacrosse ball. "No, no. I'll make you an omelette or something. There's eggs and a pepper for sure."

"You cook?"

"Yeah." The fridge door opens. Rummaging sounds. Hugh's voice hollow from in there. "That's one thing I found out, that my old man turned into a cook. So I figured I could too. When I was still at home I cooked better'n Carol. Blew Sid's mind."

"So Dot talked about me."

"Oh yeah."

Oh yeah. My old man. All right. A place to be home in.

Chopping sounds. Crunch of eggs being opened. Sizzling. Baconsmell. Sam looks at his feet. Poor old feet. He bends down, grunts, unlaces the brown leather. Still damp. I'm nuts, he thinks. And those feet'll stink like hell. Poor kid. The ancient history of your life arrives smelling like a gutter, looking for food. He decides to leave the shoes for later.

Hugh brings a delicate brown omelette folded on a white plate, with toast. Knife and fork clink on the glass table top. "You do cook! Jeez, that smells good."

He forks off a bite. Tomato and red pepper and onion steam inside. A whiff of basil as he chews. Bits of bacon.

"Aren't you eating? This thing's gorgeous."

Hugh yawns. "Nope. Gotta hit the pit soon. Work comes early."

"Oh yeah. It's only Thursday. Here." Sam slices off a portion and loads it onto toast. "Have a bite if your old man's gonna keep ya up on a work night."

"Okay. The customer's always right." Hugh takes the toast and bites.

"What d'you do, anyhow? You used to play hockey …"

"Still do. Played a couple years with the 'Birds at UBC, but since then it's just fooling around. No way I was making the big time."

Sam chews enough room to say, "Yeah, but what about work?" He swallows. "This place didn't grow on a tree."

"Would you believe, a place called Rising Sign?"

Sam feels his eyebrows jump. "What the hell's that?"

Hugh laughs. "Good question," he says. The kid really looks happy, lounged back in his chair, one leg hooked over the side. He reaches to dig around in a pile of paper on the table. "We never got to it in Victoria. This," he grabs what he's looking for and holds it out, "is my card."

Lot we didn't get to in Victoria, what I can remember. He peers at the little wine-coloured rectangle. A zodiac dominated by a fruity-looking water carrier with the name in fancy type. Underneath it says Hugh J. Wilson, Director, Sales & Promotion.

"That tells me sweet fuck all, except you don't look like no director."

Hugh throws his head back over the chair's arm and laughs hard. Sam watches his flat belly bounce under the white cotton and feels perplexed. That rabbit-tooth blonde would probably think you look sexy. But what the hell is so funny.

"That's it," says Hugh. "Oh yeah. That's what I mean. Most people look at that thing and get all serious, like it's a big deal. But my old man, my real old man that I've seen once in twenty years, thinks it's ridiculous."

Sam downs the last of the omelette and pushes himself up, suddenly uncomfortable again. "I'm sorry," he says. "I guess I don't mix in the right circles." He hoists the rye and swallows it.

"No, no," says Hugh. "Don't get me wrong. I love it."

"What do you do, push horoscopes?" says Sam, aiming himself at the kitchen and the whisky bottle.

Hugh sounds like he's having a fit. Sam feels pissed off and desperate and pours a lot of rye into the glass. The light in the kitchen bounces off white enamel and hurts his eyes. Hugh catches up to him and claps an arm around his shoulders.

"Sam," he says, "I'm sorry. It just struck me funny."

"Yeah. Have a drink." Sam splashes whisky into an empty glass.

"Okay. Look. I work for this chain that sells men's clothes – women's too, but that's new. Clothes for the Now Generation, right? If you watch TV you've probably seen the ads. We've got a store in Victoria, up on Hillside. The outfit's run by a crazy New York Jew named Benny Friedman who had a great idea and could sell women to the Pope. The main line's Aquarius and there's brassy stuff for Leos and wimpy stuff for Pisces – I shouldn't say that – and so on –"

Sam shoves away from the arm and looks at Hugh standing tanned and hard as India rubber in his kitchen. This is new. The eager kid on his shtick.

"Rising Sign was the first men's boutique for the ordinary upwardly mobile jerk. It's not Chapman's for Chentlemen or Threads for Heavy Metal. It's the Keg and Cleaver for clothes."

Sam eases his rump against the edge of the counter and stretches his eyelids.

"I went to work for them when I was eighteen, selling." The kid's implacable. "That's one of the gimmicks. Buy from kids that look like they know how to dress but couldn't know too much else. There I am, a muscle-brain in a burgundy jacket and taupe slacks selling killer threads to candy-ass jaycees and rich kids from West Van. Benny figures you win with local talent, so now I'm one of six Company Directors, Western Region – which means we each get one percent off the bottom of anything that moves from Thunder Bay to Port Renfrew. People think it's real. Nancy thinks it's very real. You don't. And that's great. Neither do I."

Sam's working on it. He makes his way back to the couch. "I guess the money's good."

"Oh yeah. Benny feeds you just enough to keep you hungry. He's big on unspecified bonuses."

Sam hauls cigarettes out of his pocket. "You got an ashtray someplace?"

"Sure. Someplace." Hugh bounces again.

"Maybe I shouldn' smoke."

"No, no. Nancy smokes sometimes. It's okay. Just where the hell is that thing?

Ah!" He flips an ashtray from a bookshelf above the stereo.

Sam pulls out an Export, sticks it in his mouth, and digs for matches. Hugh offers him a butane flame from something that looks like a black rock. The rich smoke tastes gummy in his mouth and hits his lungs with a thud.

"You went workin' young," he says. "Thought you were in school."

"Oh yeah, but I started work a lot younger than that." Sam's innards shrink from the sudden edge in Hugh's voice.

"Oh." He swigs the whisky. "I guess things were rough when I pulled out."

Hugh looks at him steadily. "I don't remember much about that. I was only five. But when Mom sold the house and we went to the place on Main Street, she waitressed for a while. Which seemed pretty awful. Then she got a job in a real estate office. That's how she met Sid. I started hustling papers, then hamburgers. Did lawns and floors for Sid. Went swamping for a while. Pulled greenchain at Alaska Pine. And went to school." Sam doesn't dare look anywhere but back at Hugh, sliding into that big hole he dug so long ago. "Sid doesn't hand out much – not to me, anyway – but he teaches ya how to make a buck."

"I shoulda sent money," says Sam. "But I kept pissing it away."

Hugh shrugs. "She opened a letter once when I was a kid. She said, 'It's a bit late, you drunken lout,' and crumpled it up and cried. I remember that. I didn't know what a lout was. I picked up the letter. There was a cheque inside. It sat on the kitchen counter for a long time. I guess she cashed it in the end."

"Yeah," he says, "she cashed it. And she sent a note saying if I'd been out of your lives that long I could stay out." He feels tears hot in the corners of his eyes and rubs them hard. Red flashes of light. The hell I'm welcome here. This isn't a drinking buddy. This is my son Hugh Wilson.

"Christ, Hugh, I dunno," he says. "It's been a mess. I didn't know what to do for so long it got to be a habit." He takes a deep, soggy breath. "I guess I shouldn't'ta come here after all." He swallows off the rye and rocks to his feet. He closes his eyes to get the level right but the aurora makes him open them again.

Hugh's there and puts hands on his shoulders, the two of them stiff as trees.

"Stop that," says Hugh. "It's okay. I've wanted to talk to you for a long time. You wouldn't let me in Victoria. But I guess I'm not too good at it."

Sam turns his face away and starts for the kitchen. "I'm gonna get another drink. Want one?"

"No. It's late. You go ahead." Hugh follows him to the kitchen. "For a long time I hated you because you walked out on us, after I stopped wondering when you were coming back." Booze splashes in the glass. "Then after a while it all seemed like it happened to someone else, in a story or something."

Sam picks up the whisky he's been pouring, a few ounces left in the bottle.

He looks at Hugh and says, "If you're brave enough to say it I better be brave enough to listen," and goes back to the couch. The night looks black as forever with lights painted on.

"Mom was pretty bitter." Hugh looks at him, then drops his eyes somewhere around the table leg. "But she was bitter about Sid and Carol, too. Carol got most of what Sid handed out because she was his kid. He was okay. He took me to ball games and showed off my hockey trophies, but Mom was jealous of Carol. And he was never my friend. When I got older I started thinking maybe you could be. You were always out there, like a mirage, like some sort of crazy hero." Hugh's eyes come up again as though in accusation. "And I began to think you were real."

"Some fuckin' hope."

"I had to go over and find out."

"Well?"

"Like I said, you were too much. The way you came on. The way you were. I'd never heard anyone talk like that before."

"You don't hang around old drunks."

"No. Come on. Old drunks don't sound like you did. About me, and the war – everything."

Sam lights another smoke and looks at it. What do they sound like? What do I sound like? All those guys in bars. Raging. Burned out.

"Maybe I never listened before," says Hugh.

"There's some deader'n others."

"You didn't sound dead," says Hugh. "You didn't sound old." He laughs. "Just strange. You scared the hell out of me."

"Hmpf. Only reason you don't wanna think I'm old is 'cause if I am, you're next. And you're right, you young prick."

"It wasn't that way at all. I thought I could be like you. A real man. The way I used to think I could be like Gordie Howe. And you just blew me away. You were a crazy hero all right – so crazy I couldn't understand you. I'd lie here at night looking at Victoria and wonder – what happened. Where you came from."

Sam looks at him. He sees red haze in the room.

"Now you come in here putting away whisky like it's water, and I find out you've been on a bad trip since before I was born. And I'm the one you call. I've never seen someone stay this sober while he tries to drink himself to death. But I still want to know where you came from."

Before I'm six feet under, Sam thinks. Came from, he thinks. Makes it sound like I got somewhere. Maybe I did. Far enough down to get up here in the air with my own kid I'm just meeting. "Sometimes I don't think I even know."

He looks at Hugh's young face swimming in the soft light. The clear faced kid in the bar who should have been a soldier. All the young men. His gut grunches.

"It's hard not to say, 'Whadda you know, you young fucker? You know cars and dames and more money in a day than we saw in a week.' You got to learn not to say that, or you're dead."

He looks up at the ceiling and sees the chief steward sitting there with a bottle of Queen Anne in his hand.

"'S funny. Heard that from a guy on the boat over here." "Is that what you think of us?"

"What?" The steward rolls drunkenly. Heavy weather. It's Hugh you're talking to, Collister.

"Us. Young people. That we don't know anything."

What to say? Sam frowns down hard to concentrate something sober in the front of his head and squelch the warnings in his gut. "It's like this place," he says. "Looks like a space-shot from outside and inside it's a movie. When I finally figure out how to work the switches in the can the lights come on and it's the star dressing room. I feel like I'm gonna dirty the rug. But it's only where you live. I don't. It's hard to believe I'm welcome."

"You are."

Sam nods. "So it seems," he says. Words pop into his skull. "Pain and time," he mutters. "Getting shot at was hell. And shooting people was worse. You don't want to talk about it." The blood slaps him in the face. "But it's all you know."

The kid is just looking at him. He feels the very large things moving together inside him.

"After you've lived a long time anyone young doesn't seem real. You get so you can't talk to people who haven't been shot at. Then you're in trouble."

"Watch that glass. It'll make a mess of your hand."

Sam looks at the white knuckles wrapped around the tumbler. "Yeah," he says, and puts it down. "I don't think you're very different from me, or Hugh, when we were your age. But Christ, it's hard to *believe* someone less than half my age is a man. And you never fought a shooting war. I hope to God you never have to, but I don't know what that's like. It's like you're from the moon. This whole damn peacetime world is from the moon. Or I am. You're twenty-five, same age I was when Hugh got it. Hell, he never *was* your age."

"Who was Hugh? I asked you in Victoria, but I mean who *was* he? How come he meant so much to you?"

The things inside Sam clang shut, hurtfully. I'm an elevator, he thinks. He sips warm whisky.

"If you don't want to talk about it —"

75

"No," he says. Then he laughs. Bloody hell … "I just don't know how." His face falls back down again. Your face sags, your gut sags, your balls sag. Jesus. He wipes a hand over his face.

"I guess the best way to say it is Hugh was a guy I fell in love with in the army. I was never queer, I don't think, but that makes most sense. If he was a woman, that's what you'd call it. Maybe I wanted a brother. I dunno. And he got gutted by a German shell in Belgium."

"I always thought you must have loved him more than me." Hugh's face in the red haze across the room. The blood's pumping out of me into this room, he thinks.

"I just knew him better," he says. "You don't love people more or less. You either love 'em or you don't. I'm just getting to know you. And that's mostly my fault."

Hugh's chest goes up and down rapidly, the hard pectorals and little peaked nipples. The breastplate of a warrior. "You're sure as hell not Sid," Hugh says. "Am I supposed to bring this guy back to life, or what?"

Sam leans forward and sets the whisky down, both hands flat on the glass table. There's tears in the kid's eyes. Hot and shiny. He feels everything break loose and tries to make his mouth work.

"You *are* Hugh, dammit. I called you after the first guy I loved in my life 'cause that was the best name I knew. If he was still around you'd have an uncle. But you're not him all over again. You're my son and Dot's son and Sid's son and your own man, built like an oak tree, pushing clothes and all right. You're *Hugh*, and that's a whole other thing. How the hell does a man get to know anybody?"

Hugh laughs, a bit hysterical, and says, "I don't know, but I think you're good at it. I think you could sell the Pope to Benny Friedman."

Sam grins. "Yeah. Maybe."

"Why did you run away?" The question sounds different, like they're both on the same side now. Sam looks at his son.

"You know that's the first time I let anybody call it that? I never wanted to believe I'd run away from anything." Ha! Bullshit. Drunken old fart. "That's what it was, though. I didn't know what I was doing, and I couldn't stand it. I fell in love with your mum because she was a good lay. And she was, dammit. And she had manners. But I never could talk to her. She stuck everything in pigeonholes. And every day I went down – on a bicycle at first to save car fare – and pigeonholed mail in Station A. That was life. And every night the sky exploded in my head. I couldn't stand it. So I ran away, and I couldn't stand that either, so I stayed drunk."

Hugh is nodding his head, then shakes it. "I don't believe it," he says. "This is my old man. I get scared sometimes because I run around doing all this stuff like it's supposed to mean something, but when you look at it it's like that business card. Nothing seems to mean anything in here," tapping his chest. "Nobody owns up to that one. Nancy just wants people to like her. Sid never talks about much but the weather and the rentalsman. My buddies figure everything's okay if you make lots of bucks and play the market right. Or they say they do. And you talk about my mom being a good lay." He shakes his head again.

"Man, moms aren't *supposed* to be a good lay. I asked her once why she married you if you were such a jerk, and she got pretty snappy. 'He was handsome and Canada seemed like a good idea at the time.' But she didn't really seem to know. She said, 'He was such a good man I would have followed him anywhere. I can't see why it all turned to drink in peacetime.' I guess I can't either. You're still quite a guy. I can see why people might follow you into a war."

Heavy Sam. "One of the funny things in a war," he says, "is you got lots of company. I was never too happy at home. I had a sister and a mother, and that was fine, but my dad was a mean cold bastard you could never please. He got chased out of England to the colonies and never forgave anybody, running that piss-ant newspaper on the North Shore. I didn't want to work for him any more so I signed up in '39 and the army got to be home. You might hate guys or love 'em, but you're all out there together tryin' to keep your tail from getting blown off. And they tell ya you're fighting to save the world. Hmpf. Then the war's over and you figure, This is it, pal. The payoff. But it all runs through your fingers. The fucking Post Office won't let you walk a route because the Germans busted your foot. Everyone's out for number one and if they drop the ashcan the whole fucking mess is gonna go ptooey.

"Y'know, when the hippies came along I figured like everyone else the world was ending. Then I found out they were the first bunch of people I felt at home with since the army. Except I couldn't talk to 'em without getting mad. Spent the last ten years tryin' to learn how. And I still fuck up."

A long silence. "Okay, Coach," Hugh says. "Okay. I kinda wish Nancy had been here." He stands and stretches. "I think we better sack out."

Sam stands up. The room swirls like water. "Fuck, I'm drunk," he says, and sits down again. Inside his eyes the aurora pulses gently in a plush red cavern. He sees the woman reaching up to draw her drapes and feels warm. "Fucking puce womb," he says.

Hugh chuckles. "Where do you get words like that?"

"A poem once. A bishop with puce gloves. Hadta look it up. Bloodhands bishop. Taupe. What the fuck is taupe?"

"Sort of grey-beige. Antelope."

77

"'S funny. That's what I thought puce was. Antelope gloves for a gentleman bishop."

"I'll go put the bed together for ya."

"Hell, couch's fine. Better'n the one I got at home."

"Oh, I'll sack out on that. That's why I put the bag out. Don't expect me to let my father sleep on the couch, do you?"

"Now look here, boy, I invite myself over here at midnight – I'm not gonna turn you outta your own bed. I slept on more couches'n you seen yet."

Hugh chuckles. "Just wait till I clean up the mess and then you move your butt in there."

Who's father now? Sam rests the glass on the couch's arm and pats the mound of cotton-ticked down with his other hand. Nice place. Nice kid. Still standing there looking at him.

"Why don't you and me and Nancy have dinner tomorrow night?"

"You really wanna show me off to your lady? I got no decent clothes."

Hugh grins, but Sam's eyes are closed. "You'll do," he says. "Maybe I want to show her off. I hope she'll do."

"Okay. Sure. I better go see Al again. I was gonna go home tomorrow." A ghost of Lily startles him. He opens his eyes. "Maybe I'll go see your mother."

"Ha ha! That'll shake her up," Hugh laughs. Then looks very sober. "I think she'll like that. I'd love to see Sid's face."

"Yeah. Is he big?" Sam's eyelids droop again as he tries to imagine Sid.

"That's a joke. I don't think he's fought anything meaner than an accountant for thirty years. Why don't we meet here around five? I'll come home for a shit, shower'n shave and we can go get Nancy. Make yourself at home in the morning – I'll leave a key on the counter. And in case you get any funny ideas, remember you're staying here tomorrow night."

"Sure." Sam feels himself stretching out so there's a lot of space inside. I'm home, he thinks. I'll go see Dot. Scared as hell when I knock on that door, but I'll go see Dot. Ready to be scared. A quiet, tingling place.

Taupe antelope. He sees a cloud of dust feather out over the low desert sun and taupe shapes bounding from the edge of it. Is there a cheetah back there spreading blood over the dun plain? And gorging on the hot meat as the dust and snaredrum hoof-beats dwindle away into the sound of time. Crunch of gristle in a very big space.

Hugh comes in from the bedroom. "There's so many things I want you to tell me about," he says. "Like Aunt Charlotte. I never met her, but she always sent me stuff. Rupert Bear soap –"

He sees Sam's head bob and fall back on the couch. He doesn't see the antelope gone into the dusthaze horizon, or the spotted cat munching what it brought down. He sees a big, strong old man in brown polyester trousers and a tan sports coat sprawled on his couch, turkey folds under his chin, belly in a grey shirt bulged over his belt.

He goes over and kneels to remove Sam's shoes and strips the damp socks away. Wrinkled feet that smell like his own. He drapes Sam's legs over the end of the couch and eases the jacket off. Then he sweeps the down bag onto the floor and drags Sam by the armpits until all of him is on the couch and his head on the pillow at the window end. Sam's eyes roll back and forth under their lids.

"What's the movie?" Hugh whispers. Or is it gonna be over before I can get there?

He loosens Sam's belt and spreads the bag over him. Like final things. He draws the curtains.

THROUGH THE LOOKING GLASS

THE AIRBURSTS arrive with the dawn, like lightning ripping the sky over his head. Razor flinders of steel flail the ground. Only a whisper to announce them, a quick strangeness in the air. "Get your heads down, you pigeons!" he roars. Drizzly dawn in a Belgian field. In the chill grey visible air, blue fireflash. Skull-splitting detonations drive his face into the freezing mud beside what's left of Hugh, stiff under a groundsheet. One of the live boys in the hole starts asking for his mother. Quietly. Steadily. Collister thinks about wanting his mother and discovers he doesn't but would like to. "Cut it out!" he shouts. "You want your mother killed too?"

"Sorry, Sarge," says a small voice.

"We're gonna kill some Germans, boy," he says. "When this lifts, they're coming down that hill and you're gonna shoot 'em. That's what they're here for."

The whispering and blasting stops. Tinkle of spent shrapnel falling. "They'll be coming," he hollers. "Spare magazines. Fire on 'NOW'."

An MG burst comes slashing out of the barn dim in the higher mist. He ducks. The fuckers, he thinks. What a rate of fire – a sound like silk tearing. Shadows out there. Germans in the drizzle. He peers over the edge. He has the Sten and Hugh's rifle. "Pick targets! – NOW!" he bellows and squeezes a long burst from the Sten as fire crackles up and down his hundred yards of front. At least these boys can shoot. The shadows shoot back. Too many of them, not enough of us. At least they can see us even less than we can see them. Grey uniforms in the mist, brown ones in the mud. The little greasegun jumps around in his hands as though it wanted to cut and run. Those guys'll be here pretty soon, plain enough in the instant before the lights go out for good. One sound he wants he can't hear, the staccato burp of the nearest Bren. Fuckit.

He bellies over the parapet and snakes for the next hole. His back wants to be steel plate and his innards shrivel. Bullets score the air and the earth, showering him with granular dirt. Ready to bury. They don't really know I'm here. I don't really know I'm here. Only a nut would be here. The ragged rim around the next hole.

"Who's on the Bren?" he shouts. "Phillips! Make noise!"

"Jammed, sir," Phillips' voice thin and hard. Sam sticks his head over the edge.

The gunner prods a shell from the breech.

"Still sergeant, chum. Get your goddam finger out."

"Done, Sam," Phillips says without a glance, slapping a curved magazine back in the gun, his partner working a rifle. The Bren barks. God bless old hands and if I stand up and run I'm a deadman. So he crawls back to his own piece of Belgium.

The two boys are working away, one with blood on his face. The Sten jams on its new magazine and he grabs the rifle. With this at least you can hit what you aim at. Hugh's rifle. A strange sideways feeling.

The Germans are getting more cautious. He sees one that looks like he isn't a bush and shoots. The shadow screams and flattens out. "Grenades!" he shouts. Discourage the fuckers. Orange flashes and thuds. More screams. The crump of German potato mashers in reply and cries of pain from his own boys. His skin tightens and blood beats on the inside of his head. We're gonna be annihilated.

He hears shouting to his right and looks. That bloody fool Halldorsen gumbooting down the line hollering orders. One officer left in two companies and he has to be a jackass. "Pull out!" Halldorsen shouts. Bent over and stumbling like a man on wooden legs, the lieutenant spots Sam and yells, "Pull your men out, Collister!"

Fucking hell. "They wouldn't stand a chance, sir."

"Pull 'em out! That's an order. Fall back."

"There's no place to fall back on. If you don't take cover, sir, you've had it."

Halldorsen screams, "Are you refusing a direct order, Collister? I'll have your balls on the Provost's charge!"

"You go to hell, sir."

Halldorsen glares, then continues down the line. No one is pulling out. A ragged shout comes downhill from the Germans. My God, they're rushing us. Halldorsen's head explodes and his flapping body falls into Phillips' hole. "Bayonets!" shouts Collister and snicks his own into place. Over where Halldorsen fell, someone is standing bent double and screaming.

"Stay down till they're on ya and keep shooting till they're close enough to stick!" Sam shouts and goes over the top, legs pumping in the stiff goop. His lungs feel like stretched rope and it seems like forever.

The rifleman Sims is covered in Halldorsen's brains and screaming like a stuck pig with his hands buried in his stomach and puke all over his boots. Phillips is shiny red as a slaughter-house, firing the blood-slimy Bren.

The madness takes Collister. He boots Sims into the bottom of the shell hole. "Shaddap!" he roars, his throat an open column of air blowing straight out of the ground. "Retrieve your rifle and use it, soldier. Halldorsen's brains aren't worth the time of day." He drags the twitching corpse of Halldorsen off Phillips' legs.

The grey air is all German. He shoots standing, watching holes blown in people. Splatches of blood bursting into the rain. Bodies melting away.

The earth explodes under Phillips and the grenade blast blows Sam off his feet. A German with Schmeisser at hip sprays a burst that would have cut him in half standing and he sees his own bullet impale the man at the second tunic button. The bolt goes home on an empty chamber.

Half-buried and flipped onto his back, Phillips empties the Bren into two Germans who loom in for the kill. Their shattered bodies dance and vanish from the thick air. Collister fumbles his full clip as the next German rears back his bayonet to plunge into Phillips. Sam flings himself full length, spinning his rifle around, butt end smashed into the German's skull below the ear. On his feet he drops the rifle through his hands, grabs stock and grip and drives in the steel. The sucking shiver of solid wet flesh runs up his forearms. Twist and yank the blade free and stick 'im again and again.

Arms grab him from behind and wrestle him around. "No! Sam! Sam!" It's the puking boy, nameless now among the dead men's faces and sheets of blood in Sam's eyes. He's soaked in sweat or blood or both, his pores drowning. Air rushes in and out of him and fills his ears with demented noise. "Let's go," he says.

He grabs the Schmeisser and full clips from the dead German. "Awright, Vancouvers," he yells, jumping onto the parapet. "Form a line on me. Let's drive these fuckers inta the ground!" And lunges into the deadly fog, the Schmeisser spitting German metal and his throat open to a shapeless cry rolling through him from the roots of time.

⊷─◦─⊶

His eyes bug out in the spectral dark he's falling into. His hands grab air. Shapes of ghost furniture. He's sitting on the couch in a cold sweat. That maze of dimly luminous white rectangles is the kitchen. Silence echoes in his head like the sound in an empty shell. Skull. A groan from the other room. Hugh's in there. I musta been shouting. He remembers Dot's face staring at him, invisible presence in the night. His arms shudder with the pull of dying flesh on steel. Her soft body to engulf, warming the cold. Blue-white flashes inside his eyes. The talk of separate bedrooms. Someone to embrace, even a man. Hugh in the next room. He shivers until his bones rattle and hugs his knees. Poor little Dot. He had taken her on leave to Devon after Rommel was kicked out of Africa and the rumour of a second front made any leave a portent of embarkation. The chills and trembling subside. In the bridal suite one morning in May he looks at her in the fresh light and thinks – My God it's pleasant to see plaster like this on the walls as the sun rises over Devon.

82

What right did I have to think that? The fair-skinned girl neither asleep nor awake beside him. The forget-me-not sky over red-and-green hills over slate roofs and chimney tiles framed in the window as in a mirror.

Kingsbridge, in pale light. The twisted streets, cobblestones erupting like swellings on a youthful face – so old. Streets before imagining. Trails among the houses while wind chased the fishermen home. A smugglers' cove. Smuggling warmth and hearth and safety to the bosoms of the men who fished and the women who kept them. A long, twisty harbour below the long, twisty street.

He caressed Dot's nipple, the one easiest to hand – her right to his left. And felt gracious, his cock coming up straight out of his balls, unlike any street in Devon, thinking, White, by God, white, this whole curve of breast down to her bones, and the hard. White. The skin of the flesh. What would have been the hang of her breasts if standing, and the skin of his balls like a plucked goose, lunging. He felt, lunging, his hand smooth over the white curve of her belly and thighs into fur and his flesh and the cunt there opening rough and warm and wet like the folds of the seabottom awakening tide. White. The knot of her skin then, pebble, the knurl of herself at the tideline as he twisted in and that hard bead ran up the back of his cock and through alleys around his balls and up the branching-out of him in breastbone ribs nipples and heart. The white gone through him, Woman, I love you, he said. The sea.

And in the fresh light of Devon he said, "Yes, Dot, goddam it, let's get married and go home and have kids."

And in the fresh light of Devon she smiled and said, "Yes," looking at him and the light that day made on the white plaster walls of the King's Arms in Kingsbridge, 1943, before the end of time and Normandy and entrails in the Belgian mud.

Lise's face. What love means, the boys staring into the ground not to see. Hearts alone in the cold earth, alone in the cold night with never a bluebird sky. The red fruit of passion. The shepherd that buries his sheep. The night of the abattoir.

⊱⊰

The light calls him. "Sam!" it says. And he awakens. The angle of the ceiling and the kitchen wall. Soft grey light. The kitchen pass-through, dim white cupboards and the bulk of the fridge beyond. Chrome backs of chairs at the dining table. The far arm of the couch, blue mound where his feet are under the sleeping bag. His mind is in his skin, like an eggshell full of slumbering trouble. He breathes. His skin vibrates. Faint electric noises. Web of wires in the walls. A sound like plaster drying. The fridge cycles and gurgles. Time, he thinks. He cranes his neck to see where the light's coming from and a white flash jumps through his spine. Innards dangerous. Don't move. White curtains. There could be anything out there. Sunday morning

10:00 A.M. Or dawn. Sunshine or clouds. But this isn't Sunday. Some other day. Hugh to work. I should do something. Do I dare look at the time? Snorfling and champing noises through the open bedroom door. Rustling. Hugh at sleep. The time. Sam raises his arm gingerly and looks without moving his head. Just gone six. The blood pressure pops you awake. He lets his arm fall and feels the blood bashing its way through stiff arteries. I'm gonna die, he thinks. Arteries bursting like old hoses in the woodpile. Bring on the leeches – Sam Collister needs to be bled. He feels cold. Not chilly, but as though he would be cold to touch, like a dead man. The only warmth in his groin. He rubs that, under the cover, and finds an erection there leaping at his hand. Damnfool organ that springs up when they hang you or when you wake up feeling half dead. He massages himself and wiggles his toes. Lonely for Lily. Lonely on the eighteenth floor. Lilynevermore. A one-night stand with a sentimental old goof. Must've got my shoes off. Jacket on a chair. What had he said to that kid? Couldn't have been bad. Echoes. Puce. A sudden chill – Hugh watching him from shadows in the red haze. *Whadda you know, you young fucker?* No. They got past that. That was the kid in the Sylvia. After all, I'm here on Hugh's couch instead of out there on the ground. Effie hits him like a punch in the gut. The black stinking lagoon. Hugh to find this wreck on his couch when he gets up. Acid snakes writhe in his bowels. Al to see. Dot to see. Dinner. Alarm buzzer at the back of his skull. He promised his boy to go to dinner. Christ. Lily's lean face like a lamp half-hidden in her tousled hair, gold-flecked grey eyes. Good woman, I love you, he says in the wherever else that Lily is. The bones of her long warm back like music under his fingers. The warmth in his crotch beads into a golden eye seeking her. Balls for brains, he thinks. Wet lips in the hollow of her thighs. Tongue tip in her smiling mouth. "Balls for brains," she says, turning them over in her fingers. Tears in his eyes and one bright drop soft to her thumb at his cock's end. Pillows and bedclothes and limbs and the dim rounded chairs.

⊶─◦─◦⊷

The white flash jolts him wide-eyed. Hugh's alarm. Elephant fumblings in the next room. Bleary Hugh stomping out. Naked tanned and muscley, a good dong on him in a dark arc over the firm summer bag. She must like that. Nancy's delight. "Morning," Hugh says going by.

Sam lies there watching his son's sculptured butt disappear up the hall. Healthy young prick. His stomach feels like a can opener ripped it up from the inside. Rush of the shower coming on. Hugh in the shower. Hugh in the showers most of a life ago, when he'd first seen a naked man as a woman might, with tenderness for that flesh and awe at the thought of loving it as a woman would, as he would a woman. The other is not the man or the woman but simply the other contained in that fleshbone vessel with hands and eyes and the genital touch of blood to blood.

Hugh appears, towelling his hair, fresh as creation. "Don't get up," he says. "I'll get you some clean socks. Remember dinner."

"Yeah," he says. His voice hurts his head. Clean socks.

"Did you put me to bed?" he calls toward the bedroom.

"Yeah. You fell asleep sitting up." Hugh returns in underpants and tosses a pair of socks on a chair. "Laundry's on the second floor if you decide to do a wash. I got a huge bathrobe someplace should fit you. Here's the key," he says, holding it up and sticking it on the coffee table. "Might as well go back to sleep. Wanna try the bed?"

"No. I think if I moved I'd fall apart."

Hugh laughs. "If I put away that much booze I'd be dead." He stops. "You okay? Thought I heard you yell during the night."

No lie. "I have dreams."

Hugh wriggles a finger in his ear and squints at Sam. "I shoulda put you to bed in the bed."

Put me to bed, he thinks. Tender hands. Smelly feet. A cool wash of embarrassment swirls through the dark syrup inside his skin. He rubs the feet together, safe and dry under the down shroud. Put me to bed. He dozes through the sounds of Hugh dressing and eating and going and drifts into the grey absence after the closing of the door. Sheets of rubbery time stretch over him as he fights the pillow and tries to roll around the ache in his back. He dreams of Lily in a laundromat and Fred sitting on the terrace of the Maltsters Arms in Tuckenhay, watching swans sail up the Harbourne River. "Sam," he says, "which way is home from here?" And Sam realizes his eyes are open, the brighter light saying, "It's time, it's time," as the swans fade into Hugh's living-room wall. His watch says ten. "I'm alive," he thinks. And needs to piss.

Swing out the legs. Feet on the floor. Steady the room.

He lurches up. Feet and legs are there, back and head and arms. He looks at his hands. Two of them. Pale, blotchy, loose-skinned. He makes fists. I'm up. Walk to the pisser, around chairs, soft rug. Groans and twinges from his bowel. Everything else numb, mostly. An ache in his chest.

Sit on the can – nothing fancy, Collister, just squat. Women piss this way alla time. His bladder lets go with a stab in his groin. Fucking gland, shut up. He stares at the brown bathroom carpet and starts sweating as a long pain slithers through his gut and blatters out in a fart that feels like hemorrhoids tearing loose. God, he thinks. A gout of acid shit on his ass and a stench that twists his nostrils. He swallows down bile and his diaphragm clenches on the gas fist punched under his sternum. Oh my, he thinks. Oh my. A long day coming, Collister. The sins of the fathers are visited on the fathers. This is alive. This is what happens when you wake up and move. Oh my.

Wipe it and get some water. He scrabbles at the soft white roll and spins it till one end comes loose and rubs his ass with the torn-off tail. You're gonna be sore, fella, by the time what's burning in there passes through.

In the kitchen he pops three cupboard doors before he finds glasses, and draws a long cold water. It galumps down his gullet and says, Jesus what'd you send me down here for, and tries to come back up. Sam grips the counter's edge and grunts, Stay down you fucker stay down, the sweat beading cold on his forehead.

I oughta do the dishes, he thinks.

He takes more water and goes to the chrome chair with arms at the dining table and sits there on the cane seat with his elbows propped. Fucking glass tables. Miracle someone hasn't been cut to ribbons. Paper napkins in an onyx holder. Onyx salt and pepper. Not a thumbprint on the smooth sheen of the tabletop like a garden pond. The kid's tidy. Or Nancy is. Whoever she is. He pictures a California blonde with a surfboard. Nancy and dinner. His stomach cringes. How am I gonna cope with all that? He could pass on seeing Al, pass on broken bones and dried blood. Pass on Dot wearing twenty years of life in real estate. If only he could pass on everything and crawl into a numb haze until he healed. Effie. Could I send her flowers?

If not for you then for Bert –

Take your flowers and get out! Vase smashed on the floor. Collister, you're an ass.

For a long time he stares at the white curtains and in their loose weave traces the acid pains inhabiting his flesh. Beyond the blank white, he imagines men and women moving through a bright day among the stark concrete and hard shadows of the West End. Blue sky and bluer water carved in angular pieces by the towers. The trees fragments of green in this Dolomite terrain. I've gotta go out there, he thinks. Vancouver like a mess of shattered teeth planted in the ground. A huge toothache throbbing at him in the white cotton light.

He goes to pull the drapes open, squinting against the glare and the grinding of the curtain machinery in his skull. It's all out there. As though *National Geographic* had photographed Collister's Vancouver Hangover. He slides the glass door open for air. Its rumble makes his teeth feel loose. Traffic noise and smell ride in on the light summer breeze and join him to the day.

Across the canyon between towers a woman steps onto her balcony in a white terry robe with a china-blue towel turbaned around her head. That's beautiful, he thinks. Bright haze of auburn hair as she sheds the towel with one slim arm curling over her head and shakes that redder light loose, high above the pavements of Haro Street.

Collister heads back into the kitchen for milk to soothe the fires below, still amazed that he can move. The strangeness of regaining hung-over life in someone else's private space.

But the engine is beginning to run. He gets the milk, which isn't sour, blessed kid, and sits at the table again.

Through her open balcony door he sees the redhead appear from shadows, woman-shaped, quick and sure, bearing that hair like a shaded lamp. She's naked, he realizes, fleshtone warm in the cool twilight of her room, paler bands at bust and hip. It's a movie, he thinks. I woke up in Hugh's goddam movie. A bachelor flat. She raises her arms to do brisk things to her hair, staring at what must be a mirror on the wall. You lovely, he thinks, seeing her as he might through a gauze curtain. The Nude of Haro Street, framed in concrete, aluminum and glass. You voyeur, Collister. He loves it. He sees her as a stewardess blown in on a Rome flight late. A showgirl restoring her bod from last night's work for the one to come. He doesn't want to see her as a whore. Ohh Sam, seduced into the day by a strawberry blonde who might as well be on Mars. Effie a swamp in him as he watches the redhead warm the day. She stoops and steps into panties, then dons a bra, her arms folded back like chicken wings. Utter ordinary grace of one moving through life at home alone. He feels oddly blessed, as though he were creating her beauty by watching it there in its private ritual. In the eye of God's mind everyone puts on their pants one leg at a time. She slips a blouse over her head and pulls a skirt neat around her waist. She's a dancer. Moira Shearer when young. What will I say to Dot? His stomach growls.

Scrambled eggs, he thinks. That's the ticket. With sautéed onions and too much paprika. And toast. His mouth waters and his stomach flinches only slightly in response. Then the dishes. Then the laundry.

The redhead is bent over in a magenta top and yellow skirt, watering plants down around her ankles from a white can. If she's not a dancer, maybe she's a painter. Late nights in the coffee houses. What do I want her to be? As though she were his own kid.

Dot, we could have had a daughter. Images of nude Hugh flicker in his mind. Weird. A son and a daughter.

He finds himself hoping Effie has kids. You're not gonna get that one to do over, he thinks. Never again. Lily seems like a big emptiness ago and the edges of himself being sucked into it. But I'll never do that again to another human being.

WHERE IT GOES

OUT ON HARO STREET everything looks foreign. Sam walks gingerly, as though he might get his feet wet. Daylight in the real world. The fountain plashes. The blue and white apartment towers. The clapboard house painted smooth cream, inoffensive, its windows blank mirrors with white trim. Concrete underfoot. Everything and himself in it frail as the reflection on a pond. In another country he walks down the High Street into a village like Port Isaac that couldn't possibly be real. Stench of fish hanging over the stone sheds at the water's edge. A place like a costume-piece decked out on the cliffs of its narrow, bent cove.

He goes to the bus stop on the shady side of Robson Street, nerves jumping to the traffic noise. Near the Robsonkellar beer parlour. The air feels dank, like a damp basement in July. Over there, everything seems too bright in the sunlight. A guy in a neon-green shirt open to the stomach comes down the hill as though it were a deck rolling under his feet. He veers to cross Robson in the middle of the block, wild white hair flowing like a steam plume to his shoulders and a cowcatcher of white whiskers fanned out over his mahogany chest. Straight out of a Conrad novel and some rummy bar.

Weaving or not, the bastard's coming right at me, Sam thinks. Bouncing off the wind of passing cars, teetering on the white lines, the apparition plunges headlong into Sam's shade and arrives like the derailed loco of a dream.

He sticks out a grubby brown hand wide as it's long. Full muscles in the forearm. It's the bloody fisherman, Sam thinks. The ancient of Port Isaac.

"Got four bits for a beer, bud?" he says. Steel-bright eyes gleam from their crow's nest skin.

"Fifty-six years old, man and boy," he says. "I was at Dieppe." He tilts his head. "Maybe you know what that's like." A pause. "Maybe you don't." He laughs. "But they ain't killed me yet, the fuckers."

Sam feels all nose and throat and bulk as he says, "Yeah, I know what that's like." He rummages a bill out of his pocket. A deuce. "You wanna take that or you wanna get change?"

The apparition laughs again. "Hell," he says, "I'll take it," and does, the brown fist closing over the salmon note.

You devil, Sam thinks. "Why don'tcha hit 'em up for the burned-out pension?"

The apparition twinkles and creases like a big leather purse. "Ha ha! Yep, I got some sand in me yet." He looks down the street, squinting shrewdly. There's a grog shop down there, reflects Sam. "Tho' I ain't what I used to be, nossir." He digs Sam in the ribs. "Guess you know what that's like, eh?" The man smells. Not bad, exactly, but he smells, and not of booze. Like men in a camp. Like men in a war. "Nope," he says, "something ain't right with my blood." He takes a swipe at the groin of his loose gabardine pants. "They say a vein's plugged down here. Wanta take my leg off, some of 'em do. But I found a guy that cut me open in two places and shot ballbearings through to clean it out."

Sam has visions of Al at the other end of this bus ride, a bag of broken sticks.

"Didn't work, tho'. Leg's shot." He laughs. "That's funny: leg's shot. Damn Germans never managed that."

"Yeah, I got a pal in the General, just goin' up to see him." The bus appears like a limbless grasshopper crawling up the hill.

"You at Dieppe?"

"No. Caen and Falaise and that little war in Belgium everyone's forgot about."

The eyes look at him. Colour of a freshly-busted axle. "Well, you're okay in my books, bud."

"Yeah, you picked me off right the way across the street." The man laughs. The bus arrives. The man sticks out his hand. Dry and soft as old dough, but strong enough to notice. The thing is, his eyebrows are black. Charcoal. "Make 'em fix that leg," Sam says.

⊱━─◦─◦──◦─━⊰

The bus goes to a place where he gets another one. People get on and off. Mucky windows. His legs ache. Winter coming, he thinks. The clear light and guys with no shirts on and young women with bare stomachs and tits flopping around like beached fish. But winter coming.

A girl with a nice shape gets on, chocolatey hair and eyes. She swings into a seat and collapses into the corner like a dropped puppet.

Jesus, he thinks. He watches to see if she's breathing. She is. Her shoulders hunch forward like folded batwings. We coulda had a daughter. He feels sad and old and useless.

Through a clean spot in the window he stares at Granville Street going by. Movie houses and penny arcades. Fourteen-year-old toughs with no asses and cigarettes hanging out of their mouths. We won, pal, he says. Even if you never saw Dieppe or even the latrines in Borden, we won, man. This is it. The payoff. He sees an old guy leaned up against a lamp post looking like he's taking a piss and Sam's insides feel like he's crying. Something tickles the outside of his nose. He wipes it away. He is crying. And snorts. Fucking sentimental hung-over asshole.

The snort comes out wet and his handkerchief isn't there. Just washed his pants, so he doesn't wipe his hand there.

Sunlight hits him as the downtown strip blessedly ends. The ships ride like big rust-streaked clouds on English Bay and the trolley crests the fat hump of the Granville Bridge, its wires singing. Down there to the west, 2nd and 3rd and 4th avenues take a chevron bend so he can see up their length, utility poles and wires, back lanes and trees, old streets caving in on themselves. Their pavements shine up the hill into Kitsilano.

Yeah, he thinks. He takes a deep breath and grabs onto the back of the seat in front of him, the whole bus shaking as it roars down the far slope of the bridge. We live here.

><+>—0—<+><

At the entrance to the ward a nurse stops him and says, "Who do you wish to see?"

"Braithwaite," he says.

"Are you a relative?"

Goddammit! "No," he says. Another one o' these bitches. This one young and solid-big, with a rope of brown hair down her back.

"Okay," she says, looking at him as though she means something.

"I'm a friend of his from the war."

She smiles. "He'll like that," she says.

He wonders. She turns toward a rack of hospital whites, a hand on his arm. "You should gown up," she says.

"To protect him or me?"

"You," she says. "He's had a lot of infection. It's probably all right now, but he's still got a bit of fever and the caution's still up."

As she helps him off with his jacket he says, "I was in yesterday." Or a year ago. "No one said anything."

"They should have." She shrugs and shakes out a gown for his arms. "If you were in the army you know how it goes. Throw this in the bin when you leave, and wash your hands."

"How's he doin'?"

Her face looks like it belongs with healing. "Fine," she says. "You've seen him. That would scare most people. But he's fine. He got more punishment than it would take to kill a lot of us. He just needs time to come around."

"It scared me all right. I thought he was a goner."

Her eyes warm and she touches his arm again. "It's not something you would expect to happen in peacetime. Especially not to a man who was blown up in the war and walked away."

"Twice," he says. "I'm glad you know that. I'm glad someone in this place knows

90

something."

"Or is willing to say it."

"You know he was a little funny in the head before this happened."

She nods. "We don't know much about how the accident has affected his mind. But he's come a long way, and he's still getting a lot of painkiller, you know. Makes you woozy."

"I couldn't figure out what to say to him. He didn't seem to be there."

Her fingers press on his arm. "He's very much there," she says. "I tend him eight hours a day, syringe fluid off his lungs, give him shots, shift him, bathe him – he's very much there." A wistful smile. "He touched my face once and just looked at me for maybe a minute. A couple of us went out after work and had a drink for that."

This is not the fat cloud. "You are something else, lady," he says. "That woman yesterday wouldn't give a dying man the time of day."

The nurse's eyes glitter. "Or a visitor. She does her job. Why don't you just go and talk to him? It's a bit like dreaming, when you hear people talking and it works into your dream. We don't really know how he sorts things out in there, but he takes it all in. And he likes it. Tell him about the weather and how you got here and what you're doing next. It beats looking at the ceiling."

"Thanks," he says. He takes her by the biceps and shakes her gently. "You oughta get a medal for what they call compassion."

>-·-→-·-◦-·-←-·-<

Al's eyes are the colour a clear autumn sky makes in the sea. Sam glances at the high white ceiling. The eyes follow him around the bed, like radar-operated guns. Sam feels conspicuously large and billowy in the white gown.

"Al," he says. "Good ta see ya lookin' alive!"

Al's mouth moves in a wobbly pucker. A drunk blowing kisses. A man dying of thirst. He wheezes and gurgles. His right hand wavers off the covers and some of the fingers twitch in the cast.

Sam grins and takes the hand like a wounded bird in his own.

"You sure as hell improve with a good night's sleep," he says.

The pucker sucks Al's cheeks into deep hollows and squeezes his mouth to a tight fleshy bud.

Sam skims the back of his hand over Al's cheeks. "No wonder you look so good. Musta got a shave from that nice broad with the big hank of hair."

Al's face relaxes and nods about half an inch.

"I got cleaned up too," Sam says, rubbing his chin that Hugh's Philishave had whined smooth. He chuckles. "Wandering around my kid's apartment bare-ass in a bathrobe, like some California millionaire."

He looks around the ward. Bent and swathed shapes. A young guy sitting on his bed playing solitaire, flipping the cards with one arm, the other about eight inches long and bulbous with dressings showing a dab of red. One-armed Jacks. Where is the Queen of Hearts to slip into place among the maimed and lonely? The old man who complained that something was wrong sits propped against pillows, listening to the radio plugged into his ear while his visitors discuss something serious in low voices in the afternoon light of tall windows. The red queen's hair shaken out in the air. A lustration.

He shakes his head. Al is looking at the ceiling again. Al lying there.

"It's a funny life, ain't it pal." Al doesn't say anything. The plastic hose leads from a steel plate in the wall to the hole in Al's throat, clouds of visible breath rasping out at calm intervals. Al doesn't say anything, but his eyelids nod. "You and me sure been in a few hospitals. Remember that pretty little nurse after we got out of Belgium? You had two good feet to my one, but neither one of us could catch her." He looks at Al as though he hadn't seen him for a long time. "You know, you old bugger, between the two of us we probably saved each other's lives about half a dozen times, without really meaning to."

He pulls up a chair and leans in toward Al. "Lots of water under the bridge since ya seen me last. I got to feeling pretty fucked up after my ticker crapped out back in '75. Not real sick or nothin'. I mean, hell, I been drinkin' like an asshole and everything keeps workin' okay. They tell me I'm a fluke. Healthier heart since it happened, or healthier heartbeat, or something."

Al receives all this quite peacefully. He scratches absently at the covers over his belly where the sutures run.

"No," Sam says, "it's just feelin' like I'm gettin' old and not doin' anything. Like it's all been a warning and I dunno what to do about it."

"Then the same day I found out about you gettin' run over I met this incredible broad." He laughs. "Broad, hell," he says. "In twenty years I haven't met a woman who's not a floozy or a nerd or too screwy to talk to and then this dark-haired thing looks at me across a bar and whammo. Jeez, you know, I was scared. A real woman, in a nice kind of place. Not pretty exactly. Kind of like Merle Oberon. No girl anymore but about fifteen years younger than me. So she invites me to her place. I still can't believe it. Lily."

Al's eyes blink every once in a long while. He looks like he believes everything. Sam sees Al seeing Lily and sees himself trying to get up the nerve to phone her once he's back home.

"Next day I get on the boat to come over here, feeling too lucky to last, and end up in the slammer for gettin' in a fight with a smart-ass kid wearing an Iron Cross and acting like he could use his dick to stir the soup. That woulda been a complete ballsup, except the chief steward turned out to be a goofy old fart like you and me who hides a bottle in his desk and hates people who act like civilians."

It's a bit like dreaming, she'd said.

"And last night I tied one on for you and me and wound up at my son's place." He takes a breath and figures that's enough about last night. "So now I'm gonna go see Dot, which is gonna be even worse than seein' you, you old bastard, and then dinner with Hugh and his lady and tomorrow I get to follow the birds back to Victoria and stop swanning around over here like a bloody socialite."

Back there, Fred's gonna be gone fishing. Home to two rooms on Battery Street. The deaf-and-dumb girl next door. The yellow wallpaper. The boys in the Beaver.

He looks up at the ceiling where Al's blue eyes are watching the story unfold. He looks back down and sees himself sitting by Al's bed and Al's eyes like two blue stars in the day. "Who's dreaming, old pal ?" he says.

>-+-⦾-+-<

He looks around because someone's there. A short, substantial-looking woman under a helmet of greying black hair. She regards him with the stoic indifference of a serf awaiting the squire's pleasure.

"Celeste?" he says.

Her face gives itself time to assess the information. Then it relaxes into half-credulity. "Sam?" she says.

"Yeah," he says, grinning. "You look like you seen a ghost." He takes her hand and kisses her absently offered cheek.

"I thought you to be a doctor," she says, looking doubtful still. Sam looks at himself. "The white robe," she says, old French accents lilting in her pragmatic voice. "I am not certain with doctors."

Sam laughs. She smiles. He is not a doctor.

"You look well, Sam," she says.

"I had a bath," he says.

"You remember I bothered you for that," she says. "We have not seen you for a long time."

"I been a stick-in-the-mud. You come in every day to see Al?"

"Of course."

He catches himself starting to say, I forgot you existed, and says, "I was in yesterday."

"Yesterday I worked so I came in the evening."

I got your note, he thinks – *Dear Sam, It is that Al has been crushed by an auto and perhaps will not be alive to see us any more* – and I forgot you'd be here. And Fanny and Bill and all those goddam people …

"He's doing well," he says.

"Yes," she says. She doesn't believe anything. She cleans people's houses and

93

offices and big kitchens in places like this. For some reason she had brought her strong back and medieval sense of order from Brittany to this barbaric land and found Al, back in the Sixties, before Sam had looked him up again. Al's live-in. Sat silent in bars with a glass of wine while Al babbled. I do not understand, she said, this life. Once she hit a man with her purse. Once she swore in French at a waiter. These were legends. She would not translate what she had said. She looked, the legend had it, like she had lost her place in the order of things. Now Al was crushed by an auto and she would tend him like a sick cat if she could till he was well. "The doctors say nothing," she says.

"It's okay, Celeste," he says. "The nurse with the long braid down her back is okay."

"She is good," she says. "She cares for him. The doctors say nothing."

Sam looks at Al and back at Celeste. He feels the load go off him.

"You can watch over him, Celeste," he says. "He'll be okay." Or you can tell us when it's time to bury him.

He puts a hand on her shoulder. "You are his friend," she says. "He is a good man."

I can't thank you, he thinks. And Al dreaming two people in the shadows at the edge of his life. Even if he lives he might be a vegetable. "I am grateful," he says.

She nods. "We are not lucky," she says. "The lucky ones do not need to be grateful."

He says goodbye to Al. "I don't know what's comin' next, pal," he says, "but they ain't licked us yet."

Outside the ward he loosens the ties of the gown and slips it off. He washes his hands again at the tap with long forearm handles and retrieves his jacket. There is someone else to worry about Al.

The nurse is bent over papers at her desk in the nursing station. The thick braid slumps in the nape of her neck and follows the curve of her back. A long fluid pull on a heavy rope and the slow swung note of a big bronze bell. He folds his jacket against his stomach and hugs it.

"Why did she say, 'Don't stay too long' yesterday?"

The nurse looks up at him. "He gets tired," she says. "It's hard work, paying attention to people." She smiles. "But he'll just drift off, so it doesn't really matter as long as you don't harass him. Sometimes he gets irritable and tries to take off his oxygen because it's cold." She shrugs. "It is cold."

"And why did you want to know if I was a relative?"

A quizzical look flickers across her face. "Because I thought you might be his brother."

"Al doesn't have a brother," he says.

The quizzical look lodges between her eyebrows. "I know. But you look like you should be."

Sam puts on his jacket and snugs his shoulders into the tweed long bent to their shape. Well, Dot, he thinks – it's been a long time.

DOT

HE MARCHES OUT of the shadow of Vancouver General. The apartment building over by Oak Street has ivy all over its liver-coloured brick. The street door says rich people live here and has the right number on it, but it's not locked. Inside, the smell of varnish and real wool rugs.

The right apartment. It even says Wilson in brass letters. He waits after the ringing of the bell. Dot opens the door and they stand like reflections on either side of the threshold as though she had looked in a mirror and seen him there. A strong face with jowls and saggy skin under the eyes more familiar than her own.

"Sam!" she says.

Sam looks at her and thinks, My God. Do I look as bad as you?

"Hello, Dot," he says.

A little thick dame with puffy powdered cheeks looking at him out of lavender-framed bifocals. Little rhinestones.

"After twenty years," she says, "just like that you stand there and say hello." She blows air out her nose. "Well, I guess you might as well come in. But don't expect me to offer you a drink."

Which reminds him he's thirsty.

He heads in across the burnished oak floor and the sedate green rug with pale flowers blooming in it. A floral sea, painted by a Fellow of the Royal Society whose mother had taught him to jack off in the coal scuttle. French-looking furniture like nervous, archaic ships, their corseted curves stuffed tight under shiny brocade. Ugly ceramic lamps. The maw of the russet fireplace plugged with an electric fire. Bits of china everywhere. On the piano a portrait photo of Hugh in cap and gown, and one of a built blonde with pouty red lips. Carol, that would be. He sails on through the arch to the dining room feeling like a large tramp steamer with engines stopped and the way coming off, Dot carried along in his wake. He fetches up against the dining table, its walnut mirror surface laid out like an ice rink, racks and glass-front cabinets of china staring down. Graceful Limoges and the oriental Victorian splendour of old Derby or Minton or something gleaming midnight blue, orange and gold amongst shadows, like fragments of Empire in a jewel box. He feels like he does in the antique shops on Fort Street back home.

"Well," he says. "Some tea would be nice."

She glares at him. "I suppose that wouldn't hurt anything," she says. The grey in her hair looks fake. Her sharp dark eyes lance around, hostile as broody starlings. She wants to know what I'm looking at, he thinks.

"Now look, Dot," he says, "I didn't come here to give you a bad time."

She lets out a little laugh. "No, you did enough of that."

He has a horrible swirl of Effie and the day before. Little plates in a rack say things like "York" and "London" and "Lake Louise". Never do that again, he tells himself.

"Look, Dot, I saw Hugh last night and just thought I'd say hello."

He pauses. Nothing happens. "There's no way of doing this right. At least I'm clean and I ain't drunk."

She puts a hand on his arm and bites her lip.

"Come into the kitchen," she says.

The kitchen is better. It absorbs less light and has corner windows looking out at English Bay and the mountains and the poles of a trolley coming around from Broadway onto Oak.

"Sit down," she says, indicating a marble-vinyled chair at the Arborite table. This he can cope with. A room with sewing in it opens off the kitchen.

"How big is this place?" he asks.

"Big enough for all four of us when Hugh and Carol were still here. Now Sid has a den and we've a guest room." She looks at him.

"I'm staying with Hugh," he says. "I was looking forward to meeting Sid," he adds, feeling mistakes would be easy to make.

"He'll be home," Dot says.

Threats and promises, he thinks. I was married to this woman. He looks out the window. If I hadn't gone to that NAAFI dance, neither one of us would be here.

Dot runs water into a kettle and takes tea things out of flat-faced white cupboards.

"Nice place," Sam says. He wants to say, You did all right, but shies away from it.

"It's about time you had something to do with Hugh," she says, looking a bit aimless by the stove and coming to the end of the table. In her natty blue summer dress with its white piping, she looks like well-upholstered pillows. "Although I can't imagine what he'd want to do with you."

She was wearing her Wren uniform when he'd first seen her, standing alone by the bar. A perfect miniature girl, dark curls around her temples, straight-nosed, bright-eyed, and shapely enough for any admiral's knee. You're pretty as a puffin, he'd said, with a much nicer beak. I'm waiting for someone, she'd replied. I'll bet. He'll just have to wait for you. She was nineteen and he was twenty-three and after they'd danced for a while he was certain the skin of his belly could feel the skin of hers through all the layers of wool while the thud of the anti-aircraft chased an intruder over London.

"He's doing okay," Sam says. "You did a good job. You and Sid. I'm just the old drunk he's heard about, and he's curious. He treated me real well. It's okay."

Later, nestling in the back of a cab, she'd nipped his nose, saying, "Well, beaky, you've finally found a bird who looks like a bird," and kissed him on the mouth.

"What have you done, Sam, really, in all these years?" she asks, still standing there, twisting her hands in the front of her dress as though it were an apron.

"Oh, I dunno," he says. "You know I worked in the bush. Went up to Kitimat for a while. Helped build a couple of mines around Terrace. Never did fit in much, I guess." He looks at his hands, curled together on the tabletop, thumbs talking to each other, no glass to cradle. Fingers like a collection of old sausages. "I did drink," he says. "Do drink."

She makes clucking noises and shakes her head. "Even after your heart attack." The kettle is beginning to growl. "It's such a pity." She looks at him. He drops his eyes to her hands, which are clenched white in a fold of blue fabric. "You were such a proud ... confident man."

Sam looks at her. She looks away, out the window behind him. Her eyes are not doing well. He keeps looking at her, wanting to say something like, Neither one of us got what we wanted, not knowing what that means, wanting to reach out and console her for his not being what she'd wanted, or for her not being what he'd wanted, wanting to change what would have to be everything. "Confident people," he says, "often don't know what the fuck's happening."

"Oh Sam!" she says. The kettle is roaring. "I'll get the tea." She goes to the counter and dabs her eye.

I loved this woman, Sam thinks. He closes his hands on each other and closes his eyes and prays. Lord, I guess I still do, and what the fuck does that mean? To love someone else's dumpy wife making tea in the biggest apartment in the world. Who used to be a girl with the cab's masked lamps bright for an instant on the tip of her nose and her heels making happy sharp thumps on the pavement of Shaftesbury Avenue while the smell of her lingered in his nostrils and drove him half crazy.

He opens his eyes. To love her like an orphan that someone else had kept out of the rain.

"There," she says, plunking a brown betty on the table and fetching the cups and the cosy. "That's done. I'll show you some pictures of Hugh."

Ordinary cups. Ordinary betty in an old rose cosy. Not the Crown Derby she'd use for the nobs and toffs. At least be thankful for that.

He follows her into the sewing room. Piles of cloth. Shelves with the spines of books. Helen MacInnes and Lillian Hellman and *The Keys of the Kingdom.* She hauls out a photo album. A plaque on the wall says, Presented to Dorothy Dowe Wilson by the Social Credit Women of British Columbia.

"Oh Sam," she says, "this is just my lumber room. Let's take the pictures back to the kitchen."

She pours him tea with sugar and milk as she had for so many years. He looks at pictures of a boy and a young man and herself growing dumpier and a skinny, sharp-faced sort who must be Sid and a blonde kid who grows less chubby and more pretty and a lot of people he doesn't know. There are Boy Scout uniforms with knobby knees and canoes and hockey togs and he doesn't want to look any more. There are no pictures of a boy younger than five. The tea is strong and good. Whatever she has said he hasn't really heard.

Dot goes to the stove and takes a pot to the sink, draining fluid from it.

"I was making shepherd's pie," she says. "It'll have to go in the oven." She takes a potato masher from a drawer and begins to assemble ingredients.

"I can mash while you do the meat," he says.

She looks at him and hands over the masher.

"Put in a bit of milk and a big pinch of salt and –"

"It's okay," he says, "I can mash potatoes."

She puts down a bowl of chopped onion and says, "Of course, you cooked in those camps. You've changed."

He laughs and looks at her square bottom and remembers when he couldn't keep his hands off her and doesn't dare remember any more.

"Yeah," he says, "I guess I have. I was on a fishboat once. Only once. We tied up in the Charlottes to wait out a blow. I was the deck hand so I had to cook, and the skipper didn't like it much. But we were alongside a bloody yacht that had a Chinaman who knew how to cook anything." He plunges the masher into the potful of boiled spuds. "Well, I had some greens and he'd run out, so we made a deal. The weather lasted three days and by then I knew enough that the skipper claimed I was the first hand he ever had could fix a decent meal. Wanted to hire me on for the next season right there. But I couldn't handle booze and the saltchuck both, so I wound up a camp cook." He grins. "You never seen the faces of twenty guys served stewed lentils with garlic sausage instead of getting steak and onions, and finding out they *liked* it. Gets awful boring, doing twenty steaks on a wood stove."

She smiles, having heard out the tale still as a stop-frame in a film. "It sounds fun," she says. "I should've guessed you'd find something good amongst the bad out there." She turns to her minced beef and the onions with a long breath in and out. "It was just so hard without you, at the beginning."

She sautés onions. The smell like a summer fairground. He leans into the potatoes.

"It wasn't no picnic *with* me toward the end either, was it?"

"No," she says. "I didn't know sometimes but you might kill me – or little Hugh – coming home drunk the way you did nights." She sighs again, stirring in the beef. "But I can see the Post Office was no good."

A ragged hallucination wrenches through him of reeling into the little wood-frame bungalow in Fraserview with bright flashes breaking loose in his head like gunfire and the whole place seeming no more than a packing crate he could smash in his hands. Dot's face pale and cowering or screaming. The sleeping child tossed like a little white boat in the broken sea.

She scoops hot stock from a saucepan.

"Yeah," he says. "I remember." He adds milk and throws in salt and pepper, whipping the crumbly mess smooth. "Haven't remembered that stuff in a long time. It hurts."

"Yes," she says.

The potatoes are done.

Dot shreds carrots into the savoury-smelling heap of steamy meat. She's doing it like there's still a war on, he thinks, leftover roast scraped to the bones and those boiled for stock to wet the chopped beef. And I bet she's got a Cuisinart or some other damn motorized chopper hidden someplace that she won't use.

"What about you, Dot?" he says. "What you been doin' all this time?"

She smiles, tying an apron around her waist. The sort of person you would hope to meet if you were a Boy Scout collecting papers for a drive.

"Well," she says, "I guess I'm still being a mum, though both my birds have flown the nest." She looks thoughtful. "It was peculiar, having a ready-made daughter when I married Sid." She uses a wooden spoon to urge the meat into a big square Pyrex dish. "I'm never sure how much I *like* Carol, you know, but I'm glad I had a girl to raise along with Hugh." She smiles again. "Girls are ever so much more fun to sew for." We could have had a daughter. Dot spreads the mixture evenly in the pan and covers it with a thick layer of mashed potatoes, which she decorates into whorls and peaks with the back of the spoon. "And she's done so well. She's off to Los Angeles right now doing tests for a big series of commercials. She did that one for Maidenform, you know, the one that's just breasts."

"Yeah. I thought her tits looked familiar."

She looks at him. "Now, Sam," she says, "don't be rude. Carol's an actress. She's done work for the legitimate stage right here in Vancouver and Sid and I joined the Arts Club and everything. He's so proud of her."

"Arts Club?"

"Oh yes," she says. "I don't understand what they do very well. But they're so intense and – dedicated, I guess, to their plays and books. I like a nice story and a little feeling. Kindness, I guess. I do volunteer things. It's important to be kind to people."

"Is that where the plaque came from?"

"What plaque?"

"That thing in there," he waves at her sewing room, "that says thanks from the Socred Ladies or whatever."

She laughs and brushes it away like a cobweb. "Oh no," she says, "Sid's forever getting elected to the riding association executive, so each year I get their annual do together for them. You know, make sure it's properly catered and has nice little paper pompoms and all. They gave me that because they said after all the years they didn't really know what else to do, the dears."

Sam looks out the window. It's that kind of afternoon at the end of July when it looks like the day could go on forever. Flocks of pedestrians like bright-coloured fish at the intersection. His wife married to one of Wacky Bennett's spear carriers. And now the torch of Aberhart handed on to Bennett Jr. who looks like a 'Lectric Shave ad.

"Why don't you show me the rest of this place?" he says. "I never seen an apartment with so much elbow room."

⊳⊶⊙⊷⊲

It is big. The guest room pale green and lonely looking, the bed wearing little organza petticoats under its licheny cover. Next door a bathroom chills his nose with white vitreous fixtures dressed in lavender. It smells of canned violets.

In Sid's den a whole wall of Carol stares at him, including a huge still of the Maidenform breasts and a signed full-face shot with golden curls and a Coca-Cola grin that reminds him of Betty Grable decorating *Stars and Stripes* while he tried to outwit boredom in a guardhouse in Aldershot. Christ. No wonder you're not sure if you like this broad. We could have had a daughter, but not like that, pray God. Big leather chairs and a TV set and fat ledgers across the bottom of a bookshelf. A desk.

"She's pretty," he says. He feels like he's sleepwalking.

"Yes," says Dot.

He realizes he's being told things, like Hugh bought them the chairs after he moved out, and the other room had been Carol's but of course everything had been redone. He doesn't think, What am I doing here? He thinks his stomach's growling and if this were a house it would probably have a gardener like him.

The master bedroom looks like the inside of a sewing box padded in various shades of green satin. Except the rug, which is white and seems about six inches deep. Ensuite plumbing in cream. Twin beds. Twin bow-fronted walnut bureaus with brass keyholes and pulls.

"We should have some more tea," says Dot. "Sid'll be here soon."

Sam sucks in his gut, says, "Right!" and wheels parade-ground fashion for the door. Scent of lilac powder in his nose.

Back in his kitchen chair, he looks for someplace to hide and regroup. He picks up a china candy dish with buttons and a hairpin in it. Poking the bits and bobs aside with a blunt finger, he finds a tarty image of HRH the Queen, dei gratia second Elizabeth, and consort Philip. No, not tarty, smarmy. The Silver Jubilee. Twenty-five years since young George cashed in his chips. Twenty-six now.

"Charlotte sent me that," says Dot, standing by the kettle to encourage it.

"Hmpf," Sam grunts.

"Why don't you ever write to her?"

Kitchen full of the smell of shepherd's pie. Time to turn off the oven. His stomach rumbles. "Nothing to say to her," he says. Not quite true. True enough. Nothing he thinks he would get away with saying. Or asking.

"Sam!" she says. "You awful man. She's always been good to you. Giving you her flat for a holiday after your heart trouble. The least you could do is write."

To say nothing of the plane ticket, he thinks.

"You're all the close kin she's got, you know. She hasn't been feeling well lately. And she cares for you, over there in England living by herself." She bangs the steaming teapot down. I think I get to pour my own this time, he thinks.

"Never could mind your own business, could you, Dot?" he says.

She flares crimson under the powder. "This *is* my business!" she snaps, eyes like little black stones. "Charlotte's been a sister to me when all I am is her brother's ex-wife. She's always sending the children little things. She's done what she could for you. She's lonely and getting older like all of us, in a place she wasn't born in and you, you thankless irresponsible lout, you might as well be dead for all the thanks she gets from you. It's always the same, isn't it? Poor Sam, big and brainy as he is, can't fit in and face the world without lashings of gin to stiffen him up. Oh, you think you're a fine ladies' man with a bit of talk and your dingus to get you what you want, but look at you now. A camp cook. And I'll warrant the drink's taken the sting out of your tail."

"Are you through?" he asks. "I oughta wash out your mouth with soap. You always could yap like a tart and that blonde floozy stepdaughter of yours has probably taught ya more. Y'know, the thing about Charlotte is she had the sense to stay in that country and stay single, not like me. Other than that I don't know a damn thing about her. Lonely, balls. If she ain't gettin' laid a hell of a lot more'n you or me she's nuttier than a fruitcake. I wish her all the luck, but what in hell have I got to say that she wants to know?"

"Men!" says Dot, slamming open the oven.

Sam breathes and says, "You shouldn't do that. It'll spring the hinges and the damn thing won't hold heat."

The hallway door opens and closes. A man's voice says in pinched nasals, "Where are you? I can't believe those crazy so-and-sos. I was in that meeting three hours and all they could decide – Oh," he says, "I didn't know you had company."

Dot is standing with the dish of shepherd's pie in both hot-gloved hands. She looks at him as though he'd come from the moon.

Sid is wearing a grass-green blazer and pale avocado pants with a white shirt stuffed in around his skinny middle. Green-and-white striped tie and white shoes. He probably has green socks, Sam thinks.

"And in all that time," Sid says, "all they could decide was to send my proposal to their finance team for study. Do you believe it?"

"This is Sam," says Dot, and sets the shepherd's pie on a rack on the counter.

Sid looks at Sam. "I was offering to buy a building," he explains.

Sam stands up and offers a hand. Sid takes it. A firm enough mitt but no grip in it. Squinty bright eyes. Sam looks into Sid's weedy hairline on a level with his nose.

"How's the welfare business these days?" Sid asks.

"What welfare business?"

"I thought that was the line you were in." Sid giggles. "Or should I say lineup?"

You smirky twerp, thinks Sam, his right hand swinging back to his side and wanting to ball up and plug Sid's puckered little kisser and knock him into the antique shop next door.

"I ain't taken a dime of welfare in my life!" Not exactly true, but the DVA doesn't count. Or Fred. Or Charlotte.

"Sid!" says Dot.

Sid shrugs and says, "Have you invited this man to dinner?"

"I have not!"

"I got a date," says Sam.

"Oh. Well, we'll have to have a drink. For old times." Sid giggles again. "You do drink, don't you?" This is the provider, thinks Sam. Shelter from the rain. Jesus.

"Put that thing back in the oven, Dot, like a good girl, and we'll go into the den."

Sid reaches out glasses and fills an ice bucket from the freezer. Dot glares and slams the pie back in the oven. The teapot sits on the table, vapour curling from its spout and lid.

Sid grabs a bottle of mix by the neck and heads out of the kitchen, calling over his shoulder, "Let's go. What can I get you, honey?"

"Nothing yet," snaps Dot. "I'll clean the sprouts. That shepherd's pie won't get any better, you know, drying out in there." Poor Dot.

"It's only food," says Sid from the hall.

"Sorry," says Sam as he goes.

"Never mind," says Dot, sounding like someone with indigestion. "I'm used to it."

In the den Sid unloads onto the sideboard under Carol's wall. He opens its doors to a gleaming crowd of bottles, bends, and plucks out a Potter's Special Old. "Rye and ginger?" he says.

"Scotch," says Sam. Fucker's true to his colours, drinking B.C. rotgut.

"Sure you're not a pal of Norm Levi's?" asks Sid, leaning in for a bottle of Usher's. "Sounds like the NDP. I thought old soldiers all drank rye and ginger. It's the creeping socialists that preach about The People and hang out in fancy bars drinking fancy liquor."

"I wish you'd cut that out," says Sam.

Sid shrugs. "Ice?" he says.

"Yeah," says Sam.

"No harm done, eh?" says Sid, pouring. He hands four fingers of cheap whisky and frozen water to Sam. "Just call a spade a spade."

"Sure," says Sam.

Sid takes his tall rye and ginger and waves Sam to one of the fat leather chairs, slumping into the other himself, a hand jammed into his trousers' pocket.

Sam sits. Hugh's chairs all gather you in like a well-caught ball.

"Your son gave me these," says Sid, patting his chair arm. "So Dot said."

"He's a good boy. Turned out well."

"Yeah." A pause. Sipping the cold varnishy Usher's. Sid's hand in his pants bunching and easing like a frog breathing. Is the bastard playing with himself? Sam looks out the window, its oak mullions sombre gold to frame the view north over roof-tops, past the BCAA building to the hazy green mountains. A fringe of ivy showing at the window's edges, corners of red bricks.

"Nice view, eh?" says Sid. "You enjoying this Social Credit sunshine?"

"Christ, man, can't you get off it?"

"No, seriously." Sid's hand comes out of his pocket to make a point. He has two quarters between thumb and forefinger. "It's the hypocrisy I can't stand. The socialists yammer for years over how we're raping the province and then they get into office, spend everything in the treasury on deadbeats – if you'll pardon the expression – and complain that we were dishonest." Sid's hand drops back into his lap, rubbing the quarters together as though to heat them up. "Every time I hear Davey Barrett preach in that squeaky voice of his, I think someone must have half strangled him and I want to finish the job. To think that he was premier of this province."

Sounds pretty much like you, Barrett does, thinks Sam. But if he'd got another term he would've done okay. The quarters rub. The man's Queeg. Doesn't use ball bearings 'cause he's not in the navy.

"So I think we've had enough NDP weather. Don't you agree? Don't you prefer the sunshine and the economy running the way it should?"

"Were you in the navy?" Sam says, feeling perverse.

Sid's eyebrows go up. He laughs. "No, I didn't have time for that nonsense." Sam feels his hackles rise and swallows Scotch. His stomach protests sourly.

"They told me I had a bad back," Sid snorts. "That just shows you. The Canadian armed forces don't have the brains of a pigeon. I took my bad back and hauled cases of merchandise around the interior in a beat-up old Ford. And if you know what the roads in this province were like then, you know that was no party."

"You don't mean it," says Sam.

"Sure I mean it. While you jackasses were off knocking up English girls and playing soldier, I was keeping the economy running."

Good God. Sam kills the Scotch and makes a face as it hits his solar plexus.

"Help yourself," says Sid.

"Yeah." Sam climbs out of the chair. "What'd you sell?"

Sid grins. "French safes," he says. Sam feels like he's groping in the elegant fog of wood-panelled walls toward Carol's many-faceted charms hanging over the booze. "Pots and pans too. Nylons. WearEver aluminum when I could get the franchise. Pens." He gestures with the quarters. "You know, all that stuff for general stores and five-and-dimes and hardware stores. Hauling that junk around in the dust and the mud and the ice. Broke more spring leaves on washboard roads than Carter has pills."

Sam pours Scotch. Drown it with ice. "So that's why you threw in with Wacky Bennett's crew? To fix the roads?"

"Sure." Sid has a broad grin for a guy with a pinched-up little gash like his.

"You're sure you're not a relative of his?"

The cackly laugh again. Dot comes in, looking worn.

"No, no, not quite. But I called at his store in Kelowna. And the one in Vernon. Had a little something going with one of his girls in that place. So almost. Not quite."

Dot goes to the sideboard, fishes out sherry and fills a little glass. Sam looks at her. She stares back, blank as a wall. He goes back to his chair.

"Well, Dot, I think your ex has a soft spot for the socialists, but he won't own up and defend them."

"Sid, you're impossible," she says. Her glass is empty already. She stands under Carol's huge breasts like a forlorn blue flower, one arm folded across her middle, the other propped against her side, holding out the empty glass.

"Have another drink," Sid says. "Sam's going to think you're a party pooper."

Dot flashes Sam a defiant eye and obeys.

"I've got a joke," Sid says. "You must like jokes, a man with your background."

Sam wraps his arms around his chest and wonders if his ribs will break first or if he'll go and beat Sid's brains out. "Why not," he says. "Everything else has gone wrong."

"A man with a sense of humour. Good, good." Sid puts the quarters in his pocket and spreads out his hands. "There's this travelling salesman, see?" Sam groans. Inwardly or outwardly, he's not sure which. "His car breaks down out in the sticks – broken rad hose, see? And he hikes down the road to this farm-house. He goes up to the door and the farmer's wife comes to see what's up. It's really hot, see, out in the interior, and he's all sweaty from driving and walking and cursing his fool car. And she's all sweaty from working in the kitchen, so he kind of looks her up and down and says, "My car's broke down and I need to do a hose job. Do you have a piece to spare?' " Sid giggles. Dot is looking out the window, breathing.

"Well, she says her hubby Stan is out in the fields so he'll just have to go around to the barn and see what he can find. Well, he does that, and out in the barn there's the farmer's daughter collecting eggs. She's only about sixteen and pretty as a picture with not too many clothes on on account of the heat, see, and says sure there's some hose and goes to help him saw off a piece." Sid can't quite control himself and wipes a tear from his eye. "Here, Dot," he says, "be a good kid and fill this up for me, will you?" handing her his glass. Hers is empty again. She complies.

"So one thing leads to another. She complains about sunburn and rubs her chest and this guy says well he just happens to have some cream in his pocket that he sells for that very purpose and since she's helping him out with the hose, maybe he could give her some and help with the rubbing. By the time they really get down to it he gives her the old proposition and she blushes and says that would be swell since the mare's in heat and all, but unfortunately she's having her monthlies. And the guy says well that's no problem. So later on he's heading back to his car when the wife sticks her head out a window and says, 'You got your car fixed yet, mister?' And he hollers back, 'No, but I got the hose and your daughter even helped me change my oil.'" Sid has a spasm and chokes out, "'She's still in the barn and says she needs a clean rag before she can come in.'" He looks at Sam.

"That's a joke?" says Sam.

"Sure. I'm laughin', ain't I?" says Sid. And he is, all right. Sam fumbles for his Exports. "I think I need a smoke."

Sid shakes his head. "We don't smoke in this house, do we, honey," and slaps her rump. "We just drip a little now and then."

"God," says Sam.

He's on his feet and moving to kill when Dot says, "Sam!" He stops. She has her hand up, like the second Elizabeth greeting a crowd. Something between a wave and a salute.

"Sid likes his fun. It's all right."

He looks at her. Colour at her cheekbones, face tight against her skull, a light in her eye that he's seen before when Hugh was small.

"He took good care of us."

"Yeah," Sam says. He feels like there isn't enough air in the room.

"I really think you ought to stay for dinner, Sam," says Sid.

Sam doesn't believe what he's hearing. He keeps moving without getting anywhere. A dancing bear in Fairview.

"He means it, Sam. If you want to stay –"

"I'm gonna eat with Hugh and Nancy" blurts out of Sam. "I gotta get goin' to Hugh's place. What's the time?" He looks at his watch.

"Quarter to six," says Sid.

"Jesus."

Sid stands up and reaches into his pocket.

"Look, old man," he says, hauling out a fold of bills, "I'm sorry you can't stay to dinner. If you're over for a few days and going out on the town maybe I could spring you a few bucks." He grins. "I know Grace McCarthy doesn't hand out as easy as Norm Levi did." He peels off a twenty. Sam doesn't believe anything. He looks at Dot, pleading for something he doesn't understand.

"Here," says Sid.

Sam looks at the greeny bill fluttering in Sid's fingers. Twenty of the fifty he's short over that punk on the ferry. The Scotch rises up his gullet and he burps acid. Damn you, you fucker, he thinks, feels his ears burning, says, "No." It comes out choking. He clears his throat and looks at the skinny little man in his businessman's clown costume.

"You don't have to feel bad about it," Sid says. "After all, it's almost family." And doesn't giggle.

"No," Sam says again. Dot's eyes on him, sadly. "Look, Sid." Sam swallows.

"No, thanks. Got it?" He breathes, down to his hipbones, it feels like. "We come from different places. You did what I couldn't do. More power to you. But I can't take your money. I don't take handouts from Gracie or any other asshole welfare minister, Socred or NDP or Rosicrucian. Us jackasses earned our keep gettin' holes shot in us. You earned yours flogging what you call junk. Your pay's better, but I'll keep what's mine."

They look at each other. "The thing is I actually believe you mean it," Sam adds. "And that's incredible. I thank you for that."

Dot sags a bit, like an overblown balloon easing down.

"Sure," says Sid, stuffing his money back in his pocket. He sticks out his hand. "Drop around when you're in town."

Sam takes the hand. He heads for the door. Sid says, "We ready to eat, Dot?"

She says nothing. They walk him to the door, evening light slanting in dusty bars over the pale-green living-room sea. "Enjoy that Social Credit sunshine!" says Sid.

Sam turns at the door. Sid unchanged. Dot impassive. A grim-faced little broad neither hostile nor friendly. Having survived.

"See ya," says Sam. And the door closes.

TOPKAPI

THE BAKED AIR and thick drowsy light tell him he's walked into sun under glass. The key strange in his hand as braille.

"Sorry I'm late!" he hollers into the hazy shower noise. Kid spends a lot of his time getting wet.

Sam sits at the dining room table and drums his fingers on its glass top. I'm starved, he thinks. His eyelids droop. Hugh's showering. Has the plan been made? Nancy. His adrenalin comes up a bit and he glances around. No sign of the California blonde. Maybe a whisky.

The thought of Hugh's rye does nothing for him.

The shower stops. He looks at the bathroom door. Like a dog, he thinks, outside the Safeway store. He listens to his blood thumping around inside him. His eyelids droop again. An old dog. Dot and Sid having finished the shepherd's pie. Or stopped poking at it. Sid watching the news. Watching the commercials. I ain't your problem any more, Dotty, and you ain't mine.

Hugh comes out the bathroom door.

"Sorry I'm late," Sam says. Hugh stands in a towel, looking chippy.

"'Tsokay," he says. He picks up a folded handkerchief. "This yours?" he asks.

"Yeah."

"You did a laundry."

"Yeah."

"Good."

The redhead morning blossoms in Sam. "Nice view you got," he says.

"Oh yeah?" Hugh removes the towel and begins rubbing absently at his hair. "Lotsa concrete."

"What's eatin' you?" Sam retrieves the hanky.

"Goddam shipment of clothes got lost just in time for the summer sale. Benny's trying to run the show from the Canary Islands, and my best salesgirl just came down with mono." He glares. "Life," he says, and goes for the bedroom. "And Nancy's kvetching about going away for the weekend," he calls, then reappears in his gaunchies. "I tell her I gotta work and it's like she didn't hear me. You know what's wrong with women?" he says, shaking a rolled-up sock at Sam. "They're women." He bends over to skin on the socks. "It's all a joke."

"Maybe I'll go freshen up," says Sam. "You still wanta do this dinner thing?"

"Sure," says Hugh, slapping hands on thighs. "Why not?" Sam starts stripping out of his clothes. "Figured out where we're goin' yet?"

"Where Nancy works. Umberto Al Porto."

"Oh yeah. Sounds fancy."

"Never mind that. It's just a place where Nancy zips around and gets all the guys eating out of her hand. Food's good."

Is that funny? thinks Sam. "Hugh," he says, "there's this little Turk place down Denman. I kinda thought –"

"Topkap's or whatever?" Hugh's eyebrows go up.

"Topkapi."

"That's just a hole-in-the-wall, man. Greaseball food."

"Nuts," says Sam. "Donner kebab's good stuff. Never seen it before this side of the pond." The kid eyes him. "Besides, I don't want to go to no dress-up joint tonight, especially not one your lady-friend works in. I can eat in Wop or Dago all right, but I *look* like hamburger and beer."

The kid's eyes sharpen and a funny grin twists across his face. "Last night, maybe," he says, "but aside from that gut on ya you don't look too bad now."

Sam looks down his bare chest at the bay stomach and sucks it in, dropping the pants he's holding in his hands. He steps out of them. The two of them standing there in jockey shorts, with socks on. Hugh raises his fists and bobs around, pawing at the side of his nose with one thumb like something out of the movies. "Well, ya big brute," he says to Sam, "wanna spar a round?" and flicks out a couple of showy jabs. Sam stands there. "I hear Gordie Howe takes on both his boys at once." The kid begins circling.

Sam raises his fists and hunches in behind them. He grins. "You silly young fucker," he says.

"Watch me," says Hugh, stepping in with a quick combination Sam catches on his arms, and out again.

"Sure," says Sam.

Hugh steps in again and reflexes at a feint jab. Sam plants his right on Hugh's chest, just inside the nipple, hard. Hugh bounces off the pale plaster wall and skids down onto his butt. The look on his face makes Sam happier than he's felt in years. Sort of surprised and pleased, like women look sometimes.

Hugh rubs his chest. "You hit a ton," he says.

Sam grins. "Yeah, if I don't have to move too much I still do okay. But if you'da been serious you coulda cracked me one in the mouth." He reaches a hand down to Hugh, who shakes his head while taking it and hauling himself up.

"I dunno," he says, "I guess. But you'd knock down a horse with one of those rights."

Sam pats him on the shoulder and gives him a pugilist's embrace – which to his surprise Hugh returns. The skin feels good, cool and sweaty.

"I do outweigh you by about fifty pounds, Hugh," he says. Hugh shoves him and laughs. "You just won yourself some

Turkish greaseballs, Sam. I'll tell Nancy you beat me up."

Sam waves a farewell hook at him and asks, "She live far from here?"

"Hell no, just down Nicola. Keeps threatening to move to Kits, but then she figures she'd have to buy a car."

"Why don't she move in with you? Or vice versa."

Hugh twiddles his fingers in the air. "Ah ah," he says. "That's the thing, isn't it? Like I said, what's wrong with women. Besides, then you'd freak out when you needed a place to crash."

Sam passes on that and heads for the can. As he's rinsing his pits the kid comes in, stuffing his shirt into his pants. Nice cream cotton pants and a shirt like the ones the faggots wear on Davie Street. Maybe they aren't faggots.

"Did you get to see Mom?" Hugh asks.

"Yeah," says Sam. "And Sid. It was," he says, "what they call bizarre." He turns for the door. "I better get dressed."

Hugh smiles. "Yeah," he says. "I bet you would've loved to plug Sid with that horse-croaker. You'd've knocked the mustard right out of him."

"Well, I didn't," says Sam. "But it was close. Dot didn't want any blood on her rugs."

Hugh laughs, high-pitched and strange, like a kid in a new school. "I'm parched," he says. "You want a drink before we go? I'm gonna have a vodka tonic."

"I thought we were late."

"Oh, hell, we were going to have drinks first anyway. And she's probably not dressed yet."

"Okay, Hugh," Sam says, "your funeral."

"Ha ha. Yeah. Lemme get some air in this place." Hugh rolls open the sliding door and goes, "Ahh!"

Sam sees the Nude of Haro Street poking at a hibachi-thing asmoke on her balcony. She's wearing a fluttery summer frock, white with what looks like a lot of van Gogh printed on it. Red-headed and delicate in the rich evening air, she looks like embers flaring out of the smoke and ash.

Hugh hands him a tall, cold-sweating glass. They go out and lean on the railing. Eighteen floors up in the last hour of sunshine, watching a woman barbecue supper. "Told ya the view was good."

Hugh looks at him. "She runs around nude a lot," he says. "Nancy figures it's the only reason she'd want to live here – to keep an eye on me and the redhead."

Sam frowns. Married kids that aren't married. He takes a swallow of the vodka tonic, which ain't bad. A long cool guzzle and the boozy quinine buzz between your ears.

"So you saw Mom and Sid."

"Yeah." Sam takes a meditative sip. "Don't know as I ever want to do that again."

"Aw, Sid's okay."

"He's a two-legged greencheese asshole. And he treats your mother like shit."

"Sid's good-hearted," says Hugh, stubborn. "Not big-hearted, but good-hearted."

"I saw some o' that. The bastard tried to give me money. Like a rattlesnake offering serum. But he meant it all right."

"Speaking of money," says Hugh, "dinner's on me."

"Okay, okay."

Some silence. The redhead reappears, followed by a skinny bearded character with a glass in his hand.

"Don't know why she puts up with it," says Sam.

"You mean Mom or that kinky piece over there?"

Sam grunts.

"She put up with worse from you, if I got it right," says Hugh.

"You got a few things to learn yet, boy," snaps Sam.

The girl's voice drifts across the chasm. "I think they're ready," she says.

"But you're probably right. Except neither of us knew better then. If that's what it takes …"

"Let's go," says Hugh, knocking back his drink.

They go down in the steel box. Sam looks at Hugh.

Twenty-five years of two lives that hardly know each other. "You and this Nancy ever think about getting married?" "Oh yeah." Floors go by in backlit numbers. "But who knows. It's a funny world these days."

The steel door slides open to a concrete catacomb, gleaming machines in the stalls. The smell of oil and cement instead of bones and putrefied dust. Bunkers and the smell of hot weapons. The distant bumping of a heavy machine gun, demented whine of its long burst raking the concrete. Germans on the hill watching the end of their Reich march in spray-swept ranks over the sea, a thousand years early. Garlicky sweat and the long snaky belts for the MGs slippery as lead fish in their hands.

The sharp scent of puke makes Sam's innards wobble as Hugh leads him to a low white sedan trimmed in black. He unlocks the door. The little plaque says Celica.

"Someone been sick in here?" says Sam.

"Beats me," says Hugh.

"Smells like it." He opens the door, Hugh gone around to his.

"Don't smell a thing. Sometimes the drunks get in here."

Don't puke, Sam, he says to himself. Don't puke. It's all in your head. He sits. Black fake leather. Clean smells of the space age. The slamming of doors.

"Who makes these things?" he asks, as Hugh starts up. "The car? Toyota."

"Fucking Nips."

Hugh backs out in a crisp swerve, brakes, and looks at Sam. "Your head does some funny things," he says, throws the Celica into gear, and roars with a sporty exhaust through the bunker corridors into sunlight.

Down Nicola toward Davie they stop in front of a renovated West End mansion.

"She lives in that?" Sam says.

"Don't get excited, Sam. She's got a one-room that used to be the butler's clothes closet. And enough plants to fill the glass house on Little Mountain." He slams his door and walks up the walk. Brassy front door with a pane of glass in it.

Where am I gonna sit? thinks Sam. This is all gonna turn real. This isn't going to be some naked redhead the other side of a lot of air. Front seat back seat. Two doors. Back of the bus, Collister. But then the lady has to get in second. Fucking cars. Fucking kid. Fucking social bullshit. What in hell am I doing here?

He feels like a large mistake parked in a small car in the wrong part of town. The wrong town, fer chrissake. I don't *belong* here. He clambers out, peers around, leans his ass against the Celica, and folds his arms over his chest.

A slender shape appears like a fish glimpsed through the glass door as it opens, and while her heels clatter down the steps Sam collects his jaw into place and catalogues the things about the California blonde that Nancy isn't. She isn't carrying a surf-board. She isn't blonde. If she's California she isn't showing labels. She looks like a cross between Paulette Goddard and Joan Fontaine. She walks brisk and springy with her hair bouncing back from her forehead like raven's wings. She's grinning like sixty and by this time she's close enough for him to see that she's too beautiful to think about. She is not blonde. She is tanned. She is not healthy-looking, she is electric. She makes him vibrate. A silver star shines from the V of brown chest in her blouse, and her eyes sparkle bright as sunlight on black coffee.

"Well *there* you are," she says, low-register alto like fingers running down his vertebrae.

"Ahem!" he says, his mouth having started to move before his head remembered any words or his throat stopped swallowing. "I'll get in the back." And turns to do that, remembering to open the door. One hand reaches with assurance to the seat's back while the other searches like a blind bird for the catch. Where would a Japanese engineer put that thing?

She reaches past him. Narrow black shoulders with monk's sleeves. Her perfumed scent hits him high.

"There!" she says. "But I'm quite willing to sit in the back, you know." Her face six inches from his, wide-spaced round eyes, forehead by da Vinci, eyelids probably by God or fluky chromosomes, and pure carbon lashes that would never need help from anybody.

"I'm five-foot-seven and skinny," she continues, "see?" and shows him a thin sinewy nut-brown wrist.

He grunts while clearing his throat and falls into the grasp of the Celica's back seat. His hands reach for the seat ahead of him to pull it home, but drop like shot fowl as she beats him to it. He watches her hip in olive-green jeans swing into the car. Hipbone like a ploughshare. Rear end by Botticelli. He has no doubt that all of her would be the same colour, warm and substantial as gumwood, pliant as reeds.

Her face turns to him around the back of the seat. "There," she says. Just her face and its blackest wings. That's it, he thinks. This woman looks like she isn't wearing anything. Not nude, just as though she were wearing nothing but herself

Hugh's door slams. Hugh is there, one big shoulder and a sharp-nosed profile. "All set?" he says.

"Should I move the seat ahead, Sam?" asks Nancy. "This jerk didn't introduce us."

"It's okay," he says.

Hugh engages the gears and accelerates Sam flat into his cushions. He watches the back of Nancy's seat, the top of her head over the headrest. If the seat broke, he thinks, she'd be here. This is my daughter-in-law, he thinks. Girlfriend-in-law. My kid's girl. Dangerous, he thinks, and his eyes cross as he looks at his knuckles while he rubs his hand over his mouth.

"Well," she says, "I'm starved for Oysters Florentine." Hugh turns a corner.

"Where are you going?"

"Topkapi's," he says.

"Topkapi," says Sam.

"Sam's choice," says Hugh. "He beat on me till I caved in."

"Oh," says Nancy. "Dreadful."

Sam considers recanting and ingratiating and facing High Wop Florentine fandangos among the bellissimi. What am I doing? he thinks. Trying to please my boy's woman or grovelling for a piece of the most beautiful ass in seven continents? His liver hurts.

"But that's okay," she says, "Turks are fun. And maybe I can convince Umberto I was checking out the competition."

Hugh laughs. "Seriously!" she says. "You can't afford to be a snob in the food business. Just think how many rich bitches shop at Army & Navy instead of Rising Sign. Do you like Turkish food, Sam?"

"Yeah," he says. "I got used to it in London. But mostly I like this Turk."

"Oh, you're friends!" she exclaims. If she were a soprano she'd be hard to take at close quarters, gushing at him. "That always makes it fun. When were you in London?"

"Oh, lots of times," Sam says, growly.

"Sam was in the army," Hugh says, "during the war."

"Oh yes, but that's a long time ago! Did they have Turks then?"

"Some. Not so's you'd notice. I got to go back just lately 'cause I had a heart attack that turned into a holiday. Place is full of 'em selling donner kebab like hamburgers." That sounded wrong. "Not that it's like hamburger," he adds.

"Oh no," she says. "What is it like?"

"Kinda like carving the outside off a baron of beef along the grain, but it could be lamb or both at once."

"Oh," she says. "Is that before or after they slaughter it?" Florentine bambinos, he thinks. God help us.

"The Turk ain't exactly a friend," he says. "I owe him a favour."

"Oh!" says Nancy. "Intrigue. I love it." Lady, he thinks, please don't be an airhead.

⊱─◦─⊰

By the time they reach the Topkapi sandwich board, day is a saffron memory fading on the higher walls of Denman Street. The belly-dance music shimmers out for them like a net floating in the lamb-scented air. It's warm enough and crowded enough on the street that Sam has a pang of nostalgia for sultry summer London and an Istanbul he's never seen.

"I think I'm going to like this," says Nancy. "I always thought Umberto's was a bit short on atmosphere."

A short, strong-looking woman with leather skin and a billowy, glittering skirt

115

slung just over her mons twirls out the door. She flashes eyes around the passersby, makes a noise like a barnload of banshees, and sweeps the three of them inside after her with an enormous scoop of her hip and a bash on the tambourine twisting at the end of her snaky arms. Her breasts are made of sequins.

Nancy throws a glance at her two men. "I *know* I'm going to like this," she says.

"You can take your clothes off any time," says Hugh. Sam shudders.

Inside it's Soho. A table of more than a dozen stretches down one side of the shoe box place. They're half cut and waving drinks around. There are brown bags under their chairs. Sam's stomach growls blissfully past the dancer's capable back at the glistering spit of meat hanging behind the counter. Nancy's long fingers wrap around his arm just above the elbow. His heart flops into his throat.

"There's a table!" she says.

The Turk appears as if by magic. "Ah, my friend!" he says, "you have come back! Good evening good evening and the young lady and gentleman. No no, not there, dear lady, here, a special table near the kitchen."

Nancy grins and says *sotto voce* to Sam, "Different priorities." He follows her slim behind, Hugh in the lead with Yusuf guiding his elbow. Even going slow Nancy puts pepper in every step.

Little brass-plated lamps with coloured shades trimmed in glass rubies and emeralds line the walls. Above them, garish illustrations of Istanbul and the great Topkapi museum.

He can almost see Nancy preen herself and waggle her tail as she settles into a chair, like a slim and lissom lady raven. Let's give this time, he thinks.

"We have menus," says Yusuf. "You have come at the right time. Everyone is here and Ishye is dancing. It is not too early." His eyes glitter.

Sam sticks out a hand and says, "Yusuf, my name is Sam Collister. This is my son Hugh and his girl Nancy." God that feels good.

Yusuf bows. "Good evening," he says, "I am honoured you have come back. They tell me in this country you cannot treat a man like a man, and they are wrong." He beams. Hugh looks like a coach who knows his winning streak has gone sour.

"Would you like to drink?" Yusuf inquires.

Sam looks at him. "You have a liquor licence in this place?"

The Turk shrugs. "The law says I need a toilet each for men and women and more tables than they will allow me to put in so small a place." He shrugs again. "So I can offer you vodka."

"Oh," says Nancy.

"Can we have some water?" says Hugh.

"Water! Of course. It is coming." He turns his head like an RSM and says, "Hassan!" in a voice an RSM would envy, a scimitar slashing silk. A boy sixteen appears. They do it with mirrors, Sam thinks. "Water!" says the scimitar. "What's the matter with you?" The boy rolls his eyes like any ordinary kid, but water appears.

"Yeah," says Sam, "sure I'd like a drink." Thinking, This I gotta see.

"Vodka?" says Yusuf.

"Please," says Sam.

"And for you?" says Yusuf.

"Yes," says Nancy. Sensible. Hugh growls and says, "Okay."

"With what?" says Yusuf.

"Perrier," says Nancy.

"I can offer you orange juice, soda pop, and of course water and ice."

Nancy purses her lips and knits her brow. Sam wants to hug her. "Nothing," she says, "just a slice of lime."

"Hassan!" says Yusuf. "The lime."

The boy's eyebrows turn into a fair imitation of Turkish script. "Dad," he says, "we don't have any lime." Yusuf glares at him. His eyebrows go back to English and he says, "Ah," and disappears out the front.

"Orange, please," says Hugh. Polite coach.

"Straight," says Sam. Yusuf looks at him with fleeting disapproval, but proceeds. He goes to the middle of the loaded table, whispers, picks up a brown bag and goes to the back. Three glasses of vodka appear, and a neatly wedged lime.

Sam says, "Yusuf, this is heaven."

"What are we gonna eat?" says Hugh, plaintive.

"Poor baby," says Nancy, long hand alighting on his arm. Hugh looks at her suspiciously, but it sounds like she means it.

As Nancy casts a professional glance toward the kitchen, Sam twists around to collar the Turk for those menus. "You will find something very good," Yusuf says. "Where they are called spicy it is true."

"Great," says Hugh, as though he'd been offered fried bread. Nancy turns a reproving eye on him and opens her menu. "Hummus!" she says. "Wonderful. I had no idea —"

"Looks like Greek to me," says Hugh.

"What's wrong with you?" she asks.

"It is the Greeks that have copied us," Yusuf chimes. "The whole Mediterranean eats our food and says it is Yemeni or Greek or Arab." He shrugs. "No matter. Ours is first, and better."

"What's wrong," says Hugh, "is that the summer sale's fucked up and sweet

Cindy's got mono from some clapmouth. Benny keeps phoning from the Canaries. It's the pits." Yusuf vanishes.

"I'm gonna have Halep," says Sam. Spicy lamb, it says. To hell with hung-over stomachs.

"Now am I going to get mono?" asks Nancy, eyebrows arched. "Not good for waitresses, you know."

"Oh fuck," says Hugh.

"How about Adana Kebab?" says Nancy. "What's Adana?"

Sam shrugs. Hugh says, "It's all hamburger anyhow."

"With some Hummus," says Nancy, "and some Jajik and some Special Turkish Vegetable Soup I couldn't possibly pronounce."

Sam begins to see method in how her mouth works. Keep 'em off balance. Dodge the bullets. Get by. She pats her stomach. "Always eat soup," she says, "to keep your tummy happy."

Tummy! thinks Sam. Her beautiful flat abdomen over there. You're beginning to make sense, girl. The good looks and the goofiness. A woman to be reckoned with. No wonder you have a hard time with her, boy.

Nancy takes a sip of her vodka, the silvery glass and its bright lime like jewels against her dusky skin.

"Hugh," he says, "you're not havin' a good time. You got a beautiful girl here, this Turk's knockin' himself out for us and it ain't gonna be hamburger you get." He grins. "Even I ain't quite the mess I was last night, thanks to you."

Nancy looks up from her menu. Veiled surprise. Hugh tries to smile. "I've been thinking about what you said about being from the moon," he says to Sam. Nancy looks back and forth between them. "Most people don't know a thing about where you're coming from, do they? I thought maybe I could. I thought to myself, 'Hugh, you think *you've* got problems.' But I do have problems. Even the kid here has problems, though she won't admit it. How can we understand you?"

Sam feels the weight of it on him. "I dunno," he says. "You had a rough day and you gotta work the weekend. Maybe we could try to enjoy ourselves."

Hugh's grey eyes level on his, clear in the exotic air. "That's what I was hoping."

"Let's order," says Nancy.

Yusuf stands, pad in hand, writing nothing while they tell him.

"What's Adana?" she asks.

"A town," he says, "in the south where it is very hot. The kebab is not so hot. Only enough to make you sweat a little." Their skins are the same colour, thinks Sam, taking refuge. I wonder if he likes skinny women. Nancy smiles. "It takes a lot to make me sweat," she says, adding to Sam's new admiration.

"Mm," she says, wiping a drip of hummus from her chin and licking her finger, "spicy."

"It ain't Greek," says Sam, breaking the flat moist Turkish bread, eyeing Hugh, dipping up a mouthful of the fluid, peppery paste.

Hugh grunts and drops a flatbread onto his plate. "It's hot," he complains.

"That's how pide oughta be," says Sam.

"Oh," says Nancy, "I was going to ask what pide was, but I was going to call it peedee, and that didn't sound right."

"Never make a false move," says Hugh, scornful.

Jesus, kid, thinks Sam, you figure you're too good for this broad?

Nancy spoons soup to her mouth, savours it, thinks a moment, and says, "What you need, Hugh, is a holiday. Why don't we go someplace nice tomorrow and get some sun for a few days?"

Hugh's clean, straight-nosed features look thickened and blurred in the ruby-lit twilight of Topkapi. He chews pide and swallows it with a slug of screwdriver. "You know I gotta work tomorrow," he growls, "and so do you."

"I'm willing to get someone to take my shift," she says. "Why don't you get Kenny to cover for you?"

"We got a boxcar of clothes lost someplace between Toronto and Tranquille. Kenny takes care of his end, I take care of mine. I'll be working tomorrow and probably Sunday if we don't get this sorted out. Why don't you just go down to the nudie beach and flaunt your bod? That's what you get off on anyhow."

She looks at him. If I wasn't around, Sam thinks, he'd get his ears burned.

Yusuf arrives with steaming plates. "You have," he says, "delicious food," and prestidigitates the crockery.

"The soup was excellent," Nancy tells him.

"Thank you, thank you," he says, "my wife thanks you. Now," he says, "you will have coffee later. I will bring more water," he glances at the plates with their peppered sauces, "in case."

"Yes," says Nancy. "Milk."

His eyebrows go up. "You know something, beautiful lady," he says. "But for spicy food the jajik is good, with the yogurt and cucumber."

"Yes," she says, "more jajik. And milk."

Yusuf looks at Sam and Hugh, uncertain. "For you?"

"No," says Sam. Yusuf looks relieved.

"I'd like another drink," says Hugh.

Sam frowns. "Hugh –"

"No no, Sam, it is a pleasure." Yusuf heads for the brown bag. "Hugh," says Sam, "that wasn't nice. You can't ask a guy for a free drink. When he's bumming it off a customer yet."

"Fiddlesticks," says Hugh. "The greaseball knows how to sell."

"Hugh!" says Sam, guttural. "Sure he'd do the same for anybody, but that doesn't mean he's an asshole."

Those level eyes. "Sorry, Sam, it's just a bad day, like you said." The eyes harden a trifle. "When you walk into people's lives out of nowhere –"

"Let's eat," says Nancy.

Sam and Hugh look at each other. Hugh shifts to his plate, attacks a piece of donner kebab, and chews hard. "Don't get me wrong, Sam," he says at length. "I just wish right now I was on a beach someplace – like Fiji maybe. Or playing left wing for money instead of this lousy rag business."

Nancy says, "Maybe we should go to Adana, if it's anything like this kebab. Mm. Cayenne sauce and meat like veal cannelloni."

Sam watches her eat while he munches halep sweet as good water and hot as a desert sun. Fresh sweat springs from his pores. Nancy's skin smooth and soft. She eats single-mindedly as she does anything at any given moment. The black queen, in spades. This is a daughter. The silver star gleams between the broad bases of her breasts.

A tambourine clash and ululating screech remind Sam that Ishye hasn't been visible – or audible – the while. She spins the length of Topkapi like a sequinned whirlwind trailing veils black and green.

"Helps ya eat better," Sam says.

Ishye dances back toward them, shimmering and undulating among the tables. Her arms are snakes mesmerizing rabbits. Her eyes pin patrons to their chairs while her breasts flutter on her chest like bright butterflies. "That's muscle control," Nancy mutters. Arms stretch toward Ishye to stuff dollar bills in her waistband. She pouts and mocks and offers her breasts to the florid-faced guest of honour at the big table. He leans his bill across, looking ready to grope as he stuffs, and she snatches it away in her cleavage, grinning like the avenging angel.

My God, thinks Sam, this one makes the broads on Davie look like rookies. He sees her navel advancing upon him and digs around for money. Make 'em pay to stay out of trouble, he thinks. That's what you get from a civilization that old.

Ishye's navel approaches like the eye in a storm. At the last moment she twitches away and extends her arms to Hugh. She stands – not stands, thinks Sam, hovers – facing Hugh, inviting him, her thighs doing eloquently explicit things under their translucent cloud of skirts, until the moment stretches beyond snapping. Hugh sits looking like a mouthful of lemon, stiff as marble.

Ishye drops her head to one side, says, "Tch, she's too pretty," and turns on

Sam. Chin raised, eyes laughing, she reels him in with sinuous arms as though he were on a rope.

He stands, the dollar still crushed in his palm, heady and hollow-gutted as a man going over the top.

Ishye dances before him, dances him out into the little space there is in Topkapi, not to fuck, he thinks, not to come up and see me, not even to perform, but to *be,* man. Dance.

His feet fumble around, his legs protest unfit for duty, all of him scrambles to remember something about dancing Greeks in late-night cafés – the closest thing he knows. He hops and shuffles and something begins to make sense. The floor begins to speak to his hips and his shoulders go back and his arms spread like wings to the Mediterranean sounds beating from a tape machine somewhere. Ishye grins like a pleased archangel. Her arm reaches for his shoulder as she swings to beside him like a closing gate and locks into step, doing ten things for his one. His hand on her shoulder finds the leather-looking skin slick with sweat and soft as petals.

As the music quickens to a rhythm his feet can no longer follow, she twirls from under his arm like pirouetting flame and falls into a shimmying curtsey in front of him. He bends to cram the dollar between her breasts, his hand for a moment flat on her chest and the heart beating through him.

Ishye rises like a dervish and flicks away. She sails into Hugh with her tambourine crashing over her head and her short body thrumming like a bowstring stretched from fingers to toes. And freezes there into sculpture. The music gone.

Hugh blushes under his tan. He slips a folded blue fin into the cup of Ishye's bra. She arches an eyebrow, pouts approvingly, and vanishes into the kitchen.

Sam stands in the middle of the floor, breathing. Applause bursts around him. Shouts from the stags. For a lady not too long on looks, he thinks, you know more about sex and showmanship than any centrefold stripper and Ringling Brothers put together.

Nancy sits at the table glowing. Something aches inside his chest. Lily all around him suddenly in Topkapi's dim jewelled night. As he settles into his chair, Nancy's smell envelops him like the Lebanese nights that man Flecker wrote hopeless poems about. Jasmine, he thinks. That's it. Jasmine and turned-on lady. An embarrassment of daughters. Lot's daughters coming to him in the cave after they'd got him pissed out of his mind. And his wife a pillar of salt for looking back on sin. Dot. The glass emeralds and rubies of Topkapi. Poor Dot never had anything too interesting to look back on.

Hugh looks uncomfortable. "Didn't know you could dance," he says.

"Yeah," Sam says, not knowing what else to say.

Yusuf, suddenly there, says, "She is very good. Not like these white girls." He glances at Nancy and adds, "Not you, dear lady. You too have dangerous eyes." He grins. "She is from Cyprus, like me."

"She sure knows how to steam the place up," says Sam. "She's wonderful," says Nancy, sounding like she knows what she's talking about.

Yusuf contemplates her with obvious approval. "You know that Topkapi was once a seraglio?" he asks.

"Seragli-what?" says Nancy.

"Seraglio. A harem. What you call a harem. Although really it is the place in which the women live."

"Would I like a harem?" Nancy asks.

Yusuf looks at her. "I don't know. With you, I think it depends on the harem. And maybe the man. Maybe you would like a harem of men. You western women – but then maybe you are not so western ... You have two men already –" He bends his head to Sam, whispering. "You do not mind?"

Sam shrugs. "No," he says.

He turns again to Nancy. "You are doubly lucky. This one is like Belisarius, strong and smart at once."

"Who?" says Nancy.

"Belisarius. A great general of the Byzantines, before Istanbul –" Hassan appears at Yusuf's elbow. "Dad," he says.

"Never mind, boy, can't you see I'm busy?"

"The people by the window want to leave."

"Well, tell them to go!"

"But, Dad, they want to pay."

"Children!" says Yusuf, scimitar. "Belisarius never lost, except in the end, to his Emperor. But that was before the Turks," and he hustles to the door, swatting Hassan aside, grinning, shaking hands, as the people by the window file out.

"This guy's a nutbar," says Hugh.

Sam laughs. "More nutbars like him and it might be worth living. You figure you could go to Istanbul and be that proud of where you come from and not make 'em feel like losers?"

"He's probably never been to Istanbul. Just another fucking Cypriot."

"Picky," says Nancy.

Are you feeling like a loser, boy? It's not only in Umberto's that all the guys eat out of your girl's hand.

"Coffee?" says Yusuf. "Turkish coffee?"

"Please," says Nancy.

"Regular," says Hugh.

Yusuf grimaces, but nods. "And dessert?"

"No," says Hugh.

"Watching your figure?" says Nancy.

"Turkish," says Sam. "And I'll try that Sutlu Borek cake."

Yusuf nods vigorously. "Pastry. My wife will be pleased," he says. "And I have something you will enjoy," pointedly at Hugh. The something turns out to be white liquor in tiny glasses that accompany the coffee and desserts.

Hugh's eyebrows go up.

"We do not serve drinks," says Yusuf. "This is raki. It is not to be had in Canada." He serves each of them a glass. "Sometimes it tastes like gasoline, but this is good. My brother has come back from Cyprus and some things he is good for."

The raki tastes like rarefied ouzo and lifts the top of Sam's head up into the smoky realm of angels near Topkapi's ceiling. A sip of the thick, sweet, terribly strong coffee dissolves all that into pure sky, black velvet and starshot as he knows it to be up there. He closes his eyes.

"Where to next, you two party freaks?" says Hugh.

His voice bores through Sam's Turkish delight like a drill press. "Oh fer fuck's sake, Hugh," he growls.

Sam opens his eyes. Nancy's looking at the kid as though there's going to be trouble. She looks like the answer poised for millenia to come in Topkapi's storefront museum night. She's all yours, kid, he thinks, not mine. I dunno, maybe she's hell to live with. Or not to live with. Lily's grown children eyeing him through wandering Jew trailing from its macramé sling.

"Let's take Sam up to Humphrey's for a drink," Hugh says. To Sam, "It's just across the street in Denman Place. You'll probably like the music."

"Old fogey music?" says Sam.

"No," says Hugh. "Lounge jazz. An old dude named Wyatt Ruther, used to lay down the line for Basie in the mid-sixties. And a lady named Eve Smith who sings and plays piano. They play pretty white up there, but it's not bad. Anyhow, I could use another drink."

Sam looks at him through dissolving Turkish angels and the echoes of halep in his gut. *Lay down the line.* Whatever that means in Count Basieland, this ain't bad, kid. Not bad at all. And glances down at the check Hassan has, like a timely genie, made manifest on the tablecloth. No raki there. No vodka, of course. A grand total of $18.25.

"Yusuf!" he hollers.

"Remember that's mine," says Hugh, reaching.

Sam growls. "Yusuf," he says, "this is criminal."

Yusuf's eyebrows go up. "Yes?" he says, and cranes to read the check Sam is withholding from Hugh.

"You're gonna go broke doing this." He waves fingers at Hugh. "My boy's gonna give you a twenty and I'll throw in five. That kid of yours ought to get something for the course you put him through. And all that booze –"

"No no, Sam. The boy will be, how you say, spoiled if he does not learn the joy of work. And the liquor …" He shrugs.

"Man, we ain't rich, but you can't afford what you did for us at this price."

"You wish to embarrass me, Sam? No, you are like what I said to you on the street last night. Look, the liquor costs me nothing. I am rich in my friends." His eyes dance. "And I am buying real estate."

Sam makes a raspberry and waves the check into Yusuf's hand. Hugh proffers a twenty. "Here," he says, "please."

And Yusuf nods. "Thank you," he says. "I am blessed with customers most of them I can like. The others," he shrugs, "maybe they will not come back." He looks at Hugh, glances at Nancy, and says with a nod toward Sam, "Your father is a man to follow. I hope you will return to Topkapi."

"Mm," says Nancy.

Sam stands, sweaty and weak in the legs but his chest happy and head light as a barrage balloon. He shakes Yusuf's hand, who says, "Good night good night" and flies into the kitchen, arms flapping about something that hasn't been done.

The boy Hassan accompanies them to the door. He says, "I keep telling my father he doesn't understand business." Sam takes his hand. "Thanks," he says. Hassan's brows arc like crescent moons as he feels the bill in his palm. "It ain't much, but do somethin' with it, and don't tell your old man."

"I will show him," the boy says, "how it should be done."

Sure, Sam thinks. Little cretin. And puts a hand each on the backs of Nancy and Hugh as they precede him into the cooler lamplit dusk of Denman Street. "Thanks," he says to them before they plunge into the July night crowds on the way to Humphrey's, "best dinner I had in years."

In the babble and crush of the street he hears voices call him. The restaurants of Soho and Bayswater and the one Jameson bought for his wife to run in Devon speak across the years and the miles from that England full of ghosts. Denizens of the Garden Square Hotel, Cockney George and the Dutchman's wife. The cranky Greek of Fournaki on the Moscow Road. Liz Jameson's foxlike smile by candlelight at the Pilgrim's Table. Old Jameson's eyes shining with history over brandy by the fire. The haunted years and lanes.

WHERE ARE THE CLOWNS

HUMPHREY'S SITS in the night sky at the top of Denman Place. A shopping mall on the ground floor. Going up in the elevator from the hotel lobby Sam thinks, It wouldn't take much longer to walk up the High Street in Totnes. This thing would make a town over there, two thousand years old. With cows outside.

He looks at Nancy standing between him and Hugh, her colour uncut by the blank fluorescent light. Just Nancy, to be possessed by no one. Which doesn't mean she's not all yours, son, he thinks, looking at Hugh paler and more Anglo in the glare, his square strong hands clasped in front of his crotch. Whatever that means, all yours. He feels very paternal and familial and kind of peacefully biologic.

When the doors slide open he hears the sound of a bass fiddle and a woman's smoky voice singing *leave your worries on the doormat,* and enters a swish-looking room all glass at the edges, full of expensive-looking people, and then a lot of lounge applause while Hugh stabs his eyes around for a table.

The woman who had been singing bows her head and smiles from a face the colour of the gorgeous walnut grand she's sitting behind. Silvery-haired Ruther is perched on a tall stool, an arm around his fiddle so you can't quite tell where the man ends and the instrument begins. Ah, a glimmer of memory: *Lay down that bass line.* From where? Music that was …

"Thank you," the woman says, looking at Sam, looking, he realizes, at everyone, "thank you. We'll be back, so don't go 'way."

Hugh's voice. "Sam," it says. Wearily, almost. A tug at his sleeve. "Over here, Sam." Sam standing there amongst tables, seeing a delectable chestnut-haired young thing with Dresden-china skin in swirls of peach and coffee paisley. Her razor-cut blond companion stares up at him with pale green fishkilling eyes. The ferryboat punk of forever ago roils up out of Sam's gut. All around his skin he feels unthinkable flame. Dresden – like you in the tens of thousands, peach-bloom lady, consumed by the firestorm. The Lancasters and Stirlings, the Halifaxes of Main Force Bomber Command thousand-plane raids to remind the Germans – all the Germans – who held the big stick now.

Hugh's standing by a table looking at him as though he were the strangest thing on earth. He turns that way with a screech between his ears like shearing metal. Nancy sits there at the table. The answer, he thinks. My daughter, my son's lover.

He sits. A patrician-looking young woman with cornsilk hair gathered in a ponytail half down her back comes to take their order. He considers her sapphire eyes and papaya-yellow dress. I'm out on the town, he thinks. Jesus, Hugh. Thanks. Ain't been like this in a long time.

"Double Scotch on the rocks," he says. Outside the glass walls of Humphrey's, Vancouver and its waters sparkle. Eve Smith's muted voice floats down from the speaker ports in the ceiling.

"This'll do," he says, "nice place." Hugh looks a bit more relaxed, one arm over the back of the bench seat, slouched against the burnt-orange cushions beside Nancy. "Don't know much about jazz, but these two sound pretty good. That big black dude musta been playin' when I was a kid. Basie, you say?"

"Yeah, Wyatt played with the Count. But that wasn't till *I* was a kid."

"Didn't hear about Basie till after the war." Sam pauses, seeing smoky dance floors in London. "Kinda liked Glenn Miller, though." He sighs decisively, plants his palms on the shiny table, and stands. "I'm gonna piss," he says, looks at Nancy, who smiles, and shakes his head. "Sorry," he says, "the price of manners is constant vigilance, for old duffers like me that ain't used to it."

Nancy laughs. She woulda giggled, thinks Sam, except she's got the sense to open her mouth. "Ladies aren't what they used to be," she says. Hugh looks at her.

"Watch out, boy, or I'll steal her on ya," Sam says and immediately regrets it. Getting careless, he thinks. Loose. "Where's the can?" he says.

Hugh just looks up at him a moment, like a man still studying new ground. Then he jerks his head back over one shoulder and says, "Through that door and up the steps."

Never mind, thinks Sam, whatever's eating at the two of them ain't my doing. No matter what you got going for you, it all gets complicated. Poor young fucker, he thinks. What a girl. And I'm the one having a good time with her.

He sighs climbing stairs. The blond guy comes trotting down. The pale green eyes flick at him quick as a springknife and the guy's gone. "Hmpf!" says Sam, climbing on. Hell of a place to put the convenience in a fancy joint like this.

But the room itself is spacious, high-ceilinged and discreetly rambling around angles in the walls to seclude one function from another. A generous room, he thinks, wazzing into the drain. Space to piss. Fucking Krauts, he thinks, suddenly angry and not sure why.

Downstairs again Hugh and Nancy are sipping their drinks. His big fat dewy-sided Scotch sits in front of his chair.

"Scotch whiskies generally taste like God's own peat bog," he intones. "It must pick the English ass. I guess that's what empires are for."

126

Nancy laughs. It's hard not to have a good time with her.

The piano puts out a rich chord note by note that didn't come from any Tannoy in the roof. He looks around. Smith is snuggling into her nest behind the mirror-polished slab of walnut and Ruther enfolds the bass as though it might have gotten lonely.

Eve turns to Wyatt. "Did you remember your bow?" she archly inquires.

"Yes, ma'am," says Ruther, slow-smiling and feeling around a scabbard slung from his stool, "if I can find it out here."

"We'd like to open this set," she says to everyone in the room, "with one of our favourite songs," the strong chords organizing themselves into a melody familiar in a way that tells Sam something is going to move him, "by Mr. Stephen Sondheim." Scattered applause.

"You know this song?" Sam asks.

"Yes," says Nancy. "Yeah, it's a nice song," says Hugh, looking out the window, thinking about something. What's gone wrong with his girl? His derelict dad? A boxcar full of bluejeans? How can you lose a boxcar full of bluejeans? Or whatever they are.

Smith's voice lilts syllables, improvising. Isn't it clear. Sometime some year. Nostalgia, thinks Sam. The kids across the table. His kids. The way we were. Were we ever like that? Nancy's eyes look at the song. Hugh seems someplace else entirely, out of time, in his transparent cotton shirt lounging there. Other Hugh in the barracks at Borden. *I feel like we've been taken out of time,* Hugh had said. Hugh from an unknown place called Youbou on Vancouver Island, familiar of deer and trees and the daughters of peculiar customers who drank Scotch and reeked of gentry. This Hugh losing a traincar of clothes. On the way to Borden the army had lost 120 men between trains in Winnipeg and found them at the Fort Garry Hotel, somewhat pickled.

Where are they now? says the song. Ruther slides his bow across the strings. This has been a song without a bass. A nice song. Ruther's bow produces one note, and the nice song becomes magic. Sam can see the bow slide back and forth, but one note hangs in the air and everything slips out of time. Nancy wearing her wealth in her skin, her eyes dark stars in the music that is the room. The live Hugh and the dead one. The sea of khaki wool clothing ten thousand frightened men. Dead Hugh's cornflower eyes look at him. Earthbrown curls and structure of bones in his face a woman could have used. "The army takes you out of time," he'd said. "Here we are not even overseas yet, taken out of time in our own country so we can dare to kill or be killed." Almost forty years ago. A boy seventeen. A man who could hit anything with any kind of gun he could hold in his hands and drive a car dead drunk through the twistedest hedgerows in England without touching

127

a leaf. A lonely kid who wondered why and wanted to go home and wanted to be a man. Who got called a fairy for his looks and couldn't punch his way through thick soup. But sneaky fast so you couldn't hit him with anything unless you held him down. Unless you hit him with a German shellburst in the mud in Belgium. A private soldier of peculiar mind who neither followed nor led but was always there like prescient thought. Who would have been a troller fisherman if he had lived, and should have married a woman like that Walloon Lise.

"Where are the clowns? Send in the clowns," he hears Eve Smith's voice sing. As though the sound Ruther has made could gather itself into words, into whatever each life is in this room, in this island of light suspended between the sparkle of Vancouver and the stars. You sonofabitch, he thinks. You gnarly magician, from rubbing horsehair on gut you get the sound of being here.

Sam raises his glass. He looks around at the clowns. The scent of peat bog fills his nostrils and tears wet his vision like a trick of light. They're here, he thinks as Smith sings it and Ruther's bow lifts off the strings and the sound ceases. Tinkling glass. The room shakes itself into time then bursts with applause. Sam stands abrupt as a stumpy tree, pounding his palms together, tears coursing down his cheeks, a noise in his throat that might have led a charge. Ruther nods, grins a very old grin, waves his bow. "Thank you," says Smith and she rolls rock-ribbed chords out of the piano.

Hugh and Nancy have clapped, Hugh gazing up at Sam rather than at the bandstand as the source of strange phenomena.

"He waved," says Sam, subsiding into his chair, snorting to clear his nose. Handkerchief out of pocket. Dab the eyes. Blow the nose. Looking at Hugh.

"They do that," says Hugh, dry.

"Goddammit!" A kid who knows lounge jazz. "Can't you appreciate anything?"

"He liked it," says Nancy, very earnest and mature and adorable, jutting out a hand each onto his arm and Hugh's. The anger in him swirls dangerous and confused. Her hand on his arm and Hugh's. One woman. Two hands. The father and the son. The lover and the daughter. Can you know that, boy? Now wait a minute. Hugh, he thinks, knowing something through that woman he'd only guessed at – the anger slapping around in Hugh. Waves of the same weather. "Were you out there wondering who your father is?" he says. *Hugh your father?*

"Where do you get this weird shit, Sam? It's like that night I went to Victoria. I don't know where you're coming from at all."

Pressure from Nancy's hand and she sits back, worried. Sam stares at Hugh's grey eyes in the inscrutable mask over anger.

Sam hears air coming out of himself. "That black man," he says, "can sure do things with a bass fiddle." He wants to go on. Stopping time. Cornflower blue eyes. The life gone out of him and no way of putting it back. No dying. No last words. Lids snapped shut. Dust in his mouth for words. "The war," he says.

Hugh's face twists. Don't work the knife, boy, Sam thinks, whatever it is. Not bluejeans.

"Does everything make you think of the war?" Hugh asks. Really asks, thinks Sam. Two-edged knife.

"Yeah," he says. "Mostly. Sometimes." And women. And the men that were and aren't, and the ones that are. And ah shit! His hands on two edges of the table want to break it like dry bread.

"I think I better take a leak," says Hugh, reaching for the bar tab tucked between the tent-card offering Kansas City Slings and Chicago Blue Tinglers and the ashtray no one's using.

Don't you understand anything, punk? he thinks and almost says to Hugh's solid back swinging out from the bench seat and two springy steps up, hand on a pillar to pivot for the door. Shouldn't wonder, growing up with Dot and Sid. But mad as hell and no wronger'n I am. Is that it? Maybe I do want you to be like first Hugh. A man who watches the fire burn and knows things. A man who stands on sheer rock and talks to birds. Like Lily, who remembers Russian churches she's never seen. And me just some drunk who walked out on you twenty years ago. His whisky's gone. I wanna talk to Lily, he thinks, the darkness in him reaching out to splotch the air like spilled blood.

He looks at Nancy. "He doesn't mean to be bad," she says, certain as she is about anything. "I keep telling myself that."

You got taken away too, didn'tcha? thinks Sam, when old Wyatt drew his bow. The woman in you has a long way to go – setting Lily's lamplike face beside her sultry glow – but it ain't going to run out before you get there. "He's having a rough time. And I'm not helping much," he says.

"Can you tell me about the war, Sam?" she asks. "I want to know." Her hands make a gesture like long birds alongside her face. "I don't know very much," she says, still certain. "Hugh's smart and I'm not. But," and the birds turn by her cheekbones as though the air had been taken from their wings as she says the first uncertain thing he's heard from her, "maybe if you can tell me –" She pauses, all the lovely lines of her scattered like a nest of sticks. He wishes for whisky. The patrician waitress bends discreetly among tables as other music goes on. *Some say it had to be you,* Smith sings.

Nancy's hand alights on his arm on the table. "Please, Sam", she says, not at all uncertain, transfixing him. "Help me," she says. "If you can tell me, maybe he can know." About the war, he thinks. About Hugh's drunk old dad. The one from

129

Victoria. The one who hasn't been home so long there isn't one to go to. About me.

He looks at her. Your eyes don't have a colour, lady. They're just a place for light to go. And what comes out is you. That's all. You. You love that boy, he thinks. Envious, in an utterly elusive way because it makes him happy. It comes to him that he hasn't seen a woman look that way about another man since Lise in Belgium wanting to return Hugh's heart to the earth. Lily looking at him.

"Yeah," he says, and believes it, a great relaxation washing over the panic. "Maybe I can." Hugh returns. Lumpy, somehow, in this place of birds and air, all the clean tidy white-and-cream package of him, a bit pink through the tan on his cheekbones, eyes too bright. I know about you, Sam thinks, you think you wanna kill somebody. And presses on, stubborn that she's right and needs an answer.

"War is waiting," he says. Jesus. Al? "And worrying and trying to think about something else instead of the guys who're gonna try and kill you – so you'll be ready to try and kill them." Am I doing okay, Al? We ain't supposed to, somehow, with these civilian kids. But what the hell. "That's not soldiering," he says. "That's war. Soldiering's supposed to get you ready for that." He takes a deep breath for Hugh, who looks dangerous. If you weren't my kid, he thinks, I'd sock you one to keep things safe. "Nancy," he says, her name a live thing in his chest. Daughter. "Nancy, somehow I'm not supposed to be saying this. It goes against the rules." Whose rules? Old soldiers' rules. The world's rules. Grown men don't cry and death and sex are dirty. Keep it in the closet so that peace may reign.

They're both looking at him as though a haystack got up and walked. But differently. The boy at war for himself, the girl at war for all of them. I'll break your face, kid, he thinks, if you don't figure out she loves you.

"You're family," he says to her, "so I'm saying it. But I have to say something about you first." He looks at Hugh and quails. "Nancy," he says. You remind me of all the women I ever cared about because you love my kid. And if I was the right age I wish I could jump in the sack with you. Except you're my daughter. That's what I'll try and tell you. "Nancy, you say you're not smart. That means you're stupid like a fox."

They laugh. Nancy as though she had heard an honestly good joke. Hugh like a man who doesn't think he's got anything to laugh about.

Ruther and Smith are doing something about when you come home again. *If you're here, I'll be gone.* It unnerves him. "I wanna tell you about Hugh, the guy this one was named after."

"He's mentioned him," says Nancy.

"We talked about that last night when I was drunk out of my skull." He eyes Hugh. "I think I managed to explain something." Not much more than a twitch in response. A glance at the bandstand. Sam takes on another full load of air.

"Hugh Young, his name was, which is almost a joke, I guess. He'd be fifty-five now. He came from a little place on Lake Cowichan. A lot of my boys did. They all signed up together. Funny how people came from all over the back of nowhere to fight Germans where all the old wars had been fought. But the army paid wages, sort of, and gave you something to eat and something to do that was supposed to mean something. I guess it did. I guess I'm glad we won that war, even if I hate it. So we went, and four years later Hugh finished his job in Belgium, ripped open by an artillery round. That's part of an infantryman's job, you know, to get killed. You can't take a piece of ground, or hold it, if the other guys are any good at all, without losing some of your own. So you got to have enough people so some can get killed. More or less, depending how you fight your war. And some guys' job is to get killed. It took me a long time to figure that out, and I didn't like it. It didn't help that I was a sergeant, which is kind of like a foreman, and my job was to keep those guys sharp and alive and more or less sane and happy enough so some of them could get killed or kill some Germans, which wasn't much better since the poor fucking Germans had the same problem. Though I did get to hate those bastards. It just doesn't make sense unless you've got a war. And even then it doesn't make sense if you think about it much. It's awful hard to stay in a war when you begin to understand what you're doing. That's why the army has to be so good at making people belong. They are your brothers in arms those sonsabitches, like they say. And if they weren't, you'd go nuts. This might sound peculiar, but if I had to say one thing that war is I'd say it was a smell. One stink made up of powder and sweat and oil and gas and burning wood and grass and rubber and burning, rotting meat – men and horses. At Caen and Falaise we smelled that one smell for weeks. It's still up here," tapping his nose, "and will be until I'm dead."

Nancy is looking at him very straight, the blood gone from under her tan, her big beautiful eyes gone even bigger and kind of flat. Hugh looks like he's desperate to disagree with something he knows he can't touch. You're mad about something else, kid, but you know it ain't this big. Good on you.

"When they were doing that song about clowns and the big guy seemed to stop time with his bow sliding back and forth on the fiddle, I saw Hugh Young. He had bright blue eyes like cornflowers and a funny mind. He used to talk about things like time and where we were in it. He got me thinking about what I was doing – I wasn't much used to looking after other people. He was the best damn soldier in my bunch because he always knew where he was in things. The order of things. He didn't have any ambition, he woulda been a career private soldier if he'd had a career, but he made the other guys, including me, feel better because he made sense of a place just by being in it. All he wanted to do was catch fish and find the

131

right lady and think about things, but he got a war handed to him instead. He was my kid brother and I loved him. When he got killed I couldn't even bury him. He had a girlfriend in a Belgian village – Hugh always had a girlfriend, but this one was something else. Lise. She came out there – God knows how she knew and how she got there alive – and she couldn't bury him either. But she knew and she came out in that parsnip field with German machine guns on the next rise and she did the best she could. That won't leave me any more than the stench will, but it's private. She had guts, that lady, because she loved him and she knew why. Never saw her again, but I learned something about loving people I'm just beginning to figure out. I've been thinking about this whole damn thing for almost forty years and I don't say it to anybody because they don't want to hear it. The ones that were there don't want to hear it and the ones that weren't there don't want to hear it. The only real sense it makes to me is that I seem to be what they call a good soldier, and sometimes I wish to God I wasn't."

"I want to hear it," she says. Brave Nancy. You too, kid, would be a good soldier. A child with a rifle on her shoulder. It wets his eyes. What's it like, not to have a war the way we had a war?

Feeling slightly crazy, he says, "What's it like to be you? What do you want to do? Why are you doing it?" and knows it is crazy.

"I don't know," she says, all the birds of her circling a question asked too soon for them to land on.

"I hope I know you in twenty years," he says.

"How can we know what that war was like?" Hugh demands of his girl. Then to Sam, "She just wants to make money and travel."

Sam stares at him. "So what's wrong with that?" she says. "You do it too. He is a good soldier. This would be wonderful if you'd stop snarling."

Ruther is tucking his fiddle away in a case the size of a sarcophagus. "Why aren't you two married?" Sam says.

"Don't you think we're too young?" she says, sounding very certain again. "Look what happens to people when they get married."

"True enough," says Sam.

"I think I'll go to the little girls' room," she says. Hugh starts twirling a swizzlestick between his thumb and fingers.

"You still mad?" asks Sam, the spent adrenalin leaving him clearer than he's felt in a while.

Hugh looks at him. The twirling stops.

"It's not a question of mad," young Hugh says. You do look like you could use some R and R, boy. "It's more like confused."

Sam waits, alert but easy, for what his boy has come to in the delicious sense of the Humphrey's night dying all around them. The Dresden-girl looks beautiful, but more ordinary, more like a pretty kid in a fancy bar than fuel for the flames. Sometimes there ain't no war.

"Nancy and I have been having our problems," says Hugh. "But I guess everyone has problems." He throws the stick onto the table. "Sam," he says, "I believed what you said about Hugh last night. And everything else. It really got to me. This morning it still made some sense, but I went to work and – hell, I don't know, maybe I was the one that was drunk last night." He's staring at the table, looking morose and feisty at once. You poor kid, Sam thinks, and doesn't dare say.

"It's like, what are you doing in my life anyway?" says Hugh, raising his eyes up to level them on Sam.

Phewee, thinks Sam, boy you do have a way. "I'm sorry," he says, "I know I got it coming, but –"

Hugh waves it away and shakes his head. "That's just part of it. I'm glad you talked to Nancy. And what can anybody say to that? We don't know what you went through. We can't." He shrugs. "I'm just confused, that's all."

"You wanna say some more about that?"

"Maybe some other time, eh?" says Hugh. "It's late."

At his elbow the waitress says, "Last call."

"We've had it," says Hugh. "Your service could be better. I gave the check to the waiter."

"The waiter, sir? Oh, that must have been the manager."

"Well, he's got it for you at the bar with my Chargex card."

"Thank you, sir," she says, more flustered than patrician, "I'll bring it in a moment."

"That would be great," says Hugh.

Sam contemplates not wanting a drink. He has a nostalgia for women. Nancy in the loo. Lily. Sitting there astride him without her clothes on, understanding things he'd never expected anyone would understand. Or seeming to. The morning of the two sons and macramé.

Dammit, boy, he thinks, I'm not gonna let you kibosh this. And Lily is probably out on the town someplace after the week's work. It's only Tuesday, she'd said. And now it's only Friday. Out on the town with some brass Adonis. What am I gonna do about it?

Nancy comes down the two steps from the dining-room level of Humphrey's. It's the first time he's seen her since she came out her door that he's seen her from any kind of distance – freestanding, as it were. She is no longer too beautiful to think about. Lightly down the steps, brisk across the floor, stern until she knows she's being looked at, when she grins – like, hey, I look like this all the time. You look, he thinks, like hope.

"Powder your nose?" he says.

"I took long enough to powder everything, didn't I?" She glances back and forth between him and Hugh. "How have you two been doing?" she asks.

"Fine," says Hugh. "Let's get out of here." He stands before she can sit. The flustered waitress with the bill. The signing of the Chargex chit. The leaving.

"You must be in a hurry to go to bed," says Nancy.

"Not with her," replies Hugh.

"Can you believe it, Sam?" she asks. "Don't answer that."

"No. But I ain't complainin'."

"Good," says Hugh, leaning on the elevator button and actually managing a smile.

TROIS GYMNOPÉDIES

SOMEWHERE ALONG Davie Street she says, "Where are you going, Hugh?"

"I'm taking you home. This is the way to your place, isn't it?"

"And it could be the way to your place, too. I just wondered. I'm going to your place."

"Nancy!" It's almost a shriek.

"Hugh," says Sam, "I beg your pardon, but –"

"You know my place isn't very big."

"It's certainly bigger than mine," she says.

"But Sam's staying with me."

"I sleep on the couch," says Sam. "And your bed looks plenty big enough for two."

"Yes," says Nancy.

The kid's embarrassed, thinks Sam. Maybe they indulge in bizarre practices. "In case you haven't noticed, Hugh, I ain't no prude."

"I noticed. I also noticed that sometimes you talk good English and sometimes you talk like a musclehead."

"Yeah," says Sam. "That would be speak good English. Peculiar, ain't it."

"I think we need a nightcap," says Nancy. "Do you have anything?"

"Not much. Wine. Vodka. Haven't had a chance to restock."

"Well, I've got a bottle of Remy –"

Hugh leaves rubber at the corner of Nicola and Davie. The Celica jerks to a halt in front of Nancy's fernpalace.

After she's gone, Sam ventures into the silence left behind the doorslam. "Sorry to meddle," he says, "I figured –"

"It's okay," says Hugh, sepulchral from the front-seat shadows. Like talking to someone in church. Hugh's fingers drum on the steering wheel. "Part of it's Nancy. She goes her own way. She's not too bright, but she gets what she wants."

Oh oh, thinks Sam. "Whaddyou mean, not too bright! You mean you think you don't want her?"

"No, I didn't say that. I don't think I ever met a man who wouldn't want Nancy. I want her but she drives me crazy. I've got too many things going on in my head."

"Oh." He's too pissed off to want to indulge in any practices at all.

"Even the gay guys in the food racket want her, for window-dressing, I guess. She suits their idea of style."

That woman's got more sense than you and me put together, but I better not tell you that. Absolutely nothing is happening in the purple mercury-lit night on Nicola. It looks like a set for a TV horror show. Hugh's still talking.

"I know tonight was my idea," says churchly Hugh. "I don't want to spoil it for everybody. Maybe I expected something different – candlelight and wine or whatever – but I haven't been enjoying this the way you and Nancy have. It started going wrong when she got mad at me on the phone because I have to work tomorrow. It's not your fault."

The dancing bear in Fairview. Take your old has-been dad and show him the town. Strange new things, thinks Sam. An upwardly-mobile kid with a fallen father and too much woman.

Clatter of Nancy's heels on the steps and quick click along the walk. She pulls open the door onto the larger presence of night and arrives in a rush of clutched objects and fresh scents. "I thought I'd grab some clothes," she says, sweeping shut the door as Hugh pops his clutch and leaves more tire marks on Nicola.

＞━＋✦＞━０━＜✦＋━＜

Upstairs in Hugh's pad the balcony door is still wide open, the room full of summer midnight. The redhead's place is dark.

"If you want to go to bed, Hugh, we won't keep you up," says Nancy. "I'm just going to change," and disappears into the bedroom. Sam reclines on the couch and pries his shoes off with his toes. Hugh begins arriving, dumping the contents of pockets onto the counter, pulling his shirt loose from his pants. Sam flexes his feet and snuggles into the cushions. Hugh picks the bottle of Remy Martin up and mulls over it. Sam remembers his jacket and sits up to take it off. Hugh gets decisive and goes to the liquor cabinet for brandy glasses, which he warms with tapwater and polishes. A neat amber dram in each.

"Just a nightcap," says Sam. "I really don't want to keep you two up." He yawns. "And I'm tired enough anyhow. I think I'll sleep better tonight."

"It's okay. I'm feeling complicated as hell, but I'm glad she likes you. I'm even gladder you like her."

Nancy reappears. The pool of relaxation spreading in Sam chokes. Lavender pants that fit like paint from the knee up, and a shiny lavender leotard. Bare feet. "There," she says, "that's cooler." Cooler. Peel on a second skin and it's cooler.

She lowers herself to the rug like a dancer and slides her legs out straight, back against a chair. Statuesque this and that, but a statuesque crotch on a dressed woman … He remembers to stop staring.

Hugh hands Nancy a glass and goes to close the drapes. He rearranges the lighting to low as last night.

"How about some music?" she says.

Hugh grunts and gives Sam his brandy. "Anything particular?"

"Quiet," she says.

Sam sniffs Remy Martin. Beatification. Churches should smell like that. Cedarchests and rosewood. He sips and closes his eyes.

Gauzy piano music drifts into his warm red haze.

"Cheers," says Nancy. Sam opens his eyes. She's smiling. Like a daughter. Hugh's sitting in the chair. "Here's to Sam," she says, raising her glass. "We're glad he's here." Hugh hoists his. She grins. "You're allowed to drink to yourself."

"Here's lookin' atcha," says Sam. Toast for toast. The two looking at him. Nancy a kind of human orchid with friendly eyes. Hugh contemplative, his eyes shadows as they had been at the other end of the long tunnel leading back to last night. It's like the bloody Underground, thinks Sam, looking down a tunnel stationed with nights and days where everyone's various selves get on and off. Long spaces between notes in the wistful piano melody.

"What's the music?" he asks.

"Erik Satie," says Hugh.

"Oh."

"They use it for muzak in the restaurant," says Nancy. "That was a funny thing Hugh said in the car, about the way you talk."

Sam laughs. Nancy's curious. How did you get to be this way, Sam? But keep 'em off balance. If they expect a question, make a statement.

"I don't notice much, unless some bright guy points it out. I guess different things have to be said different ways."

"It's true," she says, "but how do you know how?"

He laughs again. "Mostly it just comes out. I did go to high school, y'know. They did have high schools back then. Even picked up a little French – which I've completely forgot." He chuckles. "Perdu. My folks were very English. I think the old man was one of the last of the remittance men. He ran a dinky little newspaper on the North Shore, so I kind of grew up with dictionaries and ink on my fingers and the general idea that words are real the way bricks and boards are real. Worked for him for a while, reporting Sunday socials and what went on in City Hall. I still read a lotta books."

"I went to Grade Ten," she says. "What's a remittance man?"

Her capacity for that off-speed winsomeness amazes him. "A guy they didn't know what to do with back in England so they paid him to go someplace else and stay there. So I always kind of had the feeling I belonged over there, and when I got there in the war it was like home."

Hugh downs his brandy. "This is all very nice," he says, "but if I don't get to bed

I'm going to hate myself tomorrow." Standing, with his shirt out, in stocking feet, he looks between selves, unformed. Nancy puts a hand on his thigh. She has big hands, thinks Sam. And big feet.

"Is Sam going home tomorrow?"

"I think so." Hugh looks at Sam.

Endgame, he thinks. Wallpaper yellow as old grease. "Yeah," he says. "That'll be it." The poignant touch of melody like sad fingers playing inside his ribs.

"Can you drive him to the ferry?"

Hugh shakes his head. "Tomorrow doesn't even have lunch in it."

"Well then, why don't I drive you to work and take the car down to Umberto's so I can give him a ride when I'm finished? If that's not too late, Sam? About two o'clock?"

"Sure," he says, "there'll be a boat at three." Home for supper. Shepherd's pie in the James Bay? A can of beans?

"Okay," says Hugh, pulling off his shirt, yawning. "Anything else? That means you won't get your beauty sleep, you know."

"I'll have time to shop before work," she says.

Sitting like that, head turned and tilted up, arm raised, she looks like a pediment for the temple of Aphrodite. And half-naked Hugh maybe for Hermes. He bends down to kiss her. Not marble. Sculptural gumwood of living bone and tissue, Hugh's hand along her jawline. Sam looks at his own gut lying on him like a sleeping whale.

Hugh goes into the bedroom. No good night. "Don't forget to brush your teeth!" calls Nancy. He winces. Sometimes not so sensible.

She turns to him, very serious. "I know that's awful, but he really should brush his teeth."

Growling Hugh emerges, holding his unzipped pants together and saying, "Yeah, yeah," on his way to the bathroom.

Mechanized noises from the turntable. The wistful opening notes again. It's on repeat.

"Did you go back to work for the newspaper after the war?" Nancy asks.

He blinks. You could be hard to argue with, girl. Skip around all over but end up back where you want to be.

"Nope," he says. "Harry – that was the old man – died during the war." It all seems a little complicated when you look at it. Like father, like son. "I didn't like him much in the first place, but it didn't help having him go while I was across the water." Maybe that's why I came back. Like an old secret revealed. So Mum wouldn't stay lonely.

"Good night," says Hugh.

"Yeah," says Sam. On the other hand, she could have come to England. For her that would have been home. Goofy Belle retired to a village like Ashprington. God, I want to live in Devon. The brandy and piano make the room undulate in a haze of wish and memory. "I should've stayed over there, like my sister did with the Red Cross."

"What do you do now?" she asks.

"Well, lately I do the best I can."

"Doesn't everyone? No, I suppose not."

"Sorry," he says. "That's supposed to mean something but I guess it doesn't anymore. It means I take whatever comes along. I don't have a job."

"What comes along?"

"Oh, odd jobs." He grins. "There's a lotta widows in Victoria." She laughs. "Yeah, that too, but mostly I do their gardens and keep their porches from falling off." He sighs. "I've washed dishes in restaurants. You know what that's like."

She shudders. "Dreadful. Why don't you find something better?"

"The opportunities for sixty-year-olds ain't so good," he says. "But that's not the point."

Sam looks at her with what feels like a mirror of her earnestness. He can almost see reflected in her eyes the years rippling by like light on the water. Like the music going on and on.

"Nancy," he says, "the world didn't make any sense to me at all after the war. I'd been in the army seven years. It was like family. The bottom reason I didn't go for the newspapers was that it scared me. You have to do that alone. Like killing and dying and giving birth. And it makes you think about what's going on because you have to write about it. Even when I was a kid, I used to want to wring the mayor's neck, given what I knew was really going on, instead of interviewing him. After the war that was out. I'd get mad just walking down the street. So I tried to find another army, with no shooting. That was the Post Office and it was a mistake. I did a lot of things to stick my head in the sand, kid, including booze – too much booze – and running out on my wife and son. You get the picture?"

Nancy bites her lip. "Couldn't you be a commissionaire?"

He roars and again wants to hug her and wipes his eyes. "Until my heart did something funny a few years ago, I worked like a man and drank like a fish. Now it's mostly chopping wood and quiet evenings with my buddy Fred, who's level-headed. And lots of books and movies on the tube. But I ain't ready to spend the rest of my life on guard duty."

"I guess it's a stereotype," she says, "like telling me to be an exotic dancer or a secretary."

He starts. Or a waitress? "I don't know what I'd tell you to do, but not those."

She laughs. A slightly hooting sound. "I don't mean you," she says.

"Nancy!" Hugh calls, muffled by the door.

"I won't be long, Hugh," she calls back. Alto bell.

"You better not be," Sam says.

"I like talking to you. And he's being a grump."

"Keeping him awake ain't gonna help."

She wrinkles her nose. They look at each other. Sam breaks down. She's so damn nice to look at he really doesn't want her to go away.

The music seems to have been going on forever. He doesn't want it to stop.

"What do you want to do?" he asks. "Instead of the stereotypes?"

"I'm a waitress," she says.

"Well, yeah, but do you wanna be a waitress for good?"

"Why not? I make great tips."

"But, Nancy, you might not always be this pretty, and that might make a difference."

"I'm a good waitress," she says, resentful. "Besides, I'm only twenty-two and I might age well."

"I have no doubt you'll age well. That's why you might want to do something else."

"You have," she says. "Aged well, I mean."

He slaps himself on the gut. "Sure," he says.

"A lot of men Hugh's age have that," she says.

"Fat, sway-backed and spavined. An old horse. If I was a horse I'd be glue by now."

"Oh!" she says and swats the air in frustration. "You look fine, but that's not what I mean. You don't sound old. Or act old. Stop getting down on yourself."

"Thanks," he says. And believes her. Which amazes him. "But I am old. Until the last few days I've been feeling good for nothing, washed up. The other night – last night, it was – I made a complete ass of myself. Even today, going up Granville Street, I got pissed off as hell at all this," flinging his arm wide. "It just doesn't seem worth dying for. But that's all I ever did, fight a war to make this possible."

"There is Hugh," she says.

That throws him. "There's Hugh," he says. "And you." He wants to tell her about Lily, but it embarrasses him. "But that's only the last couple of days, because a friend of mine's dying in the hospital. So I get my ass over here, and like Hugh says, walk into his life out of nowhere. Before that Hugh was mostly something else to feel guilty about." He stops, staring at her toes as though they would tell him why his face feels like saggy old dough. "But he took me in, and he listened. You listened." He stares at the toes.

"At least I saw Dot again," he continues, "and now I know for sure I was a coward but I wasn't wrong." He grins. "And you two, for all your bitching, make me think life might be worth the candle after all. Maybe I can get better work. Maybe I can get myself back to England and figure out what that's about." Maybe I can even figure out what Lily's about. He sees her in their only night, grave and silent in that ancient place of unguarded selves. He sees Nancy sitting there in living lavender and gumwood. She says nothing.

"When I got up this morning, with the world's worst hangover, that redhead across the way was drying her hair in the sun. I got to thinking about going to see Hugh's mum. And I got to thinking we could have had a daughter. As far as I'm concerned, you're it."

She looks extremely pleased, and stands up. Or levitates. Smiling. "With that," she says, "she said she'd better go to bed." The dancer.

"You're right."

"Good night, Sam. Thanks for talking to me as though I'm not stupid."

"Good night, Nancy." Good grief, Nancy. "Thanks for listening like *I'm* not stupid."

She turns off the stereo and goes to the bathroom. In the quiet, that music he'd never heard before goes on like the pensive sound of time. Time remembered and time to come. A graceful song of hope and loss repeated without end, amen. He gets out the sleeping bag, looks at the bathroom door, and sits down. She comes out in a white something that makes him relieved the light's terrible. He gets out of his clothes and into the bag. She comes back out of the bedroom. "I didn't brush my teeth," she whispers. In the end she douses the light and disappears, leaving a chiaroscuro medallion of her face on his retinas.

Wait till morning, teeth, he tells his mouth.

OVER THERE

WHEREVER HE LOOKS he sees the face of the dark angel. He doesn't want to be here. On either side of him the clink of equipment and sound of careful boots in the hard mud, forms of men ghostly in the grey air. The order to advance.

No, he says. But his boots move woodenly over the uneven ground. No birds, no animals. Muffled sounds of the advance in open order. Visible breath rising into the clouds that trail low amongst them. Sound of his own exhalations loud in the falling mist. Loom of the higher ground they walk toward. Her voice says, I need to show you. You need to see. Fine bones of her face hollow with hunger and violated beauty. Lise back in the gaunt village where there had been roses and wine for them after the years of occupation. Don't go, the village had said, there are Germans. That's why we're here, they'd said.

I don't want to be here.

They walk on, nameless in the wintry land. He knows the clammy weapon in his hands won't be enough to prevent what will happen. Her sad, transparent face watches them. Men being drawn into the ground where parsnips burrow like fat grubs. He can feel the unknown lying in wait because he's been here before. He can feel it draw him down where he doesn't want to go. He says, Wake up it's not real. Her eyes compel him to go on.

The land explodes. Fire bursts from the cloud on the hill. Men crumple, their strings cut by invisible blades. Dark holes open in the earth that fills the air and colour blossoms brightly red and parsnip yellow. Bloodflowers. His boys strewn among the obscene vegetable flesh. Her tragic eyes. No! he says. Shelter in the hole. Hugh's there, high above him as he looks back, pinned against the sky by a great red blossom sprung from his belly.

No. Ease him down. The life there in warm petals splashing over your hands. Gather it, gather it, oozing through your fingers, hot rubbery meat, liver and living heart that won't stay among splintered white bone. No, and the sea of blood running everywhere away. No. Hugh. It'll be all right. No. Help, medic! No. No help. No healing can make this whole. The life gone through his hands as they try to hold it in. No Hugh. Eyes snapped shut, mouth fallen open. No words. Hands pressed into a body fallen open from hip to breastbone and Hugh spilled out of it forever. You need to see, she says. Unflinching gaze. Oh God, he says, Oh God no.

She had come to the shell hole at twilight, a slight figure crouched and quick through the gloom. No one had stopped her. The Germans had been kind.

He had looked at her face and tried to keep it from Hugh. Please, she had said. The face of the dark angel.

"Please," she says, "I must bury him." Him the filthiest bundle of rags and meat. Her face. He doesn't want to see. The live boys in the hole look at the coming night and the Germans they can't see and the frozen ground.

"No one can bury him," he says. He sees Halldorsen's head explode into a crimson cloud. He sees himself gone mad over the top, light-headed and hollow-gutted and screaming into the mist full of death. He wants to go, but her face gets in the way.

"Give me your knife," she says.

"No," he says, but he pulls it from his boot and gives it into her hand.

The two boys are staring into the ground where there are no Germans and maybe there is Lake Cowichan or the streetcars on Granville Street. She takes the knife and finds Hugh's heart amongst his ribs and wreckage and hacks it out. Blood flows again where he thought no more blood could be. He hadn't stopped her. He watches because he can't look away. Reddest fruit, Hugh's heart gathered to her breast, she crawls up out there where no one should be on the forward slope. She scrapes a hole in the mud and buries Hugh's heart in Belgium.

"You are a good man, Sergeant Collister," she says, and gives him his knife. The dark stain on her sweater. "I must go and look for vegetables now." The face of the dark angel.

He stares at the knife wiped clean in earth, the blood still caked on his hands. He stares into the ground. He sees himself charging into the mist that refuses to kill him. A scream too loud for hearing. The dark angel's face is Lily's face and her voice says, Come back. He can't go back. He is falling into the black earth. It fills his mouth and blots out his sight. Her face dwindles into distance, a star that fades as her voice fades. When it's gone I'll be gone. Sam! the voice says.

Sadness wells into his chest and throat and eyes. He's suffocating. The absence of breath chokes his mouth with dusty wool. A great weight pushes him down. He twists his head for air. A rustling white cloud brushes his nose with jasmine. "Sam!" says Nancy's voice, sleep-thick and frightened. "Sam, are you all right?"

He's half-fallen off the couch on his face on the floor. "Unhh," he says, and attempts to lever himself up on one elbow.

Long narrow hands grip his arms and she helps him restore himself to bed. He lies back and looks at her. The white gown and eyeshine in the city glow, lighter shadows on cheekbones and brow. The face of the dark angel.

"You're Nancy," he says.

She nods. "You screamed."

"Too much Belgium," he says. "What I didn't tell you. It happened in 1944 but it's been coming back in big pieces lately." He can feel his voice shake.

"Tell me," she says.

He reaches out and his hand nudges her breast on its way to find her arm above the elbow. She smiles. He can see her teeth shine. The sadness aches in his throat.

"Part of it happened the morning after Hugh Young was killed. The Germans came at us and it was just bloody murder. What tore it was our own officer, the only one we had left, Lieutenant Peter Halldorsen, a complete bloody fool who ordered us out when it was worth your life to stand up. He got his brains blown out running around right after I told him to go to hell. I went nuts." He gags.

She stretches out a hand and smooths it over his forehead as though he were a fevery child.

"I had to get pulled off a guy I kept sticking with a bayonet when he was dead ten times over. Then I took what was left of those boys straight up the hill into the Germans coming down." Her patience, sitting there. He can feel her skin growing colder. She is sitting on her heels, her hands in her lap.

"I was crazy. It was the right thing to do. It was the only thing to do. Those guys coming down the hill were trapped. They weren't going to be taking any prisoners. And they had us pinned down. Maybe I woulda done it anyway, but right then I was crazy and I think maybe I was trying to get myself killed."

He touches her face. It leans ever so slightly into his hand. The dark angel.

"Because that part was bad enough but the worst happened the day before."

The softness and warmth of her face, and slender bones close beneath the skin. As though he were touching Lise's face across the haunted years.

"When Hugh was killed we were walking across a big field where parsnips had been left to winter. It was cold and foggy and even then it was like a bad dream. An advance in open order is like that anyhow. It does funny things to you. When you know they're out there you're terrified but you have to keep walking. Even when you're pretty sure nothing's out there, you imagine guns pointed at your head. The Belgians, Lise's people, tried to warn us, but our orders didn't sound like trouble. We were expecting stragglers and little garrison units cut off by the main advance. So it was just a walk in the fog with this terrible feeling something was wrong. Then the world blew up in our faces. One second it's trying to take another step without tripping, the next it's artillery blasting the place to hell and what seems like the whole German army shooting at us from this dinky little hill up in the fog."

He feels her skin tighten.

"When Hugh was killed he was one jump from landing in the crater me and two other guys had already dived into. One jump from staying alive." The hurt chokes off his voice. "A splinter ripped him open from here to here." He takes her hand and draws it from his hip to the ribs over his heart.

"He was dead before he hit the ground, but I slid him into the hole and tried to put his insides back together with my bare hands."

Tears are running from the corners of his eyes back into his ears and onto the pillow. He touches her face again to be able to see it. She's biting her lip and under knotted brows her eyes are closed. She opens them.

"We stayed put because we couldn't go any place. By twilight things had calmed down enough that nothing much happened unless you poked your head out. That's when Lise showed up. She could have been shot a hundred times getting there, but there she was. Maybe the Germans knew. She knew. She'd come to bury Hugh. Maybe some of our guys that got out made it back to the village. I never did find out. But she knew. Except nobody could bury him. The ground was half frozen and those Germans weren't going to believe in any burial detail."

The hurt doesn't want him to go on. It tries to burst out of his chest and tear the voice from his throat. But he makes it into words because he's never been able to do that and this girl wants to know. She's let him touch Lise after all the years lost that day in Belgium.

"So she took my boot knife ... and she cut out his heart and buried it, in the mud in that parsnip field. I didn't stop her. If I'da gone out there I would've been shot dead. Then she gave me back the knife and said she had to go and look for vegetables. She had his blood all over the front of her."

Nancy gasps. Sam looks around for something else, but there isn't any. Only that day, and Lily, and this night.

"She couldn't bury all of him, but she had to do something. People might call it mutilating the corpse ... But it was the most loving thing –" he chokes – "I've ever seen anyone do. And just as hopeless as me trying to put him back together again."

"Oh Sam," she says, and brushes his cheek with her fingers, spreading the hot tears to cool. His hand aches, pressed that hard against the bones of her slender face, but she doesn't flinch. He takes his hand away.

"She was dark like you, with the high cheekbones. Maybe eighteen or twenty. All through this dream her face was watching us in the advance. I had to watch what she did because she loved him that much and she had more guts than I did. It was her face the last time I saw her. Before I went to sleep tonight the last thing I saw was your face when you turned out the light."

"How old were you, Sam, when that happened?"

"Twenty-five. Same age as our Hugh. That other Hugh was even younger, younger than you."

145

"It's hard to imagine."

He can see her trying to imagine. The knife in her hands. The look in her eyes that had reminded him of Lise, and of Lily. The hurt has dissolved into something like awe at this young woman, and all the women, that courage of hard love.

"I never told anyone this in thirty-four years. I never found the right person to say it to. It felt too bad. Too private. But the truth is I was just too scared. I don't think even Braithwaite knows. The two boys in the hole with us know, if they're still alive, but I haven't seen them since the war."

Again with this girl he feels settled, as though a decision had been taken. "Nancy," he says, "about three days ago I met a woman named Lily. In a bar. We talked for a while, and I went to her place that night. In bed with her, all this about Hugh Young came back. I couldn't tell her about it because I was crying too hard. But that didn't seem to matter. She seemed to know." He grips Nancy's hand, his fingers and hers stiff and cold. She's shivering.

"Except – my body coming out of hers – after we made love – felt like Hugh's innards slipping through my fingers after the shrapnel carved him open."

"Did you tell her that?" she asks.

"No," he says.

"I think you should."

"Hm."

"Are you in love with her?"

He peers at Nancy through the gloom and sees her face the way he had seen Lily's face in the dark, a feeling only at the back of the eyes touching, as his fingers had, the lighter and darker darknesses made of tissue and bone. He notices the warmth in his groin. It stirs.

"I dunno," he says. "I think maybe so. It's crazy. I haven't even thought of falling in love with anybody since about 1960." "People do, you know."

"She's fifteen years younger than me."

Nancy shrugs. Fifteen years ago she was seven.

"I feel like a fool," he says. The ache starting around his diaphragm mocks the ache in his bone, which jumps against the cloth like a trapped bird. He puts his hand on it, embarrassed even in the dark.

"A one-night stand with a good lady who got curious. What would she want with me? She's got two grown sons and a whole other life. But I can still taste her." He can hear the city muttering in the middle of the night and his own heart booming. "I think I'm lonely," he says.

She puts her other hand on his hand on the covers, patting it. "I'm a lot more than fifteen years younger than you, but this isn't so different from being in bed with Hugh when we talk," she says. "I think you better go have a talk with her."

"Honest to God, Nancy, it scares me."

She takes her hands from his and joins them over his middle. On her knees, like someone praying.

"Do you go to the Legion?" she asks.

He snorts. "That fucking tomb," he says. "With warm corpses in it." She's still shivering in the cool air that stirs the curtains by the wide-open door.

"I just thought there would be people to talk to there. People who know the same things you know. About the war. I don't. Lily probably doesn't."

"You know something," he says, "the both of you. You know how to be women. You know what Lise knew. The people in the Legion are so bloody righteous, with their blue blazers and their bits of ribbon. Those guys wouldn't say fuck to save their lives, if they thought a woman was around. Not in public. And the women the same. But they talk fucking any chance they get, and their guts hurt, any of 'em that were around the shooting war. They just cover it up. When somebody goes off his head they look the other way. They make me sick."

He looks at her in the dark. "Lise loved that boy so hard she risked her life to try and bury him. And she knew why she was doing it. During the occupation she'd got raped by a bunch of soldiers and then along comes this beautiful Canuck that could make people comfortable just by being there. He gave her back what those bastards had taken away. She found out she could still love a man's body with hers. And she squatted in that shell hole and told me what had happened to her so I'd let her cut out his heart."

He fumbles around with his hands, trying to pull meaning out of the air. "Oh man … That's what scares hell out of me, Nancy. Is that what love is? That hard? That hopeless? It's the best thing we can do, any of us." His hands collapse. "Damn!" he says. "I guess I am in love with her." He feels as though he is vanishing. "But making love is the closest thing I know to feeling someone die … Aside from that, and being around someone who is dying, not much has made any sense to me since the war."

He can feel Nancy sob. "Oh God," he says. He touches the wet on her cheek. "I'm sorry. I got no business talking like this to you."

"Oh yes you do." She sobs again. "I'm beginning to understand what you meant – what it takes to age well."

Groans from the bedroom and feet thumping on the floor. Hugh appears in the doorway. He flicks on the lamp, naked there as day, tousle-haired and frowzy-faced, his cock half-hard, thick and dark as sausage.

"Maybe you should put on a robe when you come out," says Nancy.

Hugh blinks. "I think it's goin' to take me a while to get used to having a family," he says, and turns around and goes back to bed.

Nancy sighs. She stands up. The light behind her makes a warm-coloured shape in the white gauze that fuses all the aches in him from his fork to his throat. The intimacy of sons and daughters. The far side of his own life.

He makes his mouth work. "You know that was a good thing for him to say. He's kind of sad and mixed up."

She nods. "But I'm a little sad too," she says. "Will you sleep?" "I think so," he says. "If not, you gave me lots of good things to think about."

She smiles, a little sad too, and bends over to kiss him on the head before turning out the light and making soft silk-like sounds into bed.

>·+>·0·<+·<

"Lily," he says and reaches out for her, the second awakening a fog of morning light in his head. The little crescendo of soft woman's cries echoes from his sleep and he reaches across under the covers for Lily. "I had a dream we were making love," he says. To no one. His arms embracing the air a foot above Hugh's living-room floor. Nancy's alto murmurs through the wall over Hugh's baritone drone. A chill runs down him and washes back into warmth. Like diving into summer water. The first awakening hadn't been Lily. It had been Belgium, and Nancy the good dark angel in the night.

He lies there nestled in Hugh's down bag, the kids' bedroom murmur washing through his ears. Small birds in the birch leaves of Mrs. Simpson's Victoria garden. English finches in the elms above Harbridge. Old Jameson harrumphing to life with morning tea while Elizabeth twittered over dippy-eggs on the cooker.

"We've been through that a thousand times," Nancy's voice cracks into his mellow-morning haze.

"Well you don't have to act like a whore," Hugh growls. Oh Christ. Sam's ears perk up and his innards slump. "But Sam's an old man! He's your *father*, for pete's sake."

"... in that flimsy thing," says Hugh. He imagines Hugh's face, looking worriedly at the wall. Can the old man hear us? Barely.

Me. She wouldn't have let him call me an old man. Politics. She likes me and I like her and she's in trouble for it.

"... dark anyway. Until you turned on the light. At least I was wearing *something*."

"He's young enough," says Hugh. "I wanted to see what was going on."

"Well?"

"Keep it down. Nothing ... kind of nice ... kneeling there ..."

"He *is* your father ... nightmare really shook him up ... how many people are carrying stuff like that in their heads ... girlfriend in Victoria ... should try talking to him yourself."

"You think I didn't? … confusing … all these years … asshole." Sam's ear burns but he wants to creep over and press it against the wall. Relieved blessedness as Hugh's voice swells. "But he's quite a guy, got to hand him that. And *strong*. I haven't been hit that hard since Byers nailed me in the Saskatchewan game four years ago."

"What?"

"We had a little father-son sparring match before we picked you up yesterday."

"Hugh!"

"I couldn't hit him. Not really. And I guess if he really wanted to hit me he would've put me in hospital. But I dunno. Here's this guy that ran out on me and Mom almost before I can remember, acted like a crazy man when I went to Victoria to find him, and he shows up out of nowhere, plastered and hopeless and, well, kind of lovable. I almost cried, seeing him passed out on the couch. Like it might be too late. He might be dead before I get to know him.

"I put him to bed, Nance. Took off his shoes and socks – soaking wet, for some reason – and tucked him in. Like a kid. My own father. And next day he's alive enough to belt me across the room and boogie it up with a bellydancer. You get into it with him like he's some trick you want to turn. And I start feeling like it would be a relief to hate his guts."

Yeah, boy, thinks Sam.

"But Hugh," says Nancy, barely audible but strong, "would you prefer Sid?"

"No," says Hugh.

"Neither would I. I've only been without a dad ten years, but you've got a chance to get yours back, and if I were you I'd take him."

Hugh sighs. Sam can hear only rustling then and dares imagine Hugh nodding as he stares out the window toward Victoria.

Playful Nancy says, "You feel like you might be interested again."

"Mm. Nice hang," says Hugh.

"Mm," says Nancy.

The rustling becomes rhythmic with breath in Sam's ear. "Quiet, very quiet," murmurs Hugh. Sam smiles. "Waking up sober," he tells himself, "ain't bad." And drifts back to sleep in self-defence in the cool rustling morning light. The L.A. Kings are coming to play the Canucks, he thinks. Purple jerseys and orange swirl around the Arena ice as he takes in the game with his kid and girlfriend-in-law, their breaths all visible in the frosty air amid the sibilant swoosh of skates.

To take Lily to England. That home place where it all began, where his father's fathers were born. To start over again. Walking the streets of young lovers among the shadows of the past as he'd done with Dot. To begin again, after the end of everything. England and Lily. If either exists. If he hasn't imagined them. To find her eyes among the macramé and eucalyptus and take her down the grand arc of Regent Street where the crowds flow like blood through the heart. To find out why Charlotte stayed. To be home again.

He comes around once more to the noise of the shower and clinking in the kitchen. Hugh setting out plates.

"Morning," he says.

Hugh grins. "How about eggs and toast and coffee?" "You look kinda improved," Sam says.

"A good night's sleep," says Hugh, and winks.

"Sounds great." The one in the shower, the other getting breakfast. Him in bed. "I'll get up," he says. But stays where he is, hands clasped behind his head, listening to the blow-drier whine from the bathroom. I wish you two'd get married, he thinks, as if rehearsing a line. Why should I think that? A home someplace. Half-remembered visions the colour of an English sky. Lily, he says in there, let's get married. Jesus. Watch yourself. Hugh in taupe slacks and a butter-coloured shirt steps from fridge to stove to counter and back again, quick and precise as a dancer. Co-ordinated. Coffee beans from the freezer. Where else. These people who have some sort of middle in their lives to balance on. The grinder's buzzing scream. He snorts, tipping over inside himself, wanting to be young again.

Nancy comes out of the loo, bundled in the thick white robe that he'd worn yesterday, the excess yardage gathered in one hand across her chest and the other across her hips. If I was young again she'd drive me nuts too. Her big beautiful feet go pad pad pad along the carpet and onto the woolly rug. What a girl, he thinks, balance returning. Good morning, daughter.

"Morning, Sam," she says, lighting up a smile. "The children are out of the bath," and marches into the bedroom.

"Right!" says Sam. He plants his feet on the floor and rises up. "You guys are healthy," he says to Hugh. "I feel like a human being for a change," stretching and whacking himself comfortably on the chest.

Hugh eyes him wryly. "Don't check into that too much. I like the image."

Sam climbs into clothes. This is sane, he thinks. Sometimes civilization is sane. Hugh plunks a mug of coffee on the table. "Why don't you start on that?"

"Yeah," says Sam. "Thanks."

The coffee vapours wander around in him like incense.

Over breakfast Nancy says, "What are you doing this morning? Want to come shopping?"

"Nope," he says. "I think I'll walk around the sea wall." He looks at Hugh. "Haven't seen much of Stanley Park since you were a kid."

Hugh's level grey eyes look thoughtful. "Wish I could come with you."

"Maybe next time," says Sam. "Look," he says, "there's gonna be a couple Canucks' exhibition games in Victoria. Think you two could make it over? I ain't got much of a place, but there's some great cheap rooms in the Cherry Bank …"

Hugh and Nancy look at each other. "We could bring sleeping bags," she says.

"You come over for a drink first," says Sam. "Or maybe I'll roast ya a chicken. It's a dump with a john down the hall." Nancy looks at Hugh. "Oh. That wouldn't matter, would it?" Hugh smiles. "It might matter to Sam."

"I got a kitchen and a sitting-room with a couch and a bed in it. It might be okay for the punk here – not that he was willing to try it last time – but all three of us in there would be like mixed barracks."

"I think we can swing a hotel. Sounds like a great idea, Sam. We'll see. That's still a while off. If we can't make it for the games, we'll get over some weekend."

"We could meet Lily," says Nancy.

"Maybe," says Sam. Jesus. What happens when you tell people things.

Nancy looks at her wrist. "I better put on a work face so we can go," she says, and stands. Her shape snug in white bouclé and the jeans of last evening doesn't make him feel any better about having no Lily for her to meet. "Umberto's at two?" she says. "It's 321 Water Street, just this side of the steam clock. Or do you want me to pick you up here?"

"No," he says, "I'll find it."

"I'll meet you in the lounge."

Hugh starts picking up dishes.

"Never mind," says Sam, "I'll get that."

"Okay," says Hugh. He puts down a plate.

Sam stands up. "Thanks for taking me in," he says. "I haven't felt this good in years."

Hugh looks at him. "Did you hear me and Nancy talking this morning?"

"Most of it, I guess."

"Well, I think she's right. About you." Hugh looks rattled and sticks out a hand. "If you hadn't showed up, I probably wouldn't have had the sense to try again."

"She's a great girl," says Sam, feeling watery. "Jesus Christ," and hauls Hugh into a bear hug with the boy's arms hurting around his ribs. "Maybe I can stop being an asshole."

><*>-○-<*><

In Umberto's Al Porto, Vancouver Harbour unfolds before him through wall-to-wall plate glass. A Twin-Otter float plane raises its roostertail spray across the middle bluewater distance and a beautiful sloe-eyed boy brings him his vodka tonic like a big dewsilver jewel.

The place is emptying quickly, latelunchers in saucer-eyed sunglasses and lineny casuals leaving soiled plates and crumpled napkins for the boy to balance away like picked bones. The airplane banks steeply against the blue mountains. A walled distance. It curves toward Victoria, the other end of the airline.

The lids sag under Sam's eyes. It's gorgeous. He doesn't want to leave.

A light hand on his shoulder. "Hi!" she says.

Sam turns his head and runs his eyes up her length. You belong here, he thinks. I don't. She sits between him and the window, her torso highlighted in fleshtone where the crests of shoulder and breast press against the crocheted cotton, her face a warm closeup set into the plateglass postcard harbour. Wish you were here.

"Nice view," he says. "You and the harbour."

She looks pleased and swivels around to check the backdrop. "I should've asked you to lunch," she says. "Have you eaten?"

"I think it woulda made me nervous. I ate the world's worst hamburger while I was walkin', but it'll do. There'll be something on the ferry." His voice flaps in his throat like a fish dying at the thought.

"Oh Sam!" She raises her voice at that feral boy. "Carmen, bring us a plate of antipasto. I haven't had lunch." Carmen slips away in gazelle-time.

"One of the advantages," says Nancy, "of working in a place that has good food." Then she gasps and jerks up her wrist to see her watch. "We'll miss your ferry."

"Never mind," he says, "they run every hour this time of year. Anyhow, I don't particularly want to leave."

"We could put you on a plane," she says.

Sam snorts. "What's that cost? Twenty-five bucks a crack?"

The hors d'oeuvres arrive, a great aromatic mound of them. "You have to pay for this?" asks Sam once the waiter has melted back into his table-clearing.

Nancy twinkles. "I'm entitled to lunch," she says, "and the manager likes me."

Sam grunts, munching peculiar delicacies impaled on his fork.

>·+◇·○·◇+·<

In the car on Oak Street toward Tsawwassen, Sam watches Nancy shift, quick and crisp, brown hand cupped at the end of its lean linkage. Driving him away, to go over the sea from this strange treasure house he's been prowling. Over the sea to two rooms on Battery Street, Fred gone fishing.

She glances at him. "You look kind of down," she says.

He stares ahead at the onrushing pavement. It's the world going around. Lily, he thinks, I want you to be there. But doesn't believe it. Bits of white line flash by beside him, wavering, flaring out. What does that mean?

"Sam?" says Nancy. Her eyes look at him quite a while, considering what she's doing – about seventy in Saturday traffic. His eyes sting.

"I ain't felt for a long time like I had anyone to leave behind," he says. Clenches his fist on his knee. Thumps it once. Don't blubber, you fucker! he tells himself.

"We'll be around," she says, bright, practical. Exotic as an orchid. Her face again, black hair shining. Below the cheekbones she is a round-faced person. Above, aquiline.

"I'm glad you don't mind me," she continues. "I've been worried Hugh's family wouldn't like me." She doesn't say anything for a spell of driving. Neither does he. He's thinking about Yusuf's glass jewels and pride.

"You know," she says, "I had a reputation as a bad girl when I met Hugh." His spine goes suddenly clear. "And I still get in trouble over it. Like this morning," she says. "And every time I get a break at work they call me a whore."

"Hugh's not so smart about some things as others," he says.

"But you are," she says. "I was afraid you might see why people call me a whore and not give me the benefit of the doubt."

"You have trouble with Sid and Dot?"

"Nope," she says. "Sid's a pussycat. And Dot is just a nice lady." She smiles. "I think maybe she likes me better than Carol sometimes."

Sam snorts. "Not surprising," he says.

"Now Sam," Nancy says, "let's stay off that."

"Okay," he says. "Is it true?"

"What?" Dodge the bullet.

"Your reputation."

"Oh," she says. A disorganized pause. "That's what I mean about you being smart about things." She skips into the inside lane and leans on her horn at a red Datsun cutting in from 67th.

"Well," Nancy says, determined, "I'm from Kamloops."

"I been there," he says.

"Okay. I can fish and shoot and drive a four-by-four. My father died when I was twelve. They used to say there wasn't a virgin there over fourteen, but that was only true in some parts of town. I've been working since I was sixteen and I haven't always been a good girl. But I never slept with anybody I didn't like and I never got a job on my back. No matter how many managers they say I've seduced."

Sam grunts. "I like you," he says. "That was a mouthful." He shifts around to face her better. "You're too beautiful to talk about, and you don't always make sense, but you're the least confusing woman I ever met."

She laughs. "I think I'll remember that," she says. "And last night."

Sam folds his hands on his stomach. They are whizzing over the Oak Street bridge. The end of embarkation leave. Down-stream, a great half-built concrete yacht rests in a cradle of weathered timbers. A thin-walled, gracious vessel looking from here small and ancient as an artifact sifted from ruins. This isn't finished, he thinks.

So he says, "But Hugh's special."

"What?" she says, startled.

"Special," he says.

"Oh. You mean my reputation."

"Yes," he says.

"You mean I'm scared because Hugh's special."

"Yes," he says.

"Yes," she says.

An arm of the bridge branches off in a direction marked Airport under the silhouette of a vaguely sinister jet.

"Hugh's special," she says. And it seems pretty clear she doesn't want to say any more. And he likes her enough not to wonder whether it's because she doesn't know more or because she does, least confusing woman he's known. After all, he's not sure if Lily's confusing all on her own or just because he wonders. Just wonders at her at all back there in Victoria on a Saturday afternoon. Only the fourth day since Tuesday and the lamp of Lily's face.

Nancy walks him into the Tsawwassen terminal stuck out at the end of the causeway a mile through mud flats, like a big concession stand in a parking lot in the ocean. In the bleak lounge outside the sign that says Passengers Only, he turns and takes her arm above the elbow, his hand big around her lean muscles. She returns the grip and presses her lips against his. A kiss like a rose.

"You're a great broad," he says, feeling thick. Feeling like this should be a different movie. She grins.

"I like you and Hugh together," he says. Not that he's lucky or she's lucky. Just, "He's a good man," he says.

"I know," she says. "Good genes."

"You'll make it all work out," he says.

Nancy's hand dives into her clutch and comes out with a folded red bill. "I thought you might take this from me. Tips have been really good."

His insides blunder and fumble like a very big seagull trying to lift something too heavy, but his fingers take the fifty. He hears himself say something that sounds like "Aw," and she's gone, " 'Bye, Sam" floating in the wake of her bouncy stride.

He buys his ticket and walks out the overhead ramp to the ferry. Poster photos of leaping whales and Indians and airborne broncos. In the midships passenger lounge, the kids are already lost in Tanks and Submarines and Space Invaders.

He finds a chair among the ashtrays and electronic explosions. Hopeless-looking people stare at the newsstand and the phone booth and the view. The travelling proletariat in vinyl jackets on the vinyl furniture, having eaten too many hamburgers, looking ahead because their eyes are in their faces. Looking at nothing. This is going home.

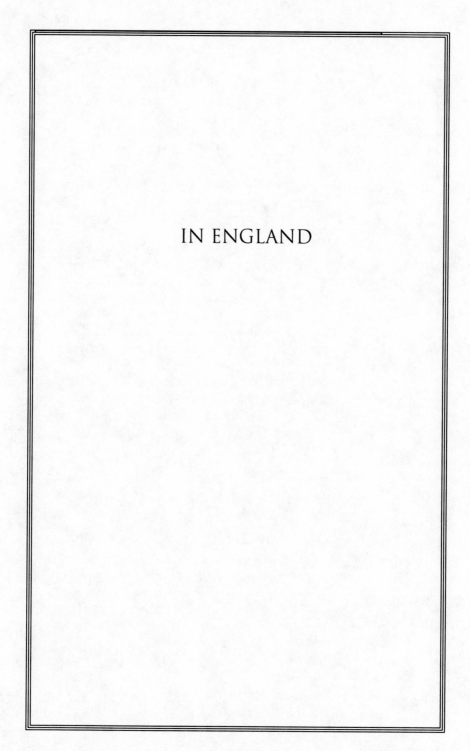

IN ENGLAND

LONDON AIR

ANOTHER DEATH.

The fields of England stand like a pinwheeling wall at the wing tip. Small, tidy, eccentric rectangles green and brown blurred by flatches of cloud. Coming down. His ears tell him, Coming down. The visible earth tells him, Coming down. To a place that looks even from here soft and older than anyone's memory.

Blurred recollections of getting here. The crossing a dream of fitful sleep, flying at what they would call Angels 40 into the stream of time. Sungleams like a pod of molten whales broaching in the black arctic sea.

Like me, he thinks, getting almost out of it.

Back in Victoria he had tried to call Lily. After the Saturday night in the Beaver and a black Sunday when he'd spent part of Nancy's fifty on fried squid in the Melos, watching the tropical fish, watching the strawberry-blonde hostess bounce her statuesque self up and down stairs, he had tried to phone Lily.

"Sorry, she's in Toronto," the young man had said. The second son. "You just missed her. She'll be gone till the end of the month." Click.

He looks up at the escarpment of cloud, white cliffs that touch the central blue. His vision goes suddenly opaque as the airplane plunges into overcast and jolts like a big bucket.

Sure. Gone till the end of August. A good half of that left yet. And how long will I be over here?

In the suddenly bright cabin lights, the lapstrap sign pings on and stewardesses hover like sheepdog angels. He feels air-conditioned and fuzzy, slithering from the throat of a nine-hour snore as the trance wears thin and the 747's engines grow loud again. He clacks his tongue in a tacky mouth. Bat guano. Too dry to swallow away the dizzy pressure on his ears.

Victoria had been unreal as a morgue full of exotic birds. Him among the droppings. His tawdry rooms on Battery Street a private cage. Wash dishes, Sam. Mow lawns. Rip out the old doghouse under Betty Newell's stairs, stench and ancient excrement and matted hair of years. Build a new one. Don't moan. After the time in Vancouver.

He had moaned. In the James Bay and the Beaver and Stubbs' and a few times in the Bastion among the street arabs and pool cues and pushers. He had gone to the Legion. Pro Patria, they called it. Something to die for. Fred sober and morose over a pair of beer each workday afternoon. Jack Frenette nervous and concerned, whomping him on the shoulder, saying, "Come on, man, sounds like you had a great time over there."

Why couldn't that damn kid marry Nancy and give him a home to go to?

The damn kid had sent him a summer-weight jacket and slacks, sandalwood and taupe, and a cream shirt.

Damn kid made him cry.

Then the letter from Charlotte.

Dear Sam,

I am writing in care of Dorothy, since I am not certain of your address. I hope you don't mind.

I have been unwell of late. The doctors tell me I have leukemia, the kind that works quickly. They say I'll not see the leaves turn.

As you can imagine, this news is not easily borne. But we are no longer young, and I suppose it's been a good life compared with most, however quickly it seems to have gone. It is, I know, not a difficult death. I am now of good cheer, with a wonderful room in St. Thomas's, looking over the river to Parliament. I know Rodin's Burghers of Calais are there in the park. I shall remember that.

I do not mean to trouble you with this – there is really nothing to be done, John Jameson has everything in hand as always – but you are my nearest kin and I felt I must let you know.

It is strange, over the years, that I have become an English woman and you have remained Canadian. Such a little time ago, it now seems, we were children in the North Vancouver forest. Is it still there? I should think not. A forest of little North American bungalows, more like.

I'm thankful that we met again a few years ago.

Think of me.

Your sister,

Lottie

He folds it and puts it back in the pocket of the sandalwood jacket. Airfare courtesy of Fred.

The 747 mushes down through the cloud base and he sees Gatwick. Last time, in the post-heart-attack frenzy, he had got pissed with a Scots karate instructor on pilgrimage to Glasgow via London. Hulks of aircraft had fringed the perimeter and scaffolding surrounded the half-built terminal. A set from a modern Italian apocalypse. Gatwick now looks more finished, a bleak and ordinary blight sprawled in Sussex under grey skies. The new port to receive overflow traffic from the colonies.

The 747 rounds off and skims the tarmac in a breathless rush the moment before the roar of reversed engines and the grab of brakes. This is England, he thinks. His dream of return to the home place now another journey to meet death.

Outside, his skin feels sticky and chill against the lukewarm, dampish air. Gatwick's cavernous industrial-nouveau interior absorbs the hundreds from Sam's flight into the hundreds from others milling like ants until they find a line to join. Like a herd of inductees. Where's a fucking drill sergeant?

Persons Bearing UK Passports look smug and arrived and generally tweedy. At this time of year. Sam finds himself wishing he bore a UK passport. Thank God he's bearing any kind of passport. If the old one hadn't been valid still he wouldn't have been here till next month. Which might have been too late. Even now might be too late.

Standing in line on shaky legs, sweating idiotically while feeling cold, his stomach querulous, he realizes he needs a godawful shit.

The immigration woman sits like a ticket-taker at her little platform desk with a racing stripe on it. She says good morning in a voice as toneless as her face. The clock tells him it's near 1300 hours.

"You haven't had lunch," he says.

He can see her general occupational suspicion begin to particularize. He adds, "The English always say good morning until they've eaten lunch."

"What is the purpose of your visit?"

"I came to see my sister in London."

"How long do you intend to stay?"

He wants to say, I don't know. "Not more than a month," he says. "She's dying of leukemia."

Something that might be a frown ripples across the bland waters between her collar and her cap. "Very good," she says.

In her uniform she reminds him of the Land Army girls almost four decades ago. Milk maids misplaced into an industrial war. She scrutinizes the mug in his passport and the one on his shoulders, and stamps a blank page. Sam goes to find a mud-brown loo and sits in the smell he's making as his last Canadian dinner passes painfully through.

He contemplates the mangled hole where a coat hook had been mounted in the metal door. The evils of English asswipe. The graffiti, heartfelt but uninspired. *Gatwick sucks. I came all this way to take a shit. English girls give head.* Tourists. It could be anywhere. But it's England. And despite it all, despite even the low-

161

slung vitreous fixture upon which he sits, he feels that he's squatting over ancient ground.

He looks up from his feet and sees a hulking shadow of himself suspended in the worn gloss of the door, faceless and grim. His scalp prickles. There's trouble here. "Whadda you want?" he growls.

The shadow's silence frightens him. Ancient ground and the ghosts of the undead. The dark bulk hunched there in front of his face. *I'm not getting out of here alive.*

⊷•◦•⊶

At Victoria Station he shoulders his way through the mob toward the ticket machines. Hordes of Londoners make beelines in all directions, heedless of the hordes of others who wander and knot like flotsam, hands gesturing for direction from the gods of Metropolitan Transport. The 20p machine lists Bayswater among the possibilities on its yellow plastic face.

A blocky, florid fellow propelled by a surge in the crowd jostles Sam's arm away before he can grab the yellow pasteboard ticket the machine spits out. The man retrieves the ticket and offers it in a stubby paw. "Sorry, mate. Bloody crush."

Sam pauses. That was nice of 'im. "Thanks, pal," he grins. "I kinda like it."

Bayswater Station looks and smells eternal. The new green paint is exactly like the old green paint, layers and layers of it so thick it looks like chipped porcelain, dark and full of time.

He follows the three others who have gotten off toward the sign that says Way Out and thinks of the one upstairs that says Way In and feels spreading through his innards the warmth of nearly forty years since the Underground first spoke to him. As if he'd never left.

At the top of the stairs he stops in the middle of the catwalk bridge that connects the two platforms. He looks down the station to the dark maw of the tunnel from which he came and inhales the fusty, ancient air, the paint just fresh enough to be identified as one element in that incremental smell. Like ragweed flowers in the alder mulch by the river when he was a boy. Like a place where people have been buried for a long time. The tunnel booms and clatters hollowly. He waits for the serried ranks of Roman legionaries to come marching from the bowels of Londinium, the sound of their sandals and shields and drums. A hot gust of wind swooshes over him. The earth shakes and a southbound train thunders to its platform. Blood-red beast.

As he goes up the last few steps, the ticket taker at the portal is purposefully not looking at him. As if to say, I've been here too long to wonder what you're doing.

Sam gives him the ticket and says, "Thank you."

"Not at all," says the man. The foyer of Bayswater Station looks like it belongs to a modest bank.

Outside, on the Queensway pavement, he hesitates. If the flat is available, why go to the hotel? Save a borrowed buck. The Queensway bustles. People and cabs and private cars and greengrocers' stands. Music from the Bistro's sidewalk café pits jazz against the punk rock blare of the sound shops. Kids in leather and chains and blue hair. Just like last time. Hip blacks and straight blacks and orientals and white and brown caucasians as Sam looks left toward Whiteley's and right toward the Bayswater Road and feels the duffle bag grow lighter on his shoulder, himself grow lighter on his feet – as though the street were lifting him onto the shoulders of its life. The eeriness persists, as though he were a lot of different people who had walked up and down this way so often in recent time and time longer ago and practically forever. I'm not really here, he thinks. They're doing it for me. Handsome Charlotte in her khaki drills, the Red Cross badge above her breast, extends her hand when they meet for tea, he and she and pretty Dot in 1943.

To the right. The estate agents around the corner. As he turns onto the Bayswater Road, he sees the sky open out over Kensington Gardens. Round canopies of trees swell into the air and grow misty across the park. Down there is Knightsbridge and the palace and the City. The river and the dome of St. Paul's. But all he can see with his eyes are the trees and the bronze sky of cloudy summer London. Warm. Humid. Huge. One of the reasons he came.

The same young Arab is there in Hartnell's Estate Agents, and his big-boned redhead secretary who looks like she would be beautiful if she had time. "Ah," says the Arab, turning surprise into delight, "Mr. –"

"Collister," says Sam, fast, just in case.

"Yes. I was sorry to hear about your sister."

Is she dead already? No. Don't panic.

"That's why I'm here. Is the flat available?"

"It is closed up. She asked us to close it up. We didn't know you were coming…"

"That's all right," he says, "I'll get a hotel. Maybe later …" "Perhaps. We should be glad to help if we can."

Diplomatic bastard. "Right."

"Give Miss Collister our best."

"Yeah," says Sam, "thanks."

The phone rings. The redhead picks it up and says, "Good afternoon. Hartnell's." The big white receiver cradles her skull like a dinosaur bone.

Sam goes out to the traffic zipping by on the Bayswater Road. "Closed up." Whatever that means, it sounds final. He longs to cross into the Gardens, which are not closed up, and wander down past the Round Pond and into Hyde Park. The exotic jungle along the Serpentine. A queer vision of Charlotte's ghost as a girl playing Peter Pan. Ghosts everywhere among the gunnera looming spiny as giant devil's club. Himself a lean figure in battle dress strolling arm in arm with Dot beyond the iron fence. Uniforms thronging the dead past. A peculiar sense of guilt.

But Charlotte isn't quite a ghost yet, and his body tells him it's time to see if the Dutchman's wife has a bed for him in the Garden Square Hotel.

On the way back up, he stops at the patisserie for some croissants and at the market for a shrink-wrapped blob of butter cheese and a pint of red-topped milk. Twelve-and-a-half p for that, which had been about nine before. How much would the hotel be? How long would the bank loan last?

"Wire me through Barclay's if you run short," Dave Hicks had said.

"I'm gonna have enough trouble covering the grand, Dave."

"Well, maybe we can work something out through the Legion fund. We are supposed to help in a crisis, you know."

A useful fellow in that tomb, Dave Hicks. Vice-president of Pro Patria and manager of the Royal on Government Street. Fit as a whip, with the dapper looks of a colonel, retired. Ex-corporal of tanks.

The tomb had treated him well. Where have you been, Sam? He had watched them play darts and kibbitzed with the new kid behind the bar and discussed the shortage of lamb kidneys with

Harold, the oldest member. One of the new Fraternals was organizing a hike to the Forbidden Plateau. How's it going, Sam? How to answer that? He had sat by the fire and moaned.

Leaving the market, he turns off the Queensway onto Porchester Gardens and up to Kensington Gardens Square. No garbage strike this year, but the place still smells urban old. And scaffolds still surround the apartment block at the head of the square. However long it's stood there, they were gutting it last time, or had been until they stalled for lack of funds. Now they are refinishing the stone. You never start fresh here, he thinks. You rework what there is. And there's so much time built in a bit more makes no difference. Ancient shades among the living who pass by, like a faint doubling of vision. Ghosting on the idiot box. Ladies of Empire escorted by merchants' sons and junior officers of the army of the Raj. He feels off-centre and queer. There's trouble here.

He rings the bell at the little window inside the hotel door. The Dutchman's wife appears.

"A single room, please," he says.

"Do you have a reservation?"

"No."

"You're mad, at this time of year."

He grins. "I know. I've been here before. Three years ago."

She glares at him. "Do you know how many people I've seen in three years? But

I always try to find space for old patrons. You are in luck," poring over her register, "you can have my last room. With bath. Fourteen pounds."

"That'll be great tonight," he says. "I just got off a plane from Canada. But I'll be here a while and I can't afford fourteen pounds a night for long."

"How long a while?"

He grins more broadly, remembering her outrage the last time. "At least three days."

She glares more intensely. "I would be mad to let a room for less than three days in the season –" She takes in his face and sounds suddenly very English. "You are having me on." He laughs. She laughs. "I'll see what I can do. Sign the register, please. You will recall that breakfast is from seven until nine."

He signs. "Is George still here?" he asks.

"Of course, George is still here! Do you think he would ever leave? All he does is whine, when I do everything for him." "It's good to be back," he says.

She looks at him from the face of a woman still surviving the German occupation of Holland. "If I had sense enough," she says, "I would no longer be here. Enjoy your stay."

He pokes his nose into the tiny hotel bar. Empty. The clock says ten to three. "George!" he hollers.

Scuttling sounds from behind the bar. George's wizened cockney face peers out from the storeroom. Hall-porter-cum-everything. "Sorry, guv," he says, "it's near closing and there wasn't no one 'ere."

"How about a pint?"

"Bitter, wasn' it? Worthington E?" When George moves, he moves quick as a fox. When he doesn't, he looks like he'll never move again.

"You remember the damndest things, George. Have one yourself. You still drinking stout?"

George grimaces and rubs his stomach. "Me plumbing's no good. I'm onta the cider now. Last step before the grave."

Sam laughs. George draws an E. White sleeves rolled up over sinewy forearms. "'Ow's your sister, then?" he asks. "You 'ave a sister 'ereabouts, 'aventcher?"

"That's what brings me here, George. She's dying. Leukemia."

"Crikey. That's a narsty one. I think I will 'ave that cider."

He lifts a little bottle off a shelf and takes for it from Sam's change on the bar. Heavy, outsize coins that let your fingers know what they're doing.

"Me sister's been poorly 'erself. Some women's thing. Took out 'arf 'er insides, they did. Not much of 'er left, 'obblin' round like a ghost. And old Reg, me dad-in-law that was, dropped dead in the street t'other day. Just round the corner for a pint and down 'e goes." George taps his chest and shakes his head. "Pump stopped." His little black eyes, gone dull as soft coal, brighten suddenly. "No use in that," he says. "'Ere's your 'ealth, guv."

"Cheers," says Sam. You good little blighter. The cool nutty English brew washing into him makes him realize how parched he is. He smacks his lips.

"I've been missing that," he says, "even if you won't have the sense to get in some Bass or DD."

George shrugs. "Worthington's what's popular. Mrs. Loo always wants what's popular. Oh oh, there she is. Best get on wif me stock-takin'. Nuffin's good enough for that woman if I work me fingers to the bone." The Dutchman's wife looks in and says, "Closing time."

Sam takes a big swallow. "You seen the Dutchman lately?" George glances at the door. She's gone. "Na, 'e's never 'ere no more. An absentee is what 'e is."

Savouring the last of the pint, Sam says, "Too bad, he's a nice guy." He yawns. "I better take a nap. Can you knock me up around six?"

"Righty-'o, guv. What room?"

"Forty-six. It's Sam, George. Sam Collister."

George sticks out a hand and shakes. A small, hard grip. "Queer," he says, "I remember everything but names."

Sam looks at the gimcrack clocks and kewpie dolls among the bottles on the shelves behind the bar. A plastic Mountie. George's mementos from everywhere his guests call home. "I'll hafta send ya a double-decker bus from Victoria."

"Coo. We've got enough of them, 'aven't we."

⊢•▸•─◦─◂•◄⊣

Sam trudges up steps. Forty-six doesn't mean the fourth floor. He's not sure it means the 46th room, either. But it does mean somewhere in the vicinity of 45 and 47, or 44 and 48. He thinks maybe they numbered the rooms from the basement up one staircase and down the other. Knock me up, he thinks. Where did that come from? I'm here two hours and I'm talking Limey. I know where that's coming from … Why I came.

Forty-six looks out over the square. It is lofty and pale and bare, with blond fifties utility furniture and a plywood speaker on the wall that looks like it came out of a Battle of Britain ops room. Its switches say BBC I, BBC II, Intercom. You can't turn it off, just from barely audible to inaudible. When you turn it to Intercom, nothing happens. Ghostly voices in the silence saying, Bandits at angels ten. Vector one-nine-zero. Break left! Break left! The distorted hammering of machine guns. A scream and the sound of a microphone frying and silence.

Sam unpacks into a rickety wardrobe and takes toilet things into the loo. White and blue tile with a bit of glaze left. Kitchen-clean. Tub wide at the shoulders and narrow at the feet. Like a coffin.

166

He sits on the wobbly chair by the drop-leaf table at the window, munching croissant and cheese sliced with a clasp knife. He drinks half the rich, warm milk. Behind its locked wire fence and shrubby hedge, the little green park looks empty. Nature by entitlement in residential London.

The buildings across the way look like this one. Several storeys of painted stone façade. Columned doorways. Inhabited by remnant Londoners from Bayswater's stylish days and the crowd of bed-and-breakfast hotels and new Londoners living cheap and making music in the streets. A lot of Empire come home to roost. London is a country, he thinks. It includes everyplace. I'll never want to leave. After Lottie dies. Good God.

In Victoria it's about time to get out of bed. He feels thick and drowsy and somewhat ill. Through the leaves he sees that the park isn't quite empty. A figure lies motionless in a lawn chair. Draped in what the English would call a rug. Probably with a book propped on its nose.

He yawns. The bed feels like a lumpy sea. He drags one edge of the coverlet over him to warm the cold that seems to be inside his skin.

In the dark sleep blue-blazered legionnaires grin and dance and gape. Lest we forget that it is sweet and fitting for thee to die, their silvery hair and medals bright as their gold-rimmed eyes and teeth. Pissing at the Club. Searching for the Men's. There's a tree in the meadow and a nightingale sang in Berkeley Square. He looks at the urinal, enamelled iron trough – rust stains, what look like blood stains, spit. When Johnny can go to sleep in his own little bed again. He leans his head against the wall and pisses at cigarette papers that bend around the bars of the drain plate. A drunken general at sea. Paint thick as armour plate on the urinal wall. Head bulkhead bloody navy, banging his forehead as the sea rolls away somewhere below his feet. Drunken admiral. Clambers up the ladder to the high bridge for admirals. Out there dawn is somebody's idea that has made the cold dark more visible. Into it, each time the sea lifts their bows closer to the sky, a very big engine hurls the Seafires away. He watches the work of the very big engine and wonders what would have happened if Hannibal had owned such huge iron hands to hurl fire at people who hid away and made him wait. He thinks of elephants and time and the commissary. He thinks of Heinz Guderian in Russia, which worries him. He sees the beautiful, bestial snouts of the guns swing 'round as though they had scented blood through the fading night, and thinks, There's something out there watching us.

In the thunder of the guns, he hears his name called. "Mr. Collister, Mr. Collister." He sees the pillow in front of his nose. "Mr. Collister, it's just gone six." Knocked up.

"Yeah, George," he hollers. The pounding stops. He does need to piss.

The dim light has some sun in it. He tastes terrible things in his mouth and sighs. Good God, here we are.

The dream lies like a pool of lead in the back of his skull. He stares at a patch of light where the wall meets the ceiling. Reflected from someplace bright. And gets out of bed in London.

Then he sees himself sitting at the table, hunched over his elbows, eating bread and cheese. God, he whispers, what's happening to me? This isn't what I came here for. And he feels very alone.

The figure at the table turns. The haggard face needs shaving, skin hanging in runnels like old leather, lids sagging below the red-filmed eyes. "I came for Charlotte," he says to it. It says nothing, eyes boring through him.

I'm lying, he thinks. I came for myself. I came to find out how come she stayed, how come I want to live here where I don't know anybody. I came because this place is old and I'd just as soon be dead.

"Get out!" he shouts, not daring to move, not able to move. He closes his eyes. When he opens them the chair's empty.

⊱─◈─○─◈─⊰

Feeling rumpled and disastrous, he swills down the remains of the cow-tasting milk to give his stomach something sensible to think about. What's sensible? Go get something to eat before you jump out the window. The prospect sends queasy riffles up his esophagus, but food is the only answer. The only answerable question.

Remembering the spectre and glancing for shapes in the shadows, he follows unthinking memory past a picture-book mews to the little Greek place called Fournaki. Candles flicker on the tabletops. Volleys of bad-tempered Greek ricochet from the walls. Across the narrow room, a straight-backed young couple prepare to dine. He thinks of Hugh and Nancy. This English pair, exquisitely discreet, matched set of lustrous, light-brown heads and silver-screen profiles. Bred to rule, like fine weapons. To what purpose now? Obsolete as the lance and the sword and the Lee-Enfield rifle. He thinks of Charlotte.

Across the river, that woman counting the days that remain. That woman he'd never taken the trouble to know. The candles on the tables flicker like the fires of an ancient army.

⊱─◈─○─◈─⊰

"It's too late, sir," says the porter at Enquiries within St. Thomas's gloom. Before Sam can get any more worried, he adds, "Visitors' hours have ended."

"Could I just go up and see her? I'm her only brother and I've come all the way from Canada …"

The porter starts to say something and stops. "I'll see if I can find someone to take you up."

168

Collister's footsteps seem to boom like a slow march as he follows a silent slip of a girl in her crêpe shoes down the panelled corridor. The girl explains to a nursing sister who looks at him with sympathetic disapproval. "You will just stand in Miss Collister's doorway, please, and not speak to her."

"Could I see one of her doctors?"

The nurse looks doubtful. "There's a houseman," she says, "but surely not tonight. Dr. Bourke, the haematologist, has offices in Harley Street. He will be in to see her day after tomorrow, in the morning."

The door swings open. A single dim lamp glows on the wall. Shadowy silence. The guardian at his elbow. Curtained windows. The muffled form on the bed, her face pale as the bedclothes. A whisper of breath through the sound of his own blood.

"Charlotte," he says.

▷─◁▷─○─◁▷─◁

Thinking it's a dream that will go wrong, he watches morning brighten his grey walls to white. A creaking sound from the next room is followed by thumping and sluicing. These noises repeat themselves in mounting chorus near and far. The honeycomb of rooms around him. His head feels creaky and full of wet cement. The ingrained smell of the Garden Square Hotel swells slowly into sickly-sweet English bacon frying and one more breakfast for the fabric of the place to remember. I'm not dreaming, he thinks. Warily he looks at the chair by the table. It's empty. George down there turning rashers, the gnome that never sleeps, ramrodding the kitchen girls. And realizes that back home in Victoria it's time to go to bed. Jesus. Then he realizes he wants to see London. Not tunnels and streets and walls, or even the breadth of the Thames, but the rambling sea of it tumbling in waves to the horizon.

"Ah!" he says and explodes out of bed onto peculiar legs. His muscles feel like fibrous cardboard. He stumps over to the window. By what there is showing, London looks lovely. A moist blue sky, cool shadows in the square shafted through with level light that greens the heights of trees brightly and gleams on the upper storeys of white hotels, islands on the dawn-coloured pool of air below his window. Even the spidery lace of scaffolding looks fresh.

Sam runs a cold bath and splashes into it. He curses and shivers and thrashes. "Goddammit!" he says. Primrose Hill is the only place he knows about where you can stand on the ground and see London.

▷─◁▷─○─◁▷─◁

A cul-de-sac between two grand houses of ox-blood brick takes him to the upper end of Primrose Hill park. Outside the gate a man in shirt-sleeves sits like a guardian atop an orderly jumble of old furniture and clothing heaped in a wooden

169

wagon. Two dark dray horses stand in their traces, nibbling at the tarmac. The man scratches his head and shifts a bureau. An icebox waits improbably next to one of the wagon's rubber-tired wheels. The wheels seem to have come, shiny hubcaps and all, from a London taxi. The man looks down at him. "Wotcher, cock," he says.

Off-balance in the face of something that seems at once significant and ridiculous, Sam says, "Want a hand loading that?"

"Ta, mate," says the captain of the apparition, "but it's where to put the flippin' thing. Can't leave it behind, it's worth a bloody fortune." He gives Sam a sly look. "When you knows the trade, if you follow me meaning."

Crazy goofs like you and George are why I wish I lived in this town. "Yeah. Why don't you leave it where you got it and come back for it?"

"Good on you, mate, that's usin' your loaf, which is more'n I can say for most. But I couldn't do it." He returns to the bureau. "Now if I shifts this lot an' chucks them rags on top …"

"See ya," says Sam.

"Cheer'o, old son, I'll get it tight in a jiff."

Sam leaves him there rearranging time at a back entrance to Primrose Hill. He walks up the easy slope under the trees.

Having exchanged words with history on a junk wagon. Knowing what's coming at the path's crest. A soft visceral eagerness runs through him.

The land falls away in a grassy swoop under his feet. Beyond the shrubbery and paths and pavilion down there, beyond the traffic on Prince Albert Road and the canal and the aviary like a great reticulate cloud full of birds, past all the jumbled beasts and landscapes of Regent's Park Zoo and its trees scalloping with lush lofty green the splendid prospect of luxury flats on Albany Street, past the serrated skylights of Euston Station and the P.O. Tower like a space-age hard-on over Bloomsbury, London rolls mistily into the forever of dockland and the invisible sea. The dome of St. Paul's floats there on the City's shrouded roofs. Far to the south an escarpment of hills lies like a deep green pencil stroke at the base of the sky.

From there the bombers had come, from the direction of France and Dover and the bluebirds over. His eyes go blurry at the huge space of air and built ground and time all around him and his innards convulse with something that feels like the oldness of grief. He sees crazed white traceries in the central blue, and birds over London.

In that air, the little birds. Dove-grey, sky-blue bellies. Little death-birds swirl like clouds of starlings, so fast, so laden with lightning – so arcane now, Spitfire and Messerschmitt, frail, buzzing wraiths lovely as finches in air the colour of pale slate among the English clouds. Air you can gather in your hands like mist to wash away the tears.

He had walked the roofs of St. Paul's and remembered men dropping bombs on London dim as a phantom in the glow of their fires. Detonations to stir the bones of Gordon and the others at their rest below. And us up here with the angels in Wren's daft galleries.

A priest to protect us. To protect his stony saints. "Why does no one," the priest had asked, "bring me up a cup of tea?" But Father, we thought up here you drank with the angels.

Huge array of pee-pot chimneys, crushed wherever the footsteps fell of those men who were only a big noise in the sky.

This is Charlotte's town. Its muffled throb presses upon him like an embrace. Charlotte is down there somewhere across the river in a room dying. And somewhere in that jabble of roofs is the office from which she sent clouds of paper scattering over the globe to raise money and food and blood and hospitals. A paper storm for years blanketing desk tops where the sun never sets and back again with unmelting snow.

He feels like he's dissolving inside, and looks around. There are passersby. Of course there are passersby. There are always passersby in London. And prams and dogs. And children flying kites red and blue, like dragons all tail and no head. Medieval banners demonically loosed to swirl in rippling hunt over the battlefield.

Charlotte, he says and doesn't care if he's saying it aloud. Charlotte, he says. They'll think I'm a native. Charlotte, why did you stay? Was it men, Lottie, did you have lovers here you could never have had at home? Or did you just have sense enough to know what you wanted? We both saw the birds, Charlotte, but did you see the dragons?

>┼●┼○┼●┼<

This time the curtains are open and the light is all from the sky. Across brown Thames, Westminster camps like a medieval host, its spires like weapons, and banners fluttering.

She lies on the bed as she did last night, pale arms along the covers, her face turned to the window.

"Charlotte," he says.

"Sam! What are you doing here?"

CHARLOTTE

"BUT SAM, YOU KNOW I never thought about those things," Lottie says. "It seemed like the thing to do ..."

"Did you have lovers, L.?" Sam feeling embarrassed. Why should a man almost sixty feel embarrassed?

"Of course I had lovers! Lovely lovers." Charlotte silent while the light fills up the room with dust. Then, "What a thing to ask a lady!" Sam watching the dust, feeling it pile up loosely inside him. He would burst like a puffball at finger-touch. Red roses by her bed. Then, "Oh Sam!", her eyes wetting down the dust. And he wraps his arms around her head lying on its pillow and kisses it. "Lottie," he says, "I wish I could have been a brother to you."

Muffled up through him comes her voice, saying from far away, "It was lonely, Sam. It's been lonely. It is lonely."

After that their breathing, the two of them while the light fills up the room and rises and falls like the sea.

"I forget," he says, "how the trees smell." He sees cherry trees when they were children, and the red roses, and hears a woman crying.

"Over here," she says, "the trees smell like men."

A curious thing to say. I wonder, do the trees smell like women to me? He thinks of the girl in the hedgerows three years ago. "Life," he says, "they smell like life."

"Oh Sam," she says, "you say such foolish things."

Beginning to remember. The alders by the river below the pasture. The acid, mulchy smell. The bugs that looked like bits of wood crawling on the stony bottom. The guts squeezed out of the fish caught by the Armenian boys from down the road. Summers in the country. A clear light like fine gold glinting up in water patterns among the leaves. The alders smelt like all of that. Summers in Haney as children – how very English. Harry and Belle, just off the boat, sent their children to the country for the summer. Despite the fact that home was the last house before the wilderness on Queens Road in North Vancouver before the war. Harry the pirate and Belle the beautiful, who so often was crying.

"You're right," he says. "England smells of humankind and cowshit in the mud."

He looks at Charlotte's face fading into the bedclothes. Red roses beside her. She opens her eyes, startling him. Grey and bright, smooth, moist.

"Were you crying, L.?"

"No," she says. "I went away."

"A woman was crying somewhere."

"I don't know." Drugged and strange. Charlotte looks like she too might be seeing the wilds of prewar Haney, when she was ten and he was twelve. The new stucco house and the three red cows. Pissing behind separate bushes and arguing over what fuck meant. The Armenian boys regarding her with what he later recognized as lust. Her slender legs the colour of the riverlight.

"What are you seeing, Charlotte?"

There seems to be less of her, as though she were passing out through her eyes to the place they see. As though the light were going out of her to illuminate what she sees. He turns to look.

"Death," she says. The sound of air. No human voice. The last of the air from the lungs. As though someone had passed behind him when no one was there. His skin chills. He looks at her and her eyes turn on him, frightening. There's trouble here.

"Charlotte," he says. The hulk by her bed. You're not getting out of here alive.

A brush of colour skims her cheeks. To make them visible, he thinks. God, he thinks, the last of the fire. And tears in her eyes. "Sam!"

"Yes, L." He takes her hand and feels his marrow shiver.

"You've seen people die, Sam," her voice skewering him with its slender, thinning edge. Get your shit together, Collister! he says to himself. "You know more about this than I do," she says.

"No, Lottie, no one knows more about this than you do." Except the dead men. And they don't know anything any more. But once they did. And he held that knowing with his life, the meat that had been a man in his arms. And the blood.

"I don't want to die, Sam."

"I know, Charlotte ... Nobody wants to die." Knowing that isn't true. The black lagoon that opens from time to time before his feet. The hulk of himself: I'd just as soon be dead. Why did I come here?

"But I do, Sam. I want it to be over." Her eyes leave him to look again at death. "I don't know what I want."

Sam draws a breath that feels like it might choke him. "Lottie, I want to know why you stayed here."

She looks at him like a scolded child who would like to cry. "They won't let me go anywhere else, Sam."

"I mean England, Lottie. I went home after the war. You stayed here."

She knits her brow. "You went home to get married. I didn't have anything to go home to."

Neither did I, he thinks.

"I could have got married here."

"What would you have done? The English didn't want soldiers any more. I had my job. This is my home," her hands moving on the bedclothes. Home is where you die, he thinks.

"I live in both places at once," he says, wondering what that could mean to her. Or if he lives any place at all.

"How odd," she says.

"I don't know why I didn't come back after I left Dot."

"You made me so angry," she says. "You know, I didn't want to come to your wedding. I was glad you went over there to do it. No one would marry me. And then you left her. And Hugh! And she was so pretty."

And so ordinary. Somewhere far away, red roses and a woman crying.

"Why didn't you marry, L.?" The eyes on him again, like bright stones. "Men wanted you." Even me, now and then. Tall Charlotte, with Harry's bones and Belle's grace. Someone should have painted her bathing in a lake at dawn. Soaping her crotch. He smiles, and feels foolish. Handsome even now, with that too-pale skin sagging in the hollows and taut over the bones. And still frightening, looking at him as though he were a loon. And no one will paint her now.

"What do you mean!" she shouts. "Sam, you can be so rude – I wish you hadn't come! Your nonsense over and over again –" A long sob arches through her, a choking noise.

He sits, feeling too big and vacant, his hands wooden as he flattens and clenches them. Is this what I came here for? "Charlotte," he says, not daring to touch her, remembering hours in bed as Dot wept. The tremors of a woman's body stiff and unhappy as a misfiring engine.

Her eyes again, wet and dark as the stiffness goes out of her. Charlotte's here, he thinks. And she touches him.

"I'm sorry, Sam," she says.

He tries to say, No, no, but his tonsils get in the way.

"Yes," she says, from far away, touching him. The air moving in the alder trees while white fluff from the cottonwoods drifted around up there in the bright blue sky. The sound of the river steady as the warm earth under their backs as the eagle wheeled across the sight of their half-shut eyes.

"I just didn't ... Well, there was Roy – but that didn't amount to much in the end." She looks thoughtful. "I think," she says, "that I was afraid of ending up like Mother." Sad Belle, translucently beautiful, who had grown sadder and more translucent until one day she wasn't there any more. Harry the bastard.

Maybe I'm a bastard like Harry, he thinks. I've thought that too often. How can you forgive me for making you cry now?

Never mind, sad Belle would say, I'll clean up. Sad, practical, half-daft Belle, with ducks. Have you put in the ducks? she said.

Then one day she wasn't there any more, and they put what was left in a grey box with chrome handles and stuck it in the ground. He had thrown the first handful of dirt, since Harry'd been put under long before.

"Was it like that for you, Sam?"

He looks up, realizing that he had been looking down. A lot of white, with red roses. A presence at his shoulder. He looks, and sees more white. Red roses in a sea of white. White blood. Charlotte's blood is killing her. Charlotte Rose.

"You should go now, Mr. Collister." The nurse. One should not make the dying shout.

"No," says Charlotte.

"You're tired, Miss Collister. You shouldn't upset yourself." "No," says Charlotte. "I'm dying. It won't hurt me."

Sam looks up and sees a pink face with blonde hair that bites its lip and says, "All right. But you mustn't stay too long."

"Was it like that for you?" Charlotte repeats, insistent. You tough woman, he thinks. You magnificent tough woman.

"Charlotte," he says, "Dot was good in bed. She was a nice girl and had a category for everything, even that. Sex was something you had after supper and before breakfast. The rest of the time you made sure nothing got disorganized. She drove me nuts, in bed and out. Eventually bed wasn't enough, so I went out and got drunk and stayed that way."

Charlotte regards him like something new.

"I don't think I understand you any more than I did," she says. "But I just now realized something. I never have liked men. Sex is still something I can't talk about easily – heaven knows why, in this state – but other than that I never had much use for men."

She looks at him some more, and says, "I suppose when one is dying one says things one would otherwise only think." She smiles. "I never did learn how to think about sex. It was something I wanted now and then. It either happened or it didn't. But I could never think of it in a – a frank sort of way. 'Fucking,' you know, as you say. I always thought that was something men said, and cheap women – that it was cheap. But you're not like that, Sam. That's what I realized. You like women, don't you? The same way you like men."

"Yes," he says, feeling strange. The awesomeness of people who are dying. This woman he'd never known before. "Yes," he repeats, nodding, feeling the way they said confession should make you feel. Released, dismissed, absolved. Bless me, he says, because she has.

"I realized that you're here because you're my friend. And that's not much thanks to me. I thought you'd come because you're my brother. The same reason anyone would come if they came. But that's wrong. All those strange things you ask me, all those strange things you say. When we were young I thought you should be a poet because I couldn't understand you. It made me furious sometimes. And your dirty language. I thought that was just what men are. But it's not true. You like people. And there's no making sense of them if you leave out the brutal things like sex and death. Is there?"

No, he says to himself. No. He knows that he is crying but doesn't mind. Something the priests had never seemed very comfortable with. If this is what I came here for, he thinks, I better do something about it.

"I came because I never spent the time to get to know you, and when I got your letter I had to come." She looks at him with shining eyes. He hardly dares go on. "I came because I had to find out why you stayed here. I love this place and I can't figure out why I left it – I don't know where I'm at home." He blows air, wondering how to say the next thing. "I've been feeling guilty as hell," he grinds out, "because it wasn't the right reason to come. But I had to find out."

"You must," she says, and touches his hand. "Why shouldn't you love this place? It's in you. I can feel it." She smiles. "That's hardly cause for guilt. It's in me too. Not that I've been much use to you."

He says something that he can't even hear, like quiet rush of wind, that means something like Thank you.

"You should write again, Sam. Not the newspapers, but books. You should write because most people don't have the – the guts to say what you say. Or know what you know."

She stops, breathing. A lot of breathing. Oh Lord, Charlotte, he thinks, Oh Lord. Why now, just at the end, this bathing at dawn? Suddenly remembering. "Charlotte," he says, "the first time I fell in love I was sitting in the currant bushes behind the house and you were a little girl in a white dress with green print on it riding the swing in the cherry tree." Their parents shouting while he ran out and hid in the currants, no power to save her, either her, little sister or mother.

A woman was crying. Then Harry erupted from the house, tiny Charlotte in hand like a rag, and the wife-mother crying. And the red roses, with Harry pushing her higher and higher, sister flying in her green print dress among the cherry leaves.

Charlotte looks at him, all her years in her eyes, a girl again, smiling, tears shining in the creases of her skin.

"Why was Belle crying?" he says.

"I don't know," she says, "but I was afraid."

"I fell in love with you because you were the prettiest thing I'd ever seen."

"You must have been six," she says, her eyes a wonder to him as she bites her lip and smiles.

"I loved you all my life," she says, "only because you were my brother." Her smile broadens to a grin. "And I finally like you, Sam."

He knows he is grinning, but the sobbing sounds in his throat keep getting in his way as he tries to thank her.

"Thank you," she says. "You must keep trying to find out."

⊳┄┤━○━┤┄⊲

"Charlotte," he says, next visit to St. Thomas's, "I've been seeing ghosts."

Her eyebrows go up. "Ghosts, Sam? Whatever do you mean?"

"Ghosts. Y'know, like in books. People that aren't there. Sometimes I feel like I'm the one that's not there."

"Whose ghosts, Sam?"

"Mine, I guess. Yours. Dot's. All kinds of people from the war time, and 'way before that. All the lives in this place."

She laughs, gently. "Well, I don't know, Sam. I know I'm the one dying, but I don't intend to become anything as frivolous as a ghost. Just a pile of mouldering bones."

⊳┄┤━○━┤┄⊲

Regent Street at the evening rush hour gathers him into the tide-change human sea going up from Piccadilly and down from Oxford Circus. It seems everyone in London is pouring through this stately curve fronted with amber stone buildings that make him dizzy following their unbroken sweep against the sky. People and buses, cabs and bicycles elbow to fender from one wall to the other, moving in oceanic time, carry him along as though he too had purpose. He brushes the sleeve of a cyclist in a bowler hat, brolly strapped to his machine, and is brushed by the arm of a woman whose tailored shoulders and brisk bottom march into the throng of backs and fronts before him. He eddies into the lee of a columned entrance and leans against the smooth square bulk of its abutment. The stone feels warm. He looks at them all coming toward him. In the heart of an army of ten million. A nation city. They round from the perfect arc he's followed into this straight gut of Regent Street. Each one has a face. Old and young, in shirts and skirts and suits. A woman in a maroon blouse, breasts dancing to the rhythm of her stride, a swatch of skirt just curtaining her loins. He looks at her strong-boned English face and sees his own mirrored in her dark electric eyes. Startled, he nods. Her nod

177

in reply says, Yes, you're here too. It would have been the same if they had both been naked. He feels naked. Not undressed, but as though he were wearing only his skin, touched by everyone. An exquisite gent in a London Fog swirling over his pinstripe suit inclines a handsome chin. They all have faces. A pair of grannies with Liberty's bags, the one with her hand on the other's arm, support each other like frail handrails through the crowd. Good afternoon for tea. A taut youth in white Levi shirt and jeans snug as a codpiece on his well-hung crotch. The faces say, You've seen us. This is how we are.

Sam goes on down to Piccadilly again for the sheer joy of it. We see how you are. You're welcome here. This is human being. He feels Charlotte's breath in him. You lived here so long, he thinks. And longs for Lily willowing beside him in this dance against death. Breath of our breath, he thinks. What am I saying? All the living and the dead pass by under the grand arced ramparts of Regent Street, like the river of time flowing in both directions. And he turns to go up again.

He finds himself in Liberty's running his fingers through piles of silk. An amber scarf patterned in maroon wraps itself around his hands and slips through them like heavy warm mist.

⊱┈╌○╌┈⊰

That night he lies in his bed listening to the presence of London, the scarf clasped to his stomach like a live thing that ebbs and flows with his breath.

With each breath the dark rushes in and out of him and he sees constellations of light burst like pale fires in space, like slow-blossoming tears. The names of Charlotte and Lily and Dot, first Hugh and second Hugh and Nancy, Braithwaite and Fred and even his own. Each life tangible as the breath in his body, full and round and warm and fleeting as starlight on the water at Tuckenhay as the swans sail into his sleep, sound of his breath and sound of London indistinguishable as dreams.

⊱┈╌○╌┈⊰

He wraps the scarf around her hands and clasps his own over them.

"I got you this because it feels nice," he says. The silk warmer than her skin on his.

"Sam, it's lovely," she says. They look at each other and the tears welling in each other's eyes. Charlotte leans up from her bed and he holds her sobs against his, afraid she might slip away and be gone like an armful of feathers.

But Charlotte's arms are strong around his neck and she pulls herself straight. "Fine pair of hydrants we are," she says and blows her nose.

"Yeah," he grins, wetly.

Her hand with the scarf in it reaches out to stroke his hair. "It's so good to have you here, Sam." Her eyes make little quick movements, twin birds taking in all of his face, all of him. "You're not afraid of death the way the others are."

"Charlotte, coming here I was terrified. But you made me so damn happy …" He shrugs. "I feel like I'm good for something and I'm not used to that."

She laughs. "You certainly are good for something, Sam. You mustn't think badly of yourself. It's such a boon to know that you'll be here when I'm gone." She's trying to say something too and not knowing how. He thinks of Regent Street. How do you say these things?

"You'll always be here, Charlotte." He waves his arm and looks out the window. "You're part of this place."

He turns back to her and sees her eyes seeing London and time.

"What have I done with my life?" she says. "All that Red Cross paper. I've made stacks of paper fly. And known a few people as far as their skins. My friend Fran has such lovely ivory skin. A few men. The frantic things that bodies do. Is that what I've done? Stacks of paper falling all over Britain and half the world. And some bodies in the dark. A few noble faces. Sunlight on St. Paul's … I've not known people, Sam. The urchins I see in the streets, the fruit vendors – not even you, my own brother."

"Lottie, you've helped people all over the world –"

"And what good's that if you hardly know the ones next you?"

"Look at me. I fought in a war and turned into a drunk."

"You don't look like much of a drunk to me, Sam. You came all this way so I would have someone close to me. There's no one here I could talk to this way."

"Maybe you're right." He grins. "I never really made it as a drunk. It just seems like a good excuse."

She looks suddenly startled. "Where are you staying? I never thought to ask."

"Up in that hotel in Bayswater you found me last time." "But you should stay in the flat!"

"I checked with the Arab and he said you'd asked them to close it up, whatever that means."

"Oh dear, yes. You see, I haven't known what to do. I thought to leave almost everything to the Red Cross, you know – with something for Hugh and Carol," she smiles, "and you. But until the time really came … At any rate, I'll instruct Hartnell's to open it up again for you. You know, he said they could rent it as an Arab flat and it would earn heaps of money. Why do you think an Arab would say a thing like that?"

"Because he's a London Arab and the others are foreign Arabs. Look, L., it's okay. The Garden Square is cheap enough."

She looks at him speculatively. She's half daft, he thinks. Seeping away, her life, like water in sand. The scarf plays in her fingers like fluid gold and dark blood.

"What have you been doing, Sam? Have you work? I had a report from Dot just last month, but I think I dragged it out of her, it was that skimpy. Poor Dot. What will you do when you go back? When this is … done?"

He takes her hand again. The silk and the pasty skin. "It's been pretty much the same since the heart attack," he says. "Odd jobs and holing up in my rooms when I'm not in a bar. But like you said about the booze, I think maybe it's time I got a proper job. Hugh's Nancy said I should be a commissionaire, and maybe the wench is right."

"Oh dear, that doesn't sound much like you, in one of those stiff uniforms. But I'm glad you've seen Hugh and Nancy. Is she nice?"

"She's wonderful."

The speculative look returns. "Sam," she says, "you've always wanted to live in England, haven't you? Why don't I leave the property to you? John Jameson's managing the cottage in Totnes and he's to be executor. You liked John, I think, didn't you?" She laughs. "I guess there are some men I've liked. To think I met him over a cream tea on holiday when I wasn't yet forty. He seems so utterly impractical, and yet his advice has made me nearly a rich woman. There's quite a bit of money, and the rentals. You could live in whichever place you choose, or sell one …"

"Lottie," he says, "no. I'm just one guy. The Red Cross …" He shrugs. "Don't upset everything you've planned just because I showed up out of nowhere."

"I'm not so sure," she says. "They had most of my life." She looks at him as though she were seeing a place to go. "You don't have very much to show for what you did for us all. And you're giving me my family back when I need it most." He can feel her in him like a pressure testing the rightness of things. Like an embrace. A particularization of London. He feels at once frightened and comforted.

He puts his hand on her shoulders and leans over to kiss her on the forehead.

"I think it's right the way it is, L.," he says. "Let it lie. You should rest."

"You could always decide when it's your turn to go," she says, like someone who has seen a truth. She smiles and holds up the scarf. "It's like marigolds," she says, "made of marigolds," and closes her eyes.

⊷─◈─⊶

In Leicester Square it's Sunday. The visits to St. Thomas's have gone on, and Charlotte is failing. In Leicester Square the people who visit mingle with the people who live there, pigeon-feeders strewing their crumbs among the sleeping figures scattered like bundles of old clothing on the lawns and benches. Like corpses. He stands by the stairs leading down to the public loos, gazing at the Ritz and the Empire and Odeon across the way. Charlotte refusing oxygen and straying more often from clarity into twilight.

One marquee shows a sere yellow picture of rolling grassland loomed over by the giant figures of two Hollywood heroes, the old and the young. A film he'd thought to see in Victoria before it got away. The other side of the world. Those film-houses make a horizon. Beyond them, invisible as prairie beyond the next rise, more buildings, more streets, squares, gardens and greens. If I walked for a day I couldn't walk out of this place, he thinks. The hugeness of home. Charlotte saying, You must find out. Charlotte.

"All right?" a parade-ground voice booms. Its owner big as a wall. Sam startles like a fish in his skin. A Guardsman, no doubt, ginger moustaches flaring over a beefy red visage no younger than his own. He remembers the answer.

"All right," he says.

"Smashing! Can't be all that gloomy, what?" A shooting stick and cap. Sam grins, feeling feeble but befriended.

"Chin up, then, there's a good lad!" the giant shouts, giving him a comfortable whack on the bottom with his stick. "March on! March on!" and marches on down into Leicester Square, a broad tweed-jacketed back implacably plunging amongst the pigeons feathered and clothed there.

Sam takes a breath and descends the steps to piss. Mosaic Hogarth in the stairwell. That savage older grief. And older still, in the tiles' blue, ancient warpainted Britons gang angrily along his shadowy way to the depths. Down there, electric light gleams on porcelain and glows in the varnished years of the wooden cubicles. The bath attendant, towel on arm, chats with a pair of gentleman hippies in expensive boots and suede-look denim. Sam makes water in the men's clubroom at Leicester Square.

The National Gallery closed for improvements. The pubs not open. Charlotte more or less in a coma. You call this life? he says to the mirror. What sorta bullshit you tryin'ta hand me? Baleful eyes of the hulk at his hotel room table glare back at him.

The mirror says, March on, you old fart, and Hogarth says the same on the way back up the stairs. He considers the Tate but can't face the chance of more Sunday improvements. This place in which he doesn't know anyone. But after all, he tells himself, the day ain't gloomy. A sort of yellowish dusty promise of rain that could mean anything. Kew, he thinks. That other Charlotte's garden, full of familiar strange things. And goes to find a train.

><+>-0-<+><

Having exchanged dour glances with the collector of ha'pennies at the gate, having marvelled at the stacks of the tiny coins on his table and what it must cost Her Majesty's taxpayers to collect them, Sam crunches along gravel paths past the pagoda – closed for structural reasons – and the structurally impeccable spar tree presented by the people of British Columbia as a kind of wooden send-up of Cleopatra's Needle. The trees of Kew, living and dead, come from everyplace to stand at spacious intervals as monuments to botany.

The growth thickens until he is in a forest. In the forest stands Queen Charlotte's Cottage, closed up because this is not a special occasion. No hunting parties closeted there so the royals can get pissed by a resinous fire. No Charlotte. The day chills as it wanes.

Further along he leans on a gate separating the Gardens from the Thames embankment. A slightly more bucolic Thames. The sky looks like varnished silver and makes the river glow as it slides beneath the acid-green foliage along the near bank. The lustrous water carries phantasms of baroque barges past his eyes and the chill wind rings in his ears like tarnished brass.

The palace at Kew would like to close because the hour is late, but he buys his ticket, and treads where the carpet leads him over bare wood floors to the chair in which Queen Charlotte died. He looks at the worn black upholstery and imagines he hears it creak as the frail body settles into it one last time, eyes if they can see gazing out that window over Thames. Hears it creak again as the body is lifted out, made heavier by the life that's gone. The light from the window. What others have sat here since? Hurry up, please, the palace is closing. Queen Charlotte's islands, wilderness west of wilderness, that belong still to the ravens and the eyes of Charlie Edenshaw.

The greenhouses are closed because the hour is late. The coldframes in this very botanical garden of the Gardens are closed because they are coldframes. Good for them. He wanders into trellised acres that look like winter. One man forlorn with his barrow tends a bed that must simply be of another season, but seems like everything around it a ruined estate. A survivor, he thinks, grubs for roots. Gone with the Wind on the eve of blitzkrieg.

Toward the duck pond, toward sunset, pampas grasses and strange fleshy little plants from Siberia. Stone beasts of heraldry guard the Victorian glass marquee of the tropical house. Inside, palm trees scrape the high ceiling, a South-Seas silhouette against the wintry sun. He shivers. The pewter scrollwork sky says it won't be summer again today. A flotilla of Canada geese show the flag to the ducks, sailing past the stone bestiary and its empty row of graceful wooden benches. Each has a little brass plaque. In loving memory of Mavis and the happy hours.

On the east side of the pond, he peers through windows of someone's mansion that has become a museum of agriculture. The history of potatoes and corn displayed in glass cases. He remembers the lone gardener. I have loved you long and silently, he says, fondling tubers out of warm earth. The maize winks its red and yellow eyes in the crystal sunset shining through the palm trees.

━•❀•━

The thin, meandering rain that had begun streaking Sam's window while the train wandered among the rooftops of Richmond and across the Thames lashes his cheek as he emerges from Bayswater Station. He has a longing for whisky.

"Mr. Collister!" The Dutchman's wife hails him as he passes her window on the hallway. "I have for you your new room. Seven pounds a night. Number 11 downstairs at the back. You will move your things, please. The maids have cleaned."

Seven pounds a night. He has visions of a broom closet. "Thank you," he says, "that'll be easier on the budget."

Her crooked, mercantile smile. "We try to please," she says. "It would have been better if you had moved before lunch. This morning you escaped me."

"I was walking. Why don't I stay in 46 tonight and you can charge me the fourteen pounds?"

She makes a face. "No, the maids have done the room. It would be wasteful." She shrugs. "The hotel is not full. Tomorrow it will be full. Do you know yet how long you will stay?"

"No."

In the bar George slumps at a table, face propped on one hand, jawing with a man and woman who look like friends rather than guests. A man in an ordinary suit plays the slot machine in the corner.

"Give us a long and short, George, will ya?" says Sam, trying to sound like a friend rather than a guest.

George finishes a sentence and stands up like taffy being pulled. "Long and short was it, Sam?"

"Right. It's bloody winter out there. And have something yourself"

"Lovely weather for ducks," George says and draws the E. "Which whisky, then?"

"Cheapest malt you've got."

"Don't have nuffin' like that, guv. Johnny Walker, 'Aig an' the Famous Grouse."

Sam sees a familiar green bottle. "Make it Jameson." That's the thing to do, phone Jameson. Drink him and phone him. He shudders. Trying the vagaries of long distance to Devon to say that Charlotte's not too good.

George hands him change and starts back to his table. "Have one with me, George."

"Next time, Sam." He cocks his head toward the table. "I'm havin' one wif me mate an' 'is old woman."

183

No invitation to join them. He swallows his Irish and sucks on the bitter E. His blurred reflection in the glass face of the slot machine says, You don't belong here.

▷—◁▷—○—◁▷—◁

With his bag slung on one shoulder and spare shirt and trews draped over the other arm, he goes down all the stairs to the basement foyer. Laundry tomorrow, he thinks. At the door of number 11 he runs into George disguised as an armful of bedding.

"Do you do everything around here, George?"

"Just checked your room, guv. Bleedin' girls didn' change the bed. I'll have 'er right in a shake."

The room, like the hallway, looks carved out of rock, like something in a whitewashed Mediterranean village. It's big enough for a bed, a bureau, and a chair, with space left over to strangle a cat. But there are French doors, gauze-curtained and pattering with rain, that must lead someplace. He stows his things and goes to locate the loo. The hallway ends next to his room in a pebbled-glass door. He opens it and peers out. Stairs going up into a yard surrounded by buildings. Other stairs going down into a concrete pit outside his French doors. Time to phone Jameson and leave George room to make the bed.

After an eternity of buzzing and clicking and static and an information operator who must be in Exeter or Newton-Abbot, he hears, "Yes? Elizabeth Jameson here," and dumps coins into the telephone.

"Hello, Liz, it's Sam Collister. Is John about?"

"Sam! Are you in Victoria?"

"No, I'm in London."

"I'll get him," she says, and through the static in the line he hears her melodious voice go, "Joh-on, Sam Collister for you." Another click. "Yes. Jameson here."

"Collister."

"Yes." Jameson says yes more often than anyone else on earth. A kind of assertion of possibility, to make sure everyone knows he's there and ready and uninformed.

"Charlotte's not in good shape. Didn't seem to know I was there today. They say she'll rally, but she won't have an oxygen tent or anything." He stops.

"Yes. Terrible thing. Good of you to come over. Sure she's better for it. Yes. I'll be up tomorrow. Can't take the morning train. Should be in by tea."

"Thanks. I'm at the Garden Square Hotel if you want to find me, or I'll see you at St. Thomas's."

The phone begins to click manically. He can barely hear Jameson say, "Damnable Post Office!" and feeds in another coin.

184

"Okay?" he says.

"Quite. I'll stay at my club. Dinner?"

"Sure. We'll see." The thought of Jameson in London makes him nervous.

"Tomorrow, then?"

They ring off. Tomorrow. Laundry and Jameson. Not dinner at the club. Hours by Charlotte's bed. Do you know yet how long you will stay? No. How long will there be Charlotte? Not long. How many tomorrows? Is this your last Sunday in England? In the world? The first day that will not repeat itself.

He stands in an absence of impulses by the phone. The bar. The telly lounge. Conversation. Bed. Something to read. To go and see *The Missouri Breaks* in Leicester Square. Lily. I gotta do something about this when I get home, he thinks. And where is that?

"Have you done?" says a woman with coins in her hand.

⋈⋆⃝⋆⋈

While he's attempting to read a Hammond Innes he found with the Bible in his dresser, a knock comes on the door. The redhead from Hartnell's is there.

"I brought you a key to the flat, Mr. Collister," she says. She looks done in.

"Can I buy you a drink?" he says.

She smiles. Yes, she would be beautiful if she had time. "Thanks awfully," she says, "but I'm knackered. It's gone ten and I haven't been home yet." Her brows knit. "I'm sorry, but we haven't had a chance to open up the flat yet. Perhaps tomorrow."

"What needs doing?"

"Oh, the furniture's all draped and things are packed away in cartons, that sort of thing."

"Never mind," he says, "I can always do that."

She smiles again, looking restless. "That's good of you," she says.

"Not at all," he says. "Thank you." And watches her red top and natty raincoat and worn brown boots up the hall. An awkward stride, as though her hips were rusty. He sees sadness the colour of the air, beyond Charlotte, beyond anything he can name. As though London were dying around him and himself with it. He wishes now for Jameson's inarticulate windy presence and a bottle of whisky by the hearth in Devon, where there would be cows to see in the morning and earth red as a banked fire on the greyest day. He closes the door and looks at Hammond Innes and chucks him away. He sits on his bed and stares at the wall and very slowly, like a trembling of the earth, begins to weep.

⋈⋆⃝⋆⋈

"Why don't you take the oxygen tent?" he asks.

"It would only prolong things, Sam," she says. "I'll not have that."

Fran, who does have beautiful ivory skin and is director of something or other, had been and gone. There was an argument about the oxygen tent while Sam twiddled his thumbs. Other visitors are not his cup of tea.

"Yeah," he says. "You talk to Bourke about it? I saw him the other day and he says you oughta have it your own way."

"Yes. Thanks for that. You treat me as I am, not like what you want me to be. Fran's a dear soul, but you think she'd know better by now."

"It's hard, Lottie, for people to let you go. I know the oxygen wouldn't help. But I damn well wish it would!"

"I know," she says, running the scarf through her hand like a napkin through a ring. "But it's all right now. I don't mind, and you shouldn't let yourself mind too much. People must let me die and look out for themselves." She smiles. "I can't say I feel the angels coming for me, but I've stopped resenting it all, you know. That's the good part." Her eyes are like windows with no shine to them. Utter transparency. He feels the wind pass through him into her eyes. A great distance. "I feel cool on the outside," she says, "but there's a fire in my bones." She raises a hand. "But you mustn't think I mind it. When the fire's gone, I'll be gone."

He clasps his hands and tilts his head and smiles. "You're amazing," he says.

"Tell me about Hugh and Nancy," she says.

>+→-0-←+<

Jameson arrives in St. Thomas's more like late lunch than early tea. "Bloody marvellous train," he says. "Yes. Couldn't believe the blighter. An express, next to it." His quick smile, moustache bristling iron grey over a crowd of teeth. Jameson smiles as often as he says yes. Dentists must hate him, a man his age with all his own choppers.

"Yes, bloody marvellous." He stands in the middle of the floor looking back and forth between the two of them. A square, thick adjutant-major in tweed cap and jacket and country-squire trousers. Sam imagines the repeated surprise of machine-gun crews as the adjutant of all people would show up under fire, his ruddy cheeks and anxious cheerful greenish eyes darting from faces to lines of fire, enfilade and defilade. In those days, Jameson loved machine guns the way a boy might love toy trains.

"You look well, Charlotte," Jameson is saying. Sam cringes. Charlotte smiles, befriended by his dotty generosity in a Devon tearoom, lo these many years ago. Jameson takes her hand, then shakes Sam's. "Yes," he says. "Good to see you, Collister. All right?"

"All right," says Sam.

Jameson, for all that he's impossible, warms a room by being in it. But he is impossible.

"Look," says Sam, "you two probably have things to talk about. Why don't I shove along now and see you later?" Charlotte nods. "You needn't stay, Sam. Come in tomorrow." He kisses her cheek. Cool on the outside.

"Dinner?" says Jameson.

"Sure," says Sam, not entirely sure. "Where?"

"Yes," says Jameson. "Shouldn't fancy the club, what?"

"No," says Sam.

"Quite. There's an Eyetie spot in the West End, then. Corner of Charing Cross Road and what have you, Cranston Street, I think, called The Inferno or some such. Can't miss it. Looks like nothing at all on the ground floor, handful of tables. But down below it's a ruddy cavern. Wonderful food. About seven?"

They both look at Charlotte.

"You'll have a wonderful time," she says. "It's Il Forno, at Cranbourn Street."

"Yes," says Jameson.

⊢·◈·○·◈·⊣

He goes to the Tate, looking for something that doesn't look hopeless. The luminous fires of Turner, as though everything were fog inhabited by flame. A placard on the wall tells him that this painter of light feared a hundred and fifty years ago that the Empire was failing. A quaint woman no more than forty adjusts with a long pole the skylight blinds that must surely have seen Victoria Regina. An archaic, gentle glow no lamp could reproduce, seeming native to the canvases on the walls rather than the sky at the ceiling's crystal-palace crest.

Outside, vinyl banners, a weary guard, an empty bench and the current of brown Thames. Schoolgirls play hide-and-seek among the Henry Moores lying like hieratic walruses beached on the lawn.

Where do I go from here? No one said it would be like this in London in late summer. Charlotte dying in this place that should have been home. Streets of stone Victorian houses, shabby, elegant, opening onto the street. Shabby men in doorways.

Livid faces. Where am I going to get to? Home in a gutter with a bottle? The seedy jacket that disappears into a crumbling pub called The Swan, a paper tucked under its stub of an arm. Five on the dot. The elegant and armless. Does it matter what town the gutter's in? If London, like the Empire, falls in on itself, we are the roaches in its walls, the ants picking its skeleton clean,

187

and that'll be a lovely bone-yard. Oh we are the ghosts of Imperial legions returned to scavenge and swill like barbarian hordes. London frightens him.

In the Underground he sees the poster image of a woman plunging through space, the nipple of one breast in her sheer blouse like a raw wound pressed against glass. When the train bursts into a station, he shrinks from the wall flashing past his nose as though its stones were a rush-hour throng poised to pour through the doors.

⊱—◦—⊰

Waiters pirouette and plunge through the crush in cavernous Il Forno, where the ceiling is an arch of shifting shadows held up by candlelight from the packed trestle tables. People looking for a place to sit, people looking for a place to piss, people trying to leave. People eat elbow to elbow. Their cheeks glisten and their teeth shine. They've put the Middle Ages underground to feed on pasta instead of wild boar. The waiters twirl in aloof frenzy, zookeepers feeding a hysteria of baboons.

Sam regards Jameson. A lesser baron, champion of geniality, moustache argent in this light, hospitable over cannelloni and Barolo.

"She won't last long," he says.

"No," says Jameson. Jameson's eyes always seem ready for tears or laughter and you can never tell which. The soft light warms them. Fireside evenings in Devon.

"But I must tell you the good you've done her, coming over like this. Yes, you know. She's turned very peaceful. Peaceful." He repeats the word, an affirmation, and knots his brows earnestly. "And grateful, you know. To you. You must know that."

He clasps his hands in front of his chin. "Can't think what else to say, really."

"Yeah," says Sam, "I know that." Poor Charlotte. He raises his glass, black-red as blood. "You're a pal, John," he says, "to both of us."

"Cheers," says Jameson. "You must come down to Devon." "When she's gone."

"Yes."

What's to do about the funeral? Death in peacetime seems more brutal somehow. Planned. Like housing for the poor. Homes for the aged and infirm. Sam sees himself in a home and shudders. Charlotte six feet under. Bang, don't whimper, he says.

Jameson raises an eyebrow. Did he hear that? Am I talking in or out of my head? But so what. More wine. "How's the book?"

"Ah, the regiment. Yes. Almost done. Into modern times now, post-Suez and all that. Colonel's tickled. Thinks it might be the thing to save 'em at the next cut. Lost his nerve, I should think, when the Greys went."

"Those bastards need a war," Sam says. "It's economics."

Jameson looks startled. "Do you want another war, Sam?"

"God no. But I ain't no peacetime soldier licking brass."

"Preparedness, old man. Standing army and all that."

"The next one's gonna be for button pushers, John. You know that. The ashcan won't need pongos like you and me."

"What if it isn't, old man? The Ruskie can field enough troops and armour to make blitzkrieg look like a schoolboy lark."

Sam tries to imagine the Red Army marching up Regent Street but can't quite make it. "Ah, bullshit," he says. "But I guess you're right. The Canadian effing forces would have a bad time with Lichtenstein, and I guess the Brits are heading the same way."

"Yes," says Jameson. "Utterly deplorable. I shall have to get this regimental thing done and get on to my South Devon history while there's still some of it left. Between the blacks and the Labour Party, we're all going to pot."

"I thought it was the Arabs."

"All the same, isn't it? The Wog makes fine light horse or a passable philosopher, but there's an end of it. Give him oil and we're buggered, not to put too fine a point on it. And have you seen what those blacks are doing in Notting Hill?"

"No. I haven't been over into Notting Hill."

"It's on the telly. A bloody riot, is what. Have a carnival and turn it into a riot. Bloody white hooligans and black ones all on the ruddy dole. There's no discipline left, Sam. Put 'em all in uniform, I say."

"A riot? But it's right next to Bayswater, which is calm as a pool of piss."

Jameson chuckles. "Ruddy colonial," he says. Someone calls for pepper through the din. A waiter advances, the three-foot wooden grinder brandished over his head like a mace. The fields of honour.

Sam scratches his head, trying to remember the street life of the last couple of days. "Y'know, I kinda thought there was a lotta cops around." Scores of them patrolling in pairs like schoolmasters. Although the helicopter had seemed a bit ominous. The man in the laundromat. "I was doing my wash up on the Queensway, with my nose down sorting through change for the drier, and a fellow asks me if I can break a 50p piece. Sounded ordinary enough, sort of East London. But I look up and the man's black as coal. I didn't know anything about any goddam riot, but we got to talking and I asked him about that, the colour problem. 'I'm a Londoner,' he says, just like that. That was his answer. Then he tells me he has a sister in Toronto and how I shouldn't leave my clothes in a machine without watching it. 'You mean someone might steal 'em?' I says. 'No,' he says, 'not a bit of it, but they might chuck 'em on the floor so's they can get the machine'."

189

Jameson regards him with serious inquiry. "Yes," Sam says. He feels foolish. "I dunno what that's all in aid of," he says, "but the guy was right. He's a Londoner. And if people don't pay attention to that, he's gonna get pissed off."

Jameson's eyebrows and moustache bristle in a fury of concentration. Sam imagines he hears the crackling of thought in Jameson's skull. Suddenly the brows arch and the eyes pop in astonishment. "You know," he says, "thought never occurred to me. The man's a Londoner. By Jove. Of course he's a Londoner. He's a bloody Englishman!"

Sam laughs. A great burst of it rocking his chair on the floor. The waiter claps him on the shoulder and laughs and says, "Dolce far niente, signore." Sam, still laughing, turns his head and says, "You stupid prick" to the waiter's back.

"It's the oil," says Jameson. "I've always believed in the oil. Had my stock in it since before the war. Steered Charlotte onto it. If Mrs. Thatcher can chase that fellow Callaghan and not make an ass of herself with the unions and the North Sea oil comes in as it should, we might get some self-respect back. Get those blighters off the dole and we might make something of this country yet. Goddam Common Market might mean something then!"

Sam grins. "Jameson," he says, "you're wonderful."

"Yes," says Jameson. "Quite. Old bore." And grins himself. Then his face straightens. "The funeral, Sam," he says. "Must tell you that. It's all in hand, nothing for you to do. She'll go to Totnes as she wishes. St. Mary's and burial on the hill. Don't have to bother your head about that, old chap." His face goes uncertain again. "Unless of course you want –"

"No, no, John. Thanks. I just didn't know." You cross-grained goodhearted sonofabitch. The red stone church in Totnes.

The dessert, an orange each, opened up like sea anemones in caramelized sugar sauce, tastes as erotic as it looks. With bursting juices in his mouth, Sam goofily sees the two of them as details in a Brueghel painting. The subterranean cathedral Il Forno feasting on the flesh of Charlotte's death.

Jameson takes the tab. "No arguments, Sam," he says.

"I don't have any, John. You're the Officer Commanding." The adjutant-major of machine guns, with everything covered. Sam feels a bit giddy. Someone else is in charge.

"Yes. Not a bit of it, you silly bugger. No rank in the mess. Caps off and all that rot. Look, why don't I get us a cab and run you up to your digs? Or would you fancy a nightcap at the club?"

"No, thanks, John. Let me walk up to Oxford Street and take the tube. I don't think I've walked up Shaftesbury since the war."

The upper end of Shaftesbury doesn't look that different. More light, but not a lot of it. A Dickensian kind of bleakness where he'd found Dot all that long ago. The place itself, near as he can tell, a union hall dark as a tomb. He is surrounded by phantom shapes and voices, their uniforms young when it all seemed real. This is where you belonged, they say. Before you went out to die.

On a triangular corner he sees a pub called The Crown displaying the yellow sign of Double Diamond. An oasis of light. He goes in.

"Pint of DD," he says, leaning his belly against the bar. Triangular bar in the triangular room. Stairs at the back lead up to the sound of more drinking overhead. A different sort of London from the one he'd left in Il Forno. Everyone looks like they're from just up the block. The ones who lived here before the Romans.

A granny sits under a mirror in a corner, at a tiny table with a pony of beer set on it like a flower vase. Sam looks for the cat, the fat tabby British puss that should be heaped comfortably as a fur muffin her lap.

I'll check out the flat, he thinks, and downs his pint.

▷┤◈─◯─◈├◁

Light from the lamps on Abercorn Place falls among the spectral humps of shrouded furniture and lies in watery pools on the floor. He stands awkwardly in the middle of the room, afraid to move. An intruder in a funeral home, not even the drip of a tap to mask the sound of his breath. Stale, uninhabited air. He sticks a cigarette in his mouth. The wavering flame picks out an empty wall, the bare corner of the mantle, the television's blank eye.

The first sweet swirl of smoke. Where to put the match. Not in the dead electric fire. He blows it out. The moment of greater darkness falls softly on his eyes. Like sleep. A ghost in a ghost house made visible by the glow of his cigarette-end mirrored above the mantle. What he came looking for. Himself in England.

He goes to the toilet, flicks on the light, raises the seat, tosses in the match, and decides to piss. The little yellow torrent's noise splashes through echoing rooms. Genteel flush. Darkness again as the switch flips under his finger.

Sam pads through the sitting-room that, three years ago, had been greened for hours each day he watched the New Zealand Test telecast from the Oval's rain-softened pitch. Boycott's century. The weedy Englishman at silly-mid-off who'd caught the meanest slicer as though he were picking lofted marshmallows from the air. Where he had seen an angelically mad Brit named Nairn make filmed journeys in search of folly, which he said meant delight or favoured abode. Love and desperation swirling with his mackintosh as he pointed to one crumbling relic of daft grandeur after another. Brunel's Folly: the Great

191

Western Railway, Nairn a demented badger sadly rooting through its graceful, abandoned way-stations. Amber light in the room while he'd prowled books that told him of Hannibal's victory over everything but time and the commissary, Napoleon pickling his favourite marshal's body in brandy, Guderian freezing his nuts off in Russia trying to pull his divisions out before Hitler caught on and yanked him back to command a Berlin desk while the divisions died. The futility of it all. The room full of teacups clinking while he didn't know what to say to Charlotte and fled back to his hotel.

He pushes open the door and wedges himself onto the cramped balcony. The flicked ashes fall on someone's car parked in the paved yard below. Poor form. Cabs turn in Abbey Road, busy as nighthawks, hunting return fares. Bare bulbs in the ceiling of a garret apartment across the way. Tawdry walls and a bald man in an undershirt staring out. Sam's gorge rises. A hallucination of puking on the sleek black roof below. Who could live up there overlooking opulent St. John's Wood in a place as seedy as his own dump halfway around the world? He stands like a big sack of potatoes crammed between the door and the railing of Charlotte's abandoned balcony, at the edge of a bleak absence around which the lit night eddies. I didn't come for this.

➤⟐〜O〜⟐◄

Along the Edgeware Road, at a place overhung by a hedge and smelling of rosemary, a younger man comes suddenly upon him. Sidelong glint of suspicious eyes, quasisexual, a London look of inquisition. Are you this way or that, and if not – beware. The fear startles him. There's trouble here. That's why I came.

The pale shadows of Charlotte's flat float in the back of his head and the Garden Square beckons in front, down past Paddington Station and the council flats and Bishop's Bridge Road where the buses run to Ladbroke Grove and Dot's flat that was. Shadows and nameless fear in the night. The underside of London and dragons hunting over Primrose Hill.

The sign of The Cavalier sways in the breeze – fancy, ruffed warrior astride an effete horse. A beer would taste good, and it's not quite closing.

Inside, the place is too bright, threadbare and whispering of cockroaches. The found-ins the same. Jesus, he thinks, As the World Turns. The bar matron looks like a whore on forced retirement. Her taps look tacky. "Best bitter," he says. She stares across the room while drawing his pint. A kid at the dart board. "Leave off that, you little bugger, it's closing!" she says. The punk in denims throws another dart.

"House darts?" asks Sam sociably, fighting the fear. She ignores him. The beer tastes like cool piss.

In the final mile home to the whitewashed cell in the Garden Square's basement,

192

he doesn't look over his shoulder at the presence there, sepulchral among the echoes dogging him through the hollow streets. Whatever you want, he thinks at it, I ain't lookin' in the mirror. And avoids the eyes he meets along the way.

◦

"Strange that you should wonder," she says. "I've been seeing blood ..." He hasn't been wondering anything, at least not out loud. And blood is what she looks like she doesn't have at all, the maroon and amber scarf like a bedraggled fire at her breast.

"Yes, Charlotte," he says, "I've been wondering. Tell me about the blood."

"It's all over the roads," she says. "The earth is red and the sheep are red and there's blood all over the road." She looks at him beseechingly. "What do the sheep want, Sam? What do the men want?"

He takes her hand, the grip of a hand that almost isn't there, like a curl of mist in his paw.

"And the dogs on the Mount are baying. All those dogs ..."

"What are you seeing, Charlotte?" Clearly not me or the Houses of Parliament or the blue air over London out the window.

"We were having coffee in Bean's, Fran and I," she says. "Fran has such beautiful skin. The coffee is good at Bean's, but the cakes are awful modern things. Down at the bottom of Fore Street, you know, by the Plains. And there was a terrible commotion in the street. Full of grockles it was, the way it gets in summer before the greengrocers close and the pubs open. Two men, you know, boys really, came running out of the Post Office with sacks in their hands, would you believe it? And guns. I think they had guns. Or something that looked like guns. It just couldn't be. But there they were, running for all they're worth, like mad things, and people spinning around falling over themselves. Not those two. Tearing by right under our noses in Bean's, our mouths wide open, I should say. A piece of breadcake half in Fran's mouth, truly. Fruiterers' trays flying everywhere, apples underfoot like, like spilled great marbles and smashed bananas and flans and grapes and tomatoes. Right by us into the Plains. There might have been a third there with the car. There was a car, an old grey thing you'd never notice anywhere, and they piled into it and flew off up the river road. Do you think there was a third?" Her eyes are looking everywhere for a third and flutter closed like tired birds. "Fran, Fran, look, they're going up Totnes Down." An expiring sound comes from her lips. "Up past the Mount at a terrible speed and the dogs baying. It must have been a terrible speed up that twisty little lane. Deep as judgement that lane is, and gates that open onto it, which should never, never be. Flew up that hill onto the downs and there was a hayrick there on the way to Ashprington where the sheep were crossing. Anyone would have known there would be a hayrick. You could

193

see it in your mind. And where could the sheep go? There is always blood on the road where the sheep have gone. Dark red blood. And the men. And the dogs. I always hear the dogs. Frightening. Awful. Awful." Chunks of metal flying down ancient lanes that had been tracks among villages for Celts and Anglo-Saxons and Normans, trampled under feet and hooves and wheels, metalled, tarmacadamized while the fields grew deeper behind deepening hedgerows, and gates opening out as they never should onto the roads covered in black blood.

From very far away, as though he were swooning, he peers through the carnage of machines and flesh at Charlotte's face, her delicate nostrils still as fluted wax and her hand joined to his. Her eyes flick open wide and bright with awe, like someone going blind, and fade to the colour of killed fish, and shut. Sam closes his eyes on the tremble of life passing through him.

But she's still here. And she smiles as though she had been comforted.

⇥·◆·○·◈·⇤

He sees it coming. London bizarre on Thames embankment, toward St. Thomas's, 8 A.M., hurrying. And he doesn't want it, but there's no way around. A thickset copper-haired bloke in a dirty grey suit and a thin, mousy stretch who looks like a seedy academic wave fists and holler at each other. The thick one chases the other off and turns away. The thin one rushes back and screams, "You filthy yob! Why don'tcher fight, why don'tcher fight, you big pillock!" stopping just out of range.

"Fight? You flamin' poofter, I'll crush yer!" One fist bandaged, the other balled to strike, the redhead charges three steps and halts as his harasser scuttles away, further along the embankment. Sam's scalp prickles. Quirky edge of fear. Walk through it.

"Spare a bob?" Sam startles. The big man's breath would stone a horse. And it's only morning. "Me old woman's burnin' up wif a fever. I'm an artist, like, an' we're for the street if I can't make the rent. Can't work the docks wif this busted mitt, can I?" shoving the bound appendage under Sam's nose. The fear impales him like a cold blade and his mouth won't work.

"Thief! You buggered me!" Close up, the frantic scholar looks filthier than his enemy. "Half a quid. You owe me half a flippin' quid!"

"Garn! toe-rag. I owe you a broken bone!" The man bristles and lunges like an enraged pig. His rawmeat face swivels back to Sam. Blood in his eye. Sam held by it. "She's a goner 'less I finds the lolly, mate. It's only six quid to keep the bailiff off. No one 'preciates art no more."

"Shove it, pal," says Sam, wrenching himself out of his rabbit fascination.

The man's good hand grabs his arm. "Don't say that, guv –" Sam yanks his arm free and bellows, "Get out of it!"

The man backs off. "Too good fer the likes of us, eh?" he hisses. Sam walks on, his back tense against attack, innards boiling.

Why the fuck should I get scared of two morning drunks? he thinks. It's funny, he thinks. It's funny. But doesn't laugh. Will there be Charlotte?

"Yankee trash," the scholar says as Sam passes. He quickens his stride.

⊳⊶⊙⊷⊲

In Charlotte's room the bed is empty. Neatly made. A bag of things on the chair says "C. Collister." Sam looks out the window. The brown river runs. An ordinary grey sky with Big Ben in it. Traffic on Westminster Bridge. Tears needle the corners of his eyes, but nothing happens. Charlotte isn't here. He picks up his hand from the window ledge and finds in it the amber scarf. A tremor shakes him, but nothing happens. Everything plain as day. What's out there is out there. What's in here is in here. No shadows, no double images, no ghosts. Nothing. What is, is.

In an underground place a white-coated man opens a door and slides out a shrouded body on the slab. Charlotte's face appears. She'd had some blood left after all. A purple pool in one cheek. Like cool dough to his touch. He takes her hand, almost pliable under the sheet.

"She's not been here long," the attendant says. Respectful but hovering. Lest he steal her.

"No," says Sam. Still nothing happens. As though the parts of himself were disconnected. Head and heart and hands. Not even the needlework in the eyes. Charlotte's not here. Or maybe she is, something of her. The warmth in the chair. The warmth in her flesh now that the fire's gone. "Goodbye, Charlotte," he says. "May it be well with us all."

He meets Jameson in the hall. "Dreadful sorry, old chap," says Jameson, reaching out a hand.

"You too," says Sam, wanting to hug him but thinking it would be unseemly. John puts a hand on his shoulder.

"I should have a drink, if I were you. Hang on a bit and I'll join you."

"If it's all the same, John, I want to go off on my own."

"Yes. Whatever you say. I'll make the arrangements and train down with her. Tomorrow or the next day. I'll call you at the hotel."

"John," he says, "I want to go down on my own."

John looks at him hard. "Yes, well, whatever you say. Funeral won't be before Monday, I should think."

"I'll be down on the weekend."

"Good. We'll have your room waiting. Leave word at the club should you want me. Sure you're all right?"

"Yes."

⊳⊶⊙⊷⊲

195

Sam's legs ache as he leans against the bar in The Crown. He's not sure where he's been except he ate half a greasy donner kebab in Soho and drank beer in too many pubs to sort out, uncomfortable amongst bowler hats and eager advertisers. He had stood like a wooden Indian in Regent Street and wandered among tourists during afternoon closing in the nave of St. Paul's, looking for a place to sit down, too tired to climb up amongst the angels. His legs ache. What do I know about mourning? he thinks. He weighs Hugh's heart in Belgium against waxen Charlotte in the morgue. Al in traction against Al blown out of a hedgerow. It helps if you can blow something up or charge the hill. If you have someone more than yourself to fight. Something in your hands. A rifle. The innards of a dead man. He looks at his hands. Two of them. They belong to someone else. A pint of beer between them the colour of cedar water running through the rain forest. How can you mourn when there's no one there? Goddamn you, Charlotte! he thinks. That frightens him. But there should have been a life. In more than thirty years there should have been a life. Lily. He wants Lily. Or a woman like Lily. There aren't any women like Lily.

Further along the bar a tarty number in fake leather pants drinks vodka-lime and cocks her hips away from her escort. An Elvis Presley remake, that one. Heavy black hair slicked back from an ominous face. A hard-on in his blank brute eyes. She has a long sensual face and a little purse slung round her neck on a thong to show off her long sleek breasts in shiny purple acrylic. "Come on, Nora," her companion says. She turns her shoulders away to parallel her hips. "Drop it, Alf, I told you the pub and that's it."

Pick your cock off the floor and go home, Sam thinks. I must be pissed. Feeling almost numb. The girl does nothing for him except to make his skin feel heavy and the pit of his stomach lonely. But he'd love to bash that brute. The punk on the ferry. Oh Lord, round and round again. Glasses and bottles glitter in the bar's oak superstructure. The beer tastes wonderful. I better sit down, he thinks.

The old one is knitting again in her angle of the wall, a vacant chair beside her. He goes over and says, "May I sit down, ma'am?" The Sam in the mirror above her looks terrible.

Her face tilts up at him. Parchment cheeks with bright spots of colour over the bones and eyes glittering behind flat spectacles. She studies him. The pile of knitting in her lap looks like the imagined cat, tortoise-shell.

"To be sure," she says.

The chair protests his bulk but stays in one piece. He feels decidedly incapable of conversation. Out the window he can see a streetlamp and the dark windows of a grey building. The old one's needles click. She wears a dark blue shawl. Her hair is almost white, gathered into a bun. She smells good, like lavender in a linen closet.

With his beer and his elbow beside her pony glass, the table is almost full. He picks up the beer.

"Mind if I smoke?" he says.

"Not at all," she says.

He puts the beer down and fetches an ashtray from the bar. She shifts the pony to make room and eyes his packet of Senior Service. "May I?" she says.

"Hell yes!" he says, and feels embarrassed.

"I shouldn't, you know, any longer. But my, those taste good."

Plain end too. My God. He lights it for her.

"Ta, luv," she says. Sam looks at her with new interest.

She sips from her glass and sits blissful in a cloud of smoke. "Ah, me porter an' me fag," she says.

"Cheers," says Sam, raising his glass.

"You're not local?" she asks.

"No," says Sam. "I'm visiting from Canada. My sister died in St. Thomas's today."

"Poor dear," she says. "I thought you looked a bit forlorn-like standing there. Died today. Dear, dear."

She shakes her head and looks at him, the cigarette alongside her face.

"Not much of a conversation piece," he says. "I'm just feeling kinda strange." That's it, he thinks. I'm next. The last Collister. Then he remembers Hugh, Wilson or not.

"You can put a plug in that, my boy," she says. "Conversation piece! I'll have no truck with conversationalists. Talk to 'emselves, mostly." She butts out her smoke and picks up her knitting. "I'm not really local myself," she says. "Lived East End 'til we were bombed out in the Blitz."

"I was here in the war," he says, "Canadian army. That was hell you went through in East London."

"I had a boy sixteen." She peers at him. "He would have been about your age now."

"I was born in '19."

"Well, he was born in '24, and that's little enough difference." She smiles. A radiance of wrinkles. "I should have had you at fourteen, not unheard of then. Never did have an 'usband, which *was* unheard of, I'll tell you."

Sam warms. You crazy old dame, he thinks.

"Dad worked in the docks," she says, knitting away, "and Mum took in sewing. Jeremy and I lived there until I came home one night an' they were gone. The whole lot of them. The whole block just a heap of bricks. Never did find Jeremy. He'd gone off twice to try and join up in tanks. Mad for tanks, that lad. But they wouldn't have 'im and he was home that night." She looks at him. "So there, you see? I should think he would have found me by now if he'd got out of it, wouldn't he? Although they say people do get amnesia. Didn't want the East End after that, I didn't. Ended up in a little flat just there," pointing with her needle, "after I landed a job in Oxford Street selling to the ladies, you know, once the factories didn't want women in the work force. And here I am." She holds up the knitting. "I should think my great-niece will like this in her pram."

He doesn't know what to say, but some parts of him feel like they're beginning to work again. "Yeah," he says, "I almost thought it was a cat."

She laughs. "The cat's under the chair if he's here at all. Boris," she calls, bending to look, "Boris, the gentleman here thought this little rug was a cat!" A moon-faced grey tom blinks suspiciously from under her long tweed skirts.

"My name's Sam Collister, ma'am," he says. "I'm grateful for your story."

She smiles. "It's all a person has, really, isn't it?" Her hand appears like a blue-veined butterfly. "I'm Cordelia. Cordelia Gilbert. My father fancied himself a bit, and I can't say I blame him." He squeezes her fingers gently.

"May I buy you a pony of porter, Cordelia?"

She shakes her head. "Thank you, Sam. Don't take offence, please, but I always gets me own."

He grunts. What other good ideas are there?

"Good heavens!" she exclaims. He hears a woman screech, "Leave off!" and glances up just in time to see leather-trousered Nora slash her drink across the brute's face. Stillness in the bar.

"Make me another, Terry luv. That 'un's done," she says.

" 'Ooked 'er by 'er privates, 'e did," says Cordelia, breathless.

The pompadoured punk stands motionless save for the vodka-lime dripping off him. Death in his eye.

" 'Op it, mate," says Terry behind the bar.

The punk says nothing. He's not even staring, just there, with his eyes open. Then, startlingly, he speaks. "But it's 'er done it. Give 'er the bounce."

"Shall I whistle up a copper, then?"

Nothing happens. Fer chrissake, thinks Sam. Guy looks like you could boot him in the nuts and break your foot. Startlingly as he'd opened his mouth, crotch-grabber pounds down his ale and walks out the door into Shaftesbury Avenue, almost taking the door with him. Better watch how you go home tonight, girl, thinks Sam.

"Shouldn't think he'd be much fun in bed," says Cordelia.

"Cordelia!" says Sam. "You got no shame?"

She grins. "I didn't always sit and watch," she says.

Sam blows air. "I'm going to find the bog," he says, propping himself out of the chair.

"It's down below," she says, waving a needle. "In the catacombs."

It is indeed. Sam winds down stone steps to a dripping cavern with cistern and urinal. The catacombs. Bright, cold, and somehow Christian.

When he gets back, Cordelia's pony sits empty by his empty mug. "Could I change my mind?" she says.

"What?"

"If you don't get mine, I'll get yours, go on, there's a quid." "Ach," he says, "old enough to be my mother and twice as ornery."

He offers the empties to Terry and says, "Pint of DD and a pony o' porter."

Terry looks at the glasses and looks at Sam. "You an' Cordelia got those broken in, then?" he asks.

"What?" The empties. He realizes he's slipped into a habit from the Legion.

The barman shakes his head. "It's a night for it," he says, upending the mug and the pony into the sink.

Safely in his chair, Sam says, "I'm getting disorganized as a kid in basic training. Where's that girl got to? If cement head's waiting for her –"

"Never mind about Nora. She's upstairs. We look after our own."

"Cordelia," he says, and raises his glass, "your dad was right."

>–•>–0–<•–<

The long-handled latch of room 11 clicks shut behind him. No rain on the French doors. He parts the curtains and looks out at the little sunken patio invisible in the dark. A few lit windows mark the walls of hotels crowded against the tiny backyard space in which a blackberry vine and other green things will be visible come morning, like an oasis at the bottom of a light well.

He digs through his jacket pockets for loose change and waste paper. His hand comes out with the scarf in it. He looks at the gold and maroon folds heaped softly in his palm. His fingers clench over it, warm edges oozing out amongst the white knuckles. A hard sob wrenches him double, and another, fists rammed into his thighs. He drops onto the bed, choking for a long time until he can draw clear breath and lay himself out full length. Listening to the sound of nothing in the room. It goes on and on. He sees the pale bulb in the ceiling looking down on him. He doesn't know if he's slept or not slept. He doesn't feel that he's there. Just the sound of breathing like the sound in an empty shell, the sound between stars. A faraway voice says, Sam. Sam, he thinks. Come back. It's time. Where have I been? he thinks. Charlotte's life mingled with his in a frail vessel soon to become, like her, a basket of bones. Am I still alive, or just part of the spirit haunting this place? The scarf looks like the only live thing in the visible world. A piece of rag. The colour of life only. Sunlight and blood. He sees the light in the ceiling looking down on a man on the bed. The futility of continued life in that wasted hulk. The man sits up in rumpled clothes, his hair sticking out from his head like straw. He turns his face to the light. One of the faces that have seen death. It's day.

I better shave, thinks Sam.

The scarf falls out of his open fist and he stuffs it into his breast pocket like a handkerchief.

> ┈┅●┉┅┈

"Mrs. Leeuwen," he says. "Mrs. Leeuwen!"

"Yes?" she says, emerging from ledgers. She doesn't look like she enjoyed what sleep she had.

"I'm leaving tomorrow," he says.

> ┈┅●┉┅┈

"George," he says, "what do you know about the Brit Museum?"

"Lumme. Full of art treasures they say it is. Elgin marbles an' what not – stuffed Egyptians, Sutton 'Oo an' the Vikings. That lot. Not my cuppa tea, museums."

"What about the reading room? I got some things to do."

"Come on, guv. I hears it's got all the books ever printed. Now what am I supposed to know about somefin' like that?"

"Do they let anyone in?"

"Search me, guv. Never 'ad the urge to try."

"Well, if they let Karl Marx in they better let me in."

"Now look 'ere, Sam, what's 'appenin'?"

"Charlotte died."

"Oh that's 'ard, that is."

> ┈┅●┉┅┈

The clerk in the little office off the corridor leading to the reading room says, "Are you affiliated with an educational institution, sir?" The prick.

"I'm a graduate of Caen and Falaise," having spied out the drill, "and I want to go in there and see about some old soldiers."

The man looks at him like someone who's seen more peculiar beasts. "Very good," he says. Old soldiers indeed.

In the hushed, bell-like hall Sam puts the notebook he got for 50p on the table. They all tell me I oughta write, he says to himself. So I'll write. He takes a piece of letter paper from the notebook.

"Dot," he writes, "Charlotte died yesterday. I thought you'd want to know."

He looks at it. It seems insufficient. He signs it, takes out an envelope, addresses it, folds up the words and stuffs them inside. The envelope glue tastes minty.

He sees another found-in staring at him as though he might be more interesting than the tome in front of the found-in's nose.

He takes another piece of letter paper and writes, "Dear Hugh, Your Aunt Charlotte died yesterday." What day is it? He copies the date from his Reader's Ticket onto the top of the sheet, then writes "London" under it. Hadn't done that on Dot's. So he takes the envelope and writes the date in the upper left corner.

"She didn't have too bad a time. A brave woman. We got to talk quite a lot before she went."

He pauses and bites the end of the pen. Sure. Write it all down. The crowds on Regent Street and the colour of Charlotte's eyes looking out the window. The Burghers of Calais. "I'm going down to Devon for the funeral. Maybe I can get my head straight down there. Right now I'm kind of out of it."

Another pause. The found-in back to work on his tome. "The time I spent with you and Nancy was great. Maybe when I get back we can get together. Give Nancy my love. I hope things are okay." He thinks about it some and writes, "Your Dad," and signs, "Sam."

When that is addressed and sealed he breathes relief and looks across the room. A stocky fellow with a fan of grey hair over his shoulders and bushy whiskers brushing the tabletop sits over there.

"Well, Karl," he says, "here we are." The found-in looks up. "Whaddya think of it now?"

Karl's blank face. *This isn't how I thought it would be.*

<hr />

The Burghers of Calais stand over him in Victoria Tower Gardens. They look at the ground. They look at the air. Their bronze faces ennoble the death they see all around them. Their bodies twist into the brownish sky like flames.

"You guys remember her," he says. "She died over there. You made her feel better, knowing you were here."

<hr />

In a little shop on Westbourne Grove he buys half a dozen bottles of cider in a box. He ferrets George out of the storeroom and says, "Stow these under your bed, mate, and get some kip now and then."

George's bright black eyes look at him a long moment. "Jesus wept," he says. He holds out his hand.

<hr />

Numbed by the rocking of British Rail, he looks out the window after miles of fields and pig farms and weedy canals to see an immense white horse carved into the face of a hill. Tiny human figures climb the hillcrest onto its back. Older than any reason why. A legendary beast that outlived its meaning. He stares at the giant chalk horse until it dwindles into distance. Then he sees the others, white dots far across the valley. He had forgotten.

THE TOPS

LORD, HE THINKS. Inside the red stone church. Dearly beloved. You really went all the way back, Charlotte – Anglican. The weedy churchyard mown flat as an old rug and headstones like dinosaur teeth. The Lord gave and the Lord hath taken away.

Blessed be the name of the Lord. They're praying, the fuckers.

I said, I will take heed to my ways: that I offend not in my tongue. Offend not, Collister. He looks at the ceiling. The groins of God. Echoing up there in the resinous scent of pews and varnished choir. Shadows. The great window's prismatic light. Lord, let me know mine end, and the number of my days. It ain't Latin, L., I'll hand ya that. Mea culpa. Mine age is even as nothing in respect of thee; and verily every man living is altogether vanity. The dead are not vain. Oh no. Hugh Young dead at twenty-one. Charlotte at fifty-seven. Where are you gone? They speak English, these priests. Lord, let me come up. All of us. Maybe twenty stiffs in dark clothes hearing the Burial of the Dead echo among the centuries vaulted overhead. The distant guns. An honour roll in stone. Jameson looking like he'd swallowed alum, and Elizabeth a pale fettered fleshly angel. Lord let me come up for I am a stranger with thee: and a sojourner as all my fathers were. Oh Jesus. Dearly beloved, our sister Charlotte Collister has been taken from us. All twenty of us. Fran's ivory skin like cold fire in her black weeds. And a pinstriped poobah Red Cross general who would rather have been Anthony Eden. Outside the sun shines on September tourists. Her good works and genteel spirit, etc. We remember them. The fallen at the going down of the sun and in the morning. Distant guns and the barrage draws near. She's in that shiny black casket, you prick, what's left of her. No children. No husband. Her parents gone unto the Lord. Oh yeah. A brother from Canada. He pulls the scarf from his pocket and wraps it tight around his hands. The earth shudders under the floor under his feet. The Lord is my shepherd. Let's get the hell out of here. Why aren't we in a pub someplace? The Waterman's Arms. Blue board with a blocky chap in white who holds an oar as though it were a cudgel and a slender boat behind. Inside, beery light the colour of good bitter and a publican who looks like his sign. His bones shake. The Wild Boar, the Two-Necked Swan, the sign of the drunken man – the sign of things as they were and of things to come. Yea, though I walk through the valley of the shadow of death. The barrage arrives. It splits open the red stone church of Totnes. Sam's flesh scatters amongst the rubble and what's left that isn't flesh swirls into space. A hot wind in the absolute zero between stars. The music of the spheres sounds like Mozart. Let us pray. He grips the wooden rail in front of him and hunches over in a cold sweat. Oh Lord, don't let me faint.

There are cars to take them up to the new graveyard on the brow of the hill. Why can't we walk? Carry Charlotte up the narrow dog-leg High Street. As it is, he lowers his corner of the coffin into the hearse and looks at Jameson, who looks back, unhappy and determined.

Yes, thinks Sam, a good soldier.

Once again he'll get to throw the first handful of dirt. Man that is born of woman hath but a short time to live, and is full of misery. Woman born of woman. Belle. Mother. Red earth. For someone who had so little blood you're going to be buried in it, Lottie. In the midst of life we are in death. A wind ruffles their hair and ripples their clothing. The priest and his two boys like black masts with their sails flapping. The wind riffles the green grass among the headstones and crosses down the long rolling slope to Totnes, a fretwork of slate roofs and white walls swooping into the junction of three valleys. The hills of Devon. A sea. England's green and pleasant land rolling up out of the Atlantic to be walked upon. He sees white crosses row on row. Name, if you're lucky. Birth and death. Serial number. Hugh planted in Belgium. They're all there. Our graves await us like the soft backs of the sea, greenly yielding to this new fertilization. Soil so often turned that it kneads like china clay, silken and shapely to creation upon creation. The earth a sea, green, that rolls over our dead and bears the living home. Little white crosses that undulate as though they stirred beneath, and a great wind rising. Their voices like Mozart tintinnabulate through the chapels their fathers' fathers raised because the ivy on the oak trees had not kept out the rain.

Jameson nudges him in the elbow. For as much as it hath pleased Almighty God of his great mercy to take unto himself the soul of our dear sister here departed: we therefore commit her body to the ground; earth to earth, ashes to ashes, dust to dust. He takes a handful of the red loam and throws it into the hole cut like a wound in the green hill. Of his great mercy. *But you mustn't think I mind. When the fire's gone, I'll be gone.* Her eyes so brightly going blind.

On the way back to the car he looks at Jameson, immaculately funereal. Himself in his summer jacket and trews, the wrong colours for death, because wearing a rental would have made him feel like a dummy. Elizabeth between them, black flounces, bosom veiled, Rosetti face pinched in disgust, plump arm in a sheer black sleeve pressing her hat flat into her pale curls so the wind cannot have it.

Not you next, he thinks, halfway into your threescore years and ten; strange match for Jameson, with your devious will and tender flesh. A spring chicken next to us. Charlotte's gone. Al's probably gone by now. Hugh's been gone since you were born. He sees white crosses and stops himself thinking how many are gone. Not you next, John. You're ten years older than me and healthy as a horse. I think I'm next.

There is a lull in the wind. Crunch of footsteps in the lane. You can almost hear the sun shining on the car. Devon smells like the warm barnyard it is. He hears dogs in the distance and turns to look. They are baying on the Mount.

▷·▸·○·◂·◁

Out the window of the Pilgrim's Table he can see the last light on a lichen-covered wall that keeps the farm across from sliding into the Harbourne River. The Devon where Charlotte will stay, and maybe him too. Rapid-fire conversation surrounds him. He doesn't want it. This window an escape. Above the licheny wall, through a mat of trees and vines and brush, the end of a stone barn, itself licheny, moss on its roof. Above that the tops of the hills, near and brown and green in the rich sunset air. Hoofbeats thud beneath the restaurant's window as a girl-child gallops her pony back and forth along the sand at the Harbourne's near edge, river you could spit across with a following wind. Smaller than the North Alouette in Haney.

There had been talk of going to the Maltsters in Tuckenhay, or up to Moreleigh. But he didn't feel like going anywhere so they'd stayed in Jameson's village and settled into the bar in this place John had bought for Elizabeth to turn into a restaurant. Though it doesn't seem she married him for his money.

So they hadn't gone anywhere. He'd wanted to sit around with John and Liz and feel like he'd been to a funeral. Then these two guys showed up. Friends of Lizzie's to pass the time. "Oh, how sad." Cluck, cluck. God.

Up the step in the long dining room, Laura Ashley waitresses waft about on the dull flagstone sheen, paisley flames of the sunset and candlelight. They minister to the horsey set from miles around, who munch steak and crab and Dart River oysters, orange sauce duck and piquant veal, quaffing French wines.

Sam sips his malt whisky. Something called Ancestor that Vaporizes on the tongue and lifts the top of your head off with a bouquet rough as cedar boards. A social afternoon isn't what he'd had in mind. Twitter and twoo. A wake is what he wants. He stares at the pint of meaty Belgian lager on the table. Are Hugh's bones growing hops over there? What will grow from Charlotte's?

The conversation crackles about him as he hunches into the high-backed settle. This is what these people do? Is this why we stayed home? Two antique dealers, freeloading off Jameson's booze. Elizabeth at her frothiest, slathering them with pet names.

On his left on the pine settle sits the antique dealer named Deaver, who could

204

be an Imperial subaltern in tropical climes. Rawboned shanks and knobby knees poke out of his tennis shorts, thatch of wiry fair hair over a sunburned brow. His blue eyes burn lunatic even in this light as he speaks. Eager Deaver, no less. Known to normal people as Jack.

"Devastating is what it is, Eliot, the prices these people want." Something about a woman near Bath.

"Dear boy," says Eliot, the other dealer, every inch the dissolute gentleman, shadows under his eyes, a touch of grey about the ears of his carefully casual dark hair, "you may be Eager, but we mustn't be eager. Unseemly to betray one's avarice, wouldn't you say?"

"Montague!" says Elizabeth in coy horror. "We must allow poor Eager his plaint." She looks like a plump and pretty thrush, changed from funeral weeds into a flouncy white skirt with bands of lace to show her legs and a loose blouse that makes you wonder where her nipples are among the ruffles and embroidered nubs and peepy-hole cutwork. The yellow curls dance like spun gold around her chameleon face. Deaver is on about the woman near Bath. "Her la-de-da house she can't keep up and wants me to help pay for. Mercy she doesn't know what she's got."

Sam feels morbid and lumpy. Jameson looks morbid and choleric beside his wife. "It's Pluck and Cunning!" she'd said in delight when the two appeared at the door of the Pilgrim's Table. Sam cringed. "Pair of bootless cadgers," Jameson had muttered. It looks for all the world as if they are courting his wife. Elizabeth. Betty. Bess. Known as Liz, who should have been Anne, a plangent, gracious sound like the lilt of her voice. What have you done, John? Half your age, Elizabeth is, old friend. Is this what happens? These flip young bastards. He thinks of Lily and the brass Adonises. Is fifteen years the same thing? And remembers that he hasn't thought of these things for a long time. What have I done? Charlotte's eyes going blind and the life passing through him like a warning. He feels reproached. And stuck here in his corner of the settle, Pluck on one side, Cunning on the other. "All the way to Bath," says Deaver, "for that. But it might come around in the end."

"Yes," says Jameson, sounding like he means No and has been waiting a long time to say it. "I do not believe that people should go about selling off precious old stuff and packing it in those container things to ship to Americans."

Everyone looks at him.

"That's rot," says Pluck.

"Boring, John," says Elizabeth.

"Would you rather some clown from London bought it?" Eliot puts in, hard edge to his voice. "Some mudlark who's made his pile in Carnaby Street, and stuffs his mistress full of chocolate before eating her out? Come, come, John. You're a realist. You see how it goes." Cunning.

"John's right," snarls Sam, wishing just that they'd either shut up or go away.

"I'd say it's none of your affair," says the dissolute gentleman. Dangerous. "We have to live here. You don't." Jameson grunts.

"The Americans buy anything," says the Imperial subaltern.

"No aspersions intended, Sam." Cunning again.

"The Canadians are just as bad," says Deaver. "They're just not so rich. Anyone calling himself a baronet can go over there and they all fall at his feet like a pack of Muslims. No reflection on you, Sam."

"He's not a Muslim," says Eliot.

"You been there, Deaver?" says Sam.

The Eager One checks his fingernails and looks at Sam. A blue jolt. "Can't say I have," he says. "No harm meant, old sport. It's just that people who insist on behaving like colonials tick me off. Shouldn't generalize. Wouldn't hurt a fly, you know." He flashes a smile at Elizabeth, who smiles back.

Those eyes make me nervous, thinks Sam. But he gets the funny feeling that those eyes view Elizabeth with compassion rather than lust. His head spins slowly like a burnt-out pinwheel. Eliot sitting there. Worn-looking. Used. Tired. A shop on the High Street in Totnes and an ex-wife named Amanda who lives somewhere about and gets pissed too often and has her transmission fall out in lonely places in the company of various men. Unflappable Eliot. Cunning. And Pluck likely would have made a good Imperial subaltern. Fuck Pluck. The decadent gentry looting one another's ancestral houses for booty to flog to the Philistines. Poor Nairn. In search of delight and the favoured abode. Shed a tear.

"What did we bury, John?" he says.

"I know what you mean," says Jameson, plummy and sepulchral.

"Terrible thing, death," says Eliot.

"Mustn't be morbid," says Deaver.

"Never. If we must have burying, let us have bunburying!" Eliot raises his glass. Sam feels his choler rising to match Jameson's. These guys are slick as grease and just as hard to swallow.

"Done!" says Deaver. "Up the importance of being Eager!"

Sam's head swivels from one antique dealer to the other as though he were caught in endless tennis. He settles for glaring at Eliot. "I'm getting tired of being outwitted by people who have nothing to say!" He didn't mean it that way, but it comes out a roar.

"You're for it now, Monty," says Deaver.

"Oh dear," says Elizabeth, "poor Sam. You've ruined the evening." She glances toward the dining room entrance. Her pout unravels into a professional smile as she launches herself to despatch departing guests. "Did you have a wonderful time?" she calls, musical.

"Scrumptious duck, Lizzie, *non pareil.*"

"I'll tell Jean-Louis. Bless his little Gallic giblets." Sam can't see her but imagines a sardonic radiance amongst the porkpie faces. "See you at Sharpleys'," she says. He glares at Eliot again.

"I assure you, it's not that we have nothing to say." The fellow has sand all right. Steady eyes. Properly ominous. The young brigadier getting a leg up on his honour. "I respect your loss," Montague continues, dipping his chin. "But hang it, man, you can't sit about being solemn as a cow. Not good for what ails you, don't you see? Shortens life, if that's what you want."

"Yes!" barks Jameson, red spots the size of shillings bright on his cheekbones. Don't keel over on me, John. They don't have shillings any more.

"Can't you guys lay off," he growls.

Eliot's eyes go steel hard. "Collister, if you wish to be treated like a colonial, we'll gladly oblige." He pauses on that. Electric silence. "But we'd prefer not."

"Certainly not in *my* place!" Jameson snaps.

The steady eyes shift. "Precisely."

"Hear hear!" says Deaver, thumping like a parliamentarian.

"Cheers." Eliot raises his glass again. "*Vive le mort*, as the French say. Don't they?"

Sam feels like a spiked gun. "Do they?" says Deaver. The waitress Rachel arrives like a tall, handsome flame in paisley, bearing hors d'oeuvres. Camembert fritters and fried zucchini.

"Isn't death feminine?" inquires Deaver. Rachel looks at him disapprovingly, her cameo profile lovely as one's mother when young. "Not this lady," she says.

"Now Rachel. Poor Deaver's quite right. The French make these distinctions and death in French is feminine. *La.*"

"I've always rather fancied death as a woman. *La belle dame,* wouldn't you say?" says Deaver. "*Quel drôle,*" says Rachel, departing.

"Exactly," says Eliot. "I'm afraid she's got you, old thing. The masculine, you see, is the dummy. *Le mort.* Bridge, you know."

"Oh, Cunning," says Elizabeth, returning, "you're not playing *bridge* are you, with these unfortunate gentlemen?"

"Wouldn't dream of it, darling –"

"Fer chrissake!" Sam explodes. "You been snorting coke? Or just getting pissed like the rest of us?"

"Did the gentleman say cocaine?" Eliot sniffs. "A line or two would be rather cleansing." He levels the steady eyes again. "But the point is not chemically altered states. The task of Pluck and Cunning is to divert the mind. To chaff the sullen vapours into heady ones. I say, John, this Camembert is divine. Would there be some leavings of duck in the kitchen, you think?"

"And how should I know? I simply *own* the restaurant. Go ask Jean-Louis."

"Moot, John, entirely. *My* restaurant you always say when you tally up the till, *your* restaurant when you see the bills. And I won't have you two traipsing through there like a pair of geese while there're guests about. *I'll* ask Jean-Louis."

"Would a single goose do?"

⊢•◆◦◦◦◄•◄⊣

When he stands in Jameson's garden looking at the sound of the river through the darkness, the geese have gone into their goose-house in the orchard. Inside French doors, Jameson hunches by the fire in his study, digging through a long box of file cards. Upstairs, Elizabeth undresses near enough an uncurtained window that Sam looks the other way, toward the gurgling black space below the house lights' glow. Singular sounds glint through the woolly night. Cow bell. Car. Dog. There are no stars. Smell of bottomland and time. The long black wall of the restaurant runs windowless, like a fortification, at right angles to the river bank.

The wind begins to blow in Sam. Things tremble. The branches of the yew tree and the branches of the elm. The weather changing. What's happening on the tops, in the higher dark? And what white-crested hills are there out at sea? The Western Approaches.

Liz's window is gone dark. Jameson sits by the fire, chin nodding onto his chest, fragments of local history scattered in his lap. Sam goes to the French doors and steps through.

⊢•◆◦◦◦◄•◄⊣

"Oldest working farm hereabouts!" says Jameson. "There's a property down Harbourneside you'll find in Domesday Book, but it's all play now. This one's not changed a stone in two hundred years."

Sam eyes the stone barns and pens, the broad-beamed, lustrous cattle red as the mud they stand in. Up the lane between hedgerows under a leaden sky. He feels tremors. Yew trees stand gallant against the air. Around that corner had been the girl and the deadly nightshade. Jameson's fat, happy yellow dog noses into something by the roadside.

"Tessie!" says John. "Get out of that." Tessie ignores him and starts trying to roll in whatever's there. Sam looks at the matted green walls. Chunks of metal flying.

"Badger carcass," says Jameson, twenty yards away. He harries the dog. "Get on, Tess! You won't be fit company for a dustman. Get on!"

The stench hits Sam. Men and horses. The girl in the hedgerow. Blood all over the roads and chunks of metal flying. The black smoke boiling from dirty flames.

208

What the guns wrought at Falaise. The stench in the back of your nose.

He hawks and spits. His head feels spinny and his skin cold. He keeps walking. "All right?" says Jameson, the dog fatly bounding ahead.

"There was a blonde girl," says Sam, feeling hoarse.

"Quite. I daresay there was. Looks like she gave you a bit of a turn. There's the cross now. Tenth century if it's a day. Celtic revival's making a lot out of these things. Dumnonia, you know."

"Yeah," says Sam, knowing only that the stench won't go away and the girl's eyes are staring at him blue as cornflowers, like Hugh's, like Deaver's, like that German kid's. Scrabbling in the grime in his kit for sulpha and bandages to stuff the fist-sized hole in the German's chest, the eyes looking straight through him. Charlotte going down. Entrails in his hands. Al's eyes staring at the ceiling. He sways into the ditch. All the eyes of the living and the dead stare at him from the dark behind the hedgerow's dusty leaves. Lily and Lise. Withered nightshade berries. His skin wet and frigid. The stink in his nose hits the pit of his stomach and his innards try to rip themselves loose.

"All right?" Jameson's voice from far away.

"No," chokes Sam and buries his face in the bristly hedge. He hangs on with both hands as the dry heaves turn to tears. Waves of them crash through him. God, he thinks. This hurts too much. God. And it all subsides. Something else, he says, give us something else. He wipes the water from his eyes so he can see. Yellow bile drips from his chin and hangs in frothy strings from the shrubbery. He wipes his chin, spits, and swallows taste of his stomach. Above him, on a crest of beaten earth by a tree, a pink lamb looks down.

He sees Jameson up a blind track that branches off from the crossroads. Pissing. The sadness of it all. One old fart puking in the hedge, the other staring off over the hills at God knows what and passing water on the crest of a ridge in Devon. No sound save the wind and space.

Jameson meets him by the ancient stone cross. "Footpath through there leads on to Totnes. You can see it all from here, how the land lies. That's what brought the Normans. Access by land and sea. Strategic." He looks at Sam and claps a hand onto his shoulder. "Sorry it's hit you so hard, old chap," he says. "Grief, you know. A hard thing."

"It's not just Charlotte. Though God knows that's bad enough. It's being *reminded*, John. The war's been coming back on me a lot. That happen to you?"

"Yes."

They start walking back down to the village. "You get older and it seems like it's all behind you," says Sam. "And what is there? In my case, a lot of shit. There's a woman in Victoria but I probably don't mean no more to her than the time of

209

day. There's my kid I haven't done anything for most of his life. Seems a man has to live for something. I gotta find a job and a decent place to live. But I don't feel like I *belong* anywhere. Where have we got to, John?"

"Might not be the best time to think about it, right after the funeral, you know."

But I'm being reminded, he thinks. He takes a deep breath. "What about you? How can you stand things like those two dealers last night?"

"That's life, isn't it? I shouldn't complain. She's a good wife. And I'm not what I once was."

Sitting by the window cut low into the thick wall of his room in Orchard House, Sam looks at the journal he bought the day after Charlotte died. The geese that had drummed him awake with beating wings and querulous bugles drift like clouds on the pool of Harbourne. He writes things down. Geese. A walk with Jameson and the dog. He grits his teeth. Puking in the hedgerow with memories of the war and Charlotte and other things. Should go to Charlotte's grave this afternoon. What comes next?

Elizabeth twitters in the hallway. He smells ironing.

The road curves past the graveyard and on down the long hill to Totnes and the meeting of three valleys fortified by the Normans. White farmhouses and grey farmhouses dot the hillsides. The wind blows. A pleasant place, even with the weather off.

"You picked good resting ground, Lottie," he says. The new grave, dirt in the grass like traces of a kill. The new-cut head-stone. Charlotte Rose Collister and the years with sharp edges where the chisel bit. He looks again down the hill. Sudden and comforting in the generations that have looked upon it.

Shall we live here? What will grow? Grass and gravestones. Fields of white crosses blooming in the wind. Vegetables growing out of Hugh's heart in Belgium. "Never mind, L.," he says, "pretty soon you'll get rained on and worn in and part of this place." One of the veteran dead.

When he opens the gate of the walled garden at Orchard House, it is late afternoon. Jameson's laundry flaps bravely under the ominous sky. Vests and pants and socks. Some white, some saffron, some blue. The ghost of Elizabeth's voice says, "Oh, I'm airing John."

In the kitchen a yellow coffee pot sits on the Aga cooker. A brindled shawl lies coiled like a cat on the rocker. There is no one about. They left their

shawls behind, he thinks, feeling absent in the empty house. Sleep, he thinks.
Food and sleep.

⊢•✦•○•✦•⊣

"Coldface?" Elizabeth chirps. "Or a dippy egg?" Outside, the morning looks
nearly black though it's gone eight. She seldom rises early and often rises
cross, but she always rises with the throat of a bird. And his nose tells him
she's remembered his coffee.

"Coldface?" he says.

She laughs. "It's the new breakfast cereal," she says. "Pluck and Cunning
won't have cornflakes, you know."

Jameson sucks tea through his moustache. "We're not having those two
layabouts for breakfast again, I hope."

She clucks. "I had a lovely tea with them yesterday at the Buttery."

"I should hope at their expense, for once. After they drink my liquor and
eat my duck whenever they want."

"Now, dear one," she says, "let's not have all that again. You were off at the
cash-and-carry when we were to have taken Sam to Dartmoor – and could
have gone riding. And Sam was off. I really had nothing else to do."

"You know damn well I couldn't go the day of the funeral and we couldn't
wait longer. There *is* your restaurant to run."

"You could have sent Jean-Louis."

"You know *damn* well Jean-Louis hasn't time."

"Well, we can't very well go to Dartmoor in this weather. Which'll it be,
Sam? I've made you coffee."

"Egg, please," says Sam.

"When you've done," says Jameson, "take a waterproof and we'll walk."

"Right," says Sam.

"You're both mad," she says. "It'll be drenching in an hour." This is awful,
Sam thinks. But at least the coffee doesn't taste like tea.

⊢•✦•○•✦•⊣

"Sharpley Barton down there," says Jameson, "and the Manor." The contour
of the ridge gives them a view across the valley. An enormous yellow stone
house far below. A white horse and a black one run from corner to corner
of the field that slopes down toward the trees and the river. Their hoofbeats
thud over the dark grass, the darker hedges and trees, the steep slate roofs of
the house dark as the lowering sky. A pale reddish road snakes over the hills
across. Beyond that, you'd swear you can hear the sea.

Jameson has been going on, pointing. Contours of the land. An eighteenth-
century house. A bridge almost old as the hills. "Sharpleys no longer own it, of

211

course. Play-farming. Blighter named Goodge who does something in oil. Never there. Twelve-metre boats and the Fastnet when he is. Very la-de-da, his wife keeps it. There's a young Sharpley in town. Headmaster at the school. Drinks too much by half."

Sam sees ghosts of men in the fields.

"Rather a comedown. His great-great-grandsire built the leats for the mills hereabouts," pointing as though he held a swagger stick to trace in the air the little canal's meander away from the river. "Not an engineer in it, but the grade's spot on. Carry water for miles. An industrialist is what he was."

The ghosts become soldiers crouched behind hedgerows, contesting the green hills of Devon. Enfilade and defilade. Hull-down positions. Death in the bocage. Death in the stables and the kitchens. Retire from untenable ground. Seek the position of vantage and raking fire.

"Let's go on," he says.

"Quite," says Jameson, a man escaped from his own kitchen and the wars without honour.

They go down into the valley and up a footpath through healthy pasture toward a bluff

"Make a circuit of the tops, shall we?" says Jameson. "Right 'round the village. Lots of up and down. Excellent for the circulation."

"Sure," says Sam.

The footpath turns into a sheep trail, by the look of it. Jameson hardly slackens pace. Sprightly old goat.

Halfway up, Sam pauses for breath and a look back. Under a canopy of trees the bluff tumbles down in grassy ledges and outcrops of rock to the tussocky field dotted with gorse. Brooding, like Hardy in Dorset just up the coast.

"All right?" Jameson calls from above.

"Fucking sheep."

"It's not the sheep, it's the men." Sam soldiers on. The sweat runs under his slicker. Here between Hardy and Cornwall, grim visions of England in the place of Walter Raleigh and Agatha Christie and cows. In Cornwall, the land and everything on it blown sideways by Atlantic gales. Through the blood pumping in his ears he imagines he can hear the hills tremble like water.

At the top they are in a wild field, long fallow and threaded with animal tracks through the matted brown grasses waist-deep. Thistles stand high as sunflowers, their heads bursting with dun fluff, like mattress stuffing.

A billowy roar from the valley behind and the wind hits. Stray bullets of rain bounce off him and crash through the dry grass. Sam turns to look down from the hill and sees history. What's that? he thinks. It beats him about the eyes. It has waves, like the sea, and a spumey mist whipping around the yew trees as the grass blows flat and flings up spray. It soaks him. The sky is around his ears. Glowing crests stretch in ranks to the horizon and nothing else is visible.

"Bit of a blow!" shouts Jameson. "It'll be force ten out there." The air is solid water and slaps at him until he thinks he hears the mains'l flapping and the earth rolls under his feet. Cold water all over him like tears. The Atlantic Ocean is in the air, and there are men in it. As he tries to breathe through the teeth of the gale a fullness gathers from the soles of his feet and swells his chest to bursting with the force that roots him there. The stays give way and the mainmast snaps and the deck comes apart under his boots. The sea is full of men. They're all out there. Every mother's son. All the men under arms and tinkers and tailors and women and children ancient and newly dead taken under the sea-green earth. And it wants him. It rears into the sky and wants him. A great glassy arch filled with faces as they lived that are not where the screaming is coming from. This is it. "It's death," he says.

"Quite!" shouts Jameson into the wind. "Can't hear a blind word. Let's get on, shall we?"

In the lee of the far slope he stumbles through bunch grass. Those aren't boots on his feet. Shoes that'll never be the same again. It's thick down here and fecund. Six-foot nettles in mulchy soil and things that look like alders. Smells of his boyhood richen the strange vacancy in him. A wooden-rail gate in a stone fence. A path next plots of cabbages and broccoli. Stone outbuildings.

"We're in someone's farm," he says.

"Public right of way. Strange lot this, never moved out of the last century. Incest, you know. But harmless."

They cross the leat on a slippery plank grown over with nettles and trudge along the riverbank on sopping turf under sodden trees. On the far side what look like young pines and firs blanket the steep sidehill. "Bit of new forest," says Jameson. "We'll go up that once we get across."

Before the bridge they emerge from canebrake into elegant grounds where the rain drips from copper beeches and stately balsam.

"Step softly," says Jameson in the downpour. "Domesday, this. Miserable son of a monkey ran me off twice. Thinks he's the National Trust and wasn't even born here. House is Georgian, but the barn's ancient. Eleventh-century foundation, they say."

Sam squelches through puddles in the needle-strewn drive. The house looks empty. A genteel sitting room sits behind glass doors, watching them. The house looks alive on its own. Sam feels that he's moving in company with a lot of time. He feels oddly all right. "All right," he says.

"Yes," says Jameson.

They cross the bridge and around a corner in the lane come into a tiny village. Narrow, blank-faced stone houses slap on the street, like a flicker of Dickens, like two rows of bread-boxes set on end. One apparently a shop. A powder-blue tin sign says Medly Tea. They're everywhere. Turn over a stone and you find human habitation.

Mercifully there is a road up the new-forested hill. They come out at the oldest working farm. Red cows stare at them from barn doors. Instead of going up to the crossroad, Jameson leads him through fields towards home.

At the crest of the hill, they can see off toward Totnes and around to the wild brown hilltop where the storm hit them. It looks like the top of a big haystack. Sam feels empty and airy. The weather has lightened to a silvery sky and steady rain. They are in an empty, close-cropped pasture with a modern shed that smells of tractor and hay. A sheep lies in the track outside the shed, mud caked in its wool, four stiff legs pointing south, pink entrails bulging out both ends.

"Bloat," says Jameson. "Fancy Smithers allowing an animal to die of bloat."

How it is, thinks Sam. The sheep and the men. This is it, all right. It's not death. It's everything. Around the next field, where they mustn't trample new hay.

In the kitchen of Orchard House they stand in twin pools of water spreading over the tile floor. The Aga sizzles. As the sodden layers peel off him, he can feel it press dry heat into his skin.

Elizabeth stands watching them, sardonic crinkles around her lips and eyes. Two old guys stripping down to sodden gaunchies plastered on like skin. Jameson bends to drag his trouser legs over his feet. One at a time like anyone else. A hard, gnarled, thickset frame. Tight pleats of pale, chilled skin. Bless your old balls, Sam thinks, fit as an oak. The warmth hiding in his bones seeps out like old wine. "All right?" he says.

"All right," says Jameson and looks up at him. They put their arms around each other's shoulders and embrace clammy flesh to clammy flesh. The wine fills Collister with warmth. He squeezes his eyes shut and in the warm reddish dark his unshaven cheek rasps against the balding pate of his friend. Elizabeth stands by the Aga, her eyes bright and moist.

><•>-0-<•><

Collister stares at his journal. Out the low window, the tentative geese dip billfuls of water from fresh pools in the grass. How do you write this down? he says. *Went for a walk with Jameson. It rained like hell.* His marrow shudders at the idea of trying to commit to paper a wall of water full of men. *Saw Domesday,* he writes. What the fuck does that mean? And scratches it out. *Old farms.*

Somewhat like Haney. A dead sheep. Alfalfa bloat? That's different from corpses bloating when they rot.

The lightness has stayed with him. This is it, he thinks, but what can I do with it? I've seen life, he thinks. Write that down and they'll take you to the booby hatch.

He looks at the geese in an even, colourless light. Ruffles of a breeze on the smooth rush of rain-swelled Harbourne.

Jameson's got troubles with his old lady, he writes. What to say about Elizabeth? *Elizabeth is like a horse looking for a race and trying to plough at the same time.* He likes Elizabeth. It would be easier if she were Jameson's daughter instead of his wife. Or maybe it wouldn't. He quivers at the thought of anyone reading this, but writes, *I love the old fart. A good man.*

He looks out the window. It's time to *do* something. He feels like a visitor.

⊰•——○——•⊱

She's reading a book when he comes down the stairs. Something fat, with a gauzy rose cover. *Far Pavilions*, it says. The old man nowhere about.

Sam looks at her bright, fox-like smile. She gets up and lays the book on a little table with graceful legs. Regency, that might be. From whose home?

"All right?" she says.

"All right." She goes into the kitchen. Sam picks up the book. Romance under the Raj. Blue mountains barred with snow. He puts the book down and follows her into the kitchen, the lightness in him like the swing of a pendulum.

Elizabeth's back in the brindled shawl looks hard-working and sensible. Winsome. The young woman tending her kitchen where he had embraced her husband in pools of rainwater. The good wife. Something pleads inside him.

"Don't screw Jameson around," he says.

"Shall we have a cup of tea?" she says. Blue-eyed face of innocence.

"Oh fuck!" he says, suddenly angry. Turned to him like that, one hand on the counter, the other half-held toward him, she's between him and the door. But he walks through her without thinking how, and on into the afternoon.

Marching up the hill his legs tell him they've already done their bit for the day. What the hell, the anger says. March on. What'd I have to do that for? What'd she have to do that for? "What's the use?" he says to a gnarled yew tree that looks like it's seen everything.

The long walk along the ridgecrest settles him. Nothing much is stirring after the storm. Over toward Dartmoor the wind has torn blue holes in the sky and fingers of sun kindle the brown tors. If she wants to be that way, he thinks. Looks after me. Looks after him, for all that. And he looks after her. His life not mine. His life not mine. Let it be a good one. What'll I do? Left, right. What'll I do?

Bring her flowers? Nossir! Play into her hands. Left, right. Never lose your temper on parade, mate. What'll I do to make it right? March on.

Going down past the graveyard, the airiness of possibility returns to him. Patches of light slide down the hillsides and over the town, pooling on bright buildings like stones in a stream. A place to live. Like the light at home in restless Pacific weather.

He feels as though he were marching in company. Charlotte and Hugh and Al at his shoulder.

Every time somebody dies I come to life, he thinks. And what do I do with it? Sweet F all. It's time to go home, he thinks, marching at the head of his ghosts into this home place in which he is a visitor. I ain't dead yet. Home to the uniform of a commissionaire? Why not.

He marches into town and drains a pint of good bitter at the Kingsbridge Inn. A tall woman in buff cape and jodhpurs boasts the merits of her stud to diminutive friends. She has a face like a horse and gorgeous walnut hair. His legs want to stay put forever but the rest of him wants to lift off and sail on, a barrage balloon bumping through narrow streets. To the railway station. The times of trains. The visitor gone home. The traveller.

He turns down Castle Street, past the bookseller's and Charlotte's cottage overlooking the valley. It's let to tourists. Outsiders. Grockles. In the clear, storm-scrubbed light he passes through the shadow of the castle founded by Normans and down the street so steep it has a handrail. A train wends its way through distant fields. Going to Cornwall, that other country. He could go to Cornwall, ancient wilderness at the edge of Britain, and drink with the ages in the Earl of St. Vincent, Egloshayle. Travelling on. He could return there like a shaggy great bird flown out of fir trees over the Rockies and the sea and walk the cliffs in conversation with jaegers and gulls.

Cornwall – old stone sofa grown over with gorse and sheep droppings – a place that isn't England. Cornishmen who have been there forever enough to welcome anyone who doesn't mind pissing in the dark on a windy night. A woolly race, hard as the stone, flint-smelling houses they inhabit in a land that bent whatever tools shaped Devon's round, English hills. And warm as the blood in their hearts' deep caverns.

But he wants the place where he belongs, maybe with Lily in it. Yes. His own thick-blooded wilderness where he's half as old as the town he lives in and the forests are full of time no one has counted yet.

Yeah, maybe that's why I went back, he says. A place where there hasn't been a war yet. He sees Fred's lugubrious face and wants to say, "All right, Fred." A place with his own people in it. All those goofy old farts having outlived one army or another, crawling out of bush camps and loading bays and chipper rooms and the rat-fucking Post Office with a pay cheque to blow on beer and a pension that barely keeps a roof over their heads. Trying, maybe, not to outlive each other. The bent-faced old guy who panhandles in a greatcoat winter and summer in front of Smitty's on Douglas Street and lives God knows where besides the public library. Guys like Al. And the kids. The young band of comrades out of arms, having had a great idea in the Sixties. Trying to learn how to get older. Asking him to write it all down. Hugh and Nancy, born into the difficult peace. The sunlight on the Inner Harbour.

He stands among people waiting for arrivals from London, feeling odd at the platform entrance, reading the schedule of trains. Like an Important Person. He has a ticket in his pocket that says London-Totnes Return. He could have supper at the Anne of Cleves and still get on the evening train. A person who doesn't belong here. He fingers Charlotte's scarf in his breast pocket. Whatever's at Jameson's could stay there. Clothes and the piss-ant journal. He could write for it. Always carry your passport. It's in his inside pocket. The air feels chill, now that he's no longer moving. He knots the scarf around his neck. The Penzance train rumbles into the station and squeals to stillness. Excited greetings, like a little tumult of gerbils. Whoever is going toward Penzance has no one to say goodbye. The trickling away on foot and in cars. The train thrums and slides on. A boy and girl with backpacks and Scandinavian accents bicker with the ticket agent. Do Not Leave Luggage Unattended says the sign on the ticket agent's wall. It might explode. He begins to feel like unattended luggage and follows the Scandinavians across the playing field into town.

A flock of schoolchildren run laps in soccer togs. Winsomeness. He sees scattered photographs yellow with time. The children that were. He sees them as all ages. Growing, blooming, withering, dying. He passes among them, their shrill voices and slender breath and sweaty fragrant flesh. An album of us all running laps through the generations in September Devon. The castle sits on the hill like a tarnished crown. Long before the Normans fortified the hill, people were learning how to live here. He feels a tug in him between the castle and the railway station. The staying and the going. His legs ache.

He detours from the Plains to look at Vire Island. The benches have been fixed. Most of them are empty. The tour boats sit across the river, looking ready for mothballs. The beer tables at the Seven Stars look out of season. It's time to go home. Enough travelling for now. It's September and Lily will be there. He takes a deep breath. Time to mend fence with Elizabeth. March back. Prepare a speech. Apologies and thanks. And Jameson. Farewell. And go home.

Up the street, gilt letters on a scarlet board say Montague Eliot • Antiquary. The man himself opens the door. Cunning. Rather beautiful he is in cream flannels and a pale grey shirt, with that absinthe look about him.

"Collister!" he hails. "What good luck. I've been looking to have a word with you. Have you a minute to step in?"

"Sure." A church-like place with the curves and patina of antique things seeming alive in the big window's soft light. Eliot goes to a writing desk glowing blond in the back corner. His feet make no noise. He opens a small drawer. Sam's eyes, not knowing quite what to do, light on a dresser with linen-fold corners like the one in his room in Orchard House.

Eliot appears at his elbow, a small maroon jewel box held out in his hand.

"I'd like to give you this," he says. "Found it in a rather fine portable secretary I picked up near Bodmin. I should think you've earned it, from what I hear."

Sam opens the box. Inside, the ribbon of the Victoria Cross rests on velvet. He stares.

"Eliot, what do you mean? I couldn't take this." He stretches it out at arm's length.

"Please do. I have no idea who it belongs to. There was no medal. And the piece itself had a chequered sort of history. Early Victorian, you know, but I couldn't trace an owner with any pretensions to the V.C. So I haven't known what to do with it, you see. Not the sort of thing one sells. And I couldn't think of anyone that should have it, until you happened along."

Sam is about to say "Jameson," and stops. Eliot meets his eyes. Cunning.

"It is in fact true, Sam, that this came to me by simple fortune. And I want you to have it."

Sam closes the box in his hand and holds it close to his ribs. "Thanks," he says, "I believe you mean that."

"I know we offended you." Eliot smiles. "Deaver and I." A very persuasive dissolute gentleman. "Truly, it must seem peculiar – Lizzie Jameson's mad gentleman callers. Half South Devon is whispering." The smile has gone. "She craves romance and intrigue. But that's all it is. You must believe that. We offer a diversion. Play the fool. A safety valve, if you will, for Elizabeth."

"It's not doing much for Jameson. You two hanging about her skirts and half the county talking."

"The man won't see what's before his eyes. There's no harm in Pluck and Cunning. No more than a pair of buskers doing a turn. And no disrespect intended."

I wish I knew you better, thinks Sam, looking at the worn handsome face and the years behind the dark eyes. But then I guess a lot of people wish that. He weighs the rough damask box in his fingers. Whatever this means, I'll bet it's more'n most people get out of you. He takes a breath. "Thanks, Eliot," he says. "I'm not going to try and tell you your business, but if you can figure a way to be easier on the old man, do it. Please."

Eliot holds out his hand and Sam takes it, feeling like his hand belongs to someone else, the Important Person of Totnes Station. A slim, hard, fleeting clasp.

"I was about to take a spin by the Table," says Eliot. "Can I give you a lift?"

Sam communes with his legs, which say Yes, yes. But he needs to make peace with Elizabeth and does not wish to arrive in company with Cunning. And there are things to do.

"Tell you what," he says, "could you drop me by the cemetery?"

"Surely."

Eliot's charger is a gleaming bone-white TD with sparkles of chrome and soft leather seats. He slings a long silk muffler about his neck before mounting. They swing out from the shadowy garage in a blare of throaty exhaust and fly up the sun-dappled reach of the High Street. Talk about romance. Sam looks for a cloud they might fly into, like the First War's Albert Ball, and never be seen again.

At the top of the hill he dismounts. His legs creak. The TD purrs and smells warm. Eliot's teeth shine. " 'Revoir," he says, and takes off again.

Sam walks down the lane and into the greeny plot of headstones sloping over the valley. The long light leans in from the west, from Cornwall and the sea. They'll just be rising in Victoria. Lily slipping silky membranes over her long body. The rain has tamed Lottie's grave. "This'll be goodbye, Charlotte," he says. "I think I've found out." Whatever that means. The castle, the playing field and the station. "You watch over it for me," he says. "For both of us."

From there he takes the Ashprington road, through the shadow of the silent Mount in a lane like a mountain defile. On the crest toward Ashprington he waits for a flock of sheep to be driven from one field to another. In their trail on the tarmac still moist-dark with rain, little blossoms of scarlet blood sure enough, and an open gate. A clear cold wind runs up his back under the skins of his clothes.

And the road rolls him down into Ashprington where waves of green billow over garden walls. A giant cherry tree stands in the roundabout of the village square. The half-timbered inn. Roses still in bloom. The village his mother should have died in.

I'll come back, he thinks, when it's spring. The blossoms of another time. As though the pages of a book were closing.

><+>-O-<+><

"You've been gone such a while!" Elizabeth chirps, sparkling. "Montague was by ages ago. I've made cakes, and we shall have duck tonight!"

"I came the long way," he says, standing there feeling knackered and high as a kite. "There were things I wanted to see. I wasn't sure you'd be talking to me."

She comes close, dancing eyes. "You're so strong," she says. "You men. You lifted me across the room as though I wasn't there."

So that's how it is. Fragrant Elizabeth in her fresh-baked umber kitchen. Play the little bunting on the bended branch.

"You should be careful reading things like *Far Pavilions*," he says. "Great stuff, but a bit soft-headed. You're no goose, Elizabeth."

"It's been good for John to have you here," she says. "For both of us. I'm sorry it had to be for such a sad reason."

"Thank you," he says. A speech. "I was afraid I might wear out my welcome." He looks out the window at the green and pleasant land, the garden wall. "It could be easy to stay forever. I think it's time for me to go before I start growing roots here in John's local history. I checked the trains. If I go tomorrow after lunch, I can try for a flight Friday morning."

"What a pity." She tilts her head to one side. "You'd best phone ahead. But tonight we shall feast on duck. Then you two men can repair to the study for cigars and brandy," she turns her eyes heavenward, "while I wear my smile to the bone on the wooden gentry."

Sam laughs.

⊱─━─◦━─⊰

The coals glow red and crumble under sated flame. Cigars and brandy.

They sit with their hands in their laps. Two old guys massaging their balls at the end of the day, thinks Sam. He grins.

"Got decorated today, John. Must be time to go!'

Jameson's eyes pop almost awake. "What's that?" Sam holds out the jewel box open on the magenta ribbon with the miniature cross fixed to its middle.

"Good heavens, man," says Jameson, taking the box as though it might break, "where did you stumble on this?"

"Montague Eliot gave it to me. More like *presented* it. Seemed to mean something by it, though I couldn't tell what exactly. Didn't know whether to shit, piss or wind my watch."

"I should say. Blackguard's shown me this. Didn't know what to do with it. Send it off to the War Museum, I said. Didn't want to do that, and I can't say I blame him. Gave it to you, did he? Presented it. P'raps he's not such a blackguard after all. Hard to tell with this young lot. Some fine iron in the man somewhere but Lord knows he hides it well enough. Should've been born fifty years earlier on. Might have done something then." He hands back the ribbon. "Keep that safe, old man. Whatever Eliot meant, you know what it means!"

"Yeah," says Sam. "You ever tell him anything about me? He made some crack

220

about how he heard I'd earned a gong."

Serious furrows wrinkle Jameson's brow. "Can't say I have," he says. "No, not likely. Elizabeth might. I've told her, you know, a bit. That action in Belgium. She likes to romance a bit, you know." Jameson looks uncomfortable.

"Sure," says Sam. Half a V.C. by irregular means for getting a hole shot in my foot and chewing out the brass. He snorts. Getting Hugh killed.

Jameson is regarding him with a sad sort of interest. "What was the outcome of that?" he asks. "You never have said, really. Took a machine gun in a barn, didn't you?"

Sam looks at him, feeling older than his older friend. "Yeah. They were all over us and I just went nuts with my lot. They were coming down, so we went up and took the hill. Like a fool I left my foot out for some German to shoot. Then we just sat there, me and Braithwaite and eighteen kids out of half a battalion that should never have been committed. Most of the rest of 'em never got outta the mud. What's there to say, John? First Army eventually caught on – they had all these panzer grenadiers tapping on their shoulder – and sent in some armour. Then a fucking red-tab captain wandered down from Corps to find out what happened. They were a bit embarrassed, those boys. Should never have sent us in there. I was in the middle of telling him what I thought about brass and ding-a-lings that order ya out when it's too late, when that bastard Braithwaite kicked me in the bad foot and explained I was a little worn out. He was the guy that had shell shock but I guess he had more sense than me. I was telling the Limey prick – sorry – that I refused an order under fire. Braithwaite tried to tell him I was a hero. I guess the guy figured the two things kinda cancelled each other out. So Al and I wound up in the hospital and never heard about it again."

Jameson breathes out as though he'd been holding his wind all night. "So," he says. "Command error. Either a court-martial or a decoration for you. D.C.M., most likely. Not a commissioned officer surviving to witness it. Bloody joke, war. I should keep that ribbon Eliot gave you, I daresay. Crime you can't wear it."

Sam's stomach hurts. He pours brandy into it to give the fire something to burn.

Jameson stands up and brings the decanter. "Something I shouldn't say, Sam, but I feel I must." He pours several fingers of the cedary old liquor into the snifter. "You say it's time to go. Back home, I take it." He puts down the decanter and stands looking at Sam, thumbs hooked in his vest like a solicitor. "I take it too that you've a fondness for Britain. A hankering, if you will. That this could be home for you."

"John," Sam says, "there's no way I could live here. I got a hard enough time making a living where I was born."

"That may be," he says. "But I must tell you you would be welcome here." He breathes. "I'm not a young man," he says. "Nor are you, but at our age ten years makes a damn sight more difference than it might do. I was never quite in the thick of it over there as you were. Too young for the first show, a bit long in the tooth for the second." Jameson looks at the ceiling as though it might be of interest. "Little as we've known one another, I can't say I could ask for a better friend than you, Sam." He looks down, eyes that always seem ready for tears or laughter. "Yes," he says. "Means a lot at my age. We have yet to hear the will. I had hoped you might stay for that. But as executor I am privy to things I should keep quiet. The thing is, Charlotte changed her will at the last moment and left you the bloody lot, near enough. And it's considerable. Frugal woman. Did well with her investments. Even after the damned succession duties you should net near a hundred a week. With the cottage on Castle Street and the flat in London, you wouldn't need more than that. I could always set you up in a bit of this or that, management you know or what have you, if a few perks were needed. An automobile here or there. You know."

John looks somewhat consumed. Sam pulls the blood and gold scarf from his pocket. It plays through his fingers almost by its own weight.

"What's that you've been wearing?" says Jameson.

"Charlotte's scarf. I picked it up in her room the day she died."

They look at each other. The coals make little tinkling sounds in Orchard House.

"What about it then?" says John. "You could stay. And welcome as the heart. She wanted it so. You've had a rough haul, but it's all coming your way in the end."

Sam sits there with his eyes wide open, sunk into Jameson's chair as though he were part of it, Jameson's brandy making vapours in his blood and in the glass wrapped around with Charlotte's heavy silk. His eyes wide open see nothing but ruddy light and Jameson's face. He hears his own blood in the large quiet night and his breathing like a slow sea.

"Thanks, John," he says. "You have no idea. Thanks, John." And sister Charlotte in her heart-dark grave on the hill. "But I want to go home."

GETTING HOME

STARING AT THE WALL

"IT'S LAST CALL," she says.

"Yeah," says Sam. Stares at his beer. Stares at the table like a ruined mirror. It's all on the table. The emptying room. Portraits of Victorian fathers on the wall. The brassy light. The last drinkers. Himself in it all, a haggard face on a heavy man like a propped sack about to fall. Sitting alone in a place where no one else is sitting alone.

This isn't good, he thinks.

The fat old whore who had tried to sit at his table. "You with him?" the bouncer had said. "I ain't with anybody," she said. And she was right. The bouncer had thrown her out for being drunk.

"You ain't interesting anyway," she'd said over her shoulder.

The fatman nearby who kept saying, Nice tits, nice tits, every time the girl waitress jiggled past. And if she didn't have a job she might've smiled at him. The vision of her slim hands groping under his billows of gut to try and make some hard meat.

Waking up in the morning with his cock in his hand saying, That's the root.

The money. If there will be any money. Of course there will be money. Charlotte's money. Blood money. A lawyers' game. After the plane ride, he'd sent Jameson a letter. Her properties should go to the Red Cross, he'd said. Could you get the legal beagles onto it? They'd all liked that. Forms had arrived. Charitable donations. Forgiveness of death duties. He'd had to ask Hicks for a beagle of his own. So there would be money. What will I do with it? Retire. He laughs and takes a drink of pissy beer. Live in a nice clean apartment someplace with other retireds. Stare out the window. Get royally pissed and wind up on a slab waiting for the furnace.

It's time to go. The lights have gone down again, but it's time to go. Cold out there. Marble moon in a blank sky. Swans on the black glinting water at Tuckenhay. We've been here before, Fred. Oh, have we been here before. Warm in here. Amber leaded glass of the lamps. Clean handsome faces of the young men rolling in after a day's work. The men who would die or would not die. The sons and the fathers. Some of them still here like him, flushed and fuzzed beyond sense in the dim mind of this place. It's time to go. But where? The empty cupboards of home. Like indigestion. He's sitting in a corner. His eyes slide sideways out the windows. This country looks too big and spread out, even in tawdry old Victoria. Too late for Fred. Fred hadn't been around much. "Mum's getting to be a full-time job," he said. Couple times a week in the Legion. At least he'd found a place and put her on the waiting list. "No more of these public bars," he said. "Can't take the fast life."

"You just don't wanna see it going by your nose," Sam said. "You gotta be careful, Whiteacre. You're letting yourself get old."

"You're only as old as you think you are, Collister. Look who's talking."

"You're only as old as you think you are but you've still lived as many years as you've lived and each day is one nearer the morgue."

"What's eating you, Sam? Sure, your sister died and a lot's happened to you since the summer. But the way you tell it, a lot of it was good. And you're going to have money coming in. You've no one to worry about but yourself. What's the beef? You know I hate saying it, Sam, but I've heard all this before and plain and simple you need to get out and do something that isn't getting pissed."

That was a speech and a half. "I need to get a job," he'd said. "Even when Charlotte's money does come through, I dunno if I want it. That's all happening in another country and it feels like it's happening to somebody else. How can I spend my dead sister's dough? Maybe I'll give it all to Hugh and Nancy."

"Oh bullshit! What about the Corps? I thought you were going to go and be a commissionaire."

"Fuck the bloody Corps," he'd said. "They'll have a job for me when I'm dead."

That immaculate dummy from the wax museum sitting behind his desk saying, "Can I help you, sir?" meaning, So you want to join the Corps. Those other grey-haired mannequins marching around in their chrome tinsel.

"I was in the army," he said. "I want to sign up."

The guy had looked him up and down. The sneer hadn't been quite visible. "You'll still have to have your references, sir. Upstanding character. Credit to the community. Medical exam. Fit for service. And we've got quite a waiting list, you know. The rate of attrition isn't very high and the economy's cautious these days, so there aren't many new positions opening up."

You fuckers live forever? "You telling me I should forget it?"

The wax man had shaken his head. "Not at all. Here are the forms. But all I can say is we'll put your application on file. Don't expect too much."

The application was still on file under the ashtray on the coffee table.

It had been like standing in the adjutant's office trying to find a way out. I was in the army. What does that mean?

"Drink up, sir," the bouncer says, picking up empties. The lights have gone bright again for the duration.

I went to a war. That's what it means. Write it down, they say. I went to a war. They said, Strip down, son. They said, Pack your kit. They said, Don't try to be a hero. King and country, they said, and handed you a rifle with which you learned to shoot the eyes out of any bull in sight. And they said, You're a leader. Take these men and keep 'em alive. Strip down a rifle. Strip down a Bren. Strip down. The proper forms are required.

The mosquitoes at Borden and aging farmers who loved a uniform to punch. The hippy kid in the Beaver. His dark earnest eyes and fire dancing in his wild hair. Write it down, man. You gotta write it down.

They had discussed fucking. The hippy said, *Man, your balls just feel like live jelly, then they go.*

A tall young guy leans boozily careful against the wall and cradles the pay phone like a tiny child under his chin. I wanna phone Lily, he thinks. Jesus. Live jelly. He rams his fist into his crotch under the table and breathes out through pursed lips.

After eleven o'clock. She might even be home. The boy who says I'm afraid she's not home might not answer the phone. Hello, she'd say. Lily, he'd say. Lily, where the fuck have you been?

The street feels like a plank that might tip under his feet. It is cold. October near gone and the Indian summer days sharpened to knife-edge nights. The boiler rooms on Battery will be cooling as the thermostat timer decides everyone has hit the sack. He could go to the Legion, which doesn't close till twelve, but the tippy street tells him he's a bit loaded for that. Wouldn't do. Mustn't look the burn-out. He could hit one of the strip bars that don't close till one. His balls tell him they couldn't stand a lot of naked pussy. Stubbs' will be closing. Sitting alone in the Beaver or the Strath, which sometimes doesn't close till everyone falls down, would be too much like going home. Which is more or less the direction his feet are going, down into James Bay. The James Bay Inn would be worse. He could go to Jack Frenette's. Jack won't be working late tonight. Jack might have some whisky. He finds himself walking down Menzies, which is a detour. But Jack's been having woman problems. Lily's place has lights on upstairs and down. He walks by on the other side of the street, veering. To go and knock on the door. To barge into whatever's going on. People brushing their teeth. Watching the news. And say, Here I am. Too outrageous. He keeps going, around the corner and down to Frenette's. There are no lights showing in the flimsy low-rent townhouse.

Sam follows his feet over to Government and along Battery.

Through the hole in the ragged hedge, windows of his rooms staring blindly into the moonlight. Jack Frenette is sitting on the steps. A round, bear-like hunch of a man, his glasses glinting, a bottle between his feet.

"Hi!" Frenette says, brittle. "Where've y'been?"

"Just went by your place. Thought you were in bed." Frenette laughs. Harsh. "Patty's got a headache. I brought a bottle."

"So I noticed." Sam looks at the ramshackle house. Frenette sounds like trouble.

"I got in a fight, Sam. I need to talk to somebody."

"This place is dead. Let's go down to the beach."

They go to the old place on the headland that had been a Stone Age camp. Eerie in the moonlight. Frenette swigs at the bottle, nervous and fidgety as a caged animal. A foreshore full of dead weapons and memories of the enemy. Like The Rumps in Cornwall. Our backs to the wall, thinks Sam. Our hands on the stones.

"This place gives me the creeps," says Frenette, passing the bottle.

Sam takes a long pull and feels suddenly too full of fire. "So what happened to you?" he says.

"A guy jumped me, outside the James Bay. I almost killed him." Frenette's voice quivers. Primeval hulks of the Olympic mountains glow across the glittering strait and disappear into the infinite dark of the Pacific. Sam takes more whisky and passes the bottle back.

"They want me to move snow for them, Sam. They know where I come from. They know I can do it."

"Snow?"

"Cocaine."

"That's crap! You've been clean ten years."

"I wanted to kill him."

"Well, maybe you should've."

"Don't you *understand*?" Frenette puts the bottle down. "Big fucker took a swing and I tripped him. Kicked him in the head in the gutter. Stomped his arm. Mighta broke it." Wildness in his eyes like bloodshot fire. "Look at my hands. *Look at my hands!*" He holds them out, shaking in the frigid air.

"Yeah. I understand." The dead men's faces. The madness that still lurks in him where the whisky burns.

"I've been out of that shitty scene ten years but it's still right there. Broken beer bottles and burning holes in your arm."

"Jack, it'll never go away," says Sam.

"I want it back. I've had it with looking after Patty and her problems. I've had it with the fucking food business. Sure I'm chef at the VI. They pay shit and I only got there by stabbing people in the back. I want out."

They're standing at the edge of the cliff. The dark ocean surges and foams over pale rock that looks like decaying flesh. "You need to relax," Sam says, and puts an arm around Jack's shoulders. Frenette springs away.

"Don't touch me, man! I'll hurt you. I'll hurt you bad."

Jesus. The fire tingles in Sam's limbs, hands poised to strike. Frenette plump but cat-quick and deadly. "Yeah, you would. But I'd break your neck." The sea on the rocks below them.

"Try me! Go on, try me."

"Shut up, you crazy asshole!"

They just stand there. Breeze icy on the skin. Frenette eases. Shrinks. Sobs. Sam moves and puts his arm around the thick shoulders, holds the tight sobs that sound like a man chipping away at granite. A man trying not to puke. "Let's find the bottle and someplace to sit down," he says.

⊷─◦─⊶

"When Hugh and Nancy finally get over here, maybe we can all go out and eat someplace where you don't have to cook."

"Yeah. I'd like to meet him. What's the word from Hugh anyhow?"

"Not much. They're pretty busy. Run off their feet working and playing, I guess."

"You sound like things haven't been so good."

"Since I got back from England I seem to have taken a nose-dive."

"Still no job?"

"Other than the Commissionaires, I ain't too long on ideas."

"I can get you on washing dishes again."

"No."

Frenette looks at the crystal mountains. "You used to cook, didn't you?"

"Yeah. But if you're thinking what I think you're thinking, thanks but no thanks. You told me too much about the restaurant racket in this town."

"Yeah, I did throw a lot of lobster at the walls when I was getting started. Fucking waiters."

"So you know you didn't get where you are just by stabbing people in the back."

⊷─◦─⊶

They walk up Menzies. The whisky swims bleakly in Sam. Gingerbread Maclure houses and stucco apartment blocks loom and recede as though he were looking through a fish-eye lens. They stop outside Frenette's tatty front yard, the two of them like what's left standing after a war.

"You'll be okay," Sam says, hand on Frenette's shoulder. "You got a lotta guts."

"Thanks, Sam," Frenette says and whacks him in the bicep. "At least you know what it's like when people are trying to kill you."

Sam stands in the mercury vapour light. Frenette goes inside. Flimsy sound of the townhouse door closing. The windows shiver upstairs and down. The sound of a toy house for shelter. He sways.

The street sings to him. It flickers as though his eyes were signal lamps. Ancient men gather in a stone room centred with fire. Their tracks become streets and the streets become cities. Many places of many people wrapped all together by their blood and memory and need to be in a place not too cold nor wet nor empty. Shaped by our fathers' fathers' hands to shelter us. And it's not enough.

Anger boils in him. The old soldier's life, his freight and weapons oiled too long ago, tumbles into his guts. *Who's the enemy?* His lungs suck air. I'm being asked, he thinks. Not Lenin's ghost like mist from the sea to answer the people's need. Not the Red Army marching up Douglas Street. *What foe?* he hears. *What weapons? What air now for the sucking in of our lungs? We are nothing now. A rabble of lonely men. Whom can we call the enemy?* Nothing but this, the weapons as worn and ready as stones boiling out of his guts. "Lord," he says. "Lord. Something else."

I'm praying, he thinks.

Lord, let us come up. In this space which is too small because we have made it so, we have let ourselves forget our fathers' hands who poured this human stone into the ground for the smoothness of our going over it. Let us come up. It is not enough to have these things, the names of God – wood and plastic and stone – to have wires through the night for force and light and warmth. Without gods. Without the beast and the tree, the things that died to be oil and coal. Without our hands on something that trembles and says, "You too, brother. You too. Be afraid." Rise up. Rise up, Lord. The spit, the tree we nail this prayer to. The sea we crawled from. The finger dredged from mud. Saying. "Adam." Say "Adam." Call us. Call us the sea. Our desires are fish in bottles waiting to be eaten.

The lights are out at Lily's place. The lights are out every place except at the tops of the poles in the street. Their blue glare bounces off glass as though the night were inside windows, watching with baleful eyes. He sits on the curb with his feet in the gutter. A dog. It circles him on clicking paws, head low and sideways.

"Give me!" he says to the dog. The dog growls back. In the street he sweeps out his arm as though it held a bone to crush the dog's teeth. Orange-furred in the streetlight the dog snaps, snarls, and wonders.

What do I dare? Sam thinks. For the dog he thinks – What do I dare? And sits in the street. Two A.M. Or three. Somewhen. What would The Man think if he came on me here? The dog wonders. Sam considers his feet, wrapped in pieces of cowhide, sitting there for anyone to see on the pavement. Blocks of wood.

"Dog!" he says. And the dog considers. On Menzies Street in the purple streetlight. He stares into the dog's nose, all that black sparkling leather, and rubs its ribs under coppery fur.

"You get in here!" Jesus. A woman on the stairs. Behind the dog. Behind the patch of grass behind the dog. The stairs of a clapboard house on Menzies Street.

The dog's woman. At this time of day.

"You get in here!"

And the dog does. At this time of day. A shapeless woman in a dress or something. Faithless dog. On Menzies Street across from the Safeway.

To call her a rotten bitch.

Sam climbs to his feet, one hand pushing off the sidewalk, the other pulling at the air. He swings around toward Lily's door. To walk through that door, smash through its glass panels and up the stairs through another door to drag her out of bed with whoever she's in bed with and call her a rotten bitch. To rest in the bosom of Abraham.

⊷─◦─◦─⊶

In the dark air he smells a panzer and wonders why he would smell it before he heard it. Was I sleeping? He sees the cars parked on Battery Street and stumbles through them. The sloppy hedge down there means home.

⊷─◦─◦─⊶

Clamped tight like a clam in the mud he huddles in the dark inside his head and listens to the sky explode. The thing about the airbursts, he thinks, like a man neither sleeping nor waking, is that they are loud. Very loud. Hard, sharp and loud, butcher's knives blown bang out of a bag, God's cleavers on the block, the blood of the lamb slapped in your face with bits of bone and brain. My boys! he thinks, and clambers out of the mud onto his feet and out into the hall, his fists bunched up in the air looking for gunners to hit, looking for citizens with white faces and editorial writers and filling his lungs with a great noise ready to burst, when he sees the carpet patterned in yellow, red and black and the silent varnished doors in 60-watt light. He remembers the sound of steel falling like ice onto frozen ground in the silence, and he goes back inside. It's worse now, he thinks. God help us, it's worse now. Jean's pale face in her doorway. Stone deaf, but she can feel the floor quake.

He sits in the dark on the edge of his bed. He sees himself sitting there. He feels like someone else, his gut resting on his thighs as he leans into the carpet smell, wondering how he got away from himself

Tomorrow, he thinks, I'll be me again.

⊷─◦─◦─⊶

When he opens his eyes, the brownish yellow light inside his head is in the room. Wallpaper looking like old grease. The light of a hurtfully clear day slants through windows pale blue with stale smoke. Beyond the bedrail and the cracked yellow wood-stain on the window sash, he can see the sun on the birchtops in Mrs. Simpson's yard. Jumble of books and newspapers everywhere. The television looking very dead. To get that fixed. An open tin of Vogue tobacco on the coffee table by the bed, surrounded by mossy shreds of weed. Spilled ash. Butts fallen from the ashtray. A half-rolled smoke.

Jeez. He feels like he's been poured full of lead. Every time his heart works, he can feel it shove against the inside of his temples. The thick air drifts over him and his eyeballs roll into his head.

He wakes up with his cock in his hand. That's the root, he says. He imagines Lily sitting on his thighs, her head tilted to one side, looking at him. He can see right through her to the blue sky behind the birch trees. He squeezes the thing in his hand like the bulb on a pump. It uncurls like warm lead. Couldn't poke a jar of jam with that.

Better eat something before my stomach wakes up, he thinks. Nothing in the house. Didn't get groceries. Stupid asshole. He sits up and waits for things to settle. Stocking feet on the floor. Got my shoes off anyhow, he thinks. The two of them like capsized boats on the rug. No Hugh to take off his socks. Jack Frenette. He shudders. Chef among the druggies. Goddam kids with battle fatigue in the glitz and glitter.

He walks over the gritty rug and into the sticky kitchen to turn on the stove. Gotta clean this place up, he thinks. He almost misses the chair when he sits down. He waits for the water to boil, getting his head organized for the next step. The smell of gas. Goddamn! He lurches up and strikes a match at it. The big soft swoosh of flame takes hair off the back of his hand. The smell wakes his stomach like a gentle kick to remind him what horrors lie buried there.

He drinks the instant coffee and gnaws a hard corner of cheese from the fridge. The bread has mould on it and the heel of milk has gone off so he drinks the coffee black and munches stale crackers. This is fucking stupid. He thinks of a restaurant. Bacon and eggs, veal cutlets or a cheap steak. But he doesn't trust his stomach for that. Not even the Melos with its delicate squid and that gorgeous woman for a hostess. And he can't afford ten bucks for lunch. I gotta go out there and buy food. He squints at the day among the peaked roofs of James Bay. Spaghetti, he thinks. Meat sauce with bay leaves and Romano cheese. Noodles not too soft and some green salad. His mouth waters but his stomach clanks like an old tin can. Shaddap, stomach, he says, you'll love it.

>+◆>-O-◆+◄

With oil heating in a huge skillet, he opens a bag and sniffs the vapours of grated Romano. He begins to feel better. Onions into the oil. Oregano and the bay leaves. Crushed garlic. Beatification up the nose.

He eats the spaghetti and the salad with garlic bread and two glasses of milk. He feels much better until he realizes there isn't any beer to chase it. And there's nothing to do but wash the dishes. He can't even offer to feed poor Jean next door by way of apology for scaring her awake last night. She's at work. Deaf and dumb though she is. Why won't that woman phone? I could clean this place up, he thinks. And has a cup of coffee instead. The kid says, I'm sorry, she's not home. The secretary in the Ministry says, I'm sorry she's in a meeting. Can she call you back? I dunno. If she can, how come she hasn't? When, he says. I'm afraid I can't say, sir. Neither can anybody else, goddammit. He'd only tried about three times, but that had seemed like enough.

He looks at the Widow Simpson's back yard. What have I been doing? he thinks. A few things. Phoning Lily. The sainted bloody Corps. Letter to Hugh. Lawyers. Six weeks, about, since I came back thinking it was all gonna be okay. Chopping wood. When was I chopping wood in Widda Simp's back yard? He gets his journal from the little table he uses for a desk. It says things like *Oct. 8. Went for a drink with Fred.* When was I chopping wood? I must have been chopping wood.

Across the street an old man in a white shirt and tie looks out a window. He looks like he's been doing it for a long time. With a tie on. When you're old or poor, every day is Sunday.

It's the waiting, he thinks. It's always the waiting that gets you. Waiting to move up. Waiting to stand down. Waiting for the pigeonholes in the P.O. to fill up and stay that way. Waiting for the woman who's always coming and never arrives. He looks at the yellowing paper on his wall. It's like me, he thinks, looking at his hands, looking at the wall as though it were a mirror.

Waiting for someone to call, for someone to arrive.

No one will call. No one will arrive.

Knowing that as a reality, the way one knows that things exist. Rocks and trees and buildings. This house on Battery Street. The table in it. The man on the bed. The whole catalogue of things.

Knowing that this room is empty save for the man in it. Knowing that this room is empty. In the morning it will be the same, even if he isn't here.

There are pictures on the dresser – a man and woman dressed for marriage, on the steps of Father Kilty's Holy Trinity at 25th and Lonsdale. I looked like such an ass when I was young, he thinks. Pretty Dot, looking old-fashioned and plump. The hair and clothes.

Flanking Sam and Dot, Belle and Harry. Oval, wistful photographs that make his parents seem like characters from *Lost Horizon*. Photographs not quite so yellow as the wallpaper. On a day like this somewhere in the sea of years he had dragged boxes out of the closet and retrieved his family. Not Hugh. He had no pictures of Hugh. Either Hugh.

So there they are among the other people who live on his dresser top, fading shadows suspended in small fragments of time sliding already over the edge of living memory. People he had never known, photographs he'd found in a junk shop one day before he got desperate enough to go for the boxes. They look like everyone else. They are everyone else, the human race on Sam Collister's dresser in Victoria, B.C. Just like any other old turkey living in two rooms on Battery Street, staring at the faces of the past. Staring at the wall.

I could go to the bar, he thinks. The James Bay. A place like an aging floozy who'd never had the sense to really turn pro. A succession of wrong men and cigarette burns on the furniture instead of a life. A place full of women like that. And guys who don't know the difference between women and any other kind of trouble.

He could call Frenette, who's probably at work and doesn't need to be reminded.

He could phone Fred. It's getting late enough he might even be home, since his mum's still there. He could pad out into the hall in his stocking feet and listen to his dime go bing in the phone and complain to Fred.

He could call Lily, but she wouldn't be there. She would have found someone else to buy her margaritas.

There are lots of things he could do.

Later on he could go for a walk down the beach and get scared by the dark sea curling white up around the rocks that look like lumps of old human flesh. That would chase him home relieved and he could write something in his blessed journal and go to sleep.

The hostess from Melos could come up and offer him a blow-job. Then he wouldn't have to do anything. He remembers her razor-cut bank of reddish hair shimmering in candlelight, her fine elegant bones. The tank of tropical fish.

After she'd done him with her mouth, she could go spit in the sink and he'd go up behind her and run his finger up and down her buttery snatch and she'd come right there in the kitchen, those strong auburn-furred lips grabbing at him like a hungry clam and her feet making sticking noises on the tacky lino floor. Among the beertops and yesterday's dishes.

The ashtray overflowing on the table by the bed. Fallen stacks of newspapers. Books with ash on them.

Read a book, Sam.

He stares at the wall.

He could go to bed and jack off His stomach tightens and feels cold. There's been enough of that. He wants Lily to knock on his door and come in and be quiet and look back at him for a long time. He wants her and him then to take off each other's clothes and sleep together until morning fills up the room with light and there are stories to tell over dishes and eggs and toast about where they have been in the night.

He gets up and takes off his clothes. He looks at his hands and his feet and his cock hanging there like something that needs to be fixed. He looks at the sagging yellow paper on the wall and sees the belly of an old man.

When we look at ourselves, he thinks, we see parts that could belong to anyone. That belong to someone else. That are not anyone. Drawings of hands and feet. Skin. It's hard to believe that anyone lives there.

He could go out into the hall to the john without his clothes on and terrify deaf-mute Jean next door, if she happened on him, coming home from work.

He hears a woman's voice downstairs. There are people in this house. But not in this room.

He puts on his clothes and opens the door. Maybe that's why we do this, he thinks. To remember who we are.

⊱—◈—○—◈—⊰

The air is sharp with autumn smoke in the slow grey light. A flat broad fan of clouds sliding in from the west. Piles of leaves smoulder in the gutters. Fires burn, they do. The day settles down; settles in; becomes another possibility gone certain. Briskly homeward people dot the sidewalks, solitary pieces of a single purpose. They glance at him like passing mirrors: a large older guy in a sports jacket looking like he's going somewhere.

Two months ago I thought I knew where I was going. He remembers the storm-whipped sea of Devon hills and Jameson's face in ruddy light. Well, I better get on with it.

He passes a phone booth that works on him like a magnet. He stops and goes back to it. He listens to its silence. He puts a hand on its chill plastic. Condensation mists the phone. Hello, she says in his mind's ear. Sam! Her face like a lamp out there in the thickening air at the phonewire's end. It's been so long. How about a margarita? Since we went sailing.

⊱—◈—○—◈—⊰

When he goes through the narrow foyer into the warm light of the Legion, he sees the back of Fred's grey head and his broad shoulders in a green squall jacket. The place is mostly empty. Old Harold in his settle by the bar, not making a speech. The young Fraternal named Purvis. The fire. Jock not pissed yet with a couple of other ex-soccer types. Frank playing chess by himself. Three Korean vets throwing darts with their girlfriends. A little group of young ones he doesn't know. Ray Frye's hundred plaques gleaming on the walls. More like two hundred by now.

"Well, you sot," he says, coming up behind Fred, "why aren't you home looking after your mother?"

Fred regards him with a baleful eye. "Fucking layabout. Do something useful and bring me a beer."

Sam bellies up and considers the price of Whitbread's. Lanny the bartender looks at him. Lanny is non-service, a veteran of hotels, professionally cheerful. "Hi, Sam," he says. "Been seeing you more often lately."

"Yeah," says Sam. "How about two Export." Lanny bends over into the coldlockers, whips out the bottles and pops them. "How's your new place?" says Sam.

"Oh, getting settled in, getting settled in. I don't think I want to move again for a while. Every time I go to unpack something I either can't find it or it's broken. Stereo worked fine when I plugged it in and now it won't do a thing. You coming to the dance tomorrow?"

"Dance?" says Sam, waiting for his change.

"Sure. The poster's on the wall. Baron of beef buffet and Zoe on the piano. Shouldn't miss it."

Sam looks at the wall. There are poppies pinned to it. *Have You Got Yours Yet?* Getting warmed up to remember.

Sam slips fifty cents back into Lanny's hand. "Thanks, Sam," he says.

"Well," says Fred, "how's life," as Sam plunks the bottles on the table and himself into a chair. It's a statement.

"Yeah," says Sam. "Like that. How's your mum's waiting list?" He pours the beer into the glass in his hand and bites off a mouthful of head.

"Still waiting."

They look at each other for a while.

"Find any lamb kidneys yet, Harold?" Sam hollers in the direction of the settle.

"What's that?" comes Harold's huge voice, like an oak barrel speaking.

"Lamb kidneys!" says Sam.

"Oh yes," says Harold. "Fine things, lamb kidneys. Pity there are none to buy."

"Saw some over in Fletcher's today. Fresh for eighty-nine a pound."

"Oh yes. What's that you say?"

"Fletcher's Meats has lamb kidneys," Sam shouts.

"Very good," says Harold. "Very good."

"Should I go get ya some tomorrow?"

Harold's face looks magnificently perplexed. A man should be able to hear, thinks Sam. See and hear and walk. Especially a man like that. D.C.M. and bar and God knows what else for things like finding the German Army where no one expected it at Second Somme. Over the hill and far away. Sergeant of Signals made like an ancient short broad oak tree out of Derbyshire.

Lanny leans over the bar and explains into Harold's ear what Sam had tried to say.

A man-eating grin splits Harold's wide serious face. "Well done, my boy, well done," he says, "thank you. But I'll have my granddaughter go 'round." Harold sits and thinks a moment. Sam and Fred look at each other. "Here he goes," says Fred. "Let him," says Sam. "True enough," says Fred.

The large wheels in motion behind Harold's solid front arrive someplace. He reaches out with both hands to the table in front of him and hauls himself to his feet like a squat crippled giant.

"It's important," he declares to the room in that voice that rumbles through walls, "it's important to remember these things." Everyone who's paying any attention at all looks to wonder if Harold will remember. He pauses and flexes the muscles of his jaw. "When I was a lad herding chickens in Derbyshire," he says, "each night we would go in from our work and give thanks for the day that had been and the food we were about to receive." He smiles around, eyes crinkling. "And good grub it was too." He draws breath and raises his glass, one hand propped on the table to help his legs. "We must give thanks to the men who are generous of heart and remember an old man's kidneys!" He drinks.

"Hear, hear," says Jock. "Is he always like this?" says a voice from the young table.

Sam hoists his beer. "Here's to ya, Harold," he shouts, "God bless!" Harold smiles around like the rock of ages on a good day, and sits carefully down.

"Well," says Fred, a celtic kind of slyness about his eyes, "you find work yet?"

"Not a damn thing."

"No word from the Corps?"

"I never did turn in the application."

Fred shakes his head. "You silly bastard," he says. "I didn't think you wanted it in the first place."

"But I got to do something, Fred. I owe money. I owe you, I owe Hicks. I even owe Frenette some. Maybe I oughta try and latch on as a rent-a-cop or a night watchman or something. You know of anyplace needs watching?"

Fred makes a noise like a horse blowing. "Maybe," he says. "But as long as you keep acting like you're headed for the morgue there isn't much point. Do you want to walk around all night packing a clock?"

"You got any ideas?" Fred stares at him. Silly fucker.

Frank contemplates the chessboard, one long hand poised over a pawn, the other propped against his temple. That man has a gentle face, thinks Sam. He sees it sighting along a rifle before the lines turned to wrinkles. Purvis is on about the Forbidden Plateau again.

"The thing is, Sam, you're going to have that inheritance coming sooner or later and you might as well get used to the idea. What you need to figure out is what you want to do. If you don't think up something that'll keep you interested, you'll end up more bored and mad than you are now."

"Fred, you're getting serious again."

Fred's eyebrows go up and he shrugs. "Who knows?" he says. "Something might come up. Why not get a job in this place? Hear they're looking for a barman."

"You crazy?"

"Well, look at me. At least I got up the nerve to put Mum on a waiting list."

One of the young ones crosses the room to the Women's. She has boot heels, tight jeans, and a tight sweater. Her beautiful blue-eyed face looks like you could use it to cut slate. He sees Lily's white trousers and soft green blouse. The forever behind her eyes.

Might as well admit it. "This sounds stupid," he says, "but what I want is a woman."

"I wouldn't mind one myself," says Fred.

"That woman," says Sam. "Lily."

"Well, I'm afraid I can't help you there," says Fred, who hadn't even seen her.

I'm in love, says Sam to himself. As though he were rehearsing. Lily, what's a sixty-year-old guy doing in love?

"How's Braithwaite?" says Fred. "You haven't said anything about him since you got back."

"Haven't heard. He's probably feeding worms by now. Or more likely sitting in an urn on Celeste's kitchen table."

Hicks comes in, dapper as a colonel. The portrait of Pepper Graham looks out from above the fire, seeing over all their heads, further than the bridge on the Sangro he'd won with his life before the Germans could blow it.

"I should forget her," says Sam.

"Not bloody likely," says Fred, "knowing you. What you should do is do something about it. Either she's a fool or you are. And I don't know her." He empties his glass.

Hicks comes over with his drink in his hand. "Am I welcome at this table?" he says. "I want a word with you, Sam."

"I was just leaving," says Fred, pushing himself out of his chair.

"Stay and have another," says Hicks.

"No," says Fred, "I'm off home. Cheer this lug up, if you can stand him."

"Siddown, Dave," says Sam, "you make a guy feel like he should stand up and salute, which sergeants do not do for corporals. Whiteacre here's going off to practise some more."

"Practise what?" says Fred.

"Playing padre." He ducks as Fred takes a swipe at him. Hicks sits, a leathery smile creasing his face below the gold-rimmed glasses. "I'm glad you're friends," he says, "or you might wreck the joint and I'd have to ask those retired athletes to throw you out."

"Is that loan getting antsy, Dave? Is that what you wanna talk about?"

"No, Sam, that loan could perish for all I care. I want to talk to you about this lounge." He looks around the room. The pony in tight clothes has sat down again. The number of people at that table has doubled. They'll be singing in an hour.

"Looks like it's doing pretty good," says Sam. "We haven't had this many young ones in a while."

"Have you ever tended bar, Sam?"

"Well no, not in a professional kind of way. Had a lot of mixing experience, though." He grins.

"I'm supposed to be chairman of the lounge committee, and we need a new barman. We're losing Ted Earle."

"What's wrong with Ted?"

"Nothing a good knock on the head wouldn't cure, but he's decided he wants to retire."

"You want me to be a bartender? There's lotsa people out there better qualified than me. Like Lanny, for instance."

"We have a problem," says Hicks. "In case you haven't noticed. We need someone who can get along with the younger members as well as the older ones. Someone people will listen to – the people that work here as well as the people that get out of line now and then. Lanny does fine managing the bar, but we've been having a lot of staff turnover lately and managing people is something else. We want a member back there. I've asked around and your name keeps coming up. We need someone like Ted, someone like you. It's only part-time, so it won't cramp your style, but it'll cover your overhead and then some. This outfit needs a sergeant, Collister, and I think you're it."

Sam looks at him. He feels like muscles that have been at attention too long are standing easy. "Thanks, Dave," he says, "that's a fine offer."

"Think it over," says Hicks. "No hurry. You could start whenever you want."

▷·◁▷·◦·◁▷·◁

Collister regards fires. From these there is no escape. The lives of men resemble fires. The collocation of lives into inferno. Burning leaves glow at the edges of the street. Their smoke spreads into the air like wash from a broad brush. The night is cold and salt and acrid, like exhalations of a burning sea. He marches at the head of a column of ghosts. Their equipment clinks in his ears. What a way to be lonely. Tending bar in the Legion.

Out the boomerang bend of the breakwater the sea slides like oil against the granite blocks. The beacon flashes. Lights in the cabins of a dark-hulled ship in the dock, ghostly voices and the clang of an iron door. Lights of a fishboat trundling out into the night. Port Angeles glows in the darker mass of the peninsula across the strait. The sound of his own feet marches over the surge and slack of the swell.

In the moments of light like fireglow under the beacon's swivelling beam, he sees large red scrawl across the lighthouse wall: *John Doe is a threat to civilization.* He grins. The longer moments of dark. He stands there at the tip of the finger in the cold night sea. He can feel the sea through his feet and his breathing swell to meet it.

><+>-0-<+><

"Yes?" she says in his ear in the phone booth. She sounds like she's expecting something to go wrong. "Hello?" she says. The weird guys that call. Her voice resonates in him like a warming of the blood.

"Lily," he says.

He waits. She isn't even breathing. "I thought I'd know what to say," she says. "I thought of so many things to say. Where have you been?"

"I been around."

He waits again. He can hear Lanny say, Coming to the dance tomorrow? and grabs at it. "You wanna come to a dinner and dance at the Pro Patria tomorrow?"

The slightest pause. "I'll be there," she says. "I'll pick ya up about five-thirty."

"No, you won't."

"Lily! What the hell?"

"I'll be there," she says. And hangs up.

xxi

LILY

THE WRACK OF a wintry day clears. Windrows of leaves like fallen men in the grass. Lord God of our fathers, be with us yet. We're still here.

He clears up piles of magazines. The dishes are done. I should wash the floor and vacuum the rug, he thinks. But she won't be coming here. Not a place to bring a lady. Abrupt and strange on the phone. The bitch. Months of nothing, and now this. As though she'd been summonsed to court. The first woman since Dot in '43 that he'd felt at home with. The pigeons of Ladbroke Grove. The first woman. But she will come to the dance. She said she'd be there. When's the last time I danced? What if she doesn't show up. He stuffs a handful of murder mysteries into the bookshelf. Murray Peden's *A Thousand Shall Fall* on the floor. He looks at the cover, a Stirling at the moment of lift-off, the moment when a twitch in the machine or the man would drop her back to earth with a bellyful of bombs. Crazy bastard. Ya done good, Peden, writing something like that thirty years after it was all over. He finds a place for it shoved sideways on top of the paperbacks. Should get that back to the library.

He wipes down the coffee table and replaces the ashtray he'd washed with the dishes. The phone rings.

Jesus. He hurries into the hall, thinking it might stop. Would she call to cancel? Would she call to apologize for hanging up on him?

"Hi," says Hugh.

"Hugh," he says.

"How's it goin', Sam? Sorry we haven't been in touch. But I had to come over on business and Nancy figured we should make a weekend of it and here we are in the Empress."

"Exhibition hockey's been over more'n a month."

"What the hell, there must be something else to do in this town."

"You got the honeymoon suite?"

Hugh laughs. "Sure thing. We're up in one of these garret rooms. Used to be where they kept the chambermaids or something. Romantic as hell. Great view."

Sam's mind begins moving again and whirls in confusion. "What'd ya have in mind?"

"Well, we thought maybe we could see you for dinner tonight. We're tied up this afternoon, and tomorrow night we have to go back."

"Oh." Sure. What the hell kind of crazy world is this? "Something wrong?"

"No, just kinda slow this morning." Slow, hell. Whatever's going on inside his head feels like pieces might start flying off.

"Look," he says, "I already got a date for tonight – remember that woman I told you about, Lily?"

"Yeah. Nancy talks about her all the time. Women are funny like that. We'd love to meet her."

"That's what I was gonna say. We're going to the Legion dance. If you don't mind a lot of old bozos like me, you could come along. There'll be some young ones too. We got new blood coming in."

"Sure. You and the Legion? Thought you hated the place." "Well, maybe I'm getting smarter in my old age. They start serving baron of beef about six. It'll be on me. It's cheap." "Great. How do we find it?"

"It's a block up the hill on that street that runs up from the door of the Beaver. Turn right. Ya can't miss it."

"That sounds easy. Can we give you and Lily a lift?" "Naw," he says, "it's a small town. See ya at six."

"Okay, Sam. Nancy says to give you a kiss."

"Yeah, she's a little kinky. Give her one back."

He hangs up and stares at the face of the pay phone. You weird fucker, he tells it. Something feels like it's squeezing the nerves behind his eyes. Little stars rise through his vision like bubbles in a glass. The whole lot of them at once. Hugh and Nancy and that woman a few streets away being strange – all having dinner with him down in the Legion hall and dancing to Vera Lynn songs.

He goes back into his rooms. His hands chase each other around like nervous crabs looking for a cigarette. I better go down there and have a beer and think this thing through. Have a look at the football game. Check on the baron of beef. Try to imagine how it's all going to be.

⊱─◈─◈─◈─⊰

When he comes back in the door on Battery Street he isn't thinking. Thinking seems dangerous. He thinks of food. Something simple and savoury to put on top of the beer and keep things quiet until dinner time. A fried egg sandwich with mayonnaise and mustard and Italian herbs. We won't think about dinner time. The mail on the table in the entrance hall. Haven't looked at the mail for a couple of days. No cheques. Nothing from England. Other people's bills. In the back, having been there a while, half buried in junk mail, an envelope addressed S. Collister in a scrawly hand.

He picks it up. Return address nearly legible on the back. Twelfth Avenue,

Vancouver. What the hell.

As he mounts the creaky stairs, he rips the envelope open with his finger. A single sheet inside, folded crooked and crunched around the corners. He unlocks the door to his rooms.

Sam, the letter says in the same spidery blue scrawl. He hears a dry, croaking voice. *You asshole I get run over by a freight train and you can't bother showing up.* It's signed *Al.*

Sam looks at his face in the mirror. It's grinning. "All right!" he shouts, and punches the air where his mirrored midriff would be. "We ain't dead yet!" Crazy old fart with his broken hands over there. So Celeste hadn't told him. Or Celeste had told him and he'd forgot.

Sam sits down at his writing table and scratches out, "Braithwaite, you silly fucker. Hell yes, I was there to see what kind of pussy you had shoving tubes up your dick, but you was too rarefied to notice. Pinch Celeste's bum, if you're able. She was there too."

He puts it in an envelope and sticks his second-last stamp on it. He looks out the window at the birch trees and the clear yellow light beginning to ease down to evening. He listens to his breathing. His shout still seems to echo in the silence. We ain't dead yet. A peculiar urge wanders up the inside of his blood. He takes more paper.

"Dot," he writes, "I'm still here. You were right about Charlotte.

"I can't say it was great seeing you and Sid, but thanks. If I hadn't been there when Lottie died, I don't think anything would ever have made sense.

"I'm glad you're sort of okay. I'm seeing Hugh and Nancy for supper tonight. He's a good kid, not much thanks to me.

"But I think maybe I'm going to be okay too. There's a pretty good job I'll probably take. Maybe I can finally be some kind of father to the kid."

He chews the end of the pen. Whatever happens with Lily. "I still fall off the wagon now and then, but I'm not going to end up a pisstank.

"Take care of yourself. Thanks again. Sam."

He looks at it. Maybe I just told myself something.

With the envelope done and stuffed and sealed in his hands, he looks at it again. So that's what the last stamp was for. Good old Braithwaite.

He breathes deep and lets it out. Now I better get the decent clothes on and get this over with.

━━◆━○━◆━━

He gets a beer and a table that's near enough the dance floor and has a view of the fire. People begin lining up for the beef being carved by a big bald old carver named Arthur who has worn his Hawaiian shirt hanging out of his pants to carve every baron of beef in living memory. He looks like a grinning Hollywood eunuch with his snickersnee out of some Turkish romance. Sam discovers that his heels have been tapping under the table to music nobody's playing yet. His stomach feels tight and acid. Shoulda had that sandwich.

He gets up and goes outside. It's mostly dark. A purply sky with big handsome clouds in it, stars poking through in the blue-black east. People are still straggling in. There'll be another wave later, when the music starts. "Hi, Sam," some of them say. He lights a smoke. The breeze nips at him and he fingers Charlotte's scarf at his throat.

Two cigarettes later he sees them coming. They don't know they're coming together, but they are, Hugh and Nancy with Lily a few steps behind, her easy stride in their brisk wake. His insides feel like air and his outsides feel numb.

"Sorry we're late, Sam," calls Hugh.

"S'okay," he says.

Hugh stretches out a hand. Nancy grins. "Where's Lily?" she says.

"Right behind you."

Lily comes up and looks at him as though she had been doing it for some time. She's wearing a slim green velour dress, belted at the waist, and green suede pumps with a bit of heel. She extends a hand from under the shawl wrapped around her shoulders. Her wrist has a silver loop around it. "Hello, Sam," she says.

Her fingers are lean and cool and noncommittal in his hand. "Oh," says Nancy.

"Lily," he says, "this is Hugh and his girlfriend Nancy."

She smiles at them. The lamp. Warm in the night under the Legion's entry lights. "I'm glad to meet you," she says.

"Hi, Sam," says Nancy, taking his hand. She tippy-toes to kiss him on the mouth and looks at Lily, pointedly. "Well?" she says. *You're the one that's supposed to be kissing him.*

"Let's get outta this air," says Sam.

Hugh takes them all in like a camera panning and shakes his head. He holds the door open and says to Lily as she passes, "We've been looking forward to meeting you," with a touch of firmness that gladdens Sam. The kid is not acting sour this time. "So have I," says Lily.

Nancy has on a creamy skirt and a black jacket buttoned to her brown neck. Her dark eyes rest on Sam a moment before she follows Lily, and her shoulders do something that looks like a raven shrugging its wings. "It's very good to see you again," she says, and touches his arm in passing.

As they settle into the table Lily sloughs off her soft wool shawl and drapes it over the chair. "I'll hang that up for you," says Sam, reaching. "I'm fine," she says. Nancy unbuttons her jacket and twists to hook it behind her, the statuesque top half of her like living marble.

My God, thinks Sam. That one on his right, Lily across from him in dark folds of green, the sea incarnate. The green hills. An oblong silver brooch simple between them. He can see nipples. Breasts just there. Her eyes smoky and hidden in the lean, glowing face. It's gonna be a long night. It's a relief to see Hugh on his left, young and muscley and capable-looking. He realizes, oddly, that it's a long time since he felt he had someone to guard his back if things got rough. It feels good.

"This is wonderful," says Nancy, casting bright eyes around. The plaques glitter on the walls, unit badges and ships' crests. The fire plays strongly in its cave. People in blue blazers and checked sports coats and frocks and younger ones in sweaters and slacks and a few in jeans flock like a zoo assortment of birds. Glenn Miller takes the A-Train on the speaker system.

Lily is looking at Nancy with the kind of patience old soldiers get. "It's nice," she says, "nicer than I thought it would be."

"Haven't you been here before?" asks Nancy.

"No," says Lily.

"Oh. Well then, this is special."

"What would you folks like to drink?" asks Sam. "And I better go sign you in."

"Yes," says Lily, still looking at Nancy.

"I'll go with you," says Hugh.

"How about a brandy?" says Nancy, shivering. "For warming up."

"Sure," says Sam.

Lily looks up at him. "I'll try a margarita," she says. "For one."

⇥◆─○─◆⇤

At the bar Sam starts signing people in. "You're only allowed two, Sergeant," Hugh says. Sam looks around at him. "Who told you?" he says.

"Put me down from Branch 176," says Hugh.

"I'll be damned. How come they let you in?"

"Because my old man's a soldier." Hugh grins. "I joined a couple months back." The grin subsides. "When I got that letter from you about Charlotte."

Sam whomps him on the shoulder, grinning and blinking a lot. "Good on you, kid." He finishes writing in the book. "If I'm not careful I might get to feeling proud," he says, more quietly. And orders drinks.

"Beer for me, too," says Hugh.

"Get out the Whitbread's, Lanny!" Sam shouts in the din. "It's time to celebrate. Room temp. You too?" he asks Hugh.

"Sure," says Hugh. "Look, how about you get the food and I'll get the booze?"

Sam pauses. "Sure," he says back. "Thanks."

245

As they each take a beer by the neck and glasses in the hand, he says, "There's something I been wanting to talk to you about, Hugh." He moves a bit away from the bar and stands in an empty spot by a post. "You know you've got a few grand coming from Charlotte's will, and some mementos." Hugh nods. "Well, it looks like she left me quite a pile, and Lord knows I can use some dough, but I decided I gotta take a job anyhow, just to feel respectable. And I don't really *need* a pile. So if you and Nancy want to buy a house or something – or just you, I'm not gonna try to tie you into anything you don't wanna do –"

"Thanks, Sam," says Hugh, his hands full of booze and glass, shaking his head. "Thanks. But no. You've got it coming to you. If I need a loan I'll let you know. Promise. Nancy too. But you keep Aunt Charlotte's money, and maybe get yourself a place that'll make a little revenue."

Sam grins. "Another slum landlord for a dad. Okay. But you will let me know? It's about time I could do something useful for ya."

Hugh nudges him with an elbow. Glass clinks. "You got me started twenty-five years and nine months ago, more or less. And you're my main guy in a way Sid'll never be. Come on, let's get back to these crazy women." He shakes his head. "That Lily of yours –"

"Yeah," says Sam, "you're telling me."

The women are into it, Nancy eager with her elbows on the table, Lily leaned back in her chair with one arm cocked in that heron pose, the other on the table as though she had just caressed Nancy's. The profile of the one enough to make your heart bleed. The face of the other. His chest aches. What is she up to? What in hell. As though he were just a kind of adjunct to her presence.

"What do you do?" Lily is saying.

"I'm a waitress."

"You're pretty enough. I get the feeling it's probably a good place."

"Yes," says Nancy, pleased. "Umberto Al Porto, down on Water Street. The food's good." She grins. "And so are the tips."

Lily grins back. "Oh to be young," she says, and looks up at the men. "Liquor parade," she says. "Grog's up."

Sam hands her a margarita. Glenn Miller and the noise of a hundred people in his ears. He feels giddy.

"Cheers," she says, and raises her glass. Her eyes are level and far away, as though she were sitting on the other side of the room. The lamp by the palisade of logs.

He pours Whitbread's and drinks it, foamy, just cool, nutty and brown.

"To us," says Nancy, raising the cedar-coloured pool in the snifter at the end of her long tanned linkage.

"I'll drink to that," says Hugh.

"Cheers," says Sam.

"Food," says Lily.

"Yes," says Nancy.

And they parade off to the Hollywood carver.

⊷•⊶

By the time Zoe arrives to tinkle the first warmup trills out of the Yamaha bar piano, the baron of beef has been declared excellent, the trimmings passable. Hugh gathers up the stripped bones of the meal. The second round of drinks had been wine.

"Whisky," says Sam.

"Yes," says Nancy.

Lily looks at him. She smiles, a sadly sort of one. "I'll take my whisky straight," she says, as if it means something forlorn to her. "Peat bog Scotch."

⊷•⊶

The band begins to play. It isn't a band, just Zoe on the piano, but it might as well be. And a lot of people singing. It's a long way to Tipperary, they sing. The notes cascade off the walls like a small fortissimo Niagara. Gentleman George of the Paul Henreid hair and long suave limbs takes Millie of course first onto the floor. Millie who might be seventy, small and neat and if you squint a bit pretty as twenty – proper, flirty and gay. They dance a quick fox trot that's a lesson in how to do something right, Millie's arm making grace notes in the air when George twirls her around. No one else clutters their floor for that first turn.

"Well," says Hugh, "we're not going to match that," as he stands up and offers his hand to Nancy.

"Will you ask me to dance?" says Lily after they're gone. "Yes," says Sam, rising. "Will you dance?" He holds out his hand. "With the old fart. I think I remember how."

She gazes at him before slowly getting up. "Never say die," she says, "can you." It sounds clear and strange and utterly obscure.

They move onto the floor. Hugh and Nancy bob determinedly amongst the swirling crowd, most of which seems to know what it's doing. *I'm her eighth old man, I'm Henery, Henery the Eighth I am,* the singers are singing. Sam puts his arm around Lily. *Not a Willy or a Sam,* they sing. Well, I am, he thinks. And she puts her hand on his shoulder and she's over there. He looks in her eyes and it frightens him so he looks over her shoulder at the little sea of moving men and women. His legs remember things, thank God, that his mind knows nothing about. Her body moves in the circle of his arm like a life that is his to touch but not to know. His to touch only because he happens to be there at the same time. In time to the music Zoe and her cluster of throats are making. Her body a place he has been, in that

247

ancient quiet space they fell into in each other's eyes, the flesh of themselves warm and wet and everything with the soundless music among the stars, her eyes now looking out over his shoulder at God knows what, his own eyes seeing nothing of what they see, her body held a space from him as firm as the pressure of her hand holding them there at other sides of the cold night water in which there are unknown fish and monsters that never see light. His hand had been on her mons and the soft lips of her other mouth. That is a place, and nothing to say he can ever go there again. Her mouth by his ear says, "You're right. You do remember how. This whole place is about remembering how, isn't it?"

And he wonders why it's so important to go there, again. At all. "Yes," he says. And knows why it's so important. The sea in which we live. The blood of Hugh in the mud and his hands and men and women who keep dancing. His hand on the small of her back feels like the pivot around which the stars turn. Hugh somewhere out there with Nancy. The fruit of my loins turning with the womb carried in the bones of the best daughter a man could hope to be given. By marriage. By anything. A sound comes out of his mouth.

"I heard you, Sam," she says. Her hand grips his fleetingly with something that isn't the force of distance. "I heard you. But I don't know.

⊱─◦─⊰

Back at the table, all of them are at least a little sweaty and warmed. His legs ache. He looks out across the floor. Sweat and tears. *Keep the home fires burning.* Vera Lynn. *I'll arrive late tonight, blackbird bye bye.* Glenn Miller going down. Millie in Fred's arms. Gotta introduce Fred. If you don't see clearly it could be 1943.

"These people are living somewhere else, but it seems like a good place," says Hugh.

"Yeah," says Sam. "If I remember right it's about the year I met your mum. And yeah, I guess it was a good place, some ways."

"If people weren't trying to kill you, you mean."

"Sort of like that. Except maybe that was what made it so good, when ya look back."

Everyone looks at him as though he had just said something. "I'll get us some more drinks," says Hugh. "Same for you?"

"Beer," says Sam. "I'm sweating a lot. Take back the empties, will ya?"

"Yeah," says Hugh, "I know."

"Excuse me," says Sam and goes over to take Millie away from Fred. "I wanna see you," he says. "My kid and his girl are here, and Lily."

⊱─◦─⊰

Fred's out there with Lily, a graceful lug beside her willowy green in the kaleidoscope swirl. *Pack up your troubles and smile smile smile.* Sure thing. Hugh

248

plunks glasses and looks at him. Sam feels bewildered about everything but the next step. "Thanks," he says. "I gotta count on you right now."

"Okay," says Hugh. No smile. Just there. Phillips making that Bren bark.

"May I have this dance?" he says to Nancy.

She bounces up, welcome splitting her gorgeous gumwood face. "You're on," she says. "I thought I was going to be a wallflower."

"That's just 'cause Hugh's on steward duty and you scare hell outta the rest of 'em."

She looks very pleased. Her body zings into his like an electric eel. He's not so much putting his arm around her as completing the circuit.

"I don't fox-trot very well," she says.

"If you knew what you were doing I'd be in a lot of trouble," he says.

To embrace this woman, he thinks. He feels as though they're flashing through the dancers crowding the floor. It would be like clasping a blade to his bosom. A keenly cutting death in this vibrant young flesh. His shoulder crashes against a bulk that's Whiteacre. Lily looks at him over Fred's big shoulder. Her brows arch. "'Ts allright," he says. "Dancing." And they're both gone.

"She's terrific," Nancy says in his ear, and backs off to look him in the face. "How old is she?"

"Forty-four. At least she was last time I asked."

"You remember what you said to me about aging well?" she says, moving in again. "Well, I hope I do half as well as Lily has."

He lets himself feel the solid fullness of her breast under his right pectoral. His balls ache. "Yeah," he says.

<hr>

He eases into his chair and watches Nancy settle like a bird that's heard the worm, like a cat that's seen the bird. Lily is dancing with Hugh. A frown pleats Nancy's brow. "What's going on with you two?"

"I wish I knew."

Nancy turns her face to him, lips pursed. Her face still startles him when she just presents it like that as though she didn't know how to do anything except be beautiful. "Give me a cigarette, Sam," she says.

"Sure." He fishes one out and lights it for her, and watches her cheeks hollow as she sucks fire into the weed. She takes a sip of her whisky and gazes out at the dancing. It occurs to him that he had once stopped asking her questions because he liked her enough not to wonder any more. And that she's doing the same for him. Least confusing woman he has known.

Zoe and the singers start doing the Lambeth Walk and Hugh gives up. Lily tries to show him a step, but he laughs it off. They come back to the table. His sturdy poise ploughs through the gaggle of bodies still trying to recapture that eccentric dance, like a stout ship in jabbled water. Lily looks like she's walking through mist. She takes a drink of water and tosses back her Scotch. "Where's the powder room?" she says to the table at large.

"Back the way you came," Sam says, "turn right in the hall."

Zoe has taken a break and the core of singers by the piano is wondering how to proceed without her. Sam watches heads turn as Lily walks across the dance floor. Some of the heads turn his way for a glance.

"The lady can dance," says Hugh. "I felt like I had four feet."

"Really." Nancy nods vigorously. "We should learn. I had enough trouble keeping up with Sam." She sighs. "If it wasn't too bizarre I'd ask her for a dance so she could show me how."

Little Tony, who was a navigator at Dresden, starts inventing progressions on the keyboard. The singers can't sing to Tony, who improvises everything out of a lyrical mind burned clean as glass by the firestorm he'd helped ignite. The bugles and time. The mad and the sane. The generals of all the men gone down to the triumph of death and putrefaction. That haunted man Horrocks. Crerar and Bradley and Montgomery. Ike. Mad Patton. Ironic Rommel. Wavell and Auchinleck and that singular man Orde Wingate. Yamashita. Poor Percival. Halsey, Bull of the Pacific. The patrician MacArthur. Heinz Guderian, whom Hannibal and Belisarius both would have loved. What do you think of Tony now, Air Marshal Harris, having sent him to make human candles of women and children in Dresden? His fingers as nimble as his sanctified mind. What do all of you think of us all who pulled the triggers and haven't had the grace yet to go away? Pepper Graham hangs above the fire, gazing into forever.

Lily comes back as Hugh is saying, "What's that job you were telling me about?"

"Bartender," says Sam, watching Lily as though she were a movie. "Dave Hicks, who's vice-president in this place, offered me a job here. That's him over there. Dapper fellow in the gold-rimmed specs."

"You going to take it?"

"I dunno. Yeah, I guess so. Funny sort of job for an old guy. Serving drinks and backchat to guys who'll never get over being young in a war. Same war I was young in. And their kids. They're all lonely, like something that's going to go extinct."

"You could be good at that," Lily says, "making them less lonely."

He looks at her grey eyes with flecks of green and gold in them. That ancient, quiet place. "Yeah. Hicks said they want a sergeant." Pull your men out, Collister! Who haven't had the grace yet to go away. "But I haven't been a sergeant for a long time." Her eyes are level on his, and she's over there somewhere on the other side of them. He can feel her breathing slow as the sea. Leave a light in the window.

"Tell you the truth," he says, "it scares me."

Her eyes don't go anywhere at all. "I think I need some coffee," she says, "before I have another whisky."

━•◦─○─◦•━

It could go on forever. It wouldn't be good, but it wouldn't be bad, and at least it would go on. He's found out about the Ministry of Education and the restaurant business and the state of clothes in Canada, Taiwan, New York, and Benny Friedman's private universe. He's said things about England, and even the Commissionaires. And Charlotte. But Zoe's long gone and the bar's closed and Hicks is trying to persuade Tony to get back on the piano and spike Arthur's *a cappella* renderings of Bing Crosby.

"Looks like it's time to go," he says.

"Yes," says Nancy. "Life begins at one A.M. Are there any good parties in Victoria? I hear it's the place for Chablis and cocaine once the fernbars close."

Everyone looks at her. Her eyes are wide. She looks like it's time for the race to start.

"Can I give you a lift?" says Hugh, turning his head from Lily to Sam and back again.

Sam opens his mouth and finds air. "I want to walk," says Lily.

"Did you walk up?" says Hugh, off balance.

"No," says Lily, "I took a cab. To the corner." She's looking again, eyes on an answer she doesn't seem to like. "I'm going to your place," she says to Sam. He makes a noise that tries to be something but doesn't get there.

Lily stands up and wraps her lilac shawl about her shoulders, Sam in the middle of rising and reaching. So he stands behind Nancy and raises her jacket snug onto her shoulders. He leaves his hands there because she's standing under them patiently as a groomed horse.

"This was good," Sam says. "Let's do it again."

"You're on," says Hugh. "If you can't get to Vancouver, I can always arrange a scam to check out the Victoria store."

Nancy spins under Sam's hands and hugs him hard. He looks at Hugh and flaps his hands and then clasps them tight on her shoulder blades because she isn't letting go. Lily keeps watching, arms wrapped in her shawl, ready to leave. That sad smile. "Good night, Hugh," she says.

Nancy raises her head from Sam's shoulder. Her fragrance blossoms over him like a magnolia night. She kisses him again on the mouth. "When you come to Vancouver," she says, "bring Lily," and leaves him on her way to the door.

"I hope we meet again," says Hugh, extending his hand. "So do I," says Lily.

"I'm half your age," says Nancy as she passes, "but I hope I'm half as good to

251

look at when I grow up."

"Thank you," says Lily. Smile and bemused shake of her head. "You will be, or there's no justice at all." She looks at Sam. "The door's that way," she says. "Unless there's a fire exit where you are going."

"The loo," he says, "but there is, at the end of the hall."

▸┼◂▸─O─◂┼◂

The door flangs shut behind them in the sudden night air by the resinous woodpile.

"Here's my arm," says Lily. "Where's yours?" And they go. Marching. He feels like swamp cedar, or a short broad oak, a blasted fir, next to her willowy ease. But they are marching, and her arm in his has no more flow than a ferrous hoop. She's mad, he thinks, or just plain weird. The moon makes purple canyons in the clouds.

"Nice night," he says.

"Yes," she says.

Her heels echo in brick and stone Victoria like the sentry marching to his post in the silence just before the shot that sounds the alarm. His own feet thump like wood. As they march past the long façade of the Empress Hotel, he begins to feel anger boiling up out of his tired legs. Is this the way to be? This haughty bitch. He feels her sinews on the inside of his arm and the weight of her body pivoted there. He wants to stop her in the purple light in front of the Empress's tourist marquee, the retired London buses parked between them and the esplanade and the moonlit harbour. He wants to twist her around to him and kiss her on the mouth with their teeth grinding under the flesh. And he knows it would get him a slap in the face or a knee in the crotch or simply her running away like a shadow under the moon.

She stands aside for him to unlock the door of his rooms. In the foyer she had stood and sniffed the fusty air. Sour. Not like Bayswater Station. No fresh green paint. Up the creaking stairs he had watched her bottom sway before him in the rich velour, the long muscles of her legs, the worn carpet passing under her suede shoes. He shudders. This will be worse. The smell of his own carpet and curtains and greasy walls. Did I make the bed? He unlocks the door and turns on the one-filament trilight. He steps aside to let her pass. The bed stands across the room like the rumpled memory of terrible nights.

"Well, that's convenient," she says.

"I'll make tea," he says.

She looks around the room and takes off her shoes. I should have done the floors, he thinks, and says, "Floor's pretty dirty."

"My feet don't mind the dirt as much as they mind the shoes," she says. "I wore them because they look good." Her toes wriggle in their nylons. She looks at the

252

pictures on the dresser. He opens his mouth to say something. She looks at the shelves. "Lots of books," she says. She sits on the bed. He goes into the kitchen and puts the kettle on. He gets the teapot and the tea and looks around.

She's standing in the doorway. The plain silver bracelet gleams on one wrist, the brooch on her chest, a small celtic simplicity. Nothing else but the shape of Lily in forest green and her speckled grey eyes looking at him out of her face like a lamp mantled in her dark hair. Strands of grey. Glint of silver. He can hear her feet stick when she moves. Her eyes wander over the kitchen.

"What a grotty way to live," she says.

The kettle begins to growl. "We got a lot to talk about," he says.

"Yes," she says. They look at each other for a long time. Her left hand rubs her thigh and moves across her breasts to massage her armpit. Then it takes her other hand and they rub each other. Sam notices that his hands are crumpling the hem of his jacket. He tells them to stop. He feels the sweat of the evening drying on him. He rubs his throat and remembers the scarf. He pulls it out of his pocket and clasps his hands in it. Marigolds. Warm blood and fluid gold. He walks across the room and holds it out to her.

"What's that?" she says.

"Charlotte's scarf. I gave it to her just before she died." The crowds on Regent Street. He brushes back Lily's hair with the fan of his hand and knots the scarf around her neck. She rests her hands on his arms and looks at him. He leans to kiss her and she turns her head away. The kettle is roaring.

"I'll make the tea," he says.

They take steaming cups into the other room. "I noticed you looking at the pictures," he says. She goes to the dresser. "That's me and Dot getting married. It's funny to see yourself a grown man thirty-some years ago. I think I look like an ass."

She picks up the photograph and looks from it to him and back again. "You're right," she says. "But you were probably good looking. I would have thought you were good looking." She would have been twelve. "Is she still so pretty?"

"No."

Lily puts back the photograph. "And these are your parents?" "Yeah."

"She's beautiful. Sort of wistful. And he's dashing. Looks a bit like a card sharp."

"You've about got it," he says.

"And all these? Are they relatives?"

"No," he says. "I don't know who they are. When I got lonely a while back I started collecting old pictures in junk shops. After the heart attack."

"I see," she says. It sounds like she does. She picks up the little maroon case. A prickle of fear twitches his shoulders. "What's this?" She opens it.

"A guy in England gave me that. After Charlotte died. He's an antique dealer and found it in some piece of furniture. It's the ribbon of the Victoria Cross. I think he gave it to me for not being a hero. Or maybe he thought I should have been a hero. He's the kind of guy I couldn't tell if he believes in heroes."

She walks toward the windows blurrily reflecting the room against the streetlamp and the moonlit birch trees.

"When I was a girl I believed in heroes. You'll probably say there weren't any, but that's what we had during the war – ration books and heroes and newspapers that said everything was all right and how many people had died.

"Ten years later when it was time to do something about it, I remembered heroes. What I found was men –" She fingers the ribbon and snaps the case shut. "Men with tombstones in their eyes. And boys like the one I married." She puts the case down on the TV set. "I don't suppose there's anything on," she says.

"It doesn't work."

She pulls the On button. The set makes a hissing noise and pinpricks of coloured light flicker like nervous stars in the blank screen. "Just as well," she says and clicks the button off.

"Why didn't you phone?" she says.

"Why didn't *I* phone?"

She looks at him as though he were very odd. As though she'd just seen him for the first time and was surprised anyone was there at all. She sits on the bed and pats it with one hand, examining the rumpled bedclothes. "This smells like you haven't changed it in a month," she says. She smiles in an unfunny way. "Have you tried some more young stuff?"

"Goddammit, Lily, I tried to call you when I came back from Vancouver!"

"I was in Ontario."

"So the kid said. Then I was in England for more'n a month because Charlotte was dying. I've been trying to call you since I got back. I either get this kid who says you're not there or I get your secretary who says you're busy."

"I get a lot of phone calls, Sam."

"From men."

"From men and other people. I work for a living, Sam, and in the information business a lot of people use the telephone. Some of them leave messages."

"And your secretaries try to protect you.'

She nods. "I think the boys forget to say some things, and maybe they don't realize it's on purpose. In the office Linda's pretty busy. Sometimes messages get lost. And if there isn't one, it's sure to get lost. How often did you phone?"

Shit – I never did leave word. He breathes. "Three, four times each place, since I got back. Till the time I got you. I thought that was enough."

She looks at him with the same curiosity. "As far as I knew you could have been dead. You appeared one night in my life and said you'd be back two days later and then you vanished. Sometimes I wasn't even sure you were real."

"I forgot I said that," he says. "I got held up in Vancouver."

The nights and the days so long ago. The punk and the steward and Al. Crazy Effie and Hugh and Nancy. The visit to Dot. The dark angel. I wish I could tell you, he thinks. There's so much I wish I could tell you. Charlotte. A wall of water full of men.

She's shaking her head. "You're not in the phone book. You're not in information. You're not even unlisted. I found that out because if you were unlisted I could have tracked you down. I can do that, Sam. I can find those things out. But there was nothing to find." She looks around the room.

"It's a pay phone down the hall," he says, feeling hopeless. Damn! He bunches his fist and bangs his thigh.

"I walked up and down Battery Street and asked people in their front yards," she says. Sitting there on his bed like one of the Furies. He'd had no idea she was this angry. "They didn't know you. I went to the Beaver and the big man behind the bar looked at me as though I belonged somewhere else. He said you hadn't been around for a while. The people in Stubbs' aren't your kind of people so they didn't know anything. I didn't try the Legion because I didn't know which one to try and I was embarrassed to try them all. I didn't think you went there anyway. I thought about putting an ad in the papers, but I do have some pride." Her eyes are bright and she stands up with her head thrust forward and her arms arched stiffly by her sides. "I want to live!" she says. "I might be crazy, and I've wondered that a lot too, but whatever you think of me and men you're the best thing I've found maybe ever. And even if I'm crazy I'm not stupid. It occurred to me, for instance, that you might start thinking I was the answer and get silly. But I wasn't worried about that. I know I'm not the answer. I'm forty-four and I've got the menopause coming and that's all right. I'm not going to get myself tied down with any man again, not even a real one. I wasn't going to get silly and ask you to move in. I wasn't going to let you get silly – but I thought we could have a nice time. But no, you have to throw your life away in these grotty rooms living like a dog, and go around drinking enough to kill a horse, thinking about death all the time. And you expect me to hunt you down and come running when there's no way to find you without making a federal case through the DVA. You just *vanished.*"

She stops. Her voice goes guttural. "Do you want to get laid?"

His mouth moves, and his hands, but the workings in his throat cancel themselves out.

She pulls up her dress and rolls down her pantyhose. The panties come with them.

"Why those first?" he says stupidly.

"Because I feel silly standing around in them," she says. "They make your ass look like plastic and lower your crotch and pinch the fat on your waist."

She reaches around to unzip her dress and it falls at her feet. She's breathing pretty hard, the muscles of her chest tense as an athlete's. Her bra is the colour of sandalwood. She unhooks it.

"Jesus Christ, Lily" he says.

"What's the matter?" she says. "I know I'm not young, but I didn't hear you complain last time."

Her skin still has a robust tan, taut at the shoulders and the tendons of her throat, soft wrinkles in the hollows between. His chest aches. She's still wearing the scarf. One end trails over her shoulder, the other spills onto her left breast. Paler tan of swimsuit marks.

"The company I keep," she says, following his eyes, "it's not recommended to take off your bathing suit." He doesn't say anything. "So I try to make up for it at home, but there's never much time." She looks down at herself.

"It is forty-four years old," she says, "but it's not bad." She pinches the skin of her belly. "Bit of a pot, more than there was a few years ago. I don't like it, but it's hard to fight." The line of dark hair runs down from her hand and spreads into the curls of her brush and over the broad folds of her groin. She smooths her hand over her flank. "Not much cellulite. I'm luckier than most. Pretty good legs – a bit flabby at the top, a bit skinny at the bottom. Big feet, but you can't have everything." Her hands rise. The left one flicks the scarf away and the two of them raise her dark-nippled breasts, as though weighing them. They are large and round and beautiful, he thinks. They look awkward in her hands. The slats of her ribs curve away behind. Not flabby, he thinks. And the moulded arches of her armpits. She's looking at the breasts. "Forty-four years old, or thirty-two, depending how you count. Nursed two kids. They still don't sag much. I don't know why, but I'm grateful."

She looks at him and slides her hands over her face. "Not much you can do about a face," she says, "except make the best of it. Like a lamp, you said. I don't know. That was a nice thing to say. When I was young I didn't like it much, but you get used to things." Her voice is going strange. Thin, angry, with a quaver like someone lost.

"Stop it, Lil," he says. He'd never called her that before, even to himself.

Her right hand snakes down over her hip to her groin and her fingers part the labia. She's looking into his eyes. "And in spite of the men you think about and the two kids, my hole's not stretched enough for anyone to notice."

He snaps. "Lily!" he shouts. "Stop acting like a goddam whore!" She flinches, and her hand bunches, but it stays where it is.

"I don't charge," she says, "when I need some cock."

"If I wanted a whore I'd go look for one in a bar!" he shouts.

She looks like she thinks he might hit her. Her hands fling out and she yells, "That's easy for you to say! Where do you think you found me!" She looks bent and clenched and ugly, her face drawn back from her teeth, her eyes bunched and blazing. Her breasts shake, like a threat, the rest of her tense as steel. "Everything's easy for you to say! You go around cutting yourself off from everything that's still trying to live. Do you need to keep proving you're an asshole?"

"God," he says. He feels enormously depressed and sits down in the armchair.

"What's wrong with you?"

The silence grows intolerable. He doesn't dare speak, but he dares even less to keep silent. "I think I'm in love," he says.

"Oh Jesus," she says, "you fool," her voice breaking, her lashes shining wet.

"I'm almost sixty. What am I doing being in love?"

"You fool," she says again. "I love you. What do you think I'm doing here?"

He feels stopped and stunned and aimless. "What would a woman like you want with a washout like me?"

She makes a sound almost like a scream and walks over to him. Moves. Arrives. "Stand up," she says. He looks up at her. "Stand up!" And when he does so she yanks the tongue of his belt out of its buckle. "Come on!" she says. "It's your turn."

His hands fumble at his waist. Like blocks of wood. Like hunks of blown tire on the roadside. Like the hands of the object of the execution. His trousers drop to his ankles. She's unbuttoning his shirt, a little grunt escaping her with each button. He looks at the scarf spilled over her shoulder like wine or blood suffused in dripping gold. Her skin has fine wrinkles, like crazed glaze on a supple, living vessel. She steps back and looks down. "You're still wearing your pants." Her silver bracelet encircles her dusky wrist. He feels his pouch hanging there heavy and obvious in the amber underpants with their ridiculous white piping. Underwear like a drum major's tunic to nestle your balls in.

"Well," she says, "do I have to do it for you?"

He shoves down on the waistband and kicks his feet free. Still wearing socks, like a fool.

She takes hold of him as though he had a soft hose for a handle.

"Most men have one of these," she says. He can feel it begin to grow in her hand and wilt again because he's thinking about it. He wants to hide. Her grip is hard and unrelenting. He doesn't recall her having calluses. Tennis, he thinks. The

tarnished Adonises. Calluses on her ass from the teak decks of sailboats? Shaddap,
Collister. Her eyes on his again. She gives him a yank that is almost painful.
"Most men have one of these, and it's a pretty good one. The only time we got
together I had the best fuck of my life, at least since I was about twenty and didn't
know any better. But the thing is –" and her other hand punches him in the left
breast "– it comes from here. You've got a heart so big I could get lost in it." She
laughs, very strangely. "And I'm a selfish kid."

He looks down between her breasts, past the little fleshy tower growing out
of her hand, and sees the arcs of skin pale between her toes, like moonflowers in
brown earth. "I want to live there," she says, "in your heart," and starts crying.
Hard, clenched crying. Her hand tight on him and the other still knotted against
his chest so the sobs jolt through him like electricity. Lise's hands slippery with
the blood they'd started flowing again, amazing that he'd had any left, that bag
of meat. The one pressed into Hugh's chest, the other like death clenched on the
knife handle. That's what love was. God. "She cut out his heart," he says, "with
my boot knife. That Belgian girl of Hugh's. Because she loved him."

Her hand eases. The both of them do, like touching. The one curled to hold
him, the other uncurling to caress his chest with blind surprise. He feels his pulse
as though it were hers. Pressing his innards back into him. "Oh God," she says, a
choking sound. "So that's what it was, that first night."

He wraps his arms around her and her hands go free and she slips her arms
around his ribs and they cry a lot, both of them.

⊱──⊰

"God," he says.

"What's the matter?"

"I think I'm happy."

She throws her head back and laughs. He can feel it all through him, through
her legs and hips against his, her arms and his arms around all their ribs, her
breasts pressed just under his. His peacefully limp cock feels the wiry warm curls
of her fork laughing. She kisses him. She tastes as sweet as morning, her lips just
hungry enough to be there. Soft and happy. His tongue grows into her mouth
and his other soft member raises flat against the rough fur of her other soft lips.

"Let's try the bed," he says.

"Yes," she says.

"Sorry about the smell," he says.

She lies back, one arm under him, and stretches. Subsides. Breathes. With
a beatified smile. "It smells good," she says, "right now." Looks at him with
sparkling eyes. "Not that it should be a habit, you understand."

He laughs. "No," he says, and rolls her onto him. That big, ancient, quiet place. Her long weight on him like a blessing. Her hair over his face scented of sandalwood and woman. Lily. Her little belly against his big one. Her hips like plough shares on his. The rough curls of their groins. They cry again. She wraps her arms tight around his neck and says, "Forgive me," between sobs. "Me too," he says.

"I thought I wouldn't be silly, but oh, Sam, I was so afraid you weren't real."

"Me too," he says, and runs his hands over her shoulder blades and the nobbles of her long spine and the good mounds of her haunches. The scarf around her neck hangs over his shoulder. Their breathing slows.

"My nose is running," she says.

He laughs, and snorts his own clear. "Good for it." She giggles and makes a warm nestling noise.

"I haven't felt this good," he says, "since –" He feels her hips slowly moving and her mons rough against him. Dot in Devon. "I never felt this good," he says.

He looks at her carefully. Her eyes and the lamp of her face. The green shadows and gold lights in her grey eyes. "I love you," he says. "That scares hell out of me. But I think that's what we're doing. I'm willing to be scared … Looks like you are, too. It's like being willing to go out and get shot at. I love you, Lil, and I don't think I ever knew how before."

"Me too," she says. Her eyes are wonderful. "You scare me pissless. But I want to live in your heart. And see you a lot. And sleep with you a lot. Sleeping with you is wonderful. In the night and in the morning and all the way through. Does that sound crazy?"

He sees things in her face and her eyes and her hair and the dim ceiling. The things he carries inside him. Jameson's face and red light like blood. The Tiger in the hedgerow and mud and men like ghosts in the mist, muzzle flashes. Hugh's dead face. The waves of time in Devon and the life going from Charlotte into him. "There's a lot I want to tell you," he says. "I've got to change my life."

She smiles down at him. Oh does she smile down at him. "Tell me about the scarf," she says, swaying to draw it back and forth over his cheek. "And turn out the light."

And he does.

⊳⊶⊙⊷⊲

"You know that little pushbutton gizmo they've got for dispensing booze and mix? I always wanted to run one of them things. In one of Steinbeck's books there's a slop-bucket under the bar where they throw all the leftover drinks. For later. Well, I figure you could do the same thing fresh with one o' them push-button jobs. The One Finger Sonata. Dazzle hell outta the customers. Have too many and ya become a zombie."

She laughs. "Zombies we've already got. Have you ever been a bartender, Sam?"

He grins. "Well no, but I done a lot of mixing." He pauses. "I think mostly he wants me to play sergeant to the bar major. Seems morale is down both sides of the trough."

"Do you mind," she says, "if I don't love you for your money?"

"Lily," he says. He looks at the other darkness of her shape in the dark. Light from the streetlamp glinting on her eyes. He feels like a night full of stars. She waits. He can hear her breathe. "Yes?" she says.

"This is so much fun," he says, and laughs suddenly. As though the sky finally got the joke. "What a pair of loonies we are."

"What do you mean?" she says. And giggles.

"That's what I mean. We're acting like sixteen-year-olds." Giddiness jiggles his voice. "We're supposed to be old and serious."

"You're crazy," she says. "I'm always serious."

Their giggles flow into each other and expand and run wild. He tries to say something and can't and she chokes on a word so he grabs her by the ribcage and she shrieks and flings all her limbs around him and they laugh and laugh like crazy people as the stars fall through them.

►─◄►─○─◄►─◄

He thinks she's sleeping. Her simple weight on him like the rhythm of breath. She breathes out as he breathes in rising and falling as he breathes out and she breathes in.

"Are you sleeping?" he says.

"Yes," she says.

The room seems made of light, as though the air were less dark than the night. Things shift and she's sitting and he's sitting looking at her, as though they hadn't moved but the room had shifted them like a compass in gimbals.

He can feel the room shake.

"The room's shaking," he says.

"I know," she says, "it's me. My heart's beating so loud I can hear the windows bounce."

And he feels a strange glory in him, as though the two of them were panoplied in light. Like they said benediction was supposed to. Lord, he thinks as the room tilts to lay them down again.

He feels her skin against his. Her breasts upon his bones and his balls between her thighs. The glory spreading through their loins which is all one place from the soles of their feet through the crowns of their heads. And it all goes on. It all goes on until the light in the room is in the sky. He opens his eyes and his gummy mouth. "Lily," he says.

She snores in his ear.

The birds are singing outside.

Lord, he says. This woman. I'm not dreaming. This woman.